SEATTLE SCORI

Ruled OUT

RUTH STILLING

Copyright © 2024 by Ruth Stilling

All rights reserved.

ISBN 978-1-0686000-3-6

Cover art by Andra Murarasu

Interior design and formatting by Summer Grove

Editing by Jovana Shirley, Unforeseen Editing, www.unforeseenediting.com

Developmental editing by Tina Otero

Proofreading by Autumn Sexton

No part of this book may be reproduced or transmitted in any form or by any means, electronic or mechanical, including photocopying, recording, or by any information storage and retrieval system without the written permission of the author, except for the use of brief quotations in a book review.

This book is a work of fiction, including names, some places, and incidents that are either a work of the author's imagination or have been used for the purposes of fiction. Any resemblance to actual persons, living or dead, events, or locales is entirely coincidental.

TRIGGER/CONTENT WARNINGS

You should be aware that while this book is a work of fiction and is, of course, a happily ever after, *Ruled Out* does contain themes of the following: sexually explicit content, strong language, abusive parents (including child abuse), domestic violence, substance abuse, off page child loss (not involving the main characters), off page parental loss, complex PTSD representation, discussion of suicidal thoughts.

AUTHOR'S NOTE

To the reader,

Firstly, thank you for choosing to read *Ruled Out*. Jessie and Mia's story is one I hold close to my heart, and I hope you will agree, is the happy ever after they both deserve.

That said, this book does contain strong themes, including discussion and representation of abuse and significant mental health struggles. I have provided trigger and content warnings on the previous page, and I would ask you to please read these carefully before continuing. The mental health of my readers is my top priority.

If you decide to continue after reading and digesting these warnings, I wish you all the butterflies, leg-kicking, and swoons Jessie can offer.

He certainly stole my heart.

Lots of love and happy reading!
Ruth x

*To the scared, shattered hearts.
If they're the one, your pieces will be enough.*

PLAYLIST

"Hometown Glory" by Adele
"Make You Feel My Love" by Adele
"Hello" by Adele
"The Scientist" by Coldplay
"Back to You" by Selena Gomez
"Wildest Dreams" by Taylor Swift
"Chasing Cars" by Snow Patrol
"Secret Love Song" by Little Mix
"Smells Like Teen Spirit" by Nirvana

PROLOGUE
NOVEMBER

JESSIE

Do you ever stare at something so beautiful that it makes you wonder if that's what true happiness looks like?

Me too.

For most people, it's the stars in a clear night sky as they shine from an alternate universe. We know they're unreachable and something we'll never get to hold or touch in our lifetime, but still, they offer hope when we need it most. They remind us that there's another, more peaceful world out there.

I'm one of the lucky ones because I get to hold on to my happiness whenever I get a chance. The second no one is watching, I get to touch Mia Jenkins like she is mine and I am hers.

She isn't millions of miles away from me; she's right here, holding my hand, reminding my body that true happiness exists even when my mind refuses to believe it.

"I wish we could stay here forever." She squeezes my hand tightly, our fingers intertwined and resting on the cold metal.

It's freezing cold as the Dallas winter draws closer, but I doubt either of us can feel the chill. Only the warm puffs of air as we speak remind us that we're crazy for sitting on the hood of my car, stargazing in the middle of nowhere.

Except I'm not looking at the stars, like Mia. I'm watching her instead, making the most of what I can get.

And I can't get enough of this girl right next to me.

From the second I walked into my general manager's office two months ago, expecting to be reamed out for another shit practice, I've been incapable of staying away from her. She's eighteen—four years younger than me—but wiser than most people I know.

Wiser than me.

Stronger than me.

With my free hand, I reach over and adjust her earmuff, whispering into the shell of her ear, "In theory, we can. If you're okay with freezing to death."

She leans back on my windshield and blows out a long, defeated breath. "Ever wonder what it would be like not to sneak around? Or maybe not to give a fuck at all?"

More times than you know.

"Yeah, but every time I do, it ends in your dad burying me six feet under."

And that's the thing—my happiness might be tangible, but it's also temporary. We sneak around, steal kisses, and carry on in private like she isn't the daughter of the GM of my team, the Dallas Destroyers—the guy who saw my raw talent in school and gave me a shot at life.

When we're together, we live in a bubble with only enough room for me and her. When her dad's away on a golf trip we take long drives into the night. When she's working in his office and he's out of town on business, we make out on his desk. There could be thirty people outside his door, but we take our chances to steal another moment. When Graham Jenkins ignored all the warnings from former coaches, telling him not to sign my unreliable ass, I doubt he envisaged the opportunity he gave me would result in my tongue down his princess's throat every opportunity I got.

Mia twists her lips to the side as I continue to watch her stargaze. When she turns her head to me as we lie side by side, her green eyes light up with excitement, and her long, dark hair blows around in the wind.

She's spectacular.

"When summer rolls around, we could go to this drive-in theater I've been desperate to check out. They show older movies. I asked Dad to take me last summer, but he refused." She rolls her eyes and attempts her best impression of her overbearing father. *"It's just a bunch of kids making out in cars and drinking underage."*

I laugh and rub the side of my little finger against hers. "Not a bad effort. All you need now is a beard, and I wouldn't be able to tell the difference." I pull my hand from hers and take her chin between my thumb and forefinger, rubbing her soft skin gently. "Oh wait, you're already working on that."

"Hey!" she squeals, swatting me in the chest.

One of the benefits of being a pro hockey player is the lightning reflexes you develop, and I easily catch her hand in mine before she has time to move away.

The cornfields whistle in the swirling wind, but that's the only sound we can hear as I pull her closer, my left hand still gripping her chin, tilting her lips toward mine. "I'll take you anywhere you want to go, Sweetheart. You and me."

"Always?" she asks, hope blooming in her pretty eyes.

I swallow thickly, digesting her plea. I never lie—and especially not to Mia. But I can't promise *always*. As much as I know we're breaking staff-player rules, I'm all too aware of the real reason Graham Jenkins would kill me if he found out I was seeing his only daughter—I'm no good for her.

And he'd be right. Having Mia Jenkins in my life is a blessing I'll never take for granted, but equally, it's a ticking time bomb waiting to go off.

So, instead of answering her question, I brush my lips against hers, hoping my mouth can show her all the things she makes me feel. Even if I can never say the words I know she longs to hear.

Her scent is a window to another existence I long to have. Her touch is a reminder that peace and happiness do exist. Her kisses make my heart beat for a reason other than fear.

Her dad might have saved me from the wreckage of my childhood and given me a chance in life, but his daughter makes me feel alive.

CHAPTER ONE

FOUR YEARS LATER—DECEMBER

FOUR YEARS LATER – DECEMBER

JESSIE

Scars.

We all have them. Whether hidden away in the depths of our brains or visible on our skin, they're there.

I have both—and all at the hands of a man who was supposed to love and protect me.

The injuries he inflicted on my body were painful. But nothing cuts as deep as the thoughts I battle every day. Or the feeling of worthlessness.

Because if my own father couldn't find it in himself to love me—something that should've been coded into him from the second I was born—then why should anyone else? Including myself.

Sometimes, the self-loathing feels like it's under some sort of control. But that's the thing with progress; it's never linear, and neither is our mind. One second, I feel great—or at least in check—and the next, I'm spiraling off the deep end. The feeling of not being able to control my emotions is frustrating as shit and, at times, fucking scary. All it takes is for the red mist to descend further and stick around for longer than normal, and I find myself teetering on the edge of doing something so final that it can never be reversed.

I know I need help, and I know I'm in the fortunate position where I have access to people who would listen. But I've already exhausted that route and endured all the poking and prodding from professionals I could stand, and being honest, the only reason I walked into the team psych's office in the first place was for my mom—if I'm not doing the things my coach and general manager want, then I'm not playing hockey; and if I'm not on the ice, I'm not supporting the woman I wish were capable of caring for me in the same way that I do her. All this trying to "fix" the unfixable and erase permanent damage, it doesn't work, only serving to unearth more pain than healing. And that's when the Band-Aids come out, trying to stem the bleeding from wounds that keep being reopened.

And talking to my teammates about any of this? I can imagine the questions right now.

"Why do you hate on yourself, Jessie? You're a good person, and you don't deserve it."

"Are you seeking help?"

"Shit, man. Talk to me. What's going on?"

"You know you can't play like this, right?"

I hate every one of those questions. It's not like I haven't asked them myself, desperately trying to find the answers. Like I haven't tried to remind myself that I'm a product of the abuse I was exposed to and not inherently broken. But when it comes down to it and I'm facing dark thoughts at two in the morning, do I believe in any of that shit?

Fuck no.

You can't just snap your fingers and break a futile cycle of self-loathing because someone tells you you're worthy. I have to believe it myself. And that's the battle right there. One I've fought repeatedly, and each time, it ends in the only "solution" I can find.

I sit at my kitchen counter and push away the empty liquor bottle I opened only a few hours earlier. Deep down, I know that no part of drinking my feelings away will ever offer anything good. However, after years of searching, my options are running low, and this is the only way I can "function" today, even if I know that long-term, it will send me to the same place as Mom.

It's true—a problem shared might be a problem halved. It also might be a great idea in principle, but in my reality, it's fucking impossible.

I'd love to be that guy and spill my guts to my closest friend, Jensen Jones, who also happens to be the goalie for the Seattle Scorpions—the team I now play for and have for the past three seasons. I'd love to lay it all out and answer the questions I know burn inside him. He's the kind of guy who would listen to everything I had to say too. He's not easily fazed, and he would absolutely go to the ends of the earth to help me in whatever way he could. I see the intuitive looks he gives me on the benches in the locker room. And I know he wants me to tell him all that I'm hiding when I head home at night and lock my apartment door.

But I can't.

I can't face—let alone share—the shame I feel when I pour myself another drink. My default setting is to withdraw and survive. Just as I did as a kid and just as I do now. And I'm good at it. Actually, no. I'm fucking great at it.

And I'll do it until I can't anymore.

Parts of my memory are blanked off from recalling what really happened in my childhood, and frankly, I'm grateful for small mercies. It's like my brain knows that no good can come from that portion of my past. I don't know if I'll ever be ready to process that kind of shit.

As for the memories I do have ... well, I'll hide those too.

And play hockey.

Because that's all I have left. The only time I feel relevant—

and more than the worthless piece of shit my father repeatedly reminded me I was—is when I'm on the ice. That's why I'm still here, living, breathing, playing, and surviving. There's no doubt he'd prefer I was six feet under, but my presence is like a big *fuck you* to him and a safety net for my mom. To provide for her in the best way I can.

So, my option? Simple. Do what I do every fucking day—brush my teeth three times over, rinse my mouth with the strongest wash I can find, and pretend like nothing happened. That, the previous night, I wasn't considering the benefits of my absence in this world.

But above all else?

Pretend like Mia Jenkins wasn't the only person in my life I didn't want to hide away from. Even though, in the end, that's exactly what I did.

Pretend like I'm not still in love with her. That I didn't fuck up my life four years ago and abandon the only light that shone into the darkest depths of my existence.

Instead, I pretend like I didn't push away someone who had given me the one thing I'd craved my whole life—love. Or the kind of stability my parents should've offered.

I push it all down and drink. Because that makes way more sense.

CHAPTER TWO

MIA

Although there are a ton of people in this bar, it sure feels like the loneliest place on earth.

New Year's Eve is not a night I like to celebrate, so I compromised and said I'd come out the night before, and that's why I'm here. But had I known I'd be spending it with half of some random guy's beer on my shoes and the Scorpions game on every surrounding screen, I'd have politely backed out of Tara's invitation.

I know I need to make an effort. Despite being a freshman, I'm almost four years older than most of my classmates, though I'm pretty sure they've experienced going out to more bars than I have in my lifetime.

Daddy's girl.

That's what I am, and I'm painfully aware of it. The daughter of former NHL star Graham Jenkins and the girl who ran off to another city to study for her dream career—the first time I ever did what my dad didn't want. The second I graduated from high school, he wanted me working alongside him, learning the ropes and moving toward a time when I'd ultimately take over for him after his retirement. That was Dad's dream and never mine. And when I told him I'd applied to college and gotten in, he was pissed, determined I was making a huge mistake I'd eventually regret.

So, I have to make a go of this. I need to prove to not only him, but also to me that I can make decisions and stick to them. Running back to Daddy in Dallas is not an option.

Even though Dad doubts it, I didn't deliberately choose this college for any other reason than my education. He thinks it's highly convenient for me to be based in the same city as his former superstar winger, who won't leave the damn TV screen above my head. Washington University happens to offer one of the leading undergraduate courses in America, and that's what I told him. I also told him he would be doing me a disservice if he thought I was choosing a college to be close to a boy who wanted to be anything but near me.

Because he doesn't.

But this man standing next to me as Tara, Hugh, Leo, and I sit at the bar clearly doesn't have an issue with personal space—or invading it for that matter.

He does realize that practically sitting on my lap won't improve his view of the game, right?

The friends I'm out with tonight are more like acquaintances. I guess I'm closest to Tara, but it's hard to get to know anyone fully after only one semester.

And I don't trust easily.

"Goddamn, he's fucking fast," Leo shouts over at us as he points at number forty-four, who's flying down the ice with the puck.

I remember when that jersey was orange instead of black, white, and gray.

I remember how unique and spicy his cologne was as it wrapped around me. I can still smell it now. I can still feel his lips pressed against mine. I'd kissed boys before, but the way he kissed me, the way he made me feel, it was everything.

"Mia?"

Blinking rapidly, I come to, and the noisy bar begins ringing in my ears. "Huh?"

I twist my stool around to face Leo, who points at my wineglass.

"Another?"

I shake my head as his gaze lingers on me for a second too long. Shit, can he tell I'm upset?

Generally, I wear my heart on my sleeve. But I'm not especially keen to show this part of it. Jessie Callaghan is a distant memory I'll bury deep in my mind. He's gone, and the last time I saw him, he treated me like he didn't even know me. Like I was dead to him.

Few people know we had a thing back when he was playing for the Destroyers and when I was my dad's assistant. Dad made sure any evidence was buried, and the press never got word of the *real reasons* why Jessie had been traded. Sure, there were rumors of a love affair gone wrong, but nothing more and no details about me.

It's easy to trade a player under the guise that they don't work on the team or that they're just not meshing well.

"Are you okay?" Leo hasn't moved since I declined the drink.

I look up at him and offer a weak smile. He's hot—I can't deny he is. The classic kind of hot—tall, dark, handsome, blue eyes. He's also a defenseman on our college hockey team—and a good one, if I believe his own hype. But I'm not interested, although I think he assumed his fake ID to buy drinks would impress me.

Negative.

Interest from guys is just—I don't know—not really *that* interesting to me. Not that Dad allowed them within twenty feet of me anyway.

And the one guy who did get close—aka Jessie—I honestly thought my dad was going to castrate him there and then when he caught us making out on my bed. Turned out, he had only played nine holes of golf that afternoon, not eighteen.

Seeing his starting winger's tongue down his teenage princess's throat was not how he'd envisaged his Sunday afternoon playing out. And neither did Jessie envisage being put on the trade list immediately afterward.

"I'm fine," I finally answer my classmate. Thumbing over my shoulder at the screen, I wince. "Just engrossed in the game; it's a close one."

Leo smirks in response, and I swear I see flirtation in his eyes, but I choose to ignore it. "I thought you'd be a Destroyers' girl. I didn't think you'd be rooting for the Scorpions."

I wince again. "Gotta support the local side."

"Holy hell, is he hot though," Tara coos from beside me.

Leo rolls his eyes in her direction and walks over to the bar.

I turn to Tara, assuming she wasn't talking about Leo. "Who?"

With her tongue practically hanging out of her mouth, she watches him move across the ice. "Jessie Callaghan. Who else?"

I can't lie. He is undeniably hot.

When my dad picked him up in his academy, something he established during his NHL career for young, gifted hockey players, I remember him telling my mom, Jayne, over dinner that he'd stumbled across this insanely talented kid from a rough area. He needed a lot of support, but my dad had never seen skating like it. His speed and precision. He basically danced on the ice.

"He's okay, I guess," I reply with a casual shrug. "Not really my type."

She quirks a brow. "Oh really? Is the rugged and tattooed Scorpions defenseman Zach Evans more your style?"

One thing I have learned about Tara is that she knows her hockey boys. Raised in Seattle, she knows the team well, mostly what they look like underneath their pads—if her wall calendars in the dorm we share are anything to go by.

I stare down into my empty wineglass and shake my head. "Not really. Plus, Zach's engaged, and rumor has it, he and his fiancée have a second child on the way."

"Lucky bitch," Tara drawls.

"He's, like, mid-thirties, and you're not even twenty yet." I laugh.

"True, but it's not like it would be an issue. Jessie though, he's, like, twenty-six, right?" She wiggles her brows at me in jest.

I'd laugh if it was funny and she wasn't talking about hooking up with my ex-boyfriend.

No, wait. You'd have to have actually been dating to qualify as an ex, and we definitely didn't have a label.

"I still can't believe you've never hooked up with a hockey player before. You could use your dad's connections." She waggles her brows at me again. "You're definitely missing out."

I pick up her empty cocktail glass and wave it in front of her. "How many of these have you had?"

She shrugs. "Enough."

I smirk. "You don't say."

"You know, I've shared a dorm with you for four months now, but I still don't think I know the real you. Don't you ever just want to let your hair down and go for it?"

"You mean, like, go out and get wrecked?"

She twists her lips to the side in thought. "Yeah, I guess. Skip class, leave an assignment until the night before. I don't think I've ever seen you break any rules. The perfect good girl." She laughs, swishing her long blonde hair over her shoulder.

"I don't see the point," I reply in an even tone.

"Why not? The first year of college is for fun, hooking up, and having a wild time. I mean, I get you're a couple of years older, but don't you want that?"

Tucking a piece of my dark hair behind my ear, I watch as the second period ends. The players skate off the ice, and Jessie disappears off camera. I keep my eyes glued to the screen and press my lips together.

"It was hard enough getting here and convincing my dad this was the right move for me. I'm not about to put my one chance at studying for this career at risk by getting wasted and hooking up. My dad has successfully kept me out of the spotlight my entire life, and that's how I like it."

Out of the corner of my eye, I see her nod and push away her glass.

"I get that. But there must be something that makes you want to go crazy."

Yeah, there is—or was. But he disappeared off camera about thirty seconds ago, and every time we've tried to reach out to each other, it all goes to shit.

I look at Tara. "I don't like doing anything where I feel out of control. So, partying and drinking just don't appeal to me."

"Because of, um ... your mom?" she asks cautiously.

Christ, I wish I'd not come out tonight.

Although she's right.

My dad has always been protective of me and my identity. But from the moment my mom died on New Year's Eve at the hands of a drunk driver, he went overboard. Images of the accident reached every news outlet from here to Timbuktu, and at fifteen, it hit me hard.

I miss my mom. I miss her smile and the way I always knew it would be okay when I saw her. But most of all, I miss her hugs.

And whether he says it out loud or not, I know that's why Dad didn't approve of Jessie, the guy who has battled addiction. Dad can hide behind his reasons—like a breach of staff-player contracts and Jessie being a "dressing-room disruptor"—all he wants, but I know the truth, and so does Jessie.

He wanted him out of Dallas and as far away from me as possible, and a convenient trade two thousand miles away in Seattle was the perfect solution.

CHAPTER THREE

JESSIE

"Callaghan, shower and then my office." As I walk off the ice with Jensen, the hairs on my neck bristle in response to Coach Burrows's tone.

"There's his *I'm pissed off, you played like shit tonight* voice and then his *this has nothing to do with hockey and everything to do with ripping you a new asshole* voice." Jensen slides his eyes over to Burrows as our coach walks into his office and slams the door behind him.

"No kidding," I reply, pulling off my helmet. "I played all right tonight." If sinking two goals and an assist amount to anything.

Jensen pushes through the locker room door with me on his heels. "Exactly. You secured us the win, so I'm saying, prepare for pain."

As we remove our pads, the boys start heading for the showers, leaving us alone on the benches.

"Well, whatever it is, it's got nothing to do with Mia. I haven't heard from her since she turned up in Whistler."

I think back to that moment only a couple of weeks ago. A whole group of us—Zach, Luna, and Aster, their baby boy; Jon and Felicity; Kate and Jensen and their twins—had all rented this house, which turned out to be more of a mansion near Creekside Village. I tagged along with Jon's brother, Adam, since my options were going home for the holidays or spending them alone.

It worked out to be one of the best Christmases I'd ever had, but the day before we were due to leave, Mia showed up at a café, where we'd all stopped by on a walk to get hot chocolate. The whole time, I'd been receiving messages from an unknown number, saying they were in town and asking if we could meet up. Turned out, it was Mia, and she wasn't just in town; she was sitting opposite me in the one open café in the village.

She only wanted to talk, but I panicked. I hadn't been prepared to see her. Because every time I did, I was reminded of the way I'd hurt her and the piece of shit I was for doing it. But despite all I'd done to her, the temptation to haul Mia straight into my arms the second I saw her was so strong that the only way I could stop myself from touching her was to run. So, that was what I did. I got up, said I wasn't feeling well, and hightailed it out of there, never replying to her messages, even though it about killed me to ignore them.

Jensen shakes his head in disbelief. "I'm not a chick, but if I were, I'd be humiliated. She came all the way from Dallas to see you, and you charged out of there and then blocked her number. Love you, man, but that was a dick move."

My cortisol levels that sit just below bearable each day surge through my body. My heart thumps wildly, and my hands shake as I remove the last of my gear and grab my wash bag.

I'm tempted to walk off and not respond to my closest friend, but I don't. "I know you went through shit with Kate, trying to get her not only on your side, but to also be with you. But this isn't some *meant for each other* fairy-tale situation, you know. I'm not like all your friends either, finding their happily ever after. Zach and Luna finally getting together after years of friendship and now pregnant with their second child. Jon and Felicity literally bumping into each other like fated mates. It doesn't work like that for people like me."

He quirks a brow, clearly doubtful.

On a deep breath, I scan the locker room again, only to find us completely alone. "Mia Jenkins might as well be some mythical creature because I have zero chance of ever seeing her again, let alone dating her."

"You fucking won't with a defeated attitude like that." Jensen grabs his shampoo bottle from the bench and fixes a towel around his waist.

"She's the daughter of a multimillionaire GM, one of the biggest names in the sport. She's destined to take over the Destroyers when he retires. She's from a good family, and she has the world at her fucking feet. I earn millions a year but seem to have very little to show for it since my parents piss it away faster than I can send it. I'm from one of the worst neighborhoods in Dallas, and my agent spends more time keeping my dad's behavior out of the press than he does promoting my hockey career. I am the last guy Graham Jenkins wants for his daughter."

Jensen runs a rough hand through his floppy, dark hair, his eyes softening as he looks at me. "You are a good guy, Jessie; your background and past don't make you any less worthy of Mia." His brows pinch together, and I know what's coming—something he's said to me a thousand times before. "I'm here for you. You can talk to me, trust me, and confide in me. I'm on your side, man. You know that, right?"

I nod weakly, averting my eyes from his face as I once again push away the help I know I should take. "I know. But I'm doing okay."

Frustration flashes in his eyes as I look at him, and he props his hand on his hip. "She's twenty-two now, right?"

I shrug. "Yeah, and?"

"And he caught you basically having sex on her bed on her nineteenth birthday, yeah?"

"Yes," I drawl, wincing at the memory—especially the look on Graham's face that summer afternoon. "But we weren't having sex, more making out."

"Whatever." He dismisses that detail. "So, you're telling me she's still being ruled by her daddy, even in her twenties?"

I nod and cross my arms over my chest. He'd better not criticize her. "It's more than that."

Noise filters from the showers, and Jensen looks over at the location of the voices and then back at me. "Yeah, you told me. You don't want to expose her to your world."

An icy sensation creeps up my spine. "I wouldn't expose the Devil himself to my world."

"Sit." Coach Burrows points to the black leather seats facing his desk.

I flop down and wait for him to finish typing on his computer.

"How much did you have last night?" He's still looking at his screen when he delivers the question.

The blood physically drains from my face. "How much of what, Coach?"

Smashing the last key on his keyboard, he finally looks at me, but I wish he hadn't.

Fucking hell, this isn't good.

"Don't play dumb with me, Callaghan. How much booze did you drink?"

I don't reply; instead, I scratch the back of my neck.

"Vodka? That's what it usually is, right? Cheap, clear, you can disguise it easily." He leans back in his chair and shakes his head at me. "I'm tempted to go check your drink bottle right now."

Silence passes between us as I fight to delay my inevitable admission.

"I lost control last night," I eventually answer. "I'd thought I was doing all right, but last night ... I wasn't good."

"Were you still pissed when you went on the ice? I couldn't smell booze on your breath, but you looked spaced out in the pregame brief. I'd seen that look on you before. You knew you weren't in the right state to play. You might do a good job of hiding things from your teammates, but I've known you since you were a kid, Callaghan. You can't fool me."

"No. I mean, not really. Just feeling the aftereffects."

He huffs out a disbelieving breath. "Jesus Christ, kid. Half-cocked and still the best player out there. Imagine how good you could be if you just got your shit together."

I don't say anything because, honestly, what is there to say? He's right. I know he is.

He sets his elbows on the desk and leans forward, a serious expression painting his face. "You're damn lucky you still have a career at this point. I thought you'd learned your lesson when I managed to convince the GM that you shouldn't be traded, that I could get the very best out of you—or at least get you to practice and games on time and not be inebriated. Your career is dangling by a thread, yet you still push the boundaries of my patience. What the fuck is going on?"

To my right, I see the picture of the team when we last won the Stanley Cup. It was Jon Morgan's—our former center and captain—last professional game before he retired. The season after that, I let the team down. My drinking increased, and much like when I had been at college and then on the Destroyers, I caused more harm than good, making bad decisions in games and mentally checking out in practices.

And I'm doing that again now. We might have won the game today, but I know I'm putting myself and others at risk out there. Hockey is my only constant, and I need it. The days when I was a boy, visiting the local rink with my papa to play for fun and hit the ice for the thrill of it, might be long gone, but the pressure to keep turning up and earning for my family is only increasing.

"Look at me." Coach tears my attention away from the black frame hanging on his wall.

"I told you"—I roll my tongue across the roof of my mouth, the sensation grounding me—"I lost control last night. There's some shit going on back home, and it got to me. It won't happen again."

"I want you to start back up with the team psych. She tells me you failed to turn up at your last three appointments. Having sessions with Ashley was a stipulation for you to stay with the Scorpions. That and"—he pauses and clears his throat—"not seeing *her* anymore."

The sessions with Ashley I can do, even if they achieve fuck all. Staying away from Mia? Now, that's much harder.

"I haven't seen her since last summer," I lie. No one needs to know she turned up in Whistler.

Coach purses his lips together. "You know my friendship with Graham Jenkins goes way back to our NHL days, and you know I did my best to convince him personal and business matters shouldn't mix, but last season, he refused to complete a trade with us because he'd found out you were sneaking around with his daughter again."

"We weren't doing anything," I reply.

Burrows's face turns a shade redder with frustration. "Son, you are a good-looking, high-earning athlete and probably the most gifted winger this game has ever seen. You can have your pick of women, but you still met up with her years later. You need to let it go. I know Jenkins, and he will never give you his blessing."

I push down the urge to tell him no one owns a person, let alone their own daughter, but I know my reply would fall on deaf ears. Instead, I run a hand through my hair and wait to see if he's finished.

More silence descends on the room as we stare at each other for a few beats.

"I have let her go," I say, the words tasting like acid on my tongue. "I haven't seen or spoken to her since you and the GM hauled me into the boardroom and told me the score. So, you don't need to worry about doing business with Graham Jenkins anymore. He got what he wanted, and you'll get what you want too. I'll check in with Ashley tomorrow."

He nods in acknowledgment and points at his computer screen. "No need. I just fired an email to her. You'll start sessions again tomorrow at nine a.m."

I stand from the chair.

"Jessie." Coach catches me as I turn toward the door.

"Yep?"

"Stay off the booze and stay away from her—got it?"

I nod in appreciation, but I'm confused by his sudden attention on Mia. Does he know about Whistler?

"Why are you so concerned about her now?"

A surprised smile breaks across his face as he leans back in his chair again. "You really haven't spoken to her, have you?"

"I wasn't lying, Coach."

Seen her? Yes. Spoken to her? No.

His smile morphs into discomfort as he shifts in his chair. "I'm not sure if I should tell you this. I assumed you knew, and that's why you've been even more twisted up and absent."

"Know what?" I bite out.

What the fuck has happened?

"She's, um ... she's in town. She left her position at the Destroyers and enrolled at Washington University."

I nearly fall through the fucking floor.

Instead, I force myself to stand and stare right through him. "Here?"

He nods. "Yep. She's been here for the past few months."

I fight with every ounce of willpower not to smile. The truth is, this is both the best and worst news I could have gotten. Two thousand miles apart is easier to manage, but in the same city ...

How the fuck am I supposed to stay away from the only woman I've ever wanted—who, years later, I still want more than anything else in the world?

CHAPTER FOUR

JESSIE

I've been sitting on my couch in my three-bedroom apartment downtown, staring at my cell phone for so long that my ass is imprinted on the cushion.

I don't have Mia's number saved on my phone anymore, and after she tried to contact me in Whistler, I threw my old one out and got a new one. It was the only way I knew I wouldn't break and reply to her messages.

But here I am, scrolling through her social media profiles. I unblocked them the second I got home.

She really *is* in Seattle.

I scroll further and stop on an image that makes my stomach roll—Mia standing next to the Space Needle with some dude's arm wrapped around her shoulders. He's tall, dark, and even I can tell he's good-looking.

What the fuck?

This was taken back in October.

Is that what she came to tell me? That she's here in town but seeing someone else?

Or is she just fucking him?

Shit, that is what she came to tell me.

The image in my hand disappears and is replaced by my mom's name lighting up my screen.

"Hey," I answer, clearing my throat.

"Jessie, is that you?"

"Yeah, Mom. It's me. You okay?"

She blows a long breath down the phone, and I can tell she's drunk. Worse than drunk—annihilated. Pure desperation engulfs me as I listen to her unsteady voice.

"Mom?" I repeat.

"I'm here, baby."

"Where's Dad?"

"I ... I don't know. He left and hasn't come home." Her voice fades out, almost like she's looking around the room for him.

"When did he leave?"

"I ... I don't know. Yesterday, I think."

"Have you had anything to eat?"

When she's this out of it, it's normally thanks to booze on an empty stomach.

"Hmm ... not—not so sure, baby."

My heart drops at the thought of her being hungry and alone. The guilt of being in a different state, trying to live my life, feels overwhelming.

"Is there food for you to eat?"

"I don't know."

"Why don't you go check while I'm on the phone, Mom?" I ask, but at this point, I'm pleading for her to go check.

"I'll be fine. When are you coming back home? You weren't here for the holidays this year. I miss you, Will."

Squeezing my eyes shut, I try to remind myself that she's pissed. That she doesn't realize she just called me by my twin brother's name—the only brother I ever had, who died a few days after birth.

"I'm Jessie, Mom. Will isn't here, remember?" I whisper.

"I know you are."

"I'll be home when I can, but the season is pretty stacked right now."

"We need some more money." She changes course, sounding panicked.

Frustration gnaws at my insides. "Mom, I just sent you a ton last weekend."

Over twenty thousand dollars. I know there's no way she's spending all this money so fast.

"It's all gone."

"Where?"

"Wayne," she sobs. "Your dad, he took it. There's nothing left in the account."

I scratch my nails down the side of my face, my suspicions confirmed. "What about that account I opened for you? I put some extra in there to keep it away from him."

"It's gone. It's all gone, gone, gone, gone, gone. GONE!" Mom wails down the phone.

I stand from the couch and walk over to the balcony doors, opening them before stepping outside. My apartment is on the third floor, and I watch as traffic and people race around below me, going about their everyday, normal lives.

"All right, I'll wire you some more."

"Another twenty?" she asks, but more like pleads.

"Yes. But if I send some extra on top, I don't want you to tell Dad. Can you keep it away from him? He's gambling it away almost as fast as I'm earning it."

"Yes, I'll try."

"Okay, I'll send it to your account. Get something to eat with it." My voice cracks with the final words because I know whatever I send will end up with him.

I know that none of this is right. She shouldn't still be with him; she should be here with me, somewhere safe and away from that life. But I can't get her to see there's a better life, out of the house, out of his grasp. Out of the bottom of a hole so fucking dark that even bugs don't nest that deep.

"I will, baby. I promise."

"*I will, baby. I promise.*"

"Promise, *promise?*"

"Promise, *promise*. We'll head to the park right after Mommy takes a nap. We'll get dressed and go out."

I waited at the end of the couch for two hours. The TV was broken from when Daddy had punched a hole through it. He had been really angry that day. I couldn't even play my favorite cartoons anymore, but at least, that time, he hadn't punched Mommy or me. It was good he wasn't at home. The house was better when he wasn't here. I didn't know where he was, but I just knew I didn't like him around. Mommy cried a lot when he was.

Mommy was still asleep next to me, but my stomach was starting to hurt.

"Mommy!" I whispered, trying to shake her awake, but she stayed asleep. "Mommy!"

She still didn't move.

As I turned over my shoulder, I knew what I had to do. She'd had too much of that clear liquid—the name beginning with a V. Every time she drank that stuff, I wouldn't get to eat, and lately, that had been happening every day.

It was okay though. I was good at feeding myself now, as long as there was something in the cupboards.

I tried to shake Mommy awake again, but it didn't work.

When I got up off the couch, my stomach growled again, but this time, it hurt. Maybe there were some of those yummy yogurts left ...

But there was nothing in the fridge, not even milk.

There was also no food in the bottom cupboards. Mommy normally had some ginger biscuits in there, but today, there was nothing.

My eyes started to sting.

It's okay, Jessie. She has something somewhere. She wouldn't leave you with nothing to eat.

I climbed onto the counter and opened each door until I found some chicken noodles. They looked old, but kind of nice.

When I found a pan, I filled it with water and set it on a burner. I'd seen Mommy do this a few times. How hard could it be?

Finally, the water started to bubble, and I opened the packet and dropped the block of noodles into the water. The smell of chicken filled my nostrils, and my stomach growled again.

I watched as the noodles broke apart and danced around in the water. It was kind of cool. Making myself some food made me feel grown-up.

Maybe Mommy would want some too.

"Mommy!" *I shouted over to ask if she wanted to share, not that there was much to go around, but I didn't want her stomach to hurt like mine. I could take care of us both.*

"Jessie?" *she groaned from the cushions.* "What are you doing?"

My eyes wide with excitement, I raced over there, ready to tell her I got food coming. But the second I reached her, I heard the pan bubble over, splashing water everywhere.

"Hang on, Mommy. The noodles are going all over the floor."

I ran back to the kitchen and tried to pick up all the slippery noodles, but they were stuck to the tiles. There was only one packet left in the cupboard. I had to save them.

"Jessie! Be careful—"

It was too late though; when I stood back up, my head hit the underside of the handle on the pan, sending the hot water into the air and landing all over me.

And it burned really, really bad.

CHAPTER FIVE

MIA

I swear my breath is freezing mid-exhale as I trudge through campus in my snow boots.

Yes, technically, we are on winter break, and there aren't any classes, but the library is still open, and I'm determined to get some extra study sessions in. The florist I work at in the center of town has been crazy busy for the holidays, and while I need and want to pick up extra shifts so I can live on more than just soup, it's left me with little time to get through my assignments.

I'm determined not to take handouts from Dad. Him paying a huge chunk of my tuition fees is compromise enough for the both of us.

Even if I have to work all hours, I'm doing it. I'm standing on my own two feet and being the independent woman my mom always was. She loved my dad with her entire heart, but she always taught me to follow my dreams and not waver for anyone. I know if she were still here now, she'd be right behind me, encouraging me to go for it.

When she passed, I was a teenager with no real idea of what

I wanted to do or who I wanted to be when I grew up. Mom had always asked me what my dreams were, but I could never answer, instead shrugging my shoulders and turning up the volume on the TV.

Her death almost broke me and Dad, but to this day, I feel like losing her finally showed me the path I wanted my life to take. I want to help people. When I get home at night, I want to feel like I made a difference for someone. Just like the people who helped me deal with and process Mom's death did for me.

Opening my own practice is my dream, but it would also be a legacy to the woman who repeatedly told me I had the ability to achieve whatever I wanted.

With no siblings and a dad at his breaking point, I had to grow up fast. I supported him with the Destroyers and tried to step up at home, too, offering to help with the household tasks my mom used to take on since she hated employing people to do them. But a career in hockey was never what I wanted, and the years I spent as his assistant made that all too clear.

The warmth of the library hits me square in the face when I push through the heavy doors. It's virtually empty as I scan myself in and make my way to a booth at the back. Even the librarians look like they've gone home for the holidays.

There's something about a library. The smell of old and new books mingling in the air soothes my senses in the best way. It doesn't matter what's going on in the world or even what decade we're in; the moment I walk through those doors, life feels timeless, weightless, and peaceful.

I dump my bag of books down on the table in front of me and I take a seat on the hard wooden chair, but quickly stand and shove my red winter jacket onto it and sit on that. I plan to be here until this assignment is complete, and a numb ass will not help my concentration.

As I pull out my laptop, I gaze around the vast space, only two other booths are taken, way ahead of me, and near the front.

One of the guys, who I assume is a senior, leans back and cracks his knuckles above his head. He must sense me staring and smiles over his shoulder at me.

Immediately, I avert my eyes back to my open laptop and focus on the screen.

Two thousand words down so far. I need to double that today to have a shot at getting this assignment turned in on time.

TWO HOURS and two packets of Chips Ahoy!—which were small, I might add—later, and I've only written a thousand words.

I'm going to be here all day, aren't I?

I reach into my bag and root around for the textbook I need next, but I can't see the bright purple spine I'm looking for.

Shit.

I left it back at the dorm, probably under my bed. Either that or Tara "borrowed" it.

I'm sure as shit not heading back in the pouring snow, so my best hope right now is that there's a spare copy around here somewhere.

Finding the reference number is easy enough, and I start to search the long shelves. The intoxicating aroma of pages fill the air as I eventually make it to the psychology section and turn the corner at the end of the stack to head down the right row.

And that's when I see it. With their back to me, another student is in the same section.

Please, oh please, don't be after the same book as me.

The black Scorpions cap he's wearing backward is the first thing I notice, and then it hits me—his spicy cologne—and I stop dead in my tracks. Even if I wanted to move, I couldn't.

And even with his back to me, I know exactly who it is. Who that hand belongs to as he examines the books.

"Jessie?" I whisper, my voice barely audible, even in the silence of the library.

The second he turns to face me, I know he's not okay. I saw him a couple of weeks ago before he fled the café, but in those few moments, at least I knew he was doing alright.

Not right now though.

He looks like he hasn't slept in days—like he did when he was with the Destroyers.

His face is... haunted.

His usual piercing blue eyes are dark and sunken, the blond scruff on his jaw is longer than I think I've ever seen it, and his complexion looks gray.

But somehow, he's still the most handsome man I've ever seen.

You wouldn't think he was an NHL hockey player and definitely not the most gifted of a generation—or maybe even several.

The man in front of me looks like he's spent several nights sleeping rough, and that breaks my fucking heart clean down the center.

Do I love Jessie Callaghan?

At one time, I was sure I did. When Dad told me he was being traded and I'd never see him again, I locked myself away in my room and cried until not just my eyes, but my entire body ached.

Ultimately, I convinced myself it was young love, and the sadness turned to anger and resentment. He never called me, and he left my messages on Read—the two blue check marks made my stomach flip in the worst way.

In the end, I was glad I hadn't given my virginity to Jessie Callaghan. Because he didn't deserve to have it.

Neither of us has moved since I whispered his name into the silence.

"W-why—h-how are you here?"

He looks back at the books and squeezes his eyes shut.

When he slides a random book off the shelf, he studies the front cover and laughs silently, but nothing about this is funny. "Figured this was the best place to start with self-help," he pushes out.

Other than a few words telling me he wasn't feeling well when I saw him in Whistler, I haven't spoken to him directly in months.

Last summer, we spent a couple of hours together when he took me out for dinner one night in Dallas. He'd finally replied to one of my texts when I'd asked if he was okay.

He was an asshole that night. He told me he wanted me, but that we couldn't be together and I was better off moving on and being away from him. The cold way he delivered it cut through my bones.

I know I shouldn't have gone to Whistler and waited for him in that café. I should've listened to him last year. But when Coach Burrows—my dad's closest friend and a guy I've known for most of my life—invited me to his house for Thanksgiving last year, I couldn't help but overhear him telling his wife that Jessie and his friends were spending the holidays in Creekside Village. I wanted to see him, to see that he was doing okay. To tell him I was doing what I'd threatened so many times—leaving the Destroyers and following my dream of studying psychology.

But the second he flew out of that café, I knew I'd made a mistake, traveling all that way from Seattle. I knew I had to let him go.

And I did, as much as it hurt to accept that we were over.

So, why is he here?

"You want to study psychology?" I reply, still in a daze that he's standing in front of me. "Do you go here? Like, as a student or something?"

Why the fuck would he be a student, Mia?

He still doesn't look at me fully as he continues to stare down at the hardback in his hands. "Why didn't you tell me you'd moved to Seattle?"

At last, when he looks at me, I see it—the pain. My jaw is agape as I struggle to contain my reaction to his appearance.

"I did. Well, I tried to tell you back in Whistler, but you ran out on me, leaving me in a random café with your friends. You know, the super-famous hockey friends you have. And their wives or girlfriends and babies."

Fuck me, that was embarrassing, as they all stared straight at me. I swear one of them—the goalie, Jensen Jones—knew exactly who I was.

He'd either seen one of the *very* few public photos of me and Dad and recognized me—which I doubt—or Jessie had told him about us.

Part of me hoped for the latter, that he'd missed me enough to talk about me.

He blows out a silent, humorless laugh and drums his fingers on the front of the book. "I needed to see you. To check you were okay. I was told you were studying here, and I knew there was only one subject you'd take. So, I took a gamble and came here." With his free hand, he scratches the back of his neck. "Third day's the charm."

My eyes go wide. "You've been coming here for three days?"

"Yep." He pops the *P*.

He takes a couple of steps toward me, and every single hair on my body rises in response to his movement.

I point at the book still in his hand. "Are you actually a member of the library and going to check that book out?"

When he comes to stand only a foot or so in front of me, I look up at his six-three frame. I'd still need to stand on my tiptoes to kiss him.

I can smell the booze on his breath. Something I used to gloss over when my dad discussed Jessie's state of mind in board meetings. Something he started hiding more and more successfully with strong mouthwash and gum back when he played for the Destroyers. Something I'm sure he does before he sees his current teammates. But today, I can tell he's too far gone to care.

He hands me the book and shakes his head. "Nah, I came to talk. Is there, like, a place we can get a drink or something around here?"

I quirk a brow in response. "Sure. If you can promise to stay in this café for longer than thirty seconds."

CHAPTER SIX

JESSIE

"What are you looking for?"

Mia sits opposite me, watching me look around the small boho-style café opposite the college library. Other than a couple of students getting takeout coffees, we are the only people in here, and no one has recognized me—thank fuck. I'm not surprised; I look like shit, and I could tell Mia noticed when her mouth popped open in shock after I turned toward her in between the shelves.

Fuck, was I relieved to see her. Not having any idea where she was staying or if she was even on campus at this time of year, I knew I was taking a risk. But jumping the barrier in the library and hanging out at the back after every practice was worth it. I had been ready to give up and message her on social media, but I wanted this meeting to be in person. That way I could look at her. Smell her scent. And the second I did, I knew I had to spend more time with her. So, I suggested grabbing a drink.

Beyond this moment, I'm not sure what I expected to get out of coming here. But my feet kept taking me back to the library, even though I knew she'd see me in this state.

I've hit the bottle hard each night since Mom called me and asked for more money, triggering memories. And then seeing that guy's arm around Mia in front of the Space Needle. I guess I came here wanting at least one answer. Even if it's none of my fucking business.

Is she dating?

"Making sure Graham didn't bug this place."

I look at Mia as she holds a cup of cocoa between her hands. Her deep red nail polish matches her red half-finger gloves.

"He's not that controlling," she replies, blowing away the steam.

This is awkward. I don't know why I expected it not to be. The past couple of interactions we had have made it exactly that, and it's all my fault.

Every time I've seen Mia since that day her dad caught us on her bed, my brain has done the exact opposite of what my heart wants.

Just looking at her unearths all the worst emotions within me —hurt, rejection, a complete feeling of worthlessness. I'm not good enough for her. I know I'm not. I never will be. And deep down, I know she feels that too.

But looking at her also stirs an insane need within me.

"Are you seeing him?" I blurt out of nowhere.

Fuck.

My heart pounds in my chest as she cocks her head to the side and sets her mug down on the table. I'm hot and sweating, and my breathing has turned erratic.

"What do you mean?"

I pray I don't leave marks as I drag my nails down the sides of my face. "You know who, Mia. Space Needle Guy."

"Space Needle Guy? Jessie, are you okay?" Mia tucks a piece of her silky, dark hair behind her ear.

She had bangs cut in since I last saw her properly, and, fuck, is she gorgeous. Her rosy cheeks are prominent and draw me in.

But, as always, it's the gold speck in the green iris of her left eye that captivates me. It sparkles like glitter.

"I'm fine," I say, shaking away my thoughts and trying to concentrate past staring at her. My head is still fuzzy as fuck from last night's vodka.

"I don't know who Space Needle Guy is, Jessie." Mia's eyes go wide as if she suddenly connected the dots. "Wait, you mean Leo?"

She half laughs as if it were the most insane thought ever, and relief washes through me, making my head feel slightly lighter.

"Yeah, Leo, if that's his name. He had his arm around your shoulders."

She blurts out another laugh. "He's just a friend, and he was showing me around the city. Tara, another one of my friends, took the photo. We all took photos of each other."

I wouldn't know. I only focused on the one of her.

She straightens slightly in her chair and picks her mug back up, her face changing from amused to annoyed. "What does it matter anyway? And why were you looking at my profile?"

Yeah, why were you looking, Jessie?

I've got no answer to that, so instead, I scuff the floor lightly with my sneaker and lean my forearms on the table, twisting my hands together.

When I bring my attention back to her, it's clear she's watching, maybe even appreciating the way my biceps and forearms flex with the motion. I run hot most days, so a T-shirt and thick coat are all I need, even in a Seattle winter. When your trauma-affected body runs on cortisol, you rarely feel the cold.

"So, you're single?"

Jesus fucking Christ, Jessie, rein it in. You shouldn't even be talking to her, let alone checking on her dating status.

"Yes," she drawls. "I am still single. I'm also well overdue on the assignment I was working on in the library."

I pick up my glass of water and take a sip, trying to push past her need to leave and study. I'm not ready to let her go yet. "How's college going?"

"Are we friends now or something?"

She still looks annoyed, but past that, I can see the hurt in her eyes, like she's finding seeing me difficult. I've given her zero answers since whatever we had ended, and I have zero to offer her now too.

"Do you want to be, Mia?"

She runs her tongue across her perfect white teeth and then thumbs to her bag. "Yeah, sure. Let me just give my dad a call, and you can call Burrows, and we can run it past them. I'm sure they'll be fine with it."

"Couldn't give a fuck what they think, Mia." It's the truth. I couldn't really.

Sure, I need hockey, but Coach isn't about to trade me if I can clean up my act and stop turning up to games and practices half-cocked. I've got a lot of respect for what Graham did for me as a boy, but I'll be goddamned if he dictates who I can and can't see, even his daughter. If I can avoid him getting his hands around my throat, I'll survive.

The real issue is me. It's always been me, and it always will be. I live two lives. The Jessie I want Mia to see and the one who lives back where I grew up—South Boulevard–Park Row. I'll never shake my past while it remains my present.

"I'm worried about you, Jessie."

I know she is, and I know it's partly responsible for the pain in her eyes.

"I'm fine. I'll be fine." I take a deep breath, filling my lungs. "I just heard you were living here, and it would've been weird if I hadn't come to see you. There's ... too much history between us not to," I say on an exhale.

She smiles, and fuck if it doesn't make me want to smile too.

"Do you ever think about that day in my bedroom?" Mia keeps her green eyes on mine, searching me, maybe even pleading for her answer once more.

"I think about a lot of moments, Mia."

Her eyes begin to shine, and she swipes her long hair over her shoulder in haste. "What moments?"

The kind of moments I've never been able to—and never want to try to—re-create with any other woman.

A smile creeps onto my face; it's subtle, but it's there, and it lifts me when I see it reflected on her. "Secret moments."

I watch as she bites on the inside of her cheek and looks off to the side.

"Special moments," she adds.

A few beats of silence pass between us. The temptation to climb over the table separating us, haul her into my arms, and take her back to my place is overwhelming. Graham could arrest me on the way there, but I'd still find a way to lay beside her tonight.

If only it were that fucking simple. Jensen would tell me it is. But he doesn't know shit about me. No one does. Not even Mia.

And I'll never let her either—because at that point, she'd have seen too much. She'd be in too deep in a life I'd never let her get mixed up in.

Shame, guilt, anger, and hurt ripple through my veins.

Mia checks her watch and then looks back at me. Part of me knows she wants to stay, maybe even come back to my place just to talk in private, to be around me a while longer.

"I need to head out. This assignment isn't going to write itself." She shrugs on her jacket, and her scent finds its way over the table again, making my pulse pick up. She rises from her chair in a hurry and grabs her backpack, throwing it over her shoulder.

I remain seated as she comes to stand next to me, her hands dangling by her sides. Without thinking anything through, I bring mine next to hers, gently wrapping our little fingers together.

Her breath catches in her throat at the contact, causing her to pull away, and instantly, my chest shrinks at the loss.

"Bye, Jessie."

She looks at me one last time before she takes off, leaving the memory of where it all went wrong hanging between us.

CHAPTER SEVEN

MIA

"Are you sure your dad isn't going to be home for a while?"

"Yes. It's Sunday, and golf takes top priority."

"Mia, I don't want to fuck this up. With you, with him, with us."

Jessie pinned me against my living room wall. Well, my dad's living room.

I was pulsing, throbbing, begging him to take me, to take my virginity and own me. God, he was sexy in all the best ways.

"You won't. He won't be back for hours."

We kissed and kissed. My knees felt weak, my stomach swirled with need, and my heart raced faster than it ever had.

"I shouldn't be here," he whispered against my mouth between kisses as I rode his knee, desperate for more friction.

I was soaking through my jeans so badly that I should've been embarrassed, but I wasn't. I didn't care. I was ready to have sex with him.

"Maybe we should've gone back to my place," he said, his voice shaking with uncertainty as he took in our surroundings.

With my hand around his chin, I pulled his gaze back to mine. "Don't overthink this. He isn't coming home."

"He'll kill me if he catches me with you."

His darkened blue eyes trailed down my body. I felt alive, possessed, and so fucking needy.

"He'll punish you too."

"If you don't want me, just say it."

My brain was in overdrive. Did he want this? He'd kept going on about my dad, but all I wanted was for him to forget and live in this moment with me. To undress me piece by piece. To slide inside me, even though I knew it would hurt. That was what I needed. Nine months of yearning, kissing, meeting up in secret, and going out on dates had led to this right here. It was my nineteenth birthday, and I wanted the best present ever. Him.

"Jessie," I whimpered as I continued to ride his thigh.

"What do you want, Sweetheart? Me? Because I'll gladly give you all of me."

I melted. Right there and then against the outdated wallpaper my dad had insisted was still on trend.

"I want you," I groaned back. "I want you to take me on my bed."

He pulled back and looked at me seriously. He knew I'd been holding off, so for me to say this, to be so sure, it said everything.

"A-are you sure?"

We'd not said those three little words ... yet. All we'd been doing was sneaking around. Not only was it against our contracts to fraternize like this, but Jessie was also essentially betraying my dad.

Betraying his trust.

Betraying everything he had done for Jessie by being here with me. By wrapping his little finger around mine and following me as I walked him into my bedroom, where I let him lay me down on my bed.

My body language told him everything he needed to know—that I was ready.

I knew he'd slept with a lot of girls at college. He was barely sober and the wild child of the NCAA, and Dad stuck with him through thick and thin. He'd ignored all the warning signs in favor of Jessie's insane talent.

But I was enraptured by him for a totally different reason.

I was in love with him.

"Take off my clothes," *I whispered in his ear as he climbed on top of me on the bed.*

I had to admit, even though we'd never given ourselves an official label since we were so unofficial in everyone else's eyes, the fact that he was four years older than me and hot as hell did things to my teenage heart.

Every girl wanted him.

Every girl had posters of him on her wall.

But he wanted me.

To an outsider, he was living the American dream even though, underneath, he was broken. But that didn't matter to me. I knew who he really was. Kind and thoughtful.

All Jessie had told me was that his childhood wasn't good, but I knew that was just surface level. That he was holding back details for my—and probably his own—sanity.

When he peeled my purple cami top over my head, I was relieved when the breeze from the ceiling fan in my bedroom hit my burning skin. It was one of the hottest Dallas summers on record, but I was on fire from more than that—from the way he looked at me.

"You're so damn beautiful, Sweetheart," he cooed as his eyes drank me in.

I wasn't a girl who'd been blessed with big boobs, but I believed him —that I was beautiful, sexy, desirable.

"Take your shirt off," I moaned into his mouth, and he smiled against my lips, bracketing me in with his arms. I'd never seen his bare chest, but I knew his body was gorgeous. I could feel it under my touch.

His body tensed at my request. "In a second. This is about you. If I'm going to take something so precious to you, I want you to remember it for all the right reasons. I'm so fucking serious about you, Mia."

I pulsed again—from my hairline all the way down to my toes. "I'm serious about you too, Jessie."

I tugged at the waistband of his athletic shorts, wanting more, but he pulled my hand back and pinned it above my head, the other one meeting it soon after.

"No hurry. We've got hours, right?"

I nodded and smiled blissfully as we continued to make out on my bed.

"I want to cherish you first." He looked down at my pale pink bra, a cheeky smirk on his face. "Have you ever been with anyone else, Mia?"

I shook my head quickly. "No. Never." I was kind of intimidated, knowing he was older than me and had way more experience.

"I'll take care of you. Just trust me."

And I did, with my whole damn heart. I knew he would never hurt me. That he would never take this moment lightly.

"It might hurt a little," he said, kissing his way across my collarbone. His hand wrapped around my back, searching for the clasp on my bra. "But I'll make it good, I promise."

"Can we go slow?" I asked. My body started to tremble in all the best ways.

Jessie smiled as, finally, the clasp on my bra popped open, and I arched my back to give him the freedom to take it off, for him to see me for the first time.

"That's the only way I plan on taking you, Sweetheart," he rasped. "I can't wait to see you. I've been thinking about this moment since the first day I saw you."

I whimpered with need, "Then see me."

"What in the ever-loving hell is going on?!"

Oh no.

No.

No.

NO!

I didn't understand. Why was Dad home? He always played eighteen holes with his friend Mike Burrows on a Sunday—or at least when he was in town and not in Seattle, coaching the Scorpions.

Jessie flew away from me so fast that he almost hit the ceiling fan in the process. Backing away from me, from where I was still lying on the bed, he shook his head vigorously. "Graham, this isn't what you think. I'm in ... I mean, I care so m—"

"Oh, I know what I see here all right. You trying to take advantage of my daughter!"

My dad strode over to Jessie, who was thankfully still fully dressed, and I quickly refastened the clasp on my bra and reached for my cami.

"I-I'm not trying to take advantage of anyone, let alone Mia," Jessie replied, and his eyes flashed to mine for a split second.

"Don't look at her. Don't even think about her ever again. You disgust me, Callaghan. How many chances—how many lifelines—can I throw you? Hmm?! You're just like your father, aren't you? I should've listened to your former coach and cut you loose while I still could, before you made a play for my daughter."

My dad took a step back and screwed his nose up. "I swear to God, I can smell booze on your breath."

"Dad!" I futilely pleaded into the tense space. "Dad, you've got it all wrong. He's my boyfriend." I sat up on my bed and pulled my knees up to my chest, giving us a label I knew we didn't officially have. "We've been seeing each other for a while."

What I'd thought would pacify him only seemed to enrage my dad further.

"How long?" he roared.

"A while. Since September maybe."

My dad's head whipped back to Jessie, and he grabbed him by the throat. "You, my boy, are finished. You'd better hope there's a team out there that's willing to take your sorry ass because I am done with you. Done!"

My sobs were uncontrollable as I scurried off my bed and chased my dad through the living room. He still had Jessie pinned by the throat. I was sure he could fight back, but he didn't. He let my dad lead him through the house and toward the front door. Away from me, from us.

"I don't want you anywhere near my daughter, anywhere near my team, and I never want to see you again. Your agent will hear from me directly."

Dad slammed the door in Jessie's face and then turned back to me, fire still burning in his eyes.

"You don't understand, Dad. It's not like that. He lov—"

"He loves no one but himself." He cut me off. "Boys like him are brought up to survive and take what they can, when they can take it, and I'll be goddamned if that includes my daughter. Tell me you haven't been in the car with him after he's been drinking. Tell me you aren't that stupid."

"He wouldn't do that, Dad. He cares for me."

Dad pointed behind him and toward the front door. "You keep hanging around him, and you'll end up like your mother—dead and in some ditch." He closed his eyes and blew out a long breath. "Have you slept with him?"

Tears started to fall from my eyes, and my voice cracked as I said, "That's none of your business."

Enraged, he took a step toward me. "Oh, it really is my business, Mia. You're both my employees, and you are my daughter, living under my roof. Sneaking him back to your bedroom when you think I'm not around to catch you. So, I'll ask again. Have you slept with my winger?"

"No!" I croaked out, embarrassment and anger breaking my voice. "No. He was waiting for me to be ready."

He shoved his hands into the pockets of his beige golf pants and dropped his eyes to the floor as he shook his head. "After everything I did for him."

I flew back to my bedroom and slammed the door behind me. The smell of Jessie's spicy cologne was still fresh on my pillow.

I snatched up my phone and typed out a panicked message.

ME

> He's just mad, but I know he'll come around, Jessie. I know it. I'm so sorry.

I waited and waited for a reply.

Finally, when the ticks turned blue, I prayed for him to start typing a response.

But he didn't.

He'd chosen to run away, and he had taken my heart with him in the process.

CHAPTER EIGHT

JESSIE

I don't know why I left her college campus a week ago and hoped—maybe even half expected—to hear from Mia.

But I do know why I haven't messaged her myself. One, we never exchanged numbers, and two, I know I need to stay away.

Just because she's in the same city doesn't mean I can see her. It doesn't mean I can ask her to let me take her out so I can try to make up for the multiple occasions I fucked up.

But knowing what's best for her doesn't override my need. Is she thinking about me? About us?

Part of me hopes her memory replays that day in her bedroom on repeat, just as mine does. All of me wishes Graham hadn't walked in on us. How far would we have gone? I'm betting all the way. I know that's what she wanted—to hand herself over to me. She trusted me to take care of her. And I would've gone to the ends of the earth to make it special for her.

I still would.

To think some other guy has had that privilege with Mia makes me sick to my stomach.

I stare down at the pucks laid out along the ice as we warm up for tonight's game.

"You gonna start taking shots at me or what?" Jensen shouts over at me.

It's a big fixture and I'm already MIA. Worse than normal.

"Yeah, sure."

Hit after hit, slap shot after slap shot, gets harder and harder, and I take each one faster than the next as I work my way through the line of pucks set up for me.

Jensen stops nearly all of them, which is unsurprising given his insane talent. But some are so fast that he barely gets a chance to move as they go rocketing past him and into the net.

The final puck leaves my stick in a crack that rings above the noise of the crowd and music, and Jensen stands dead still in the center of his goal.

He pulls off his helmet and slowly skates over to me, his eyes fixed on mine the whole time.

I've barely spoken today. At morning skate, I was pretty much nonverbal and the same again in the locker room.

What the guys expect from me is to be a joker, the first one to rip the shit out of himself or say something stupid. Masking like that is actually pretty easy for me; it's less exhausting. When you act like the fun guy, no one asks questions. But today, even that's too tiring.

"Want to talk about it?" Jensen finally speaks.

I flick my eyes left and then right as I chew on the corner of my mouthguard. "Here?"

"Nah, later. At Riley's Bar maybe. We can step away from the guys for a second."

"I'm not going out," I reply, pushing back away from him, ready to start the next phase in the warm-up.

"The fuck you're not. Kate, Luna, and Felicity are there tonight since we got a sitter, and you are a part of this team, a part of our group. It's been too long since we all went out like old times."

"Not up for it," I bite out, my bad mood getting the better of me while I focus on rounding up pucks.

"You're coming." Zach comes to a stop beside me, spraying ice.

"Well, now, our captain and enforcer has spoken, so get out of that one, Callaghan." Jensen smirks.

Looking between them both, I prop my hands on my hips. "Why are you so fucking bothered? I need a night to myself."

"You've had enough of those lately," Jensen counters.

All the guys know I've had my battles and that my childhood wasn't the best, putting it lightly. But they have no idea about my secret drinking. But the worse my drinking gets, the harder it is to keep hidden, especially from an intuitive Jensen. I know Coach has kept what he knows between himself, my therapist, and our GM, but it's only a matter of time before the fucked-up Jessie literally fucks up on the ice.

"Put your postgame pants and shirt on after the game, Jessie. I want you at Riley's for at least an hour," Zach insists. "No excuses."

"Has your barber gone on strike or something?" Kate—Jensen's wife and a scary-as-hell litigation lawyer—sits herself down opposite me in our usual private booth at the back of our regular postgame hideout, Riley's Bar.

"Still as bratty as ever, Mrs. Jones," I retort and run my hand along the scruff of my jaw.

She's not wrong; I look like shit.

Since Jensen finally convinced Kate that they were each other's endgame and not enemies, I've seen more of her than I ever did in the previous years we've been a part of the same friend group, even though I've always lingered on the fringes.

"Look, all I'm saying is, the NHL pays well enough for you to afford a razor, right?" She smiles around the rim of her wineglass.

"Or better still, maybe do a commercial deal for men's grooming. I could see you in front of your mirror, smiling away, while some cheesy song played," Felicity—Kate's best friend and also a lawyer—adds.

I lean forward on my forearms and eye her with a quirked brow, my jovial mask sliding right into place. "Your British accent is fading. You're starting to sound American."

She throws a hand to her chest and leans back in the booth. "Really?" Shrugging a shoulder, she looks around the bar—no doubt for her husband, Jon. "So long as it's only his accent and not his bad jokes that rub off on me, I'll be good."

Jensen slides in next to Kate and immediately kisses the top of her head, sending a pink flush to her cheeks. Never did I think this woman would melt for any guy and definitely not for the former bad boy and my best friend, but maybe anything is possible if it's truly meant to be.

My attention immediately drifts from the conversation about the game we just won tonight and across the room.

A woman in a red coat stands in the main bar area, talking to a couple of friends. I know it isn't Mia the second my eyes see the woman's long brown hair, but disappointment still rolls through me.

She turns her head over her shoulder, locking her brown eyes on mine. She's pretty and definitely my type, but other than appreciating how she looks, I feel nothing. I might as well be staring straight at a blank wall since there's zero physical reaction.

Quickly, I avert my gaze and immediately find another pair of brown eyes.

"All okay there, man?" Jensen knocks his beer glass against mine. I haven't touched a drop from the moment he set it down in front of me.

"Yeah, just not thirsty."

I could easily be on my third drink by now, but tonight, I'm trying to be strong because the second I taste this beer, it'll be too late. I'm all in with no going back until I wake up on my bathroom floor the next morning.

For me, the worst thing about alcohol addiction is being sufficiently aware of my triggers, but too fucking weak to resist.

And that's how I feel when I pour myself a drink—weak. In that second when I put the glass to my lips, I know this decision is on me, and so are my actions that follow. The pounding head and fucked-up mentality—I'm answerable for it all.

Alcohol physically poisons your body, but its true toxicity manifests in what it does to your self-esteem. It robs you of everything.

And in my mom's case, her hope.

Jensen continues to stare at my glass and then back up at me. "Can I get you a soda or something?"

I shake my head and then notice the way Zach observes us from the opposite end of the booth. Our captain misses nothing. His fiancée, Luna Johnson, continues to laugh and joke with Felicity and Kate as they talk about her pregnancy, but that couldn't be further from the mood settling between us guys.

I'm on borrowed time with this team—I know it. These boys are like brothers to me, and Burrows has given me more chances than I deserve.

Ultimately, I know I'll end up benched or shipped off to the farm team—or worse, traded. I've got a reputation for being a locker-room disrupter and a handful to manage, and at only twenty-six, I would be on my third NHL team since barely graduating from college.

Realistically, how many teams would want to take me on?

Realistically, how long have I got before the last decent thing exits my life?

I look back up at Jensen and blow out a long breath, studying the beer in front of me before bringing it to my lips.

CHAPTER NINE

MIA

January is a depressing month. I don't care how people try to spin it as a "fresh start" or a "new chapter." I hate it. It's cold—no, fucking freezing actually—and the days are short and dark.

It's also the first month I lived without my mom.

So, yeah, January can go fuck itself.

My plan is to live in new-year ignorance and spend the rest of it in class or the library. And that's where I'm heading back from right now—or at least trying to make it back as I slide along the icy path leading off campus.

It's past ten p.m., and instantly, I regret not leaving earlier to catch the last bus, even if it's only a two-minute ride to my dorm. I left my car back in Dallas since I figured getting around a big city like Seattle would be easy enough.

But apparently only if you make the last transport.

"Mia."

Coming to a skidding stop as my snow boots fight to find a grip, I know without looking that Jessie is behind me, and it breaks my heart to hear him slur my name in a way that tells me he's had way too much tonight.

"Mia," he says again, and I turn to look at him.

Compared to the last time I saw him, he's dressed differently. He's wearing his postgame dark blue suit and shoes tonight, but no winter jacket.

"Jessie?"

Despite his state, he looks hot as hell as he leans against a streetlight, wearing a black beanie, his dark blond hair peeking out around the sides.

Somehow, his blue eyes shine tonight, and his rosy cheeks pinken further as he smiles when I walk toward him.

"Hey, Mia," he says, his eyes casting down my red winter jacket, not stopping until they reach my toes—a little like the tingles his gaze sends through my body.

"W-what are you doing here?" I ask.

I haven't heard from him in a week—since I walked out of the café and proceeded to sob into my assignment when I got back to the library. Seeing him was the best and the hardest thing for me—perhaps for both of us.

He pushes off the light and closes the few feet remaining between us.

At first, I think he's going to bring a finger under my chin, demanding all my attention.

But he doesn't. Instead, he reaches to the side of my head and pulls one of my fluffy black earmuffs away from my ear. He leans in closer, and the warmth of his breath fans my face, intensifying the tingles.

"I wanted to see you. I hope you don't mind."

As he pulls back, he smiles down at me, and I can't help it when I smile back, my knees shaking, but not from the cold.

But here's the harsh reality I'm faced with: I know he wouldn't be here if he were sober and thinking straight. Sober Jessie would be willing his feet to walk in the opposite direction of me, but his inhibitions have been drowned in a ton of booze.

"How much have you had?" I ask quietly, keeping my voice soft so he knows I'm not mad. Because I'm not. I'm never mad to see him.

He brings his pointer finger to his still-smiling lips. "Shh. Probably way too much. Enough for me to be standing here in front of you. I knew you'd be studying tonight." He leans forward and lifts my other earmuff away from my ear. "You've always been a good girl like that."

His words shoot straight through me, but his flirtatious tone sets off a flurry of butterflies in my stomach.

"I picked up extra hours at the florist, so I'm behind in my classes."

Shock paints his gorgeous face. "You have a job?"

I laugh, my breath forming a cloud in the freezing air. "I can work, you know."

"Oh, I know."

He brings an arm around my waist. I don't know who is watching, but I don't care as he pulls me into his warm body.

"But why? Hasn't Graham got you all set?"

I shake my head. "This is for me. Being here, standing on my own two feet."

"I'm proud of you, Mia," Jessie whispers into my hair. "So fucking proud." His voice cracks on the final word.

I know I shouldn't, but I'm going to ask him back to my place anyway. Unless he calls an Uber, he has to walk way too far in the freezing cold, which I worry he's already done to be here tonight.

"My dorm is a ten-minute walk away," I say quietly.

"Mia." He pulls back and squeezes his eyes shut.

"You can't go back across town like this," I plead. "I can get you a coffee and some food."

He scrunches his nose up and then buries his face in the crook of my neck, inhaling deeply. "I hate coffee. You know I do."

"Well, at least come back to my dorm and out of the cold."

He releases his hold from around my waist and glides his hand down my right arm until our fingers touch, and it's then I feel how cold he is, even through my glove.

"Jessie, you need to get warm."

"I'll be okay," he replies.

But that's not a chance I'm willing to take. I don't think about it for a second longer when I wrap my little finger around his and lead him into the night and toward my dorm building.

A FEW STUDENTS are still hanging around in the halls when we enter my building and make our way up the stairs. Jessie pulls down his beanie to hide his identity as best he can, but panic still races through me. What if he's recognized? There's no way our picture wouldn't find its way onto the internet.

I walk us faster to make it to the privacy of my dorm and blow out a relieved breath when we finally reach my door, and I slide my key into the lock.

"Do you live alone?" Jessie asks from over my shoulder, his hot breath fanning across my neck.

Shit. Tara.

I turn to look at him. "Wait here for a second."

Our dorm is small, but it has everything we need—from a tiny white kitchenette with two stools at a breakfast bar and a small living space with a gray couch. Then we have a shared bathroom and a bedroom each. I let Tara have the bigger room since she had more stuff when we moved in.

But when I push through the door, everything is dark, and the door to Tara's bedroom is open with no one inside.

She must have a shift at the bar near campus tonight.

I flick on a floor lamp in the open-plan space and wave Jessie inside. "I have one roommate, Tara, but she isn't home, thank Christ."

He looks around and smiles, pulling off his black beanie to reveal his sexy, tousled hair. "Nice place."

"Are you being sarcastic?" I quirk a brow as he closes the front door behind him.

"No. Seriously, it's … kinda cozy. Reminds me of when I was at college."

Jessie wobbles as he takes off his shoes at the door and then looks at the bedrooms. "Which one is yours?"

I point to the one on the right. "That one. I'll bring you some water or something, just make sure to take your shoes with you. Otherwise Tara will notice."

"Are you sure?"

I nod my head and pull the fridge door open. "I have no idea what time Tara is due home, and trust me, she will recognize you. So, unless we want to stay up half the night, explaining why you're here and definitely shouldn't be, you should go ahead."

A couple of seconds later, a lamp switches on, and I hear the springs on my bed squeak as he takes a seat.

"Do you want some Tylenol?" I ask, setting a glass down on my nightstand in front of me.

Jessie shakes his head. "No thanks."

In the soft lighting of the room, I can tell his eyes are still glazed, but he's more with it than when I first saw him outside.

I knew he was battling with his mental health when he played for the Destroyers, and I knew he went to therapy. Dad had mentioned Jessie had an idiot father and needed more support than the average kid, and all Jessie would tell me was that his childhood was very different from mine. Back then, I was really young and didn't know how to ask, but now, sitting on my desk chair in front of him, I want to know more. The reasons behind his actions.

Does he drink to forget? To numb the pain?

Silence stretches between us. Eventually, he leans forward and attempts to pick up the water, but his coordination is shaky, and he almost knocks the glass off the table.

"Does this make us friends now?" he asks with a lopsided grin.

"What? Me taking you in so you don't freeze to death?"

His shoulders shake as he downs the water in one gulp.

"Can I ask you something?" I say cautiously, unable to stop myself from wanting to know more about his state of mind.

"Sure."

"Why do you do it?" I nod at the glass, hoping he'll get the meaning behind my vague question.

He looks at the empty glass in his left hand and then sets it back on the nightstand, blowing out a long breath. "Drink?"

I nod slowly as he looks at me for a brief second and then down at the floor.

"Because I have zero self-control." He shrugs, looking around my room and then finally back at me. "And sometimes, it's easier to be numb."

"To pain?"

"Yeah. To memories. Invasive thoughts don't have the same effect when I give less of a shit." He looks me in the eye once more.

With alcohol in his system, I get the feeling he's opening up to me more than he normally would. I got that same feeling back when I was younger.

What happened to him to make him feel this way?

Part of me feels guilty for wanting to push him further, but maybe this is my chance at getting answers as to why he's always kept me at arm's length. I remember my dad shouting at him, saying he was just like his father. I asked Dad over and over what he'd meant by that, but he refused point-blank to talk about Jessie. To even acknowledge his existence.

"Did your dad do something to you?" I whisper into the silent room.

His head darts to me, panic across his face. "Why are you asking about my parents?" he rushes out, pulling at the collar of his dress shirt.

"I just remember something my dad said that day when he caught us. Something about you being like your father."

He runs a stressed hand through his hair as his jaw tics. "I'm nothing like that piece of shit."

My stomach clenches at his honesty, but my heart breaks at the realization that my gut was right. His troubled past has everything to do with his dad. His troubled past is still hurting him today.

"Jessie"—I twist my hands together in my lap—"were you, um ... were you abused when you were younger?"

Whenever he went home to visit his family, he'd come back in a different state of mind—a bad one—and a couple of times, I noticed bruising on his cheek, but chalked it up to a hit on the ice. Or at least tried to convince myself that was the reason.

"I told you back then that my childhood was nothing like yours, Mia," he finally answers. "Nothing like a lot of people's."

The door to our dorm opens and then closes with a bang.

"Mia?" Tara shouts.

Jessie's eyes bug out as he looks around the room in panic.

"It's okay. She won't come in without knocking first," I whisper.

"Mia? Are you in?" she repeats.

"Yeah," I shout back.

She knocks on the door.

"Don't come in!" I hurry out.

"Why not?" Her voice turns cheeky. "Got some company in there?"

I roll my eyes at Jessie when he smirks, but really, I'm more frustrated at her timing. I know we've lost our opportunity to talk.

"Yeah," I finally answer.

"Ooh, not such a good girl after all. Have fun!"

A few seconds later, the TV in the living room switches on, and I look across at Jessie. "Best make yourself comfortable for the night."

He looks at the single bed he's sitting on. "Do you have some spare blankets? I can take the floor."

"Only out there." I point to my door. "And if I head out in search of spare bedding, she's going to be hungry for answers."

He nods. "I can sleep without bedding; it's fine."

I cock my head to the side. "Are you for real? This dorm was freezing last semester—never mind January—and that floor looks about as comfortable as my seven-inch heels on a hot day."

He shrugs and stands from the bed, pulling back the covers for me. "Just get in, Mia."

CHAPTER TEN

JESSIE

I knew from the moment I saw the time that I was screwed. It was past nine at night, and my curfew was over three hours ago.

It wasn't like it mattered though. It wasn't like I was coming home for any reason, like for food or a hot shower before school the next day.

There was never any food.

The bent wheels on my bike rotated more slowly the closer I got to home. I didn't want to go back, and I wouldn't ever if it wasn't for my mom. She needed me to help her to bed each night, but lately, I had been more there to stop the beatings from Dad.

Last night, I'd stepped in front of one of his hardest punches yet. My ribs ached real bad from that, but I tried not to let it show.

He was smart. He only ever took his anger out in places where we could cover the bruises.

There was a Wendy's across the road from our street, and I was hungry.

While I had been at my friend's house tonight, his mom had offered me dinner, but I had been too proud to accept, even though I was losing weight.

I pulled a couple of cents out of my pants pocket, nowhere near enough to cover a burger or fries. But that didn't stop me from crossing the street and heading toward the drive-through.

I'd done this a couple of times and risked being caught on security cameras each time. But I figured, What the hell? They can lock me up and fucking feed me at the same time.

I pulled my hood up and over my head; it hung low enough to hide my identity. And I waited at the back of the dark parking lot. The restaurant wasn't busy, but when a car finally pulled up to place an order, I knew that was my chance.

Sometimes, I couldn't pull it off because they parked too close to the serving hatch. But the woman driving had overshot it. She was in a brand-new Mercedes, which stood out in this part of town. I was sure she had a few more dollars to replace her meal.

As she placed her order, my legs trembled as I pushed on my pedals and edged toward the back of the car, still camouflaged by the darkness.

It was now or never. My chance to eat or go another night hungry.

Whatever was at home, I wasn't going to get a chance at. The only thing waiting for me was a beating, and my best shot at defending myself was to keep growing so that one day, I'd have a chance at knocking the fucker out.

Twelve-year-old Jessie stood no chance.

But sixteen-year-old Jessie might. And I couldn't wait for the day I could give it back to him.

Handing over the cash, the woman waited for her meal.

I knew the server could see me if they looked to the side, but I had to take my chances, and so I edged even closer, the bright lights from the drive-through stinging my eyes.

"Okay, here we are. I have a cheeseburger, fries, and a strawberry sh—"

I took off just as the server leaned out the window with the food, snatching it as I raced past the window. My heart thumped wildly in my chest; pure adrenaline raced through my body.

"Hey, what the hell?!" the server shouted after me, but it was too late.

I was gone, taking a right along the sidewalk and back into the safety of the night.

When I found a playing field, I pulled behind a row of trees and dropped my bike down out of sight.

I'd done it. I'd pulled it off.

Tonight, I'd get to eat.

I'D THOUGHT *tonight was my lucky night.*

Hot food and no one around when I got home.

That was how I liked it.

Even my mom wasn't on the couch when I walked in the front door.

Maybe she'd not drunk as much tonight. Maybe she was turning a corner.

Hope bloomed in my chest as I made my way to the kitchen and filled a glass with water.

The house was fucking freezing, and I shivered when the ice-cold liquid ran down my throat.

I couldn't remember the last time my dad had paid for the heating. Not that he had a good job to afford it. Not that any of his wages went toward the family. He either drank, smoked, or gambled it away.

I couldn't wait for the second I could get a job and have my own money. I'd make sure Mom and I had food every day, and I'd hide every last cent from Dad. Maybe even my dream of making it to the NHL would come true. Mr. Jenkins was pushing me hard in his hockey academy. I needed to stay strong to have a chance as a hockey player and have a shot at escaping this nightmare.

Quietly, I took the stairs one at a time, desperate not to wake them both up. If Dad didn't notice how late I was, maybe I'd get away with no beating.

Nothing was worse than the end of my dad's fist.

But I immediately wanted to take that thought back when I opened my bedroom door and saw the bare space.

It was all gone. My bed, my nightstand, even my fucking clothes were gone from the rail they'd hung on in the corner of my room.

Both windows were open, and the icy air clung to my clothes, seeping deep into my bones.

I didn't understand. Other than Mom, everything else was the same as when I'd left earlier.

"Looking for something, boy?"

I didn't turn around. I didn't need to.

The first hit was to the back of my head, knocking me straight off my feet, and I crashed into the bedroom wall.

The second hit was to my ribs, but this time with his foot instead of his fist. I didn't know how he had done it, but he'd managed to catch me right in the place he'd hit me before. The hit to my stomach caused me to puke, throwing up most of what I'd eaten.

I couldn't get my breath as I clawed at the floor, trying to get away.

Another hit was coming—I could feel it.

I could tell by the evil way he laughed.

"Fight back, boy. What kind of man are you?"

Tears streamed from my eyes. But not from the fact that my dad was beating down on me. I'd stopped crying about that years ago.

I'd have to love him to care about what he thought of me. What he did to me. Now, the pain was only in the physical torture he handed out.

"Where's my stuff?" I choked out.

A dark laugh rumbled from his chest. "For every hour you were late, I got rid of a piece of furniture. Last to go was your bed."

"Where am I going to sleep?" I forced out the words, past the lump forming in my throat. I could taste blood, and I knew I'd bitten my tongue when I hit the wall.

He bent down, close enough so I could smell the booze and nicotine on his breath. "On the floor. Like a fucking rat." He spit into my hair.

I curled in on myself, willing my body to disappear, for me to vanish into nothing.

I'd be happy if I stayed that way too. Nonexistent.

A sob left my chest. I couldn't cry. I couldn't let him think he'd won or that I cared.

"Where's Mom?"

He didn't reply, turning to walk toward my door. But before he slammed it shut, he faced me, his hand on the door handle. "She's in the hospital. Consider yourself lucky. I'm tired of having to keep her in line."

Panic raced through me. "You hurt Mom?"

He spit on the floor in front of him. "She's fine, but those stairs can really fuck a person up. She needs to be more careful. Don't even think of trying to sleep on the couch because that's where I'll be tonight, listening for you."

"Why?" I asked, just before the door slammed shut.

I wanted him to leave me the hell alone, but more than that, I wanted him to just tell me why. Why was he so fucking angry with me all the time?

He stalked back into the room and grabbed me hard by the hair, practically ripping it out at the roots.

I squeezed my eyes shut as he brought his face close to mine. I didn't want to look at him. He was the devil.

"Open your eyes before I cut off your lids!"

I wouldn't put it past him, so I did.

And when he finally had eye contact, his lips—stained blue from too much alcohol—curled into a sneer. "Because you are an oxygen thief. You had to be the only one, didn't you? You had to take it all from your twin."

He dropped my head to the floor with a thud, and I lay still, hoping he wouldn't come back. Trying to figure out what hurt the most—my ribs, my head, or my right leg as an unbearable ache radiated down to my toes.

But none of that could drown out the pain of losing my brother or the guilt that racked through me for being the one to survive.

As much as I hated Dad, he was right. I didn't deserve to be here.

Not even sleeping on this goddamn floor.

CHAPTER ELEVEN

MIA

Waking up to Jessie Callaghan asleep on my bedroom floor was not how I imagined my Sunday morning playing out.

The heating in this place is crap at best. In the end, I managed to dig out my robe for him to use as a makeshift blanket.

When Tara had gotten home, I hadn't known what to say. It was like our conversation and the questions I asked him had faded into the background, and like a switch flicked in his head, he closed off, and I didn't dare push further for fear of him shutting down completely.

I know he's there, on my floor. I can hear the soft sound of his exhales in the silent room. Part of me wants to climb down from my bed and join him. Part of me wants to snuggle under the robe with him.

I consider what he would do if I did. Would he snuggle back or race out of the room?

"Mia?" he whispers. "Are you awake?"

"Yeah."

I lean down to see him, and his eyes have regained their sharpness.

"What time is it?" he asks on a yawn.

I reach across for my phone and light up the screen.

Christ. "It's only six a.m. Do you have practice this morning?"

He shakes his head, staring up at my ceiling. "Nope. Day off today." When he turns to face me, a sweet smile pulls at his lips. "Cheat day."

I know what cheat day is; the players talked about it all the time when I was working for my dad. Twenty-four hours where they could ignore their nutritional schedule and indulge. "Pancakes?"

He tucks his clasped hands under his head on the one pillow I could find, turning to face me. Even though we're lying separately, my body heats like we're right next to each other, and I can't help it as I fantasize about what it would be like to spend a night with Jessie Callaghan.

I wonder how many women have had that pleasure.

"Pancakes sound perfect," he coos.

We lie, staring at each other, perhaps for a beat too long.

Is he thinking about lying next to me?

I break from my own thoughts as I sit up, and Jessie does the same, the tension between us mirrored.

"How was your sleep?" I ask casually.

"Actually, not too bad." He runs a hand through his messy hair.

And that's when I see them.

From this angle, I can see down the neck of his T-shirt, and the black tattoos covering his chest are unmissable. I wonder how I never noticed them before. How long has he had them?

"I-I didn't know you had tattoos. They're beautiful."

His discomfort at my statement is obvious as he stands and walks across to grab his button-down dress shirt, no doubt to cover himself properly.

I never expected my observation to cause such a visceral

reaction, but it's clear his tattoos are significant, and I want to know more.

I have zero idea what we are to each other, but he's the one who came to me last night, and that has to count for something.

"Yeah, had them done a while back." He shrugs on his shirt and begins hastily buttoning, working his way from the top down.

"What do they mean, Jessie?" I ask, my knees automatically coming up under my chin as I continue to watch him dress.

"You sure ask a lot of questions."

"And you sure know how to avoid giving answers," I counter, grabbing a tie from my nightstand and throwing my hair into a messy bun. "I thought it was an innocent thing to ask."

Once finished buttoning, he drops his hands to his sides and makes his way over to me, where I'm sitting up in bed.

His eyes drift down my top half until he stops on the print of Darth Vader on the front of my shirt, and he flattens his lips together, clearly trying to hold back laughter.

"Don't deflect with Darth," I scold.

He slept in his pants, which are now wrinkled, but somehow still hug his thick hockey thighs perfectly. Grabbing his socks from the side of my bed, he sits next to me and begins pulling them on.

I don't speak. I want him to be the next one to say something. To offer me *something* about his past that I know is connected to the artwork that covers his chest. But I know this isn't going to be easy since he's now sober and fighting me with everything he has.

"You know when someone tells you not to push the red button?" he asks, still focused on his socks.

I pinch my eyebrows together in confusion, even though he isn't looking at me.

He must take my silence as acknowledgment since he continues, "Well, this is me telling you not to push it. Don't try to deep-dive into something you know nothing about, because believe me, there's nothing good for you there."

"What do you mean?"

When he turns to face me, his expression is a warning. Not in a bad or angry way, but a concerned warning for me to stay away. "Why do you think I never invited you to my parents' place when we were seeing each other back in Dallas, Mia?"

"Because we were a secret?" I reply quickly.

He edges closer to me, and I lean toward him until we're only inches apart.

"Yeah, we were. But I told you, judgment from your dad was an issue, but not the real one."

"Your parents. It has to do with them, doesn't it? Are they bad to you?"

He reaches out and tucks a stray piece of hair behind my ear, his sharp eyes searching mine while his hand pauses on my cheek. His touch causes me to hold my breath.

"It has to do with my entire life, Sweetheart."

Sweetheart.

I remember the last time I heard that name leave his lips. It was right before my dad stormed into my room and kicked Jessie out on his heels.

"Nobody's life is perfect," I whisper. "Look at mine. My mom was killed by a drunk driver, and my overbearing dad tries to run my life for me."

"I know." He blows out a breath. "And trust me, that's why you don't need me around you. You've been through more than the average twenty-two-year-old, and I'm not about to invite you into my nightmare."

His hand hasn't moved from the side of my face, and I reach up, placing my palm over his. He dwarfs me in size.

"You can't hide away forever, Jessie. Human beings aren't meant to be solitary."

"No, you're right; they're not. But nothing about my past or present is humane." He shifts closer, his breath tickling my lips. "I'm still working on my future."

"Let me help you. Let me be your friend," I plead quietly. "Don't shut me out, Jessie."

He wets his lips and then casts his eyes to my mouth. "You want to be my friend?"

"Always. Why do you think I came to Whistler that day? I care about you."

When he squeezes his eyes shut, I know he's fighting something.

"You smell insanely good."

"I do?"

He nods his head. "Just like I remember."

I pluck at my shirt and inhale the strawberry fabric softener. "I started using a new brand."

"No. You, your smell. The way it makes me feel so many things. I can't describe it, but it's just ... you."

"What emotions, Jessie?"

His tongue peeks out and runs across his bottom lip. "Safe. But also out of control, and that scares the shit out of me because I know how easy it would be for me to take what I want and say to hell with the consequences."

My heart thunders in my chest.

So much of me wants to kiss him, but the teenage Mia screams from the back of my mind to stop. Too many sleepless nights and unanswered texts should have been proof enough that Jessie is no good for me, for my heart.

But I so want him to kiss me. To take us back to the time we once shared.

My uncertainty must have found its way to my expression as he drops his hand from my face and pulls back slightly.

"We should head out for those pancakes before your roommate wakes up."

He goes to stand from the bed, but I grab his hand at the final second.

"When you said *working on your future*, do you mean you're trying to get better?"

I'm not an idiot. I know his drinking is more of a self-medication for the pain he must be feeling. He pretty much admitted that last night.

He closes his eyes. "Yeah, I'm working on it. Just a lot going on in my head, Mia."

I nod. I know he isn't bullshitting me. Jessie might've withheld a lot of details from me, but this is the furthest I've ever gotten. Still, I feel like if we hadn't been interrupted last night, he might've told me more about his past.

"I'm not the fragile flower you think I am, you know? You can talk to me about even your darkest parts."

I want to tell him after my mom died, I went through a cycle of depression, and I want to tell him when he left, I went right back there.

But that's not what he needs to hear. Jessie needs to hear that he's a good person—because he is. He rains enough judgment down on himself.

"I know, Mia, and I'm not treating you like one. But sometimes, you have to put your trust in someone one hundred percent, and right now, I'm asking you to do that with me. It's my duty to protect you from your dad's wrath, but mainly from me."

CHAPTER TWELVE

JESSIE

It must be some kind of record when I'm the first to get to the gym on Monday morning.
Fuck me, even Zach isn't here.

My next therapy session with the team psych, Ashley, is scheduled right after this, and the thought of walking into her room and talking with her settles heavily in the pit of my stomach. There's only one person I'll consider sharing with.

Maybe Mia thought I'd opened up with her because of the alcohol, but the truth is, that night in her dorm room, I wanted to talk—or at least offer her a part of me.

That was, until her friend arrived home and interrupted us.

The temptation to pull out my phone, scroll to her contact—which I have saved under *S* for the nickname I gave her years ago—and type her a message, asking how her day was, is overwhelming.

I'd thought I knew Mia Jenkins, but on Sunday morning, she surprised me—she didn't judge me for the state I was in on Saturday night. All she wanted was to understand, and she started with my tattoos. She asked questions about me that I wanted to answer. I'd meant it when I said she made me feel safe. She always had. But in that moment, on her bed in her dorm, I'd never wanted to kiss her so badly. She'd caught a glimpse of the real me, the ink that represented so much. She didn't get irritated when I struggled to explain what they were and how they had gotten there. Instead, she sat and ate pancakes with me thirty minutes later. Talking to me about hockey.

I know she wants me to open up and tell her more.

And I want to let her right the fuck in, crack the door and give her access to all of me. If only the monsters I can't control wouldn't walk through with her.

"Fuck me, you're here—and early. Put the flag out or something." Zach walks past me, heading to the changing rooms.

I pocket my phone and follow behind him.

"You disappeared fast on Saturday night." Zach pulls off his jacket and starts changing his sneakers. "One second, you had been having a drink with us all; the next, you were making your excuses to head to the restroom and never came back."

I pull at the back of my neck. "I told you I wasn't up for going out. I had a drink with you guys."

"Would've been nice if you'd at least answered our texts and calls. You know, to let us know where you were."

I would have if I'd known myself. But somehow, *I'm in a random bar and on my fourth scotch* didn't quite sit right.

"Yeah, sorry, man," I reply.

Three more guys enter the room, followed by Jensen. He doesn't even acknowledge me as he pushes past and immediately begins getting changed.

Shit.

"How're June and Will?" I ask, approaching cautiously.

One thing about Jensen Jones, no matter how pissed he is, the second you mention his wife—or in this case, his kids—our crazy-ass goalie melts into a puddle.

"Don't try that one," he bites out, still not looking at me.

"Huh. That moody then?"

"No, Jessie. Just fucking perplexed as to why you constantly go AWOL." He turns to me, a serious look on his face. "Are you seeing her again?"

My eyes flare, and he clearly catches himself as his head darts around the locker room. Thankfully, everyone is busy laughing and joking, and some others, including Zach, are already in the gym.

"I've seen her, yeah. *Seeing* her? No."

"And that's where you were on Saturday night, right?"

"Yeah. I went to her. To talk."

Jensen's eyes soften as he sees the anguish in me. "You know that I'm here for you too, right? You aren't alone."

I drop my head between my shoulders and exhale slowly. "I know. There's a lot that's changed for you though, man. With Kate and the twins. You have a lot going on, and I don't want to get in the way."

He reaches out and sets a hand on my shoulder. "Jessie, you are never in the way, and when you're ready to talk, I'm always ready to listen. I just get concerned when you disappear and ghost us. It happens a lot."

I nod once and grab my wrist tape from his bench, trying to deflect from the conversation. "This is mine."

He snatches it back and rolls his lips together. "Look at it as penance for ignoring my texts all weekend."

I roll my eyes. "You're so fucking needy. Also, you didn't answer my question. How're my niece and nephew?"

He zips his bag shut and smiles. "June and Will are good. Kate's fucking stressed though."

"Why?"

He dumps himself down on the bench, bending over to do up his laces. "Her maternity leave ends in a month. She's stressing over going back—how many hours to do, what her cases will look like when she takes them back from Nina 'Bitchface' Higgins. She's giving herself a hard time, feeling guilty about leaving June and Will." He blows out a humorless laugh. "I don't think it helps that we barely get any time to go out together. I think what she needs is a date night with me, but our nanny just quit since she's getting married and moving away, and I'm not about to invite her parents over to sit for us."

Kate Jones could rival me in the closed-book department. What I do know about her is, her family sucks ass—other than her brother, Easton, who works in the Middle East. From what Jensen has told me, Violet and Henry Monroe are lucky to be free people after being caught up in a huge tax scandal. Pretty much all their assets were seized and sold to pay off bills and unpaid staff wages. They swapped their huge mansion for a modest two-bedroom house, and Kate hasn't seen them in over a year.

"Well, I could help."

I gotta admit, avoiding his texts on Saturday was a shitty move. Babysitting June and Will is the least I can do. Not to mention, I love the twins with my whole damn heart. I'll never forget the time Jensen told me he had named his son after my brother.

I swallow down the lump forming in my throat. "If you want?"

He smirks and stands from the bench. He's only got a couple of inches on me, but in his mid-thirties, he sometimes feels like the father figure I never had. "You ever change a diaper before?"

If you count the times I had to change my own, then yeah.

"I can manage. When do you need me?"

A cheeky smile spreads across his face as he takes a sip of water from his bottle.

I hold up a hand. "I don't need the freaky details, just where and when and for how long."

"This Friday night. It's our last game before the bye week, and I want to take her out to the same French restaurant I took her to a couple of birthdays back. Probably be a few hours, max."

"Yeah, sure. Sounds good."

Walking back out into the gym, we're met with blaring music and a horde of guys working out.

Coach stands in the center of the room and raises a brow at us. "You planning on joining us this morning or what?"

"Yep." Jensen pops the *P* and then turns to me. "When you're ready to talk, just know I'll be waiting."

MIA

> J
>
> Still thinking about those pancakes …

My phone buzzes on my desk, and Tara's eyes dart to the screen, lit up with Jessie's message.

"Ooh." She leans in and speaks low so the professor can't hear. "Is Pancake Boy the same guy on the other side of your door on Saturday night?"

On a side-eye, I pick up my phone and drop it into my bag.

"It is, isn't it? You guys were quiet on Saturday. I didn't hear a thing."

I side-eye her again. "I hope you aren't expecting details because I have none to give."

She visibly deflates and sticks out her bottom lip. "Does he have a name? I assume it begins with *J*."

In my head, I cycle through possible names starting with *J*. I feel like I have to offer her something to at least not raise suspicion.

"Jay," I hiss.

Fucking Jay? Imaginative, Mia.

She balks. "What?! As in Jay Macintosh, the football player in his senior year? Well, he is always in the library, so that wouldn't surprise me. You two probably hook up near the Historical Romance section."

My brain whirls in panic. Christ, is that the guy who smiled at me that day I saw Jessie?

"No. No, not him," I rush out quickly.

The professor stops talking, throwing daggers our way. He begins speaking again, and I duck down slightly.

"You don't know him. He doesn't go here, hence why we were sneaking around."

"Like, an older guy?" she whispers back, her eyes wide.

"Yeah, exactly." I cringe. "But it's nothing serious. I doubt I'll see him again."

"Ohh, a one-and-done type of arrangement." She leans back in her chair and chews on the tip of her pen. "I didn't have you pinned as someone who does that, but fair play, girl."

I can't help it; a smile spreads on my face, but not for the reasons she's thinking. If only she knew the truth ...

"We're all headed out on Thursday night. There's this bar in town that Leo keeps saying is really great. Wanna come? If you aren't seeing Pancake Boy, that is."

"You mean Jay?" I correct her, feeling ridiculous for keeping up the lie.

She taps her pen against her lips in thought. "No, I think I prefer Pancake Boy. Anyway, are you coming or not?"

I would rather stick pins in my eyes, but unfortunately for me, Thursday isn't a night I have a shift at the florist, so my excuses are running low.

"Is it better than the place we went to for New Year's?"

She shrugs. "Apparently. It's got a private area in the back, and Leo is talking about booking a booth since it's his birthday this weekend."

"It is?" Shit, I didn't know that.

She nods. "I had no idea what to get him, so I just picked up a gift card for the record store he likes downtown."

I don't think flowers will be his thing, but cash is really short right now. "That's really thoughtful. I haven't gotten him anything."

"Well, if Pancake Boy really was a one-and-done deal, I'm pretty sure I can think of a couple of things Leo would thank you for," Tara adds.

I press the pen harder into my pad as I continue to try to focus on the class and take some kind of meaningful notes. "Oh, yeah?" I ask innocently.

She scoffs quietly. "Oh, come on. You know he has the hots for you."

"He does?" I continue to play along.

"Yes," she hisses, garnering another seething look from the professor.

"You're going to get us kicked out of this class in a minute."

She leans forward and begins writing. "And we couldn't have that, could we? Good girls don't get kicked out of lectures."

I inwardly roll my eyes. I'm ready to change the conversation —or better yet, put an end to it altogether. "What's the name of the bar?"

She stops writing and looks across the room, clearly trying to remember. "I know it's a sports bar. I want to say it begins with an *S*."

"Helpful," I reply dryly. I don't know why I'm so damn moody, but I am.

"All right, don't get your panties in a twist," she replies, pulling out her phone and quickly typing something, although I can't see to who, and I get back to note-taking.

A couple more minutes pass, and finally, I feel like I've rejoined the room and started to follow the class. Although Jessie's unanswered text plays in the back of my mind, firing off excitement in my stomach. Once I'm out and away from prying eyes, I'll reply to Pancake Boy.

"Aha!" Tara announces. "I was close with the *S*, just one letter off in the alphabet. Riley's! That's the name of the bar."

CHAPTER THIRTEEN

MIA

Okay, well, Riley's Bar is clearly the place everyone goes to after Scorpions games.

"Are you sure about this?" I tap Tara on the shoulder as we push and squeeze our way through the mass of bodies.

Nearly getting taken out by a big, brawny dude, she turns back to me. "Yeah, I told you, Leo booked a private booth."

As I grip my bag closer to my side, embarrassment no doubt paints my cheeks redder than my reaction to this hot-as-fuck bar. The gift I got him is kind of embarrassing, but I couldn't think of—or afford—anything else. Especially when we've only known each other since the start of the school year.

"I'm going to head to the restroom," I announce as we finally reach the other side of the crowd and I can breathe again.

Swiveling around to me, Tara smirks. "You look perfect, babe, but I can understand why you'd want to look your best for Leo."

"More the fact that I actually need to pee," I reply dryly.

I'm at that point where I've given up on trying to correct Tara about Leo. He's nice to look at, but he does nothing for me.

The cooler air from the bar restroom hits me as soon as I push through the door, and I shake out my long hair and pull off my jacket, instantly feeling the benefit before looping it over my shoulder bag.

"Unbearable out there, right?"

A petite brunette looks at me in the mirror as she washes her hands and then begins drying them on paper towels.

She's pretty—really pretty. Definitely older and somehow kind of familiar.

And British.

"Yeah. Kind of wish I'd worn my hair up tonight." Trying to gather my it into a tight, high ponytail, I begin searching through my bag for a hairbrush and tie. "Dammit." Pulling out the brush, I set it to the side and then root around for the black hair tie I'm sure I picked up from my dresser.

"What's the matter?" the pretty brunette asks as she begins applying hand cream.

As I drop my shoulders in defeat, I try one last time, looking in a zipped side pocket. "Ugh. I was sure I'd brought a tie with me."

"I got you."

When she bends down to her side, that's when I see it—the large black tote bag next to her feet. She sets it on the counter and then pulls out a cosmetic purse, handing me a black tie with a smile. "Here you go."

It's a tiny gesture, but coming from a stranger in a big city like this, it somehow means something. I take the tie from her as my eyes snag on the impressive emerald rock on her left hand.

That's some ring.

"Thank you. That's really kind."

As I gather my hair, she stands, watching me in the mirror, her head cocked slightly to the side.

We stare at each other for just a couple of beats, but it's not uncomfortable.

"Are you here with friends?" she asks, her English accent noticeable.

"Yeah," I say on a semi-sigh. "We're celebrating a birthday. We have a private booth in the back."

"Oh, that's where we're sitting."

"You come here a lot?"

She smiles and begins applying some gloss. "Yeah. Typically when we're celebrating a win."

"Scorpions girl?" I ask.

Her face seems even more familiar as she fluffs out her thick chocolate-colored hair.

"You bet. You?"

"Getting there, I guess. I've always followed the Destroyers."

For a second, I think about telling her who my dad is, but right at the final moment, I change my mind. There's something about her that draws me in. Apart from Jessie, she feels like the closest thing to someone I can trust since arriving in Seattle. Still, I don't know her.

"Well, I won't hold that against you." She clips the cap back on her gloss and tosses it into her cosmetic bag. "I can definitely recommend the cosmos here if you're a cocktail girl."

"Oh, I don't drink much, but thanks, although I might make an exception tonight. I think my student budget could stretch to one."

She smiles again and turns to me. "You're new to Seattle, right?"

Raising an inquisitive brow, I turn to face her too. "I am. Other than the Destroyers, how could you tell?"

She runs a manicured hand through her hair, her smile growing wider. "Because you have the same look on your face when I came to this city—overwhelmed. It's fine though; people are kind of friendly when you get used to it."

She throws her bag over her shoulder and makes for the door, stopping just before she gets there. She walks a couple of paces back to me, holding out her hand. I take her soft palm in mine.

"Felicity. Nice to meet you ..."

"Mia."

"Pretty name. Well, Mia, when you head up to the bar—there's one in the private area—just mention that the drinks are on Felicity Morgan." She squeezes my hand. "And happy birthday to your friend."

I'm pretty sure my eyes are bugging out of my head as I finally place her face, although she clearly doesn't recognize me. I saw her in the café that time in Whistler. "Call me crazy, but are you Jon Morgan's wife?"

She throws her head back and laughs sweetly before focusing her green eyes back on me. "I am. You really are a hockey fan if you know who I am. I try my best to keep my face out of the spotlight as much as possible."

I'm a hockey fan, but I also have a good memory.

I nod as our hands break apart. I want to tell her I know the feeling of wanting to stay anonymous all too well.

"Well, thank you, Felicity." I point at my hair. "For the tie and the drinks."

I'd usually never accept anything from a stranger, but there's a strong part of me that doesn't want to reject her kindness.

Felicity walks back over to the door and pulls it open, casting an appreciative gaze down my outfit. "Nice skirt and boots."

"THAT WAS the longest pee in history," Tara drawls as I walk back into the main bar area.

"Sorry. Got to talking."

"To who?"

"Oh, no one in particular."

I could tell her Jon Morgan's wife, but I decide not to. Felicity clearly values her privacy, and I'm not about to send Tara on a hunt for famous hockey players. As harmless as she is, I can see it ending with her trying to take sneaky photos for social media.

We begin walking toward the private area at the back of the bar. It's cordoned off with red rope and several security guards.

Tara quickly gives Leo's and our names, and the guard nods and unclips the rope so we can walk through.

"I feel like royalty!" she says, taking my hand in hers.

"Underage royalty," I mumble under my breath.

She brings her pointer finger to her mouth. "Shh! You'll blow our cover and my expensive fake ID!"

I roll my eyes for the hundredth time tonight as we turn a corner, and that's when it hits me—Tara's back against my chest, to be specific.

"Oh. My. God!" she squeals.

Thankfully, her shriek doesn't garner too much attention over the music, and I look around to see what she's so giddy over.

"Over there!" she hisses, pointing without shame. "Jessie fucking Callaghan! Oh my God, and Jensen Jones, the goalie."

My face heats with the fire of a thousand suns right before the panic hits. Sitting around a black leather booth is none other than half of the Scorpions team. Felicity has her back to me as she sits next to her husband, one of the most famous names in the NHL.

But it's Jessie that I can't stop staring at. He hasn't seen me as he sits there, smiling and laughing with his teammates. His white dress shirt is rolled up to the elbows with a couple of buttons undone at the top. His disheveled blond hair hangs over his forehead, but doesn't cover his piercing blue eyes. The scruff on his strong jawline is short and definitely tidier than when I previously saw him.

His appearance makes me happy. Like, today, he's doing okay.

To look at, he's delicious. But to see him smiling tonight is everything and more. I just hope it's genuine. Although I want to speak to him since the last time I did was a couple of texts about pancakes, there's a part of me that hopes to stay anonymous. It's not like I can join him. It's not like we can sit across the table and share a conversation.

It's not like we can ever admit we know each other. Not if I want my dad to stay out of jail.

"Over here!" a voice shouts from across the room.

Leo waves his hands in the air, attempting to attract our attention.

Tara grabs my hand and pulls me in the direction of our table. "Girl, I need to find an excuse to talk to Jessie!"

"Just leave it, Tara. They're having a night to themselves. They don't want to be bothered," I reply.

We dump ourselves down into the booth, and I cast my eyes to the right side. They're around thirty feet away from us, but Jessie's back isn't to me, and if he looked up and to his left, I'm almost certain I'd be one of the first people he saw. But his attention remains focused on his friends as he takes a sip of beer and sets his glass back down on the table.

"Right, so happy birthday and all, babe. But, please, tell me you guys have noticed who is behind me." Sitting opposite me, Tara inconspicuously tips her head over her left shoulder, gesturing toward Jessie's table.

"Leo won't shut up about it." Hugh chuckles, taking a sip of his beer.

"I say we tell them it's my birthday and try and get autographs and pictures."

I quirk a brow at the three of them. "You guys seriously have zero chill. Just let them be. This is a regular hangout for them, probably because they don't get bothered by the public."

"And how would you know it's a regular spot for them?" Tara returns a raised brow.

Because Jon Morgan's wife just told me.

I shrug a shoulder. "Intuition. I'm sure they've tested out loads of bars over time."

Leo edges closer to me as we sit next to each other. It's

subtle, but obvious enough for my cheeks to no doubt flush again. "Can I get you a drink, Mia?"

"I can get them," I rush out, already starting to slide out of the booth.

"They have servers on staff tonight," Leo counters.

"It's fine. I, um ... I want to order a cocktail, and call me weird, but I love to watch them make it. All part of the experience."

Leo chuckles and points to the table number. "Just put it on that, and we'll split the bill at the end."

"It's fine. I got it. Birthday gift," I reply. "Same again?" I point to Hugh's half-empty beer and then to Leo's.

"Yes, please," they both say in unison.

"I'll go for a porn star martini, please, babe." Tara closes the cocktail menu in front of her.

"Okay. Got it." I say over my shoulder as I head for the bar, all the while keeping my eyes trained on the floor and away from Jessie.

CHAPTER FOURTEEN

JESSIE

She thinks I haven't noticed her.

The truth is, the second she walked around that corner, I almost dropped my beer in my lap.

Because. Wow.

Did she know I would be here tonight?

The short, pleated black skirt and knee-high leather boots she's wearing are doing things to me I can only hide while sitting down.

Fuck me, Mia. What are you trying to do to me?

It's been years since I touched her, but in that time, she's grown into a literal goddess.

As Mia rises from the booth, she leans forward to grab her bag. She's wearing thick black tights, but I can still make out the curve at the bottom of her ass. Her tight purple sweater creeps up slightly, and a slither of her lower back comes into view.

Stop staring, Jessie.

She whips around, saying something to her friends over her shoulder and then makes a beeline for the bar, her head down and eyes on the floor.

I know she's trying to avoid me. The second I saw her, I had to fight with everything I had not to let my inward reaction show on the outside.

Not only will Graham Jenkins put out a hit on me if he knows I'm drinking in the same bar as his daughter, but he'll also demand she return to Dallas. Jensen's right; she's old enough to make her own decisions. But I'm not about to come between Mia and her dad. He means the world to her, even if he's an overbearing asshole at times. He's all she's known since her mom died.

I sip my drink and watch from the corner of my eye as she comes to stand at the bar, waiting for the bartender to finish up with another customer.

Felicity sits at the end of our booth, a glass of wine to her mouth and a smile on her lips as she watches me track Mia's movements. I know she has no clue who Mia is to me, but my appreciation for how fucking stunning she looks is unmissable.

"I gather you weren't expecting to see her tonight," Jensen quietly says from across the booth.

"Nope." I smile and look at him. "She's here with her friends."

And Leo. Unfortunately, I wasn't the only one to appreciate her a second ago.

The need to stride over there and tell him to keep his eyes to himself rolls through me. I've got zero claim over Mia, but if there's one element of this fucked-up mess the possessive part of my brain wants to have a say on, it's that no other guy can claim her either. And Leo one hundred percent wants her in his bed tonight.

Trying my best to keep my reaction casual, I attempt to engage in the conversation between Zach and Jon.

"Look, all I'm saying is, it's time, buddy. You have Aster and another baby on the way in August. I've got the time and the resources to make your day unforgettable." Jon presses his lips together and leans forward on his forearms.

"Let me plan your big day. I can have you hitched in the offseason."

Felicity holds up a hand to her husband. "Whoa, whoa. Got the time? Jon, you're the head coach of my son's team. You leave the apartment at, like, eight a.m. and don't come home until midnight some nights. I have no idea what you do in that time, but something tells me you haven't got the capacity to dabble in the wedding-planning business you keep threatening to start."

Zach rolls his eyes from beside me. "We're getting married this summer. But we're thinking of doing it abroad. Maybe in the Caribbean." He pauses and eyes his best friend and former captain carefully. "Just me, Luna, Aster, and an officiant."

I swear I can hear the audible gasp come from Jon's mouth. "So, no one else there? Like, no one? Not even your family or Luna's mom?"

Zach shakes his head. "Luna's mom is too busy with her new husband, and my parents won't mind as long as we're happy. We want to do it on a beach since that's where everything sort of happened between us."

"Well, I think it's really sweet. When Luna told me and Kate, we both thought it was a great idea. At the end of the day, a marriage is about the couple, not the glamour."

Jon sets his glass down, practically choking on his beer, and I take the opportunity to watch Mia walk back to her booth with a tray of drinks.

"So, let me get this straight." He looks at his wife. "You knew about this, Angel?" He then shoots daggers at Zach and then at Jensen. "Let me guess ... you knew about it too?"

"Yep." Jensen pops the *P*. "Not long though. Maybe a week or two."

"Fuck off!" Jon announces, hurt on his face, his head whipping to Zach. "Oh, you are so not being for real right now."

Zach narrows his eyes at Jensen as Felicity fights to hold back laughter. "Always a fucking troublemaker. No, Jon, he hasn't known for two weeks. A couple of days, tops."

Jon sits back in the booth, which clears a direct path to my view of Mia. Although I really fucking wish he hadn't when I see the way Leo has his arm wrapped around her. He kisses the top of her head as he looks down at a black photo frame in his hand.

Fuck, is that the Space Needle picture? Why the fuck would she give that to him?

"Make sure you grind down on the other side too; it keeps the wear even."

My eyes flick back to Jensen as he points at my clenched jaw.

"I'm fine," I bite out.

He looks over his shoulder and then back at me, a twisted smile pulling at his lips. "Yeah, you look relaxed, almost happy to see that dude all over your girl. I'd be fine with it too."

"She isn't my girl," I say, my molars meeting again.

"She is," he replies.

"Maybe we can have this argument another time, yeah?" I side-eye the rest of the table, all deep in conversation and trying to console Jon.

Jensen folds his arms over his chest and leans back in his seat. "It's called manifestation, buddy. Manifest that she'll be yours, and she will be. When she's ready."

I lean forward and shake my head at him. "And like I told you, this isn't the same thing as you and Kate." The sentence comes out confident, but I know deep down that shit isn't true.

He says nothing, simply taking another sip of his beer.

"What?" I say to him, frustration seeping into my tone.

"Didn't say anything, Jessie."

"Might as well. You've never held back before," I chide.

He chuckles low and points his finger at me, shaking it slowly. "It's like I once said to Kate. Your body doesn't lie to me, even if your mouth does."

He then motions behind him toward Mia's table, and I close my eyes in added frustration.

"Invite her to come help babysit June and Will tomorrow

night. They're a handful these days, and you could probably use an extra pair of hands."

My jaw goes from clenched to slack. "Are you serious?"

He quirks a brow. "Deadly. Tell her I roped you into it, even though we both know you're obsessed with my babies, and that you need an extra pair of hands and thought she might like it. It's a chance to talk to her without fear of being caught by someone." He puffs out a humored breath. "And fuck knows do you need to talk. Or maybe even fuck ... actually, no. Not in my house or around my children."

My brows shoot to my hairline. "You really are unbelievable—you know that?"

He shrugs. "Tell me something I don't know. But you gotta admit, it's a great idea."

"Yeah. If it wasn't fucking weird, asking her to babysit my goalie's children when she's never even met you guys before, then it would be a great idea."

Jensen lifts a shoulder and pushes his empty beer glass away from him. "When you come up with a better idea to spend the time with her you so clearly want and away from prying eyes, then I'm all ears. Until then, I'll wait."

MIA

"Seriously, I love it." Leo brings me into a hug again as we shrug on our jackets at the door to Riley's Bar. "I know it's only been a few months, but it feels like our group is really close. It's nice to have a picture of everyone together."

I inwardly cringe again at the gift. All I could think of was the picture of the four of us standing in front of the Space Needle. So, I grabbed a black frame from Target and wrapped it up.

Picking up flirtatious signals has never been my strong point, but even I can tell from tonight that Leo wants more than just this frame for his birthday.

Trying to remain friendly but uninterested is impossible. He's edged closer to me all night, and I lost count of the number of times he brought me into a hug, even kissing me on top of my head at one point. If Jessie saw—which I doubt since I'm certain he's not noticed me at all tonight—then I know it would bother him.

Or maybe I'm just fooling myself. He told me nothing more could happen between us. He couldn't have made that any clearer.

"Okay, I'm going to head out and flag down a taxi," Tara shouts over the music.

I point behind me. "I'm going to use the restroom before we leave."

Tara smiles and pushes through the door, Hugh following closely behind. Leo lingers for a beat, unsure of what to do.

"I'll meet you outside," I say. "I'll only be a second."

He nods and follows, finally leaving me with a moment to breathe.

The two free cocktails I had, courtesy of Felicity Morgan, are definitely more than I would normally drink, and it kind of shows as I wobble my way to the restrooms.

Just as I'm about to push through the door, a hand wraps around my upper arm, pulling me away from the entrance and into an opposite room. I'd squeal if I had time to register what was happening, but then a light flicks on in the dark space, and Jessie's face comes into view.

His blue eyes are darker than usual, but not as glazed as they were the last time I saw him. He hasn't been drinking heavily tonight.

"Fancy seeing you here"—I look around the space filled with boxes, mops, and various cleaning products—"in this closet."

He bites on his bottom lip as he casts his gaze down my body.

I can't tell if it's to fight back his laughter or in response to my outfit. "I haven't seen you with your hair like that in a long while." His voice is playful as he flicks the end of my ponytail, which rests over my right shoulder.

"It's hot and stuffy in this bar, and Felicity Morgan gave it to me when I arrived."

His eyes flash with something—maybe excitement, perhaps realization. "As in Jon's wife?"

"You were sitting with her all night. You should know who she is."

He shoves his hands in the pockets of his fitted black dress pants. "All right, smart-ass."

I chuckle and look around once more. "So, what exactly are we doing in here?"

He runs a hand over the scruff on his jaw, and his previously confident demeanor turns sheepish. "I, um ... Christ, Jensen, why did I let you talk me into this?" he mumbles.

"What are you talking about?" I reply casually. In reality, I'm anything but casual, as my stomach does flips. *What is he going to ask me?*

"Okay, so this is going to sound a bit crazy, but ... I need to babysit Jensen's twins tomorrow night. He's taking Kate, his wife, out for a date night. He kind of roped me into it since he didn't have another option with the late notice. I wondered if you wanted to help me. June and Will are amazing, but kind of a handful."

I point at my chest in disbelief. "You want me to help you care for the children of probably the most famous goalie in the NHL?"

He nods, wincing slightly. "Thought it might be a chance to talk, you know, privately, without people walking into your dorm or in a packed bar. I'm going home for the bye week afterward, and I ..." He looks off to the side and blows through his nose. "I wanted to see you before I left."

"Jessie ..." I blow out a breath. "My head is spinning. You

spend half your time shutting me out or running away, and now you want to spend more time with me. Then, the other night, I thought you were going to k—" I stop myself quickly.

He bites down on his bottom lip again. "Finish your sentence, Mia."

"It's fine. I'm just confused—that's all."

He steps forward and leans over me, his palm braced on the wall above my head.

My knees go weak. *Oh shit, is he going to do it now? Kiss me?* In so many ways, I know it's a bad idea, but there's not a chance I'd stop him.

"I know, Sweetheart. I am too. But I think you've worked out by now that I can't stay away from you, even if I know this is a bad idea and your dad would likely kill me."

His breath fans my face as he brings his other slightly callous palm to my cheek. "Watching you give Leo that gift and then him touch you in public when I can't go anywhere near you—it's like pouring gasoline on what we've had simmering for fucking years."

My legs are about ready to give out from underneath me as I try to find a response. *He noticed it all.* "It was just a photo of the group of us. I didn't know what else to get him for his birthday."

He chews on the corner of his mouth. "He wants you naked and in his bed for his birthday—that's what he wants."

"And what do you want?" I whisper.

He presses his body into mine, eliminating the space left between us. I can feel him, what this is doing to him. "You know what I want, Mia. I wouldn't be pulling you into dark and dingy spaces if I didn't. What I really want is to hold your hand, take you to fancy restaurants, and show you the man I want to be for you."

Neither of us moves an inch, waiting, willing, desperate for the other to make a move and break the tension that's so thick that it could be cut with a knife.

But if anyone needs to make the first move, it's him. It has to be Jessie. It's not my career on the line, it's not me who my dad will murder, and it's not me with traumas that make me feel like I'm not enough.

I'm also not the one who ran away and left calls unanswered and messages on Read.

I push against his chest, and he takes a step back, diverting his focus from my eyes to the floor.

Disappointment shoots through me. It shouldn't be this hard for two people to kiss.

Maybe we aren't meant to be; maybe there are too many barriers between us. Whatever this is, I know I won't be strong enough to resist him if he makes a move.

"Okay, I'll help you tomorrow night. Just give me the address, and I'll meet you there."

CHAPTER FIFTEEN

MIA

Kate and Jensen's house is just on the edge of town and is huge and kind of spectacular in all white with a beautiful front porch.

I hand the driver cash and step out of the taxi and onto the sidewalk.

From the second I agreed to do this tonight, I've been nervous. I've seen Jessie more times than I can count, but I've never met Jensen and his wife, Kate; they're all highfliers in their fields and older than me.

After I walk up the porch steps, I knock a couple of times, using the brass door knocker, and step back, waiting for someone to answer.

My stomach knots again with a mixture of excitement and anticipation.

Through the stained-glass window in the front door, I watch as a figure I know to be Jessie approaches and pulls open the door.

He smiles at me warmly. "You made it."

In gray sweatpants and a tight-fitting white T-shirt, he looks even hotter than he did in his postgame suit last night.

"Hey," I say, stepping into the hallway and bending down to unzip my leather boots, pulling them off my jeans.

He tracks every movement I make, not once taking his eyes off me. I know he doesn't because I don't take mine from his either.

As soon as I stand up straight, he wraps his arms around my smaller frame, planting a kiss on the top of my head.

I look up at him and smile. "Was that deliberate?"

He chuckles and kisses the top of my head again. "Sure was. Leo might've had his chance last night, but tonight, it's my turn."

He pauses for a second, his eyes scanning my face. "Thank you for coming tonight. I know this is kind of weird for you."

Jessie loops his little finger with mine, and we walk down the hallway and turn a corner, entering an open-plan living space with a kitchen set at the back. The dark blue kitchen cabinets are a stark contrast to the soft blue walls. The design of the house is an L-shape, and around the corner, I see a large dining table with a chandelier directly above it. The house is modern and sleek but really homey.

Jessie guides me over to a couch. A flatscreen TV sits on the far wall, and all around, there are houseplants. There must be at least twenty that I can see so far—some big, some smaller, and some hanging from the roof.

"Kate's into plants," Jessie explains as we sit next to each other, watching some random children's program I've never seen before.

I nod. "Where're June and Will?"

He thumbs over his shoulder. "Kate and Jensen are about to head out, so they're changing them into pajamas before they go. The twins only need to stay up for an hour after they leave."

I narrow my eyes at him playfully. "You couldn't watch them for an hour without help?"

Returning my expression, he shakes his head. "Nope, definitely not."

I go to open my mouth and reply, but I'm cut short by a female voice from behind.

"Okay, I think we're all set. June is having some trouble going down at night and sometimes keeps her brother awake, but eventually, they both drift off."

Other than for a very brief moment in Whistler, I've only seen the occasional photo of Kate and Jensen together in the press, but much like Jon and Felicity, Zach and Luna, it's clear they keep their private lives out of the spotlight. I knew she was pretty, but as I watch her walk toward us, a baby in each arm, she could be shooting for the latest top-model awards.

She's kept her focus on her children the entire time, but as soon as she looks up and sees me, she stops in her tracks. "Oh, hi."

I lift my hand and offer a tentative wave. "Hi. You must be Kate."

A little like Felicity did last night, she cocks her head to the side and smiles. "Yeah. And you're Mia, right?"

"And I'm Jensen."

In the flesh and standing up rather than sitting in a booth, the Scorpions goalie is kind of an intimidating figure. His dark hair and dark brown eyes match June's and Will's perfectly—a complete contrast to Kate's light-blonde hair and blue eyes.

Jensen takes Will from Kate's left arm and then lowers him to the floor, setting him on his feet while holding onto his hands above his head to give him balance. "These two troublemakers are well on the way to racing around our house."

Will looks up at his dad and then slowly takes a step forward. On wobbly legs, he does the same again.

From Kate's arms, June makes a frustrated noise and points at Will. "Oh, so you want to join your brother, huh?" Kate sets her down, too, and begins walking June toward us alongside Will.

"Look at you two go." From beside me, Jessie smiles over his shoulder and then leaps to his feet, rounding the couch in record time. "Come give your uncle Jessie a squish."

Immediately, Jensen lifts Will from his feet and passes him over, his arms outstretched to Jessie. His dribbly chin rubs on Jessie's shirt, but that clearly doesn't bother him as he holds Will with one arm and reaches out for June with the other.

"Bring it in, Juney Baby."

Kate rolls her eyes as she passes Jessie her daughter. "How many times have I said Juney Baby is not her real name?"

Jessie shrugs and plants a kiss on top of her mass of dark hair, sending my heart fluttering. "Neither is JJ or Princess, but you two use it all the time."

I chuckle, and Jensen and Kate look over at me.

Kate points at me in jest. "Oh, don't you go encouraging him. This boy doesn't know his limits."

"Okay, so they just need warm milk before bed, their teeth brushing, and the latest story read to them. In theory"—Jensen drawls the final word—"they should go to sleep easily since they didn't have a long nap today."

"Yeah, and don't I know it?" Kate brings the back of her hand over her mouth as she yawns. "We won't be late, trust me."

"We'll see about that." Walking over to his wife, he takes her left hand in his, and it's then I notice the huge black diamond on her ring finger. "A couple of mojitos, and you'll be into it. Or maybe even me if I can help it."

Kate shakes her head, pats him on the shoulder, and then looks over at me and smiles. "These boys always think they have the upper hand. What they fail to realize is, behind the scenes, we call the shots." She checks her watch. "We'll be home by ten."

With a kiss to June and Will's foreheads, they both make for the front door before Jensen stops and swivels on his heel, pointing over at the kitchen. "There're snacks and drinks in the fridge if you want anything. Thanks for this."

A few seconds later, I hear the soft click of the door closing behind them and then an engine firing up on the driveway.

Jessie turns to me, his left brow quirked. "I think Will might have already pooped."

"Okay," I say, rising from the couch and walking toward them. "How hard can a diaper be?"

He passes me June, and I take her into my arms.

"Not that hard," Jessie confidently says, walking toward the hallway.

We climb the glamorous wooden staircase and make a right at the top. The nursery is a stunning sage color with light wood furniture and white decor. As soon as we enter, my eyes are immediately drawn to June's and Will's names on the wall above their beds.

"They're really cute." I point to the wooden name plaques as I bounce June in my other arm.

Despite me being a total stranger to her, she giggles and looks up at me with her big brown eyes.

Jessie looks over to where I'm pointing "Yeah, they were a gift from me. Brought them over the day Kate got back from the hospital." He focusses back on Will, laying him on the changing table.

Maybe I should be surprised at Jessie's thoughtfulness, but I'm not. Through the aloof exterior he tries to portray, I see him —the soft guy who, over time, has lost the ability to open himself up to show love and be loved in return.

"Nice names too." I look down at June in my arms. "You've got a really pretty name, not one you hear too often either."

Jessie doesn't respond to the smell as he tears off Will's diaper and quickly bags it before wiping him down and grabbing a fresh diaper from the side. "Kate chose June's name, and Jensen chose Will's," he replies, still focused on changing Will, but has no issue with completing the task easily.

"You really didn't need my help tonight, did you?"

He pops the buttons on Will's pajamas, picking him up and then the diaper, ready to throw it in the trash. "Not with the diaper. I've changed a fair few in my time."

"How? You're an only child." My question is definitely more of a statement.

Looking down at Will, he offers him a small smile and then the same to me. He opens his mouth, but hesitates, clearly thinking about what to say. I notice the pull within him—he wants to tell me more—but at the last second, I see him close off.

"Yeah. Yeah, I am."

As we creep out of the nursery, Jessie bends down to flick on the nightlight and leaves the door off the latch, the baby monitor in his left hand.

I pull my phone out of the back pocket of my jeans, checking the time. "Right on schedule, Staff Sergeant."

"Want to give me a little salute to go with that?" he retorts.

I look down the staircase toward the kitchen. "Nope, but what I do want is ice cream."

We make our way into the kitchen, and I take a seat at one of the barstools as Jessie pulls open the freezer door.

"Okay, we have vanilla."

I scrunch up my nose. "Nah."

"Oreo?"

I wave a hand in front of my face. "Overrated."

"Chocolate Fudge Brownie?"

"Gimme." Flipping my hands toward me, I beam in delight at the tub of Ben & Jerry's as Jessie slides it across the counter, followed by a spoon.

"What are you smirking at?" I say around my first mouthful —it took me exactly half a second to pop the lid and dig in.

He shakes his head and takes the stool next to me. "Nothing. Just know that's probably Felicity's stash you're eating."

I stop chewing immediately. "Seriously?"

"Yep. I mean, she offers to buy your drinks for the night, and you repay her by eating her favorite ice cream. You're a bad friend."

That's when I see the second spoon in his hand. "Don't think you're sharing this. If I'm going down for ice cream theft, then I at least want to enjoy it all to myself."

Setting his spoon down, he rests his elbow on the counter and watches me side-on, his face resting in his palm as he continues to smile softly.

"What now?" I say, managing to scoop another load of ice cream onto my spoon.

"We have at least three hours to kill. How about a movie?"

I pause, remembering the last time we watched a movie together, and my thighs squeeze together at the memories. "What kind?"

"Your choice, ma'am."

I stand and clear away the spoons and ice cream and take them to the kitchen, and then walk across to the couch and pull off a couple of blankets from the arms. "Are you taking that one?" I point at a second couch opposite and throw him one of the blankets.

Jessie looks surprised as he catches it against his chest and makes his way toward the other couch. "Yeah, sure."

As much as I'd love to snuggle up with him and watch the latest action movie just released on Netflix, I know a dangerous idea when I see one. I haven't changed my mind since last night in the bar; if anything happens between us, then he has to be the one to make the first move.

He grabs the remote from the coffee table and starts flicking through the latest releases until he lands on the one I was hoping to watch. "This one?"

I adjust some of the pillows behind me, getting myself comfortable. "How did you know?"

Jessie starts the movie and kicks his feet up in front of him, a wry smile pulling at his lips. "How could I forget? You enjoyed the first one so much."

CHAPTER SIXTEEN

MIA

We timed tonight to perfection. With my dad out of town on a golf stopover, there was no way he could catch us.

I waited at my window, pulling the curtains back every couple of minutes to catch a glimpse of Jessie's black muscle car pulling up along the sidewalk.

We'd snuck kisses every now and then—either in my office when no one was around or in the dark of the empty player parking lot.

But tonight, I hoped we'd have more time alone, and heat thrummed through me at the thought.

After nearly ten minutes of back and forth to the window, two headlights shone into the living room as Jessie pulled up outside the gates to our driveway, and my phone buzzed in my pocket.

> J
>
> I'm here, Sweetheart.

I giddily smiled down at the text.

> ME
>
> Okay, coming out now. Shall I bring snacks for the movie?

> J
>
> Taking his daughter out and eating his snacks. You make me want to do bad things, Mia.
> *wink emoji*

Grabbing the snacks I'd already packed, I made for the front door and out to his car.

When I pulled open the passenger door, I was immediately hit with air-conditioning and the beat of Nirvana. The cool air was a relief against the hot Texas summer. Even though it was early nightfall, the outside temperature was still crazy high.

Jessie put the car into gear and revved the engine as I clipped myself in.

"I would have gotten out and opened your door for you"—he ducked his head and peered out the windshield and then his side window—"but we both know I'm going to be seen."

I shrugged my shoulders. "My next-door neighbor, Maybell, is likely already asleep." I paused and looked at him, my lips tipping up at the corner. "Or at least she was until you woke her with your car. And I doubt anyone else around here cares."

He leaned across the center console, tipping my chin up with his forefinger as brushed his lips over mine. "Such a brat."

"You love it," I replied, kissing him back and wanting more.

He pulled back and looked at me, his hand resting on the stick shift between us.

We didn't say anything as he backed out and into the street, heading toward the drive-in theater he'd been promising to take me to since the night we had gone stargazing.

Tonight, they were showing an oldie but one of my favorites—The Fast and the Furious.

Taking my hand in his as we hit the freeway, Jessie smiled over at me.

"You're going to witness plenty of cars faster and louder than this in about thirty minutes, Sweetheart."

I balked at him. "You know I've seen this movie, like, a thousand times before, right?"

"You have?"

I nodded. "Yep. It's one of my all-time favorites." I chuckled cheekily. "It has absolutely nothing to do with Paul Walker though."

He let go of my hand for a split second, shifted gears, and then retook it. "Is that right?"

"Yep," I teased, popping the P, entirely too excited about the night ahead of us.

"Well, I'm not sure I want to go and see this movie with you anymore."

I stuck out my bottom lip, mocking him. The streetlights flashed inside the car as we sped along the freeway. "Awww ... well, I guess we could go somewhere else. The snacks will go to waste though."

Jessie squeezed my hand tighter as we came to a halt at a stoplight ahead. He turned to me, his lids slightly hooded. "Nah, we can still go watch the movie. I'll just have to make sure your attention is on me and not Paul."

I HAD no idea what part of the movie we were on, and I didn't care either.

All I could think about was which part of my neck he was going to kiss and suck on next.

"Come over here, Mia," he whispered into the crook of my neck as he leaned across the center section of his car. "Sit in my lap."

Every muscle in my body contracted as I lifted onto my knees, almost bashing my head on the roof in the process, and climbed over into his lap. I was wearing a skirt with no tights, but I didn't care if I flashed him or anyone else in this theater. I wanted Jessie to see me.

I knew I was wet, soaking through my panties. Part of me wanted to warn him I'd leave a mark on his jeans, but another more dominant part was too embarrassed to say anything. Jessie had been with so many more girls than I had boys, which was zero in total before him. I wanted to act confident, even if, inside, I was shaking with anticipation.

He flicked a button on the side of his seat, lowering it slightly. "There. Now you're not crushed against my steering wheel."

Bringing his palms around the nape of my neck, he continued to kiss me, the scruff of his jaw rubbing against my face.

I could feel it—his hard length—as I adjusted myself on his lap and braced my legs on either side of his seat, straddling him. I wanted him so badly, but I knew we couldn't go much further tonight. The blacked-out windows of his car gave us some privacy, but I didn't want to lose my virginity in a drive-in theater, even if it was with the right boy.

Jessie brought his hand to my waist, slowly grinding me on his hips. "Tell me if it's too much, if I'm too much, Sweetheart."

"It's not too much," I whispered back into his mouth, turned on by his presence, his tongue, his cologne, but mostly the hard bulge beneath me.

He teased the waistband of my skirt, running his fingertips along the front. His light touch sent shock waves throughout my body as he caressed skin that had never been touched in this way.

"I really want to touch you some more, Mia."

I whimpered. I wanted it so bad. "Where do you want to touch me?"

He dropped his hand from my waistband as he slowly worked it down the flimsy material of my skirt until the back of his hand rested on his thigh.

He teased the hem of my skirt between his fingers. "Under here. Is that okay?"

My ability to speak had deserted me, and all I could do was nod as I rested my forehead against his and rose up onto my knees to give him the access he needed.

When his warm, rough palm met the inside of my left knee, his fingers began dancing toward my apex. I was so turned on; it almost hurt.

"I want to make you feel really good, Mia."

As soon as his fingers found the fabric of my underwear, my breath caught in my throat. "Oh my God," I gasped.

"I haven't touched you yet, Sweetheart," he replied.

"It already feels so good. I just hope I do it right for you."

Jessie pulled back, his bright blue eyes shining in the lighting from the theater. "Do it right? Mia, I'm ready to blow straight into my pants—you turn me on that much. I'm fighting with everything I have to hold it together."

I kissed him hard, my tongue swiping against his. The way he could make me feel everything, but mostly in this moment, the way he could make me feel safe, secure, and confident to go further than we ever had before.

"Touch me," I pleaded.

His fingers found the edge of my panties. "I can feel how soaked you are for me. I promise I'll be gentle."

I waited to feel him, for his hand to find my center and do all the things I'd fantasized about in my bed, when his phone buzzed in the center console, and Mom lit up the screen.

It was like a switch flicked in his head. Relaxed and happy Jessie was gone, and in front of me was a guy panicking to grab his phone.

His cell was still ringing in his hand when he picked it up, but he didn't answer it.

"Why didn't you pick up?" I asked, confused.

He shook his head and adjusted himself beneath me. I could tell he wanted me to climb off, so I did, making my way back to the passenger seat. He didn't fight me to stay where I was, and he didn't seem sorry for breaking away from me when I had been about to hand myself over to him.

He looked in his rearview mirror and cranked the engine on the car.

"W-where are we going? The movie isn't finished," I asked, a lump forming in my throat and tears welling in my eyes.

I was embarrassed and shocked by the way he was reacting to a simple call from his mom. Was this just an excuse for him to get out of a situation he didn't want to be in with me?

I thought I was what he wanted.

"I'm sorry, Mia. But I need to drop you back at your place. We'll do this again another time."

Through glassy eyes, I looked over at Jessie's worried face. "Is everything okay?" What I'd meant to say was, Is it me?

He nodded once and hit the road, heading back to my house. "Everything's fine. I just need to be somewhere."

CHAPTER SEVENTEEN

JESSIE

S

> So, I went for blueberry pancakes this morning.
> I'll hand you this round; they are superior and
> an excellent pre-shift breakfast.

Mia's text comes through just as I'm getting ready to board my flight back to Dallas. The thought of going home for four days in the bye week is anything but the rest and recuperation the break in the NHL schedule was originally designed to provide. And based on the phone call I took from Mom last night, I'm about to walk into hell and a whole lot of painful memories. Each step I take toward boarding the plane, my lungs find it harder to inflate.

But hearing from the girl I want to kiss more desperately than I need air right now somehow has me smiling like a fucking Cheshire cat as I hand over my boarding pass to be scanned.

>   ME
>
> There's an even better pancake house I go to with the boys on cheat day. I'll take you there when I get back.

What are you doing, Jessie? You're supposed to be staying away from her, not fucking taking her out.

> S
>
> You're heading home right now then?

My chest deflates when she doesn't accept my offer to take her out.

>   ME
>
> Yeah, about to board, so I gotta go.

Stay away from her. Keep her safe.

Though my body doesn't get the memo from my brain as my fingers type out another message before I switch my cell to airplane mode and pocket it.

>   ME
>
> I'll text you when I land. Have a good shift at work.

I PULL off my black hoodie when I step into the Dallas air. It's only fifty-eight, but the climate is a whole world away from Seattle.

When I played for the Destroyers for a grand total of one season, the team paid for a rental, and I planned to buy a place for myself in the city, using my signing bonus. That never happened though. Somehow, my parents managed to spend every last dime in a matter of months, and when my season hit a tailspin and my drinking increased, I knew I was on my final warning. Good thing I didn't commit to anything since I'd have another expense in a city I had no reason to be in.

Heading for the pickup zone, I put my bag in the open trunk and climb into a taxi, hesitating as I consider what destination to provide. Mom is my priority, but the selfish part of me wants to head straight to my hotel, grab a shower, and make for the bar. I despise myself for thinking about it, especially when it's not even one in the afternoon.

"Where are we heading then, buddy?" The driver eyes me through the rearview mirror.

I pull at the back of my neck. Going "home" shouldn't be this fucking difficult. "South Boulevard–Park Row," I finally say on an exhale.

The driver nods once and narrows his eyes in question.

I know he recognizes me but is working to keep his reaction hidden. There are two kinds of people when they see a famous athlete from their hometown. The squealers, who don't know what to do first—jump up and down, grab their friends, or take a photo and post it on their social media. Then there're people like this guy right here—the play-it-cool types.

But I know what he's thinking: *Why in the hell is Jessie Callaghan heading to the worst part of Dallas in his bye week?*

The streets pass by in a blur for the entire twenty-five-minute drive, and when we pull up outside the house I hoped I'd never have to see again when I moved out for college, I'm hit with a repeated realization.

Nothing has changed.

I remember when I was ten, and my dad told me if I painted the front porch, he would pay me twenty dollars. To me, that was like winning the lotto. Three entire days, I worked in the summer heat until I could barely move my wrist. The day I finished, I couldn't wait for him to get home from whatever bar he was at and show him. The money could buy me more candy than I could carry, but it was his pride that I was really craving. His acceptance of me.

For once, I just wanted his hand around my shoulder instead of in between my ribs. Yet that was exactly what happened when he got back home that night. It was almost dark when he flew into my bedroom and pinned me against the wall, screaming at me that the finish was shit, that I'd missed parts. He pulled the twenty-dollar bill he'd been waving in my face for days and slammed it flat against my forehead, still screaming in my face.

I never did get the money. Instead, I'd gotten an even bigger beating for being a "useless little prick."

I climb out of the taxi and hand the driver some cash, pulling my bag out of the trunk.

The front yard is overgrown, and the old tan leather couch that was in my baby photos still sits out front—Mom's favored smoking spot. The porch hasn't been touched since that day, and as I take the couple of steps and pull open the screen, I don't know what's going to give out first—the wood beneath my feet or the door barely hanging on its hinges.

My parents see more per month from me than some families do in a year, but zero of it goes where it should. They wouldn't even let me buy them a new house; they wanted the money for other things.

I know it's coming; as soon as I step across the threshold, I'll smell it—the memories, the pain. Trauma hangs in the air in this place, its presence ingrained in every wall. The few photos my mom hung portray smiling faces, but every square inch of this house is a lie.

If you visit in the daytime, you'll smell the stench of old cigarettes and liquor. But you'll have to hide and wait until the sun goes down and nighttime falls to witness the truths. To catch a glimpse into the horrifying secrets the Callaghan family hides.

Still standing in the entryway, I close my eyes and take a deep breath, pushing through the front door.

The living room is like it always is—gray, worn, and a fucking mess. Mom is as she always has been—and probably always will be—passed out on the couch with an open and half-finished bottle of vodka balancing dangerously on the edge of the coffee table.

Fear rocks through me as my heart races in my chest. My body begins to burn from my toes all the way to my cheeks, but my hands feel ice cold as I breathe in through my nose for four seconds, hold for another four, and slowly exhale.

Over and over, I work to center myself and temper the response my body defaults to. When the anxiety attacks first started to happen, I was convinced I was about to go into cardiac arrest. Pain shoots through my arms, tingling into my fingers, and the familiar wave of nausea rolls through my stomach.

Shutting the door behind me, I turn and take in my mom once more. From the outside, you step directly into the living room. There's no hallway or separating door to the living space, and the outside elements whip around the room, blowing frail strands of blonde hair around my mom's pale and motionless face.

Her breathing is shallow, but I can make out the movement of her chest underneath the baggy and threadbare sweater she's worn pretty much every time I've seen her.

It's useless, trying to wake her since she isn't really sleeping. She's intoxicated, passed out. Her body is alive, but her mind is dead to the world. The addict in me—which is fighting so fucking hard to break out as it takes her in—feels a sense of envy toward her numbness, her lack of fucks toward herself and the rest of the world. But the fighter in me carries my feet toward the kitchen to find cleaning supplies and a trash bag—a routine I could carry out in my sleep.

An hour later, I've scrubbed every countertop and thrown out every bottle and empty packet of noodles and ginger biscuits I could find. I've heard Jon, Jensen, and Zach talk about home cooking and meals their parents made as comfort food. Jon would frequently travel home to Bellevue and return a day later, reminiscing about how he could never top his mom's cooking.

That's not something I can relate to. The empty food packets stashed throughout this house represent much of what I remember from my childhood. When I was older and she was occasionally sober, I asked Mom to tell me about my brother, about the boy she cried about daily. It was clear she'd never dealt with his death properly, and Dad wouldn't even acknowledge his existence, throwing out the baby clothes they'd bought for him and refused to use for me.

Just before my papa passed, I remember him pleading with Mom to talk to someone about my brother's death since he could see the way it was tearing his daughter apart. But she refused, burying away her feelings. Instead of getting the help she needed, she leaned on the familiar and drank herself into submission.

And that's where she's been ever since. Locked in a world of pain, only numbed by addiction.

"Jessie?" Mom's weak voice calls from behind the couch. "Are you home?"

"Yeah, Mom. Just figuring out what you have here. I'll head out and grab you some food," I reply, pulling open each cupboard door and then the fridge to discover nothing inside.

"We ran out of money again."

I squeeze my eyes shut and close one of the cupboards slowly, gripping the loose handle tightly. "I know. You told me on the phone last night."

"It's not enough, baby. We can't get by on it."

Frustration races through me. "How can twenty thousand every week not be enough?!" I bite out, desperately trying to rein in my anger.

From the kitchen, I see a hand shoot out and snatch the vodka bottle off the coffee table. "Because it's not. Wayne is spending more, and I can't keep him out of that account."

I want to plead with her to come back with me to Seattle. I can get her away from this place, enroll her in a program, and help fix her. The number of times I've begged her to pack a bag and leave with me for Seattle. I'd find her a place away from Dad. I'd appoint lawyers since I have connections, dissolve their marriage, and file orders against him coming anywhere near her.

But I don't think she's ever been tempted to accept my offer. This house is a link to Will and my dad as the man she fell in love with years ago. She can't see that he's morphed from the asshole he was back then into the full-blown monster he is today. Or maybe she does. She cries like she knows it deep down. But to break the perilous cycle she's in, she has to *want* to get better, to be better. She has to want change and be prepared to fight for it. Being in this place and seeing my mom in this state chips away at my own armor, and I know too long spent here will inevitably drag me down too.

It already is.

I pull my phone out of my back pocket, and a text from Mia, asking me how my flight was, lights up the screen.

Her words are like a lifeline to me, a tether to another world and a different, happier Jessie. I want to reply, but I know I can't. I can't do to Mia what this place does to me. I need to swing by the store, make sure Mom's okay and fed, and then get the fuck out of here and over to my hotel.

CHAPTER EIGHTEEN

JESSIE

> JON
>
> Since all you lazy bastards don't have any games this week, how about you come watch a master coach at work?
>
> JENSEN
>
> Oh, look, Princess—a stampede of responses.
>
> KATE
>
> I'm not getting involved.
>
> ZACH
>
> Didn't see you complaining when you had bye weeks. In fact, I clearly recall you running off for extended weekends away.

Pausing in the freezer aisle of the grocery store, I quickly type out a message.

> ME
>
> When is the game?

> **JON**
>
> Finally, a mature response.
>
> **FELICITY**
>
> Look who's talking …
>
> **JON**
>
> Jessie—I'm talking exclusively to you at this point—the game is this Thursday night. I can get as many tickets as you need.

Since I only plan to spend three nights in Dallas—which is three nights longer than I want—I figure, why not?

> **ME**
>
> Okay, I'm in.
>
> **JENSEN**
>
> Kate has the twins, so count me in too. She's being a star and giving me a night off. I think it's time I saw your prodigy play in the flesh.
>
> **KATE**
>
> Wife points.
>
> **FELICITY**
>
> You won't be disappointed; my son is killing it in the NCAA.
>
> **JON**
>
> Yeah, he is, Angel. Joint top goal scorer right now.

Memories of my time playing in college come racing back. Well, the memories I have anyway. Those three years looked a lot like Jon's rookie years in the NHL—drinking too much, fighting, and, yeah, being the resident playboy. Don't ask me how many girls I fucked before pretty much kicking them out once I was done. I'm not proud of my behavior. They knew what they were getting with me—that I wasn't in it for a relationship. I had a contact list in my phone longer than the receipt for this grocery shop will be. Difference is, Jon actually cared about his career, and he didn't start fights in the locker room. It's safe to say I was a dick at college.

JON

Are you coming, Captain?

ZACH

If I do, will you promise to shut up about attending our wedding?

JON

I'm still not over the fact that you want to have it alone. Without us. Without my skills at your disposal.

ZACH

There's literally going to be three of us plus an officiant. How much planning does it need?

JON

You underestimate the little details that can take your day from good to spectacular.

ZACH

Okay, I'm not going to the game. Count me out.

ME

Jack's a winger, like me, right?

JON

Might be even faster than you. Need to watch your back when he breaks into the NHL.

ME

He's that good?

JON

Yep, but don't tell him I said that. Cocky little shit gives me enough back talk already.

FELICITY

You gotta admit though, he was right about that power play last week. You made the wrong call.

ZACH

Changed my mind. Count me in.

JON

Fucker.

KATE

Okay, I'm off to stare at a wall. Jon, you need three extra tickets.

LUNA

And to listen to Jack more often.

ZACH

Bahahaha. That's my Rocket Girl.

As I push the cart of groceries through the empty aisle, I close out the group chat but pause when I see another message from Mia.

S

How's home? It's freezing here.

ME

You need to get that heating figured out in your dorm. If it's any colder than when I was last there, it's practically freezing. I could see my own breath at one point.

S

Tara has already complained about it, but it's an old building. They said we need to get additional heaters if we're that cold.

ME

You should definitely do that. It's not healthy to sleep in the freezing cold.

I should know.

S

Yeah, I know. I'll buy a couple of storage heaters when my next paycheck comes in.

ME

Which is?

S

Week or so.

Right before I reach the counter, I stop and open up my browser, buying a half-dozen top-of-the-line storage heaters, then set them for next-day delivery to her dorm building.

ME

Use the extra blankets you have and complain to the maintenance team again. They need to check the furnace.

S

Okay. When will you be back?

ME

Three nights here, and I'll be back on Monday night.

I want to tag on *can I see you?* to my message, but I resist.

S

Okay. Be safe.

WHEN I WALK BACK into the house with three hundred dollars' worth of groceries, Mom is exactly where I left her—on the couch, scrolling through TV channels.

I carry the bags through to the kitchen and begin restocking the cupboards. "See you got a new TV," I shout over my shoulder.

Mom hums in acknowledgment. "Wayne got it a couple of weeks ago."

"What happened to the old one?"

Silence.

No money for food or supplies, but plenty to go on a state-of-the-art flat screen. Figures.

"What happened to the TV, Mom?" I push, turning back in Mom's direction and making my way back to the couch with two bottles of water. I offer one to her and perch on the arm at the other end.

She shifts uncomfortably and then leans across, taking the water and looking at me for the first time since I got here. Her blue eyes are dull and glazed.

I look down at the coffee table and pick up the open packet of ginger biscuits set in front of her.

I reach inside and fetch one out, breaking it in half and handing the bigger piece to her. "Eat this and take a few sips, Mom. You need it."

She shakily brings the biscuit to her lips and crunches down, chasing it with a small sip of water before setting the bottle on the coffee table. "The last one couldn't get all the channels he wanted."

That's the biggest pile of horseshit, and she knows it.

"Didn't punch a hole through this one then?"

"Jessie," she drawls, "just leave it, yeah?"

Slowly, she shifts her body forward and gets up. The black leggings she's wearing hang off her legs. Since the last time I saw her, she's lost even more weight. "I need to use the bathroom."

I watch as her frail body climbs the stairs she's fallen down more times than I can count.

"I'll make us some food," I say, downing the rest of my water and heading back into the kitchen.

It must be ten minutes when I finally hear footsteps

approaching from behind me as I stand at the burner, stirring pasta sauce.

"Can you help out and grab a couple of plates?" I call over my shoulder.

"Enough for your old man?"

I stop stirring and turn around to face my dad. He looks like he hasn't shaved in a week, the dark blond stubble on his chin long, and his floppy hair sticks out of the sides of his Scorpions baseball cap.

That's the thing about my dad—he hates the very bones of me, but enjoys telling everyone who I am and how he got me into hockey. In reality, he did nothing for my career except hold me back with injuries that weren't sustained on the ice. The only people who looked out for my career were my papa and Graham Jenkins, and neither of them ever knew the truth about my father.

As I stand, facing him, his eyes laser-focused on me, I know it's not a question of if he's going to attack me, but when and how.

I cross my arms over my chest and pin him with a mocking smile. He doesn't need to know that behind my confident exterior, I'm a trembling mess, waiting on his inevitable strike.

You're not a kid anymore, Jessie. You can take him.

"Just enough for us both. I didn't know when you'd return. Today, tomorrow, next week. Maybe never," I eventually answer.

A subtle sneer traces his lips. "I live here, and I own this place. Of course I was coming home."

Turning back around to the burner, I point at the top-right cupboard. "There's extra pasta in there if you want it."

The tickle of his breath on the back of my neck is the first thing I feel, then the constricting vise grip as his palm squeezes my shoulder. Tighter, harder, with increasing brutality.

"Make me some *fucking pasta*."

Normally, it's unwise to poke the bear, but when the animal is Wayne Callaghan, it doesn't matter what you do. I could roll over and ask him to tickle my stomach, but that wouldn't serve me either.

I pause on stirring and take hold of the pan handle. "You didn't say please."

He knows I've got scalding pasta sauce at my disposal. I've never hit him first—ever. But I have always defended myself in any way possible.

When I feel him back away, my lungs inflate once more.

My phone buzzes in the back pocket of my jeans, and before I can stop him, he rips it out, tearing the denim.

"S? Who the fuck is this?" His voice is a mock tease as he turns the screen to face me.

It's just a picture of Mia's hand as she holds a fork, ready to dig into a stack of pancakes. There's no way he can recognize her from that photo alone.

Thank fuck.

"No one you know." I don't turn around to face him. In fact, I barely move a muscle as I work to keep my response neutral.

"You know what they say about girls with red nail polish." He chuckles low, sucking in an appreciative breath.

I say nothing as he slides the phone back into my ripped pocket.

"They suck dick really fucking well."

I shake my head, mimicking his chuckle. "I think that sexist line is exclusive to you."

"You really think you're above me, don't you, hotshot?" He steps closer again, and I turn off the burner. "But you'll never escape this life, and you'll always just be a little rat that murdered your brother."

The red mist descends, and I spin on my heel, for once ready to land the first punch.

But maybe I poked the bear a little too hard this time because I buckle over in agony.

He landed the first hit, just like he always does. But something about this doesn't feel right. I lift my head and look at him, my knees ready to give way beneath me and the room spinning three sixty degrees. That's when I see it—the brass knuckles on his right hand.

He brings them to his mouth and kisses them gently, a disgusting sneer returning to his lips as he winds back for another shot at my ribs. "Welcome home, Jessie."

CHAPTER NINETEEN

MIA

Nearly a week and nothing.
No word from Jessie.

Last time, he at least read my messages; this time, he's not even opened them.

I wrap and tie a bunch of red roses, handing them over to a customer before passing them their change.

I wish I could be angry with him for ghosting me because then I'd be able to shake the nauseating dread swirling in my stomach. The more hours that go by without a response from him, the more I worry he's gone off at the deep end. It's also impossible to be angry with someone when they deliver a half-dozen heaters to your freezing dorm.

But he didn't even reply to my thank-you text.

"There's only a half hour left, and we're quiet. Why don't you take off, Mia?" Carly, my boss, pokes her head around the corner of her office door.

"You sure?" I reply.

I don't mind waiting. Today's shift has at least somewhat distracted my mind.

Carly holds out a white envelope in her hand. "Here's your paycheck and a little tip to say *thank you*. The Christmas period was heavy, but profitable. I wanted to share some of it with you."

I take the envelope from her hand. "Thank you."

She smiles at me warmly and closes the door to her office as I grab my jacket off the hook on the back and begin slipping it on.

"Um, are you still open?" A British voice filters in from behind me.

I turn around to see Felicity standing at the counter, a bouquet of pink roses in her left hand.

"I can come back tomorrow." Her eyes go wide as she recognizes me. "Oh, Mia. Hi again."

"Hey," I greet her, walking across to wrap the flowers. "No, we aren't closed. I was just about to head home."

She passes them to me and watches as I begin rolling them into white paper.

"I didn't know you worked at my favorite florist."

I shrug. "It's part-time. I pick up hours when I can. Helps to pay the bills."

As I look up, she nods, her green eyes meeting mine. She doesn't smile though; her expression is more worried. "Are you okay?"

I snap off a piece of tape from the dispenser, securing the wrap. "Yeah, I'm fine."

It's then I make the fatal mistake and look at her again. The warmth in her eyes tells me she's not buying my bullshit, and I blink back the moisture building up on my lashes.

Reaching into her tote bag, she fetches out a fresh tissue and hands it to me.

I figure it's useless hiding my upset, and I dab at my eyes, smearing mascara on the tissue.

She takes in a breath through her nose and pauses, the silence stretching between us. The only sound is heavy rain pounding the sidewalks outside.

"Look, Mia. We might not know each other that well, but I want you to know whatever it is, it's safe with me."

I look down and shake my head. "I can't say."

"Is it Jessie?"

My head whips up to her. "Jessie?"

She nods slowly and hands me a twenty. "Don't be mad. But Kate Jones is my best friend. She mentioned you were round at theirs last week, babysitting the twins with Jessie." A delicate smile pulls at her lips. "It didn't come as a surprise that you were seeing each other. I had seen the way he looked at you in the bar."

"W-we aren't seeing each other." I drop my shoulders and sigh. "We shouldn't even be friends."

Frantically, I grab a random green ribbon and begin tying it around the bouquet.

She reaches out and places a hand on top of mine to steady me. "I don't need to know details, but Kate told me that you've known each other a long while."

On a long breath, I finish the bow and look up at her. "We do. But it's complicated. We aren't supposed to know each other anymore. The thing is, I'm worried about him. I haven't seen or really heard from him since he went home to Dallas last weekend."

Felicity presses her lips together. "Neither have we. He was supposed to be at my son's game last night, but he didn't show. He sent a text saying he was sick and couldn't go."

My brows knit together. "Sick?"

She nods. "He texted the boys and said he had the flu and that he'd see them at practice tomorrow."

"He hasn't replied to any of my texts," I say, my worry only increasing.

"He probably doesn't want you to stress about him."

I huff out a laugh and hand Felicity her change. "A little too late for that."

"Why don't you go round to see him?" she suggests.

Huffing out another laugh, I grab my cell and bag from the side and check the screen—still no messages from Jessie. "I would if I knew where he lived."

She looks genuinely surprised, but doesn't say anything.

"Like I said, we aren't supposed to see each other. It's a long story."

Felicity takes out her phone and begins tapping on the screen. "One involving your dad, I'm guessing."

She sets her phone down on the counter, the screen lit up with an address. When she leans toward me slightly, I catch a hint of coconut. "Like I said, I don't need the details, but I do know the owners of large NHL teams, thanks to a hockey-mad husband." She nods her head at my paycheck envelope on the side, which has *Mia Jenkins* scrawled across the front. "I might be reaching here, but would I be wrong to hazard a guess that Graham Jenkins is your father?"

I nod once.

She smiles and taps the screen on her phone with her pointer finger. "This is Jessie's address."

I pick up a pen and scrawl the address on a piece of scrap paper. "You don't miss anything."

"Lawyer, babe. It's my job to notice things."

I set the pen down and smile at her. "Kate didn't tell you who my dad was? I guess she knows too."

She picks up the flowers and hugs them to her chest with one arm, adjusting her emerald scarf with the other hand. "No, she didn't. She only mentioned you when I accused her of eating all my ice cream. There are some things Kate won't go down for."

I bark out a laugh and then wince. "Yeah, that was me. Sorry."

Felicity chuckles and then offers me a warm smile, pulling up the hood on her coat and getting ready to leave. "I won't hold ice cream against any girl." She pauses. "Go see him." Felicity turns to leave, but then stops.

She sets the flowers on the counter between us, and then picks up the pen, quickly scribbling a number next to the address. "This is my contact. If you ever need anything, you know where I am."

The rain beats against my umbrella as I stand at the entrance to Jessie's apartment building.

What am I doing? If he wanted to see me, he would've replied. He didn't have a problem texting his friends.

My doubts aren't enough to stop me though as I walk into the building with a drenched bouquet of flowers being squashed under my arm as I shove my umbrella into its holder.

"Can I help you, ma'am?" the doorman asks me as I continue to frustratingly fight with the umbrella.

"Huh?" I look up at him, my slightly damp, dark hair stuck to my face. I stand straight and smile at him. "Yeah, I, um, have a delivery of flowers for Mr. Callaghan." I point at the small card with Jessie's address across the front.

A crease forms between his brow. "I haven't seen Mr. Callaghan in a couple of days. He might be out of town. But let me try his number."

My eyes flare wide. "Oh, um … I mean, it's a surprise delivery. He isn't expecting them."

He smiles at me empathetically and walks across to the desk. When he lifts the phone, I watch as he waits a few seconds before speaking and then nodding once.

"Mr. Callaghan says you can bring them right up," the doorman says, walking back over to me. "He's in apartment number three twenty-nine on the third floor."

My stomach twists as I ride the elevator to Jessie's floor. There's every chance he knows it's me coming to check on him, pushing him to see me when he doesn't want to. But I keep walking anyway, my body refusing to listen to the doubts swirling in my mind.

I get halfway down the hallway when his door number comes into view, and I stop. I could just knock and leave the flowers by the door and then hightail it out of here.

I turn on my heel. *Or I could just leave altogether.*

"Mia?"

Slowly spinning back around, I see Jessie standing in his apartment doorway. His hands are tucked in the pockets of his gray sweatpants, and his fitted black shirt clings to his ripped torso.

Awkwardly, I raise the flowers. "Just delivering these. I heard you were sick."

He smiles, but not his usual easy smile whenever he sees me. He's trying his best, but I can see the pain he's in.

As I walk toward him, he looks more like he did that day in the library—pale, washed out. Full of anguish.

"You don't look well."

He rests his head on the doorframe. "Want to come in?"

"Sure."

Jessie's apartment is exactly like I imagined it to be—a bachelor pad. A large black L-shaped couch sits in the middle of a living space and is the first thing you notice as soon as you enter. The couch faces a stone wall with a fireplace and a huge flat screen TV above it. There's a coffee table set in front of the couch, which sits on a gray rug, the only thing that breaks up the wood-effect tiles, which run the length of the open living space and into the gray kitchen.

The place is modern and really large.

Jessie points to my coat. "You want me to take that?"

Alternating the bouquet between my hands, I shrug off my jacket and hand it to him, but as he reaches up to hook it on the back of the door, he winces.

"What's the matter?"

He shakes his head. "Nothing."

"Jessie," I drawl, "I'm going to be really honest with you right now." I take a deep breath as he looks at me from a few feet away. "I should be really pissed at you for ignoring me all week." I exhale and tuck my hair behind my ears. "But I'm too busy worrying about you. What's going on? I heard you're sick with the flu. You look pale, but it's not from that, is it?"

Jessie steps forward a couple of paces, taking the bouquet from my left hand. "You're so pissed at me that you brought me flowers?"

I quirk a brow. "They were more of an excuse to get past security since you weren't expecting me and they wouldn't know who I was."

There must be only a foot separating us when I see the dark circles under his eyes.

"Shouldn't it be the other way around—me buying you the flowers?" He smiles softly at me.

I shrug and look down at the battered yellow roses. "I saw Felicity at the florist, and she said you didn't turn up at a game last night. She said you'd texted the boys to say you were sick. But you hadn't replied to me, and I got worried. So, she gave me your address. I thought about leaving you alone, but I …"

When he brings a palm to the side of my face, I tingle at his touch.

"I'm okay, I promise," he whispers. "Nothing that I haven't been through before, Mia. I can handle it."

"Then why did you go MIA on me again?" I ask. I close my eyes as his thumb strokes my cheek once. "Something happened back home, didn't it?"

When I open my eyes, his tongue pokes out and slides along his bottom lip as he looks at me.

"What did I say about not pushing red buttons?" Jessie takes a step back, his hand leaving my face.

He turns to head toward the kitchen, but instinctively, I wrap an arm around his waist to stop him.

"Wait."

Jessie shoots back and groans quietly; he tries to hide his reaction, but I don't miss the wince as he hisses in response to my touch.

All my alarm bells go off at once.

"Jessie?"

Clearly trying to push past what just happened, he strides across to the kitchen, his hand clamped over his side as he fills up the sink and drops the flowers into the water.

"Jessie," I repeat, and this time, my voice is serious.

He doesn't turn around or even acknowledge me as he leans over slightly, bracing his hands on either side of the sink.

I'm across the kitchen and behind him in no time.

As I place my hand over one of his, I whisper softly, "Let me see what's hurting. Please."

He shakes his head. "No."

"It wasn't a request, baby. Let me see." The nickname I used to call him slips out before I can stop myself.

He drops his shoulders, maybe in defeat. But for once in his life, he doesn't fight me as I slowly peel up the Dri-FIT shirt.

I don't know whose gasps they are, but they fill the silent apartment as I take in his black-and-blue torso.

He continues to allow me access, and I peel more of his shirt upward, taking in the marks.

It's horrific, heartbreaking, sickening. These injuries are the kind only another human could inflict. They aren't from hockey.

"Jessie, please tell me ... was this from your dad?" I don't sound surprised because I'm not. The nausea swirling in my stomach the past few days was a result of what I'd already known.

He nods once, but doesn't say anything more, almost like he's accepted that I'm not backing down. I've pushed the red button and seen a glimpse of the real world he lives in. But I'm not pulling away at the sight of his bruises.

My breath catches in my throat as he slowly turns around to face me. The front of his torso is arguably worse. His skin is so black and blue that it's hard to make out the tattoos I asked him about in my dorm.

"Jessie, you need to see a doctor."

"No, I don't."

"You do. I—you—"

"I don't go and see doctors, Mia. I never have, and I never will. If I show up looking like this, then they'll ask questions, and when I don't answer them, they'll start talking to the team."

"But you're in pain. This looks really bad," I say, tracing a very light hand over some of the marks.

"This level of pain isn't anything I can't handle. I'm used to it."

"But this could be really serious. I've never seen any—"

His palm lands on my cheek again, cutting off my rambling, and I look up at him with glassy eyes.

"I need to see it all." I tug upward on his shirt, asking him to remove it. "Take off your top and show me all of it. Everything you're feeling."

"This doesn't scare the shit out of you? Knowing my own family, my own flesh and blood, did this to me?"

I shake my head. "It sickens me, and, yeah, it's shocking to know your dad could do something like that. But nothing about you could ever scare me. I'm more interested in making sure you're okay."

"I don't believe you."

"Tough."

A cocky smile pulls at his lips. "You can be really stubborn sometimes—you know that?"

His face contorts with pain as he pulls off his top to reveal more of his upper body. Bruises stretch from his waist to his shoulders with some starting to turn yellow, but they're especially bad across his rib cage.

I shake my head and look at him. "Is this why you didn't call me? Because this had happened and you didn't want me to know?"

Jessie continues to stare down at me as I take in his injuries, which have given me more answers in thirty seconds than I've had over the past four years.

He huffs out a dry laugh. "I didn't want you to see me this way, and I was in too much pain yesterday to go watch a game. Even with my pain threshold, the guys would've noticed."

"I don't see how we can have a friendship if you won't tell me what's going on."

Jessie squeezes his eyes shut and leans down to my height. When he rests his forehead against mine, my body trembles at the contact.

"We aren't friends, Mia."

My heart drops. "We aren't? But I thought that's what you wanted?"

He puffs out another humorless laugh and his breath tickles my lips. "I've got plenty of friends in my life, male and female. But none of them makes me feel the way you do. They show up for me, yeah, but I don't want to show myself to them. Only you. I've never shown my bruises to anyone, except you just now."

I want to tell him the same, but I don't. Instead, I place a warm palm over his heart.

He reaches up and takes my other hand in his, bringing it to his lips and kissing the tips of my fingers tenderly. "I've been wanting to kiss you from the second I found out you were in Seattle. No, from the second I walked out of your house that day Graham caught us. But I've never wanted to kiss you more than at this moment right now. I'm sorry for being a fucking idiot and ignoring you. Sometimes, letting in the person who sees you the most is the hardest thing to do."

He kisses my fingers again and then pulls back slightly, his heart beating rapidly under my palm. "If I said fuck it and took you into my bedroom right now, would you stop me? Would all this be too fast, even after years of being apart?"

My heart races at the same speed as his, reminding me of the last time I felt this way. I'd just turned nineteen, and I was waiting for the boy standing in front of me to remove my bra.

I cast my eyes over his battered but still-beautiful body. "The only reason I'd say no would be to stop you from hurting yourself further. You're in pain, and I don't want to be the reason you hurt more."

He runs his fingers through my hair as he rests his hand at the nape of my neck, drawing me closer to him. "Yeah, it hurts, Sweetheart. But trust me when I say that the pain in my body is nothing compared to the thought of spending another fucking second without touching you like you're mine."

CHAPTER TWENTY

MIA

Jessie's lips crash down onto mine. At first, the kiss is rushed and every bit the way I imagined him kissing me after so long without each other. But then he slows down, gently brushing his mouth against mine.

His heart has gone from fast to practically beating through my palm. Only our hands and mouths are making contact, but somehow, I feel him everywhere.

When he reaches down and wraps his hands around the back of my thighs, I instantly know what he wants to do, and there's no way I'm allowing it.

I shake my head and reach for his hands, taking them in mine and interlacing our fingers. "No. There's not a chance I'm letting you carry me."

He stops mid-kiss and speaks against my lips. "You think after years of picturing you in my bed, I'm not going to lay you on it myself?"

I look to my right and down the hallway. It's easy to tell which bedroom is his since his door is wide open and his bed is visible.

When I turn back to Jessie, his eyes burn with need.

"I want you to lead me to your bed and watch as I lie down in front of you."

Resting his forehead against mine, Jessie closes his eyes and exhales. "I'll let you win this round. But there's something I will absolutely not compromise over."

I roll my lips together, my core tightening at the sultry tone in his voice. "Oh, yeah? What's that?"

"You can call the shots on the way you get into my bed, but I get to say when you leave it."

Oh Lord.

My body overheats, reaching boiling point in record time.

"Do we have a deal, Miss Jenkins?"

I nod lightly as our lips brush together.

"Words, Mia. Let me hear you say you're mine to do as I want, for as long as I want."

Our hands are still interlaced, so I separate them and wrap my little finger around his.

When I take the first step toward his room, I turn and look over my shoulder at him and smile. "I'm yours, Jessie. For as long as you want."

As my back hits the gray sheets on his king-size bed, I don't take in the rest of the room. Only the man hovering over me as he stands at the foot, his bottom lip pinned between his teeth.

I know his mind is in overdrive, and so is mine.

"I need to tell you something," I say as I hold my weight on my elbows.

Jessie slowly crawls over my body, his attention locked on me the whole time. "Okay, Sweetheart."

My cheeks heat at what I'm about to say. "I—I don't know how far we plan to go right now, but I need you to know that I'm ..." I cast my eyes down my body and then back up to his face. "I haven't actually been with anyone. Ever."

I watch as a small crease forms between his brow, almost like he's struggling to process or maybe even believe what I said.

"Are you telling me you're still a virgin, Mia?"

I bite the inside of my cheek—hard. I know I shouldn't be embarrassed, but I am. I'm twenty-two, and I still haven't slept with anyone.

"I've messed around a bit," I say, feeling kind of infantile in front of Jessie Callaghan—a man with experience.

He doesn't say anything, just continues to stare at me, the furrow between his brows still there.

"Say something," I plead, desperate for him to tell me it's okay.

When a smile breaks out across his face, my face mirrors his own.

"Just to be clear, what you're telling me is that no other guy has had the pleasure of having you beneath him in his bed?"

I shake my head and whisper, "No, not in any bed."

His smile grows wider as he continues to hover over me. I want to check he's not in pain like this, but if the look on his face is anything to go by, I know he's doing just fine.

"Do you remember that time at the drive-in theater?" he asks.

I bite on my bottom lip, the best kind of nerves shooting through me. "Mmhmm."

"I knew we couldn't, but I wanted to take you right there and then. All I could think about was pushing your panties to one side and sliding inside." He looks off to the side and shakes his head slowly. "Then my mom called, and we had to leave."

"I remember," I reply, pushing away the humiliating memories.

"Well, that's not going to happen tonight, Sweetheart."

"I hope not," I tease.

He pulls back and stands from the bed, walking over to his bedroom door. Jessie reaches into the pocket of his sweatpants as he takes out his phone and tosses it, and I hear it land on something soft.

I giggle, and he turns back to face me, taking me in with a

feral need in his eyes. A look similar to the one I saw in the closet at Riley's Bar.

"Back then, I told you that I'd go at your pace. And nothing has changed." He walks back over to the bed, but doesn't climb on, instead dropping to his knees in front of me. "The only thing that has is the knowledge that I can never walk away from you again. I've tried staying away. I've tried putting distance between us. I've tried pretending like we don't belong in each other's lives. But we do, Mia. There's too much of you flowing through my veins for us to be apart anymore. Time has only made me want you more than ever before."

My heart goes from beating through my chest to almost stopping completely when he leans forward and wraps his hands around mine, pulling me to a sitting position in front of him.

When his fingers find the hem of my black sweater, every nerve fires off in my body, settling between my thighs.

"We've wasted enough time messing around. I want you in my life, in my bed, in my arms, if that's what you want too." He pulls my sweater up, exposing my navel, and then he stops, looking me dead in the eyes. "I just have one last thing to ask of you."

"Okay," I whisper, my voice quivering, just like my body.

"Let me give you every part of this Jessie, the Seattle Jessie in front of you right now. Because that's the man you deserve."

"What about Dallas Jessie?" I reply, my eyes starting to blur. "Seattle Jessie is an amazing hockey player with a posh apartment and a smile that lights me up. But Dallas Jessie is the one my heart remembers."

I lift my arms as he pulls my sweater over my head, leaving me in my plunging deep-blue bra. His eyes travel to my chest for a second, but then quickly find mine again. He leans in and kisses my collarbone, his lips causing me to pulse all over.

"The Jessie you knew in Dallas is kneeling in front of you right now—he never left, Sweetheart. It's what's in Dallas—the other part of my life—that I don't want to get you tangled up in.

Let me protect you from it because there's nothing there that's good for you or us. It won't be this way forever."

I know there's no other way. This is not something he's willing to move on. "Okay."

He smiles at me, kissing the side of my neck. "Thank you."

"I never want you to shut me out and leave me on Read again."

He shakes his head into the crook of my neck. "I promise, I won't. I did it to try and keep you at a safe distance, but I don't want to fight us anymore, Mia."

"Me neither," I whisper, steadying my trembling body as I reach out and hold on to his muscular shoulders, cautious not to hurt him. "We just need to work out how to tell my dad now."

His hands fall to the waistband of my jeans, and he undoes the top button and pulls down the zip. "That's a problem for tomorrow. We'll work it out, I promise."

I lift up and let him peel down my damp jeans.

The look in Jessie's eyes as he carefully undresses me is reminiscent of someone receiving their dream gift on Christmas morning. With his bottom lip caught between his teeth, he sucks in a sharp breath. "Is this from the rain, or are you that soaked for me?"

I let out a needy whimper. "Both."

Chuckling, he tosses my jeans to the side. "Has anyone ever gone down on you, Mia?"

My face heats, but this time, it's not from embarrassment. "No. I've never actually ..." I trail off, not sure how much to offer him. Even though it's Jessie, the whole idea of telling him I've never had a proper orgasm feels strange.

I've gotten myself to that point, yeah. But never all the way.

"Never what?" he pushes.

"I don't think I've ever actually orgasmed."

His eyes grow wide. "Really?"

"Nope," I say, crossing my arms over my chest. "At least, I

don't think so. Ridiculous when you think about it. I'm twenty-two."

He kisses me and loops his hand around my arms, uncrossing them. "I never want you to think of yourself as ridiculous again. But, Sweetheart, if you'd had an orgasm, then you'd know."

"I kind of guessed that. It doesn't matter what I do; the toys just don't get me there, and then I phase myself out and get more frustrated."

A filthy smirk spreads across his face. "You know the easiest way to get you there?"

"How?"

"My mouth."

My core throbs. "Is that what you want to do to me?"

His hands fall to my panties, tugging them down my thighs slowly. "I've wanted your pussy in my mouth from the moment I laid eyes on you, Mia. And given that was fucking years ago, I'd say *want* is now the understatement of the century. So, let's go with starving."

I throw my head back and laugh, but then stop as his hands come to the insides of my thighs, parting me open as I rest my feet on the edge of his bed.

"Lie back for me," he whispers.

I drop from my hands to my elbows and watch the way he takes me in.

"Yeah, it's no use," he drawls. Lust lacing his tone. "I'm gonna need this over my shoulder."

I balance my leg over his shoulder as his eyes find mine. When his tongue swipes across his bottom lip, so does his finger through my pussy, and then he brings it to his lips, tasting me.

My jaw hangs open at the way he groans in pleasure. Like I'm the best thing he's ever tried.

"I need to be honest with you, Mia. I know you want me to go slow, but I need to devour this pussy."

"Do it," I tell him, a determined edge to my tone.

As his tongue passes through me for the first time, he

watches the way I react. I squirm as he brings one hand to my entrance and the other around the leg on his shoulder, holding me steady.

"Ready to experience your first orgasm, Sweetheart?"

Words fail me as I nod. His confidence to get me off is, without a doubt, the sexiest thing I've ever witnessed.

Jessie eats my pussy like an ice cream that's melting. The wetter I get, the more he laps at me, his tongue moving up and down my entrance. Sometimes, he sucks me into his mouth, massaging me with his tongue; other times, he enters me with it, fucking me slowly.

"Oh my God!" I cry out as his fingers join his tongue, toying with my clit.

Jessie growls into me, anticipating that I'm close as I squeeze around his tongue. The vibrations add an extra layer of intensity, which fires off sparks as they dance beneath my skin.

"I—I'm right there. I can feel it. Jessie, I can feel it."

"Come for me, Mia," he growls against me. "Let me be your first and only."

I fall over the edge, my entire body feeling like it's shutting down, but never more alive at the same time.

I thought I'd cry out when it happened, but I don't. I shake and shudder and whimper with desperate need as Jessie kisses my clit, sucking it into his mouth to prolong my high.

God, he's so damn good at this.

He drops my leg down and comes to a stand, hovering over me, his arms braced on either side of my body. "Kiss me; taste how beautiful you are."

I'm hesitant, but I trust him. There's never been anyone I've wanted to give myself to more. I lean forward, and his tongue enters my mouth, teasing me with it.

"Now it's time for you to hold up your end of the bargain," he finally says, his blue eyes darkened with lust.

"Ugh." I blow out a mock laugh. "Such a drag to sleep in your bed tonight."

Jessie smiles at me sweetly, his eyes somehow even darker than before. "You're so damn cute—you know that?" He runs a hand across the scruff of his jaw. "Thinking my bed is for sleeping."

My core tightens again. "What else would it be for?" I ask innocently.

I climb off the bed and pull back the sheets, my eyes tracking Jessie as he rounds the bed and comes to stand next to me, wrapping a piece of my hair around his finger.

"Well, first, I vote that we eat because I don't want my girl to go hungry."

"And then?"

He leans down and kisses me, my taste still on his lips. "And then I'll eat some more."

I whimper with need and drop my eyes to his sweatpants, a wet patch clear against the light-gray material.

He follows my stare and shrugs his shoulders with a casual laugh. "Yeah, I blew straight into my pants at the same time you came. Turns out, feeling the girl of my dreams unravel into my mouth was even better than I'd imagined. Hence why I'm desperate for the next round."

I smirk, feeling like, somehow, we're now on a level sexual playing field. "Just like you nearly did at the drive-in theater."

His fingers move from my hair to underneath my chin as he tips my face up to look at him. "Absolutely, Sweetheart. But just know, the next time it happens, I'll be inside you, doing exactly what we should've been doing for all these fucking years."

CHAPTER TWENTY-ONE

JESSIE

"Whatcha making?" Mia asks, padding through to the kitchen.

She took a shower and announced that my bathroom could swallow her entire dorm in one. It's nothing compared to Jensen and Kate's new place, but it's still a lot more than most people have.

"Grilled cheese, but it's technically not cheat day for me, so I threw in a tossed salad."

She snorts a laugh and makes an appreciative noise at how good it smells. "Can you cook?"

It occurs to me that in the nine months we were seeing each other, I never got a chance to cook for her since we never went back to my place; the only time we ate together was if we snuck out to a restaurant or grabbed something in a drive-through.

Mia approaches and then hauls herself up onto the countertop to sit beside me; this already feels different from how we were together in Dallas.

Better different.

Flipping the grilled cheese, I look over at her, unable to stop my eyes from trailing down her body. "Well, I wouldn't describe this as gourmet food, but, yeah, I know my way around a kitchen."

I pass her a glass of water, and she takes a sip.

"Who taught you?"

I run a rough hand through my messy hair, which definitely needs a cut. "Myself." I want to offer her more, but that's the God's honest truth. This isn't some cute story about how my mom taught me to peel potatoes and prepare a Thanksgiving meal when I was ten.

I watch the way heat warms her cheeks, almost like she's working that out for herself. Years back, when Mia once asked about my parents, I told her their names were Wayne and Alice but left it at that. She now knows my dad is a straight-up asshole, but describing my relationship with Mom is going to be tougher and something I don't know I'll ever be able to explain. She isn't a bad person, and I love her with everything I have, but she has made bad choices that have torn me apart.

The team psych, Ashley, along with countless other professionals, have tried—and failed—to talk to me about her. I guess I just refuse to throw her under the metaphorical bus. At one time, I was angry for the way she seemed to accept Dad's behavior, but now, all I feel is sadness and desperation on her behalf. Hoping that one day, she will accept one of the many opportunities I give her to escape his clutches.

Mia clears her throat and takes another sip of water. "That's impressive—teaching yourself, I mean."

The need to share everything with her pools in my gut, screaming at me to follow my instincts and trust her with my secrets.

I flick off the burner and come to stand between her legs, resting my palms on either side of her. I'm still shirtless, but changed into black athletic shorts. I can't remember the last time I was so fucking turned on that I blew into my own pants. I should feel even a hint of humiliation at my dick's lack of control. But I'm not. Going down on Mia, being the first guy to do that or even give her an orgasm, is way too fucking amazing to worry about my inability to hold it together.

She's still a virgin.

I had every intention of being inside her all night tonight, despite the pain my body is in. But the second she told me, I knew her first time had to be something special.

Did she hold out for me? Warmth spreads across my chest at the thought.

I bite on my bottom lip as I take her in. She's dressed again, back in the clothes she arrived in.

"You haven't tried my cooking yet, so maybe reserve judgment on how impressive it is until you have." Offering her a cheeky smile, I rub my hands up and down her thighs, feeling her jeans are still damp, although that's not the real reason why I want her out of them. "You got dressed."

She shrugs, the redness staining her cheeks getting deeper. It's so fucking cute to watch my sassy girl show her shy side. "These are all I have with me."

Leaning in and brushing my lips against hers, I shake my head softly. "Incorrect, Sweetheart. You have my entire wardrobe at your disposal."

She giggles and then kisses me back. "Your stuff would drown my five-feet-four ass."

The urge to gather her up and march us back into my room for round two overwhelms me, but I hold off, remembering we have food to eat. As I wind her long, dark hair around my fist, I feel the way my dick grows at the thought of doing exactly this while I slide inside her from behind.

Soon.

"That's the idea. Utopia would be you waltzing around my place, wearing nothing but my name."

I watch the way her throat works as she digests my fantasy. And I have fantasized about Mia in my jersey way more than I ever had the right to do after I walked out of her dad's house and ignored her messages like a goddamn coward.

When I release her hair, my hands wrap around her gorgeous, round ass, and I pull her into me, noting she's at the perfect fucking height.

"We need to eat this food." I kiss the tip of her nose. "But I want you to know, I'm sorry for running away from us. I let you down. I had known the risk of getting caught when we started seeing each other. I need to be honest and tell you that I never expected you to be my forever girl—because girls like you don't happen to boys like me."

When she opens her mouth to speak, I know she's going to protest and tell me that's not true, but I stop her with a finger to her soft lips.

"The happiness you brought me back then felt too good to be true, so I lived in the warmth of your addictive sunshine for as long as I could. All cards on the table—it still kind of does feel surreal, having you here. But you didn't rule me out, even if your dad did. You've given me a second chance, and I want to be a man you can call yours and be fucking proud of it. Even if it takes time to separate my past from the present, I'll do it for you, for us. So, while I work on fixing myself and believing I'm lucky enough to have you in my life again, I want you to work on trusting that this time, I'm in it for the long haul. Your dad might want to murder me, but no matter what he does, I'm not going anywhere, Sweetheart."

Mia's eyes turn glassy as she looks at me, but doesn't say anything.

When I pull her into my chest, she releases a silent sob against me.

"I'm sorry. I didn't mean to make you cry, Mia."

"No." She shakes her head. "No, these are happy tears." Pulling away from me, she wipes under her eyes. "Just ... why now? I came here, expecting to deliver some flowers to a guy who didn't really want to talk to me, and now, all this."

I cock my head to the side and study her. "I really did a shit job of showing you how I felt back then, didn't I?"

She blows out another sob.

"I fell for you years ago, Mia. Do you know how unnatural it's been for me to hold back from you? Then you walk into my apartment and do something no one has ever done."

"What's that?"

Squeezing my eyes shut, I force back tears. "You saw me, my scars, my bruises. You didn't freak out or want to run away, just like you've never judged me for drinking to numb my pain. That night, back in the dorm, when I told you why I turned to alcohol, there was nothing but understanding in your beautiful eyes. It might take me a while to get there, but I know you're the only one I want to show myself to. And when you find someone like that, you never let them go."

Mia presses a kiss against my lips. I'm almost sure the food is cold by now. Not that I give a fuck.

"But you don't want me to be a part of your whole life, the part back in Dallas."

"Mia, my dad is an abuser and a really bad man. In a different state is the closest he will ever get to you—I'll make sure of it. But the demons from my childhood live on inside me—I know they do. Keeping myself straight and not drinking is the only doubt I have about us because if I head down a pathway similar to my mom, I'll break your heart, even if I never mean to. That's what I'm protecting you from. I'll show you my bruises, and I'll answer the questions you have, I promise. But that doesn't mean I have all the answers to everything."

I point at myself and look at her. "There's only one circumstance where I'll walk away from you: if I'm going down, there's no way I'm dragging you with me."

MIA

Wearing an oversized T-shirt and with a cold grilled cheese in hand, I crawl into Jessie's bed.

I'm still trying to process everything he said to me in the kitchen, but right now, the high I'm riding on is blocking out my ability to form coherent thoughts.

Does Jessie Callaghan love me? Has he always loved me?

He didn't say the words, but I know he wants me, and I have to give us a shot. My euphoria is so intense that even my nineteen-year-old self is kicking her giddy feet, pushing back memories of heartbreak.

He climbs in beside me and takes my plate while I make myself comfortable under his arm. "Comfy now?"

I wriggle a bit more for effect and take the plate back, instantly taking a bite out of the grilled cheese. My mouth waters. This is seriously good. "Even cold, this is the best I've had."

Jessie flicks on the TV mounted on the wall in front of his bed and begins scrolling through options.

"Your choice tonight," I say, taking another huge bite of the grilled cheese.

Selecting one of my all-time favorite shows, *Dexter*, he settles back behind me and starts eating his food too.

"I'm sorry if I get crumbs in your bed." I wince, brushing off a few that already stand out against the dark gray comforter he has.

Jessie shrugs. "It's fine. I can change the sheets tomorrow."

"You don't have a housekeeper to do that?"

"Nope." He takes my empty plate and sets it on the floor with his. Adjusting himself to look at me, he bites down on his lip, almost like he's working himself up to say something. "I don't own this apartment. The team paid for it as part of the contract I signed. Even though I was forced out of Dallas, the Scorpions wanted me bad, so my agent negotiated in a housing arrangement for however long I'm on the team. I earn well, yeah, but I get taxed a huge amount, which swallows a large chunk of my take-home pay."

"So, your wages are only in the lower hundreds of thousands per month," I jibe. "I know how much you were earning in your first year at the Destroyers, baby." I pat his cheek mockingly. "You must be rolling in it now."

Jessie kicks his feet out in front of him. "I send a ton home every week."

"To your parents?"

He nods slowly. "I know it ends up in casinos, liquor stores, and the pockets of hookers since my dad can't keep it in his pants. But I can't leave my mom without food. Every last cent I send, my dad steals, even from the bank account I set up for her a while back. So, I send more. I know it's not a solution, but the guilt of not helping her when I earn big eats away at me."

"H-how much do you send, Jessie?"

He pinches the bridge of his nose and whispers, "It's been twenty thousand a week for the past six months."

"Nearly half a million dollars?!" I burst out. "They've screwed you for all that money!"

"At least."

My heart cracks. "Jessie, that's so much money. Money for your future. Your career won't last forever. God forbid, but it could end tomorrow."

"I know. That's not where it stops though. I have fines coming out of my ass for showing up late to practices and games. I pay my agent and PR team way more than their average clients since they're constantly putting out fires my dad starts. He might hate me, but he doesn't hide the fact that I'm his son. Neither does he hide what he gets up to in public." He blows out a defeated breath. "You remember my black Mustang?"

I think back to the secret kisses we shared in it. "Yeah."

"He totaled it a couple of months back. When I'd left for Seattle, I'd said he could use it. But he never got it insured. He got pissed one night at a bar and drove it straight into a store window. I paid for the damages and to keep the news about who had done it buried. Just lucky it was the middle of the night and the store was closed. And the fact that he didn't kill anyone."

Nausea swirls around in my stomach as my mom flashes in front of me.

Jessie turns to me, his hand coming to the side of my face. "Shit, Mia. I'm sorry. I didn't think about your mom." He scrubs at his face with his other hand. "See what I mean? He's already hurting you. *I'm* already hurting you."

"It's okay," I whisper, picking up the remote to silence the TV. "The only time you hurt me is when you shut me out." I climb over him until I'm straddling his hips, and I feel the way he responds immediately.

He looks deep into my eyes, hands falling to my sides as he pins me to him. "What do you want, Mia?"

I bite my lip nervously. "I want to taste you. Give you what you gave to me earlier."

"Mia, you don't have—"

I stop him with a finger to his lips. "I know, but I *want* to."

My heart races as I lift off him and pull back the comforter, staring down at his cock, which is obviously huge, even beneath his athletic shorts.

I pull at his waistband, and Jessie raises his hips, making it easier for me to remove his shorts.

I expect him to be wearing boxers, so when his cock bobs up and rests just below his navel, I gasp at the shock.

Jessie chuckles, running a hand through my hair until it rests at the nape of my neck. He pulls me into him. "Have you done this before?"

When I told Jessie that I'd messed around with guys in the past, this is what I meant. In my heartbreak, I had gone out with a couple of girlfriends from back home. They convinced me the best way to get over whoever it was that had broken my heart— since I wouldn't tell them—was to get under someone else.

Big mistake.

The guy I met at the bar told me we'd only make out in his car. We didn't. He didn't force himself on me, but he did make it pretty clear that the goalposts had changed when he unzipped his pants.

I could've gotten out of the car and gone back into the bar. But I wanted to prove to myself that I was over Jessie.

I had tears in my eyes the entire time, and I hated it. So, I vowed never to touch anyone else again. A stupid and unrealistic promise—I knew that. But unless it was Jessie I was touching, I just wasn't interested.

Wrapping my hand around his shaft, I pump him once, and he groans in pleasure. The sound shoots straight through me, pooling between my legs. I look at him; he asked the question, and I don't want to lie.

"Once."

A crease forms between his eyebrows, almost like he's regretting asking me. "Did you like it?"

I shake my head. "No. Because he wasn't you."

His dick leaks in my hand as it grows even bigger. I'm nervous. I can't pretend that my inexperience doesn't affect my confidence, but I'm determined to make this the best blow job he's ever had.

I take him into my mouth and swirl my tongue around the tip, and he groans way louder than the last time, his fingers twisting in my hair.

His response spurs me on and fills my chest with warmth, letting me know I'm making it good for him.

He's huge—so much bigger than the guy from the bar, but going down on Jessie is also so much easier.

Because it's what I want. *He's* what I want.

Cautiously, I take him all the way to the back of my throat and gag as his hips shoot off the bed.

"Oh Jesus, fuck, Mia," he cries out.

His pleasure only urges me on. I want to pull my panties to

the side and sit on him, taking his huge dick all the way inside me.

But more than that, I want him to finish in my mouth.

"Sweetheart, I'm not going to last another ten seconds with the way you're sucking me so good."

I release him with a pop, my confidence only growing with every moan that tumbles from his lips. "I've always wanted to know what you look like when you come."

My mouth finds his dick again, and without having any idea if it's good for a guy, I start to pump him as my hand and mouth work together in synchronization. He swells in my palm, and I flick my eyes up to where Jessie braces his arms behind his head, clenching his jaw.

When he releases into my mouth, I don't feel the disgusting urge to spit him out, like I did with the guy at the bar. I swallow every last drop of him, savoring the way he tastes.

With his jaw now slack, he watches the way I take him further down my throat, and when he shudders, I lick the tip of his dick, proud of the way I just made him feel.

I barely have time to register what I just did when he loops his arm around my waist, flipping me onto my back as he hovers above me.

"Did that not hurt you?" I say, my eyes on his bruises.

Kissing me passionately, he breaks for a second. "Like I said before, Mia, I'm used to these bruises. There's also no better pain relief than feeling your body in my hands. And right now, I'm on top of the fucking world."

CHAPTER TWENTY-TWO

MIA

Only a matter of weeks ago, I was wondering what it would be like to spend a night with Jessie Callaghan.

This morning, it's no longer a fantasy. With his arms wrapped around me, pulling me into his chest, I've never felt safer or more wanted.

Sunlight fights to break through the gaps in Jessie's bedroom blinds, and I let its warmth settle on my face. Just like that Sunday morning in my dorm, all I can hear is Jessie's steady breathing, but this time, I can feel it, too, as it tickles the back of my neck.

"Turn around for me, Sweetheart."

The gruff of his early morning voice shoots a delicious tingle through my body, reminding me of the way he kissed and nipped at my neck all night.

He wasn't lying when he said I was cute for thinking his bed was for sleeping.

Slowly, I turn in his arms. At some point last night, his T-shirt that I was wearing landed on his bedroom floor, but never made it back to my body, leaving me topless and in only my panties.

"Morning," I say with a stifled yawn.

Pulling the duvet from around my shoulders, Jessie exposes my breasts. They're hardly award-winning, but just like that day in my bedroom, he drinks me in like they're the sexiest thing he's ever seen.

He offers me a sleepy smile that fires off butterflies deep in my stomach and leans in for a gentle kiss. "I gotta leave for practice in a half hour."

Jessie pulls me closer to him, his hard cock pressing into my stomach.

Maybe I'm naive or perhaps still struggling to believe this is all real, but the question threatening to fall from the tip of my tongue must also be written right across my face when he pulls his head back from another soft kiss and tips my chin to look him in the eyes.

"Ask me, Mia."

I chew on my bottom lip, suddenly feeling like a young schoolgirl. "The first time, when we were sneaking around, we never actually talked about what we were to each other, but this ti—"

He rolls me onto my back, cutting me off with his mouth. His top half hovers over me, his fingers twisting and playing with my messy bed hair. His tongue feels warm and soft as it massages against mine with a deeper level of passion than any previous kiss we've ever shared.

As he grinds against me, I know he wants to go further, and I do, too, but I know he won't, not with only minutes left together.

When he pulls back from the kiss, his long fingers continue to dance in my hair as I look up at him, completely at his mercy.

"You are one hundred percent mine, and I am completely yours. I'd say calling you my girlfriend would make it official, but, Sweetheart, I never stopped belonging to you. We have to be careful about how we play this. We need to tell your dad when the time is right and when you're ready, Mia. But do not doubt for even a single fucking second that we are anything but each other's." He chuckles happily, the sound doing things to my heart. "I'm going to let you go for a few hours while I head to practice and you go do some studying and shit."

"And shit." I giggle into his chest.

Jessie rolls us back so we're facing each other, and he squeezes me tighter against him. "Yeah, and shit. But once you're done, I want you to text me so I can send a taxi to your dorm to come get you and bring you right back here. To my bed, where you belong."

Every nerve in my body fizzes with anticipation and excitement. "I'd like that."

A cheeky smile breaks out across his face. "I bet you do."

I bite down on my bottom lip, needing to address something else he just mentioned. "When are we going to tell my dad?"

Underneath the duvet, Jessie wraps a leg over mine. "ASAP. There's a risk we're gonna get caught, and it only grows the longer we keep sneaking around. To you, I'm just Jessie, but to the public, I'm the starting forward for the Scorpions. I get photographed a lot, mainly when I least expect it. That would be the worst way for him to find out."

"Are you scared?"

Jessie's brows pinch together. "Of what?"

"Of him finding out, of what the Scorpions will say. You were supposed to be staying away from me, remember?"

He shakes his head. "Nervous of Graham's reaction? Yes. Scared? No. Once your dad figures it out, he can't control us, and, yeah, Coach Burrows will probably be pissed, but in reality, there's fuck all they can do. If they trade me, they trade me. I've made my bed, and I'm lying in it with my girl, no matter what."

"I think you underestimate my father and his hatred of you."

Jessie kisses my forehead, resting his chin on top of my head.

"And he underestimates how far I'm willing to go for his daughter."

Silence stretches out, the faint noise of the world passing by beneath us. We both know this is risky, mainly for Jessie, but also for me.

I love my dad with everything I have, but he's a stubborn man, and I can't help the niggling worry that by choosing Jessie, I might be simultaneously setting fire to the relationship I've built with my father. I've already lost one parent, and even though he's wrong about Jessie, there's a good chance he'll never forgive my betrayal. Walking away from the career he wanted me to have at the Destroyers hurt him badly, but going behind his back again might be something we never recover from.

JESSIE

I've done some difficult things in my twenty-six years, but leaving Mia in my bed this morning while I hauled my ass to practice was fucking tough.

The way she watched and laughed while I raced around my bedroom, getting dressed, has gotta be one of the highlights of my life.

Having Mia, the girl I can finally call mine, wake up next to me was everything, even if I did have to tear myself away and leave her with a key to my place forty minutes ago. She might think the key is a temporary thing so she could take a shower and get dressed without rushing. But I have zero intention of removing it from her key ring.

So, when I push through the locker room door on time and without a hangover, the golden-retriever smile I wear is, for once, not forced. The genuine bounce in my step is every bit exhilarating as it is a foreign feeling.

"Wow, I'm practically blinded by sunshine." Jensen nudges into my shoulder when he comes to stand next to me at the benches.

I don't say anything as I take a seat and begin lacing up my skates, the smile still plastered across my face.

He comes to sit next to me and dips his head down, speaking quietly. "You just left her in your bed, didn't you?"

Finishing up one skate, I shift the other foot forward and begin lacing it. "Yep."

He throws his head back and laughs way louder than he likely intended, and Zach's head whips over to us.

"Share with the group," he says, inspecting one of the blades on his skates.

I pull off my hoodie, feeling thankful I wore a Dri-FIT today since the bruises marring my torso will be hard enough to practice with, let alone explain to my teammates. Especially when I can't chalk these up to a hit, like I have in the past.

I look at Jensen, who raises a brow at me in question.

I know what he's thinking—I should tell Zach the reason behind my smile and I should trust the guy who's given me no reason to doubt him over the years I've known him. When Jon needed Zach to stand by him and have his back, he did.

The rest of the team starts to make their way to the ice, but there are still a few minutes until practice starts, so I wait a couple more seconds for the room to clear and then turn to Zach.

"I don't know exactly how much you know already, but remember when I was traded here?"

Zach's eyebrows shoot up in surprise like he didn't expect me just to come out and tell him whatever it was. "Yeah, there were rumors of a love affair gone wrong."

I nod and scratch at the back of my neck. "I know you're my captain, but I need to know I can trust you as a friend."

"You can trust him," Jensen interjects, looking at Zach.

With a single tip of his chin, Zach stands and waits for me to continue talking. I take a deep breath and prepare myself to do something way out of my comfort zone—share my life.

"Right after I was signed, I met someone."

Zach takes a seat on the bench next to me and begins lacing up his skates. "A girl?"

I side-eye Jensen. "Yep, and, well, she worked for the Destroyers."

Zach's head shoots up. "You broke staff-player fraternization policies? Shit, man."

I wince and run a hand through my hair. "Annnnd ... she also happened to be the GM's daughter."

If the bench wasn't between his ass and the floor, I'm pretty sure Zach would be flat on his back right about now.

"Say fucking *what?*"

"We got caught one day in her bedroom by her dad, and I got put on the instant trade list. After nine months of sneaking around, I had known it was getting riskier, but I couldn't stay away from her."

Zach comes to stand in front of me. He props his hands on his hips and shakes his head. "And you can't keep away from her now."

"Never have been able to. Tried my fucking hardest, but ... she's ..." I drop my hand from my hair to my side. "She's everything to me. Just like Luna is to you, like Kate is to Jensen, and like Felicity is to Jon. She's *the fucking one*, man."

"He just left her in his bed," Jensen adds.

Zach runs a hand over the scruff of his jaw. "I'm guessing Graham Jenkins doesn't know about this—you know, given the fact that you're still breathing?" He winces. "Jesus, that guy made me look like a teddy bear on the ice."

"He has no idea. Mia and I need to work out the right time to tell him."

"Burrows is gonna be pissed too," Jensen says, fixing a final pad in place.

I nod. "Yeah, I know. But if I can prove to Graham that I'm

serious about Mia, then I have an outside chance of not being murdered."

It's not lost on me that, at this point, neither Zach nor Jensen knows about the depths of my past or the real reason Graham thinks I'm bad news for his daughter. Right now, those are truths I only want to share with Mia.

Zach points to the clock above the locker room door, indicating we need to head out onto the ice. "For what it's worth, here's my best advice. You are the most gifted player I personally have ever seen, but speaking honestly, I don't think we've seen the best of you. Your eighty percent is another player's dream game." He looks me dead in the eyes, offering me a captain's stare. "Bring it. Turn up for practices early; stay behind until the Zamboni hits the ice. Show them *why* you are so valuable to the team. Send a message to Graham that you're every bit the player and man he wants for his daughter and make it so Burrows has no choice but to keep starting you, even when he wants to bench your ass for being a stupid prick."

"I loved all of that up until the final two words."

Jensen snickers at my side, but Zach maintains eye contact with me.

"If you bring your best, then you have no reason for them—*or me*—to question you. That buys you time and respect for when you go to Jenkins and tell him you're fucking his daughter again."

I roll my tongue across the roof of my mouth and smile at Zach. "Jesus, now I know why Jon always said you're the guy to go to when you got issues. Technically though, I've never fucked his daughter."

Jensen chokes on his own breath. "You're telling me you had the girl of your dreams in your bed and didn't fuck her?" He holds up a hand. "Sorry, make love to her."

I roll my eyes. There's zero chance of me telling them she's a virgin and that her first time with me is going to be one she'll never forget. Although I know if I did say it, they'd ten out of ten get it.

"We literally made things official last night, and we had a lot to work through, like over four years of shit to straighten out. I'd hurt her bad when I left Dallas and joined the Scorpions."

Zach turns to leave, and I grab my gloves and follow, Jensen right on our heels.

"She's the girl we saw in the café at Whistler, isn't she?" Zach asks.

"Yeah."

Zach stops just before we hit the ice and looks at me one final time. "Give the fans the best show of their lives, make yourself untradeable, and show her dad that he made the biggest mistake of his life, trading you in the first place. Then tell him about you and Mia."

He shoves his mouthguard in and steps onto the ice, skating toward the rest of the team.

I feel a gloved hand land on my shoulder; the pain from the bruising is still there—a faint reminder of everything I'm still hiding.

"I know this might sound fucking weird, but I'm proud of you, man. Going after what you want. And for what it's worth, Zach is dead right."

"Thanks," I reply, my throat growing thick.

Jensen tips his head at the ice. "Time to see the real Callaghan, starting now."

CHAPTER TWENTY-THREE

MIA

By the time I get back to campus and walk toward my dorm building, it's past ten in the morning. Tara generally sleeps in on the weekends, but if she's up, there will definitely be questions for me and where I've been.

Suspicious Tara is the worst. When it comes to gossip, she's like a dog with a bone.

But last night will be worth every single question and raised eyebrow. Last night was, without a doubt, the greatest night of my life.

The skip in my step only gets lighter at the thought that tonight, I get to do it all again with him.

Sharing a bed with Jessie is incredible, but just having time to spend alone, away from prying eyes, without fear of being caught, is all I've ever wished for—all we've ever wished for.

I'm not sure if it's hit me yet—Jessie Callaghan is mine. *My boyfriend.* Even if we are a secret to the outside world, when we're alone and inside four protective walls, we're everything to each other.

He made the move I'd been desperate for him to make. He

let down his walls when I asked—virtually pleaded with—him to show me his wounds.

He kissed me. He asked me to be his.

He promised me he wouldn't walk away from us again.

And I believe him. I believe in us.

There's still so much shit to work through—I know that. I'm not eighteen years old and surviving on the next time I'll see him. For us to be permanent, I know Jessie needs to believe he's everything I deserve.

"Mia?"

A gloomy mist has settled on Seattle this morning, and as I take a few more steps toward the entrance of my building, the orange-and-black cap I only know one person to wear stands out in the haze.

I should feel warmth wash over me as I take in my dad's familiar face and broad stature. But I don't. I guess that's partly due to his unexpected visit, but mostly because of the confused scowl he wears.

"Dad?"

Fetching my keys out of my coat pocket, I scan my fob to enter the building and hold the door open for him to walk through.

"Early study session?" he asks, not bothering to tag on a greeting.

I haven't seen him since I left for Seattle. The longest time we've ever been apart.

He steps inside and takes a look around.

When I moved here, he arranged a moving van, but never came with me. I know it hurt him for me to walk away from a career he'd envisioned me to take on. Mom had had me when they were both twenty-five, and now that he's forty-seven, I know he has one eye on passing the Destroyers over so he can concentrate fully on the academy.

The academy that funded Jessie's career and college tuition.

My cheeks flush as the lie tumbles from my mouth. "Yes, I

have multiple assignments due. Early mornings are the quietest in the library."

Dad nods, and his eyes flick to my sweater, which is peeking out from underneath my unzipped coat. "Strange top to study in." He points to the white logo of the florist I work at, which stands out against the black material.

Shit.

"Only thing I had clean," I counter.

I begin taking the stairs, hoping he will follow and drop his inquisition.

"Thought I'd travel to see you; the team has their bye week."

Sliding the key into my lock, I pray Tara isn't on the other side of the door, ready to blow my cover. "How long are you here for?"

"Until tomorrow morning. I'm here to see you first, obviously, but I'm also here to watch an NCAA game. One of the guys I'm putting through college is playing, and I want to check on his progress."

"I see."

As soon as I push through the door, my stomach flips as I set eyes on Tara sitting at the breakfast bar. Other than Leo and Hugh, she's the only person I've told who my dad is. It's not exactly a secret, but it's also not something I choose to advertise around campus.

At the sight of us, she drops her half-eaten bagel onto her plate. "Hey."

"You must be Tara." My dad strides across the room, his hand outstretched for her to take.

With his back to me, she shakes my dad's hand and then flicks her eyes to mine, surprise written across her face.

I shake my head slowly, a desperate attempt for her to read between the lines and play along with my story.

"You're the same major as Mia, right?"

Picking up her bagel, Tara takes a bite and focuses her attention back on Dad. "Yep," she says around a mouthful.

He thumbs over his shoulder to where I'm standing behind him, and I close my eyes, saying a silent prayer. I know exactly where he's going with this. If Tara blows my cover, he'll know I wasn't at the library. And knowing my dad, there's only one conclusion he'd draw as to why I was trying to hide my whereabouts.

"Didn't want to join Mia for an early morning study session?"

Tara swallows her mouthful and then rubs her hands together. Confidently, she slides off the stool and carries her empty plate across to the sink. Turning back around, she faces my dad. "Nah. I worked a late shift last night and don't have the same commitment as Mia."

Every knot in my stomach unravels as I blow out a silent, relieved breath.

Propping his hands on his hips, he swivels back around to me. My dad is very rarely surprised or wrong, and I can tell by the look on his face that he's both things right now. "Can I use your bathroom?"

Thankful I cleaned it before my shift yesterday, I point to a closed door. "Go ahead."

As soon as he disappears inside and we hear the lock turn, a cheeky smile spreads across my roommate's face.

Thank you, I mouth.

She picks up her phone from the counter and walks over to me. "Welcome. I've hidden enough from my parents to know a girl in need of an alibi. I guess Pancake Boy wasn't a one-and-done arrangement after all."

The temptation to spew more lies and deny that I was with anyone last night fights to be the next statement out of my mouth. But Tara just surprised me and did me a solid in the process.

I pin my bottom lip between my teeth, remembering the way Jessie's tongue slid against me, desperate to feel it again tonight. "I guess not."

With my jacket resting over the back of my chair, I take a seat in the same boho café Jessie and I were in only weeks ago. My dad pulls off his cap and hangs it on the back of his chair, shaking out his messy, dark hair and looking around at the decor. He's more relaxed than he was when I saw him outside my dorm building.

"Okay, I have a gingerbread latte with extra cream and a black filter." The barista looks between us both, clearly not recognizing Dad.

He was one of the biggest names and enforcers in the NHL. But unless you're a Destroyers fan or you've followed hockey for years, it's unlikely you'd know who he is.

"Latte for me, thanks," I say, taking the large coffee from her hands and holding it between mine, the early February air still freezing my fingers.

Dad shrugs off his jacket and picks up his coffee, taking a sip. "I'm sorry I haven't been in touch all that much. The season has been crazy, and we're struggling to find a replacement for you. You did a lot around the place."

Guilt washes over me as I take in my dad's face. The stress of losing Mom understandably aged him several years, but somehow, in the few months I haven't seen him in the flesh, the lines around his green eyes look deeper.

"Marie wanted my job when I left. Did she not take it?"

He shrugs his broad shoulders. "It didn't work out."

I spoon some of the cream into my mouth. The air between us suddenly feels heavy and awkward again.

"I thought you'd take the chance to get away—you usually do in bye weeks."

Memories of that season flash through my head. When Dad went on a short vacation to Mexico, Jessie and I took full advantage. Crossing my legs over, I remember the way he pinned me against Dad's office door as I shamelessly humped his thigh. Smiling around the spoon, I also remember the panic when we both noticed the security camera set up in the corner of his office.

It took Jessie ten minutes to find the recording and delete it, and then we made out for another twenty. Let's just say, Riley's Bar wasn't the first time we'd been up close in a closet.

"What time is the game?" I ask.

Dad checks his watch just as I feel my cell buzz in the pocket of my jeans. There's a chance it's Jessie since practice will be over by now. Excitement races through me, but I fight back the urge to check who it is with Dad sitting directly across from me.

"Early evening, but I have some calls to make in the meantime." He takes another sip of coffee and sets it back down on the table. "What about you? Got plans? You can come to the game with me, if you want? It's your college team playing."

No can do. By that time, I'm hoping to be in your former winger's bed, preferably underneath him.

"Tara and I are heading out tonight." I have genuinely never lied so much in my life.

Dad nods his head, clearing his throat. "You're being, um … safe, right, Mia?"

Even while I'm twenty-two, talking about sex with my dad has never been more embarrassing.

"Really?" I drawl. "Are we having this conversation? I'm not sixteen anymore."

Shifting in his chair, Dad rests his forearms on the table, pinning me with a serious stare. "I was a college student once, and I know dudes operate mainly with their dicks."

My brows shoot to my hairline. "Yeah, well, no danger of that. No one is interested in me, and I'm more likely to have a love affair with the librarian than I am a student."

Dad sits back in his chair, crossing his arms over his chest. "Have you heard from Callaghan?"

It's right about now that I wish I'd joined the on-campus

poker team as I try to keep my face expressionless. "Jessie?" I question.

A wry smile traces his lips. "You know exactly who I'm talking about, Mia."

"Why would you ask that? You know I haven't heard from him since the summer."

"Because you're in the same city."

I lift a shoulder. "So? And I don't see why you have such a problem with him. It's been years since all that went down. He's probably got a girlfriend now."

Me.

"Because boys like Callaghan are the worst of the worst when it comes to thinking only with their dicks. I'd rather you date some hotshot on the college team than him."

"Drop it, Dad," I grit out, anger beginning to swirl in my stomach.

"You were a conquest to him, Mia. He's a bad person from the wrong side of town. You know the drunk that killed your mom was also from South Boulevard, right?"

I press my lips together and shake my head at him, looking down into my half-finished coffee. "You're a snob—you know that? You weren't exactly from a good part of town when you met Mom, but I didn't see Grandpa judging you."

Dad checks his watch again, grabbing his cap and jacket from the back of his chair. He pulls it on and then reaches into his wallet, pulling out a twenty-dollar bill for the check. "I also didn't sneak around behind his back for months and then leave her brokenhearted when I got caught."

He sets the bill down on the table and offers me a warm smile, clearly trying to avoid an argument.

"I don't see that he had much choice since you threatened murder and then kicked him off the team."

Standing from his chair, he rounds the table and leans down, setting a chaste kiss on top of my head. "Still defending him, even now. Move on, Mia."

When I push back my chair, it makes a squeaking noise across the floor. I grab my jacket and bag from the back of it and follow him out of the café.

Once outside, I turn to look at Dad, who thumbs behind him in the opposite direction. The freezing wind whips around us, blowing my hair across my face. Moments like this are when the pain of losing my mom feels the harshest. I know if she were here, I'd be able to talk to her about Jessie.

I know she'd see it from my point of view.

I know she wouldn't just give him a chance; she'd tell my dad to back off.

My eyes start to blur as I blink several times to hide my emotions. "Good luck with the game tonight."

I can tell he wants to say more, and as he watches my eyes glaze over, he knows he's upset me. Graham Jenkins has never been a mean person, but Mom's death definitely changed him. Bitterness and anger found their way into his personality and never really left. If anything, it's grown worse over the past seven years.

At twenty-two, I should be able to talk freely with him, and he should respect my decisions, even if he doesn't always agree with them.

When Mom died, it was like time stood still, and in my dad's eyes, I stopped getting older. Maybe continuing to treat me like a fifteen-year-old was—and still is—his way of hanging on to the past and keeping me protected, all at the same time. What he failed to realize is I did a lot more growing than the average teenager.

As much as his overprotectiveness has held me back from pursuing what *and who* I want in life, I don't have it in me to hurt him further. My breaking from his Dallas chains hit him hard enough, and telling him that I'm involved with Jessie again without him losing his shit feels just about impossible.

I step forward and reach up to kiss him lightly on the cheek. "Talk soon."

CHAPTER TWENTY-FOUR

JESSIE

> S
>
> So, I got your text, but Dad showed up at my dorm building. Then he took me for coffee and grilled me about you. I'm grabbing my overnight stuff, and I'll be over.

I'm halfway through prepping the salsa for the ground beef tacos I'm making for Mia when her text comes through. I wipe my hands on a towel and quickly unlock my phone.

Graham is here?

> ME
>
> Shit. Does he know?

> S
>
> No. But surprisingly, Tara covered for me after I told him I'd been studying early at the library. She knows I'm seeing someone, but not who. I'm getting in the taxi now. See you soon.

> Have you had dinner?

> No. When I did make it to the library, I worked through the day and forgot to eat. Starving!

> I made tacos.

> OMG! Ground beef?

> Of course.

> The man of my dreams.

When I hear a key slide into the lock twenty minutes later, I shut the burner off and head over to the front door.

"Does it ever stop raining or snowing in Seattle?" Mia steps inside, pulling down her hood and kicking off her boots at the door.

"You get used to it," I say, taking her bag from her shoulder and setting it down on the floor.

"My fingers are freezing, and all I did was walk from the taxi to the lobby," Mia says on a shaky breath, fumbling with the buttons on her red coat.

I step forward and take her hands in mine, warming them through.

She looks up at me, the golden fleck in her left eye shining underneath my apartment lighting.

"You're freezing, Sweetheart."

"It's cold outside, and the taxi driver was too cheap to use the heater."

I unzip my black training hoodie, and her eyes fall to my bare chest.

"Bring it in. I run hot."

Mia steps forward, snuggling into me, and I wrap my hoodie around her.

"My mom used to call these under-jacket hugs."

"She did?"

"Yeah." I rest my chin on top of her head. "She said they

were the best type of hugs—warm and cozy. She had this one jacket that was so big that she could zip us both up in it."

Pressing her lips against my chest, she places a gentle kiss over my heart. "The day my mom died, the last thing I did was hug her. I'd been a brat all morning and wanted to wear my school skirt short, like the other girls in class. She wouldn't let me."

She takes a deep breath and exhales, the warmth of her breath picking up my heart rate. "We fought from the moment I woke to the second I left the house. But before I walked out the door, I got this urge to make it right, you know? To hug her. So, I did ... and that was the last time I saw her."

Reaching down, I bring my hands under her ass and lift her up so we're nose to nose.

"Jessie," she protests, "you're still in pain."

With one arm supporting her, I wrap her left leg around my waist. "And I told you what my best pain relief is. I'm fine, Mia."

Gently, she wraps her other leg around me and then kisses the end of my nose. "I'll never stop worrying about you."

"I know, but I'm telling you, I'm good." I look around at the kitchen. "I had this special night planned for us, starting with tacos, followed by a movie and ending with you in my bed."

Her green eyes turn darker as she looks down the hallway toward my bedroom. "I have this feeling that tacos are just like grilled cheese—best served cold."

"Funny you should say that because I've heard the same."

She giggles as I walk us through to my bedroom and kick the door closed with my foot.

"I wanted to do this so badly yesterday," I say, laying her down on my bed, and I watch the way her dark hair fans out against the crisp white bedding.

"You changed it," she says, running a palm over the cotton duvet.

I shrug off my open hoodie, leaving me in only low-riding black jeans. "I didn't want there to be crumbs when you got back into my bed tonight. My goal is to keep you in here for as long as possible."

Crawling over her, I pull at the hem of her deep red sweater. She sits up fully, and I pull her top overhead, revealing a lacy, similarly colored bra. It's stunning against her fair complexion.

I pause, taking in the sight of her beneath me. "You look like pure perfection."

She brings one of her hands to my cheek, pulling me down for a kiss. "My thong matches. I wanted it to be the last thing you removed before you took my virginity."

My callous palm meets her soft, flushed cheek. "You want this tonight, Mia?"

"Yes," she whispers into the silence of my darkened room.

My trembling lips meet hers, and I kiss her deeply. The second I close my eyes, images of nineteen-year-old Mia lying on her bed flash through my mind, along with the pain etched across her face when I let her dad lead me out of the house and away from us.

"Are you on birth control?" I ask, reaching behind her and popping the clasp on her bra.

Her full breasts spill free, and I lean down, taking her right nipple into my mouth.

She throws her head back and moans at the sensation, the sound shooting straight to my dick. "Yes, I never stopped taking it."

My mouth moves from her nipple to the crook of her neck, kissing my way up to her left ear. Blood pulses through my body, gathering in my rock-hard cock. Though it's not the pounding of my heart rate, nor is it the rush of adrenaline I feel right now, that overwhelms me. It's the sight of Mia as she looks up at me with so much trust that has my emotions spinning out of control.

"I know I hurt you when I left that day. I know you thought I walked away from us. You had every right to be pissed at me, and I'm so fucking sorry," I whisper into the shell of her ear.

"There's never been anyone else, Mia. Not since the day I met you, not after I got traded to Seattle. You're the last girl I laid down beneath me, and if I'm lucky enough, you're the only woman I'll ever get to call mine."

MIA

My eyes sting in the best possible way when Jessie hovers over me, whispering into my ear.

"You haven't been with anyone since ..." I trail off, still trying to process everything he just admitted.

So many times, I was convinced he'd moved on. I spent weeks, maybe even months, avoiding news outlets and places where there was a risk of seeing him pictured with other women on nights out. I have no doubt there were some posted, but to know he never went further with anyone, to know he waited for me ... if I ever had any doubts about sleeping with him, they'd be out the window right about now.

Slowly, he shakes his head, his dark blond hair falling over his eyes. "No. My head told me to try and move on. That I'd fucked everything up with you and you were better off without me. But my heart never did, Sweetheart." He brushes his lips over mine. "When you love someone the way I love you, they're impossible to forget. I never wanted to forget the way it felt to be yours."

I open my mouth to speak, to check that he just told me he loved me, even though I know my ears heard him right. But he presses a finger to my swollen lips.

"Here's another thing about me. I might be about to take it slow with you tonight. I want to savor the way you wrap around me. I want to draw out every orgasm I give you—and there will be multiple, Mia. But you need to know I have a dirty fucking mouth, and it's desperate to tell you all the things my hands, tongue, and dick are dying to do to this stunning body of yours. You'll never wonder what another man feels like because you'll know there is no one else in this universe who can fuck you like I can."

Straddling my body, he sits back on his heels and brings his hands to the waistband of my black leggings, peeling them down until I'm left in only my thong.

His gaze drops to my lace-covered pussy, and an appreciative rumble emanates from his chest. "When I push inside you for the first time, do you want to still be wearing this hot-as-fuck scrap of lace?" He drops down onto one arm and pins me with a feral stare, running his hand over the soaked material. "I know you're gonna be so damn tight, but with the way you're weeping for me, I'll slide right inside you easily."

My core clenches at his dirty words. "Push them to the side. I want you in me right now."

Jessie comes to stand over me, and I scoot back into the center of the bed. In one move, he pushes his jeans and boxers down, and they pool at his bare ankles as he steps out of them.

He reaches over and grabs a pillow from the top of the bed, handing it to me. "Put this under your head, Sweetheart. I want you as comfortable as possible tonight."

My pulse throbs in my ears as I follow his commands.

As he kneels on the bed, his thick thighs on either side of my body, I watch the way he works himself above me, the tip already shining with his needy release. I know what that tastes like, and instantly, I want him in my mouth again. But tonight, I want him inside me way more. Somehow, he looks even bigger than he did last night.

"Are you sure you're going to fit, Jessie?" I ask on a shaky inhale.

He crawls over me, nudging my legs apart with his knees. "I'm not gonna lie to you, Mia. You're gonna be so damn full of me, especially when I finally come inside you. But there's no way my dick isn't sliding into that pretty, wet pussy of yours, and when I sit all the way inside, I'll hit spots you never knew existed. You think the orgasm I gave you last night was good? You'll be chanting my name all night."

With two fingers to his mouth, he sucks on them slowly and then runs them across my bottom lip. "Open for me."

I swirl my tongue around them, and I watch the way his throat bobs on a deep swallow.

"Good girl."

When he pulls them out, they're already wet from us both, but as he spits onto them, my pussy clenches. I'm so fucking turned on.

"You're ready to take every inch of me. But I want more than just my cum inside you. Spread your legs further, Sweetheart."

With his hand at my apex, he shifts my drenched thong to one side and rests a finger at my entrance. I feel my breath hitch in my throat with anticipation.

Jessie's attention moves from my pussy to my eyes. "Breathe out, baby."

On my exhale, a single finger enters me slowly, and a cheeky smile tips up the corner of his lips as he watches my jaw fall open.

"You're already so good at this, sucking me right in."

He continues to slide inside me carefully. At one point, I feel a tiny pinch as I take him further, but the pain is everything I'm ready to hand over to him.

When he pulls his finger out, I watch as his eyes hood at the sound of me taking him, and he pushes back in, another finger joining.

"Two this time, Mia. I'm so fucking proud of you for taking my hand so well."

He pumps in and out of me gently, and the sound of my pussy fills his bedroom.

"When I lick you from my fingers, I want them to be soaking. Now come for me."

When he drives deeper than he's gone before, scissoring his hand inside, white-hot pleasure rockets toward me. My hips shoot up off the bed, and he cups his hand over my pussy, his thumb working my clit. It's enough for the simmering heat to spark, and it sends me up in flames as every nerve fizzes in my body, burning in the best possible way.

"Jessie!" I croak, my voice failing me. "I-I'm coming ... s-so hard."

Just like he promised, he draws out my orgasm until I'm a writhing mess beneath him. He pulls out his fingers and smiles at me.

"You've always followed the rules like a good girl, Mia." He brings his fingers to his mouth, stained pink from where no one has been before, and sucks each in turn, his eyes fluttering shut at the taste of me. "Who knew Daddy's little princess could taste so damn sweet?"

I let out a needy whimper as he brings those same fingers back to my pussy, swiping them through me once.

"Are you still coming for me?" he says as he wraps his now soaking hand around his impossibly hard length, working himself up with my release.

I nod, looking up at him. "I think so."

When he notches himself at my entrance, he drops down into the missionary position, his forearms bracketing me in as his lips hover millimeters above mine. Pushing back some hair from my slick forehead, he kisses me softly above my left brow.

"I promise I'll go gentle with you. Breathe with me when it stings."

I wrap my legs around his waist, pinning him in place, and I feel the way his cock pushes just inside. The sensation is everything.

"I want it to hurt," I say, bringing my hand around the nape of his neck. "I want to be able to feel you when I wake up tomorrow."

When he pushes his hips forward, our jaws simultaneously fall open at the incredible feeling we've only fantasized about until now.

"There will never be a time when you don't clench your thighs and feel me, Mia."

He must be halfway in when I feel the first stab of pain, and I wince. Jessie kisses me through it, retracting his hips before pushing in again.

It hurts. I can't lie and say it doesn't, but it's the best kind of pain, as it flirts with insane pleasure.

"I want you all the way in me," I beg, pressing my heels into the top of his ass. "Touch that spot you keep talking about."

Jessie pushes further inside, and within a second, he's so deep that I can barely breathe.

"Are you ready for me to move, Sweetheart?" he asks on a choked breath.

I nod quickly. "Yes."

He moves in and out of me in smooth, languid strokes. Brushing his lips over mine with every inward thrust.

"Are you okay?" he whispers into my mouth.

"Keep going," I plead. "Make me come again, Jessie."

Finding the place he promised he would, he thrusts into me harder than before. It must kick up his pleasure as he moans into my mouth. "Mine. Always have, always will be. You're mine, Mia."

"Show me. Come inside me."

"This tight pussy is going to pull every last drop from me, Sweetheart. Do you want it now?"

"Yes," I chant, my body burning, another explosion ready to blow me apart at the seams. "I want to come with you."

Our joint cries fill the room as he fucks me straight through my second orgasm and immediately into a third.

"I'm coming again."

"Me too."

I half expected Jessie to bury his face in the crook of my neck when he comes, but he doesn't. I feel the way his dick throbs, and all the while, he moves his lips over mine, kissing me as he comes inside my pussy.

I have no idea how long we stay like that—joined together and kissing until my lips and chin are sensitive from his scruff. His messy blond hair is over his eyes, some of it stuck to his damp forehead.

Pulling back a couple of inches, he tucks a piece of my hair behind my left ear, his smile way lighter than I've ever seen before. "I'm so happy."

Earlier tonight, he told me he loved me, that he always had. But somehow, these three words have my heart about ready to burst.

"That's all I've ever wanted. For you to be happy."

This time, his head does fall to the crook of my neck, and he exhales a long breath into my hair. "Your dad can deport me to the other side of the world, but it'll never keep me away. I exist only for you."

CHAPTER TWENTY-FIVE

JESSIE

"What exactly is it you want?"

"Simple, Richard." Graham leaned forward and addressed the head of his legal team, resting his forearms on the boardroom table that separated him from me and my agent, Steve Waters.

He'd removed his hand from around my throat when he dragged me out of his house yesterday, but I was convinced he was still throttling me in his mind. His hands shook with rage as he reached into the middle of the table and turned the volume up on the conference call he'd urgently requested.

"I want to discuss the immediate termination of Jessie Callaghan's contract with the Dallas Destroyers."

Steve shifted uncomfortably in his seat. I'd called him last night to warn him this would be happening, but he still looked surprised when Graham declared his intentions.

Holding up a hand, he opened his mouth to speak, but Graham immediately shut him down.

"I don't want to hear it, Steve. You have represented this boy"—he pointed to the middle of my chest with venom—"since I made the biggest *mistake of my life—signing him. This time, he's gone too far, and he's not only a danger to my team and the future of the Destroyers."* He paused and cleared his throat. *"He's a danger personally too."*

Steve turned to me then, his brows knitted together, his shoulders slumped in defeat. *"Someone needs to fill me in. All you said last night was you'd fucked up again. I assumed in the same way—too much booze, or you needed me to deal with your dad and the press."* He looked back over at a red-faced GM. *"What do you mean, a danger personally?"*

Mia's face flashed through my head, her tears staining her cheeks. I imagined the state she'd been in when she texted me over and over again last night. I read each one and typed out a reply to nearly all of them. But I never hit Send on any. I couldn't bring myself to say goodbye, even though I had known that was exactly what this was. There was no way Graham would settle for anything else.

Graham lowered his voice and leaned closer to the phone speaker. *"For the sake of my daughter."*

"Oh fuck," Steve interjected.

Graham nodded at Steve, and his eyes flicked to mine. *"For the sake of my daughter,"* he repeated. *"This is to go no further than these four walls and whoever I trust. The fraternization policy between staff and players is clear. Ordinarily, it would be non-playing staff that leave. But there's not a chance in hell I'm throwing my daughter's career under the bus. She's destined to take over the team. She's damn good at what she does, even at such a young age. She's learning the ropes and fast."* He leaned back in his leather seat and crossed his broad arms over his chest. *"But for all her potential, she is still nineteen years old and impressionable."* Uncrossing his arms, he pointed at me again, and accusation laced his tone. *"And you took advantage. After everything—all the years I put you through college, paying for taxis and equipment to get you to practice and games because your parents drank away any donations I made—this is how you repay me. You looked me in the eye and told me you wanted to be the best, to rule the goddamn league. You told me you wanted the world and you'd make sure I'd never regret my decision to stick by you. I boarded planes to speak with your college coaches and convince them you were* worth starting. Fuck me." He ran a furious hand through his hair. "I even cleaned up your puke when you drank yourself silly at frat parties. And, yes, I know you spent more time fucking girls than you did on the ice."

I felt the blood surge to my face. I had no response, no leg to stand on. Every decision I'd ever made worked against me in that moment. "I'm sorry, Graham."

"Fuck off," he scoffed at me.

Steve opened his mouth to speak again, but Graham shoved his hand up in the air. As he leaned forward across the table, further than he had before, I could feel his disgust absorb into my bones. Graham's face was twisted with hatred, all too similar to my dad's.

Oxygen thief.

"My late wife always used to tell me to trust my gut. Especially when it came to you, Jessie. She said you were the right boy from the wrong side of town and you needed more support than most. She said she could tell you wanted this, even if you were messed up." His voice shook with emotion. "She'd kill you herself if she knew your true agenda. All you wanted was our only daughter."

"It wasn't like that." My hands were freezing cold, the pain was shooting into my chest, and my heart was hammering at an unsteady rhythm, reverberating throughout my body.

"Was she a bet?"

My head whipped up to him, anger swelling in my gut. "Mia is everything to me."

He huffed out a disbelieving laugh. "You're just sorry because you got caught before you could put your dick in her." He paused again, straightening his tie, before he pinned me again with a glare. "You'll never see her again. I'd be tempted to say you might catch a glimpse of her when you play away games, but I doubt your career will last more than a season with the way you're playing. I'll be calling in my final favor on your behalf, if only to get you off my team and out of my fucking life. But mark my words, Callaghan. You so much as LOOK at my daughter again, and you won't have legs to skate on."

Silence stretched throughout the room.

Steve dropped his pen to the notepad in front of him as he pushed it away, resigned to my fate. "What's this favor you're speaking of, Graham?"

He picked up his cell phone and started tapping on the screen a few times. "Mike Burrows is a former teammate and a good friend. He's got serious pull with the GM of the Seattle Scorpions. I know they have been watching game tape of Jessie for some time. They were interested at one point and likely still are if we can bury this scandal and Callaghan can keep off the fucking bottle."

"We will need to look at the terms of Mr. Callaghan's contract with regard to a trade deal," Richard added.

Graham shook his head at the speaker. "You mean the contract he's already in breach of? This is misconduct of the highest order. As far as I'm concerned, he's a free agent."

Steve threw me a despondent look and drummed his fingers on the table. "I don't want this to be dragged out. Jessie needs to be on his new team ASAP. If we can get discussions off the ground, I want negotiations to follow quickly afterward."

Graham nodded vehemently and pushed back his chair; he was done with the conversation. "Agreed."

I was barely able to inflate my lungs. I needed to get outside. I was either going to pass out or puke at any second.

"Like I said, Callaghan ..."

I paused on my way out of the room and spun back around to eye Graham for what I knew would be one of the last times.

"Not one fucking word about this from you, not even to your parents. This trade is by mutual agreement. You're a disturbance, and you dislike the way I run things, and I can't see a future here for you anymore."

I nodded as he turned and walked out of a second door leading to his office.

He had it all wrong if he thought I'd be breathing a word of this to anyone, let alone my dad. He always told me I was a fuckup, but if he knew, he'd have the evidence to prove his theory right.

I flew out of the room and left Steve to finish the call with Richard.

The hallway out to the parking lot was thankfully empty. I didn't want anyone to see me like this, especially not the rest of the team. They were already pissed at my performance and the way Graham had given me way more chances than they would ever get.

I got right to the end of the hallway when a hand landed on my shoulder from behind, spinning me back around. Other than Graham, this was the last person I wanted to see.

Tate Coulson, our captain and experienced hard-ass defender. Other than Zach Evans, who played for the Scorpions, he was the guy no one wanted to mess with in the league. I didn't like the way he looked at me. I knew he wouldn't start a fight right here, but I could tell he knew what had happened. He was close with our GM. Unlike me, when Graham had put Tate through his program, Coulson had taken the opportunity with both hands. He was one of the first success stories for Graham's foundation, and at this point, he was more like a family member to him. He'd also known Mia since she had been really young. Part of me thought he wanted her, but he wasn't that fucking irresponsible.

"So, the cat finally ran out of lives," he sneered, getting right in my face.

"Leave it, Tate," I replied, stepping back toward the door, feeling less sure that he didn't want to get into it right here.

He shook his head and tutted at me. "The GM's daughter. I mean, I always knew you were a fucking idiot. But I never thought you'd bury your career with a sex scandal."

"Fuck off. You got what you wanted; I'm gone."

I pushed at his chest, and he stumbled back from me, fire burning in his eyes.

"I don't think you realize how much Jenkins did for your sorry ass. He believes you're the best. And I'm not just talking about a generation; I mean the best ever. Period. But you know what I see? I see an average player. A rookie too scared to shoot for his potential, combined with a selfish prick consumed by addiction. Yeah, that's right; I know about your little secrets. Too wrapped up in finding your next drink to give a fuck about anyone. When Graham called me last night, he told me how gutted he was to lose you, even after everything. You know what I told him?"

"What?" I spit.

Reaching out, he fisted a handful of my orange-and-black hoodie. Spitting on my Destroyers logo, contempt overwhelmed his features. "I told him he'd dodged a bullet. But Mia had avoided a fucking land mine. You're not destined for greatness, only the fucking sewer."

I thought about what it would feel like to connect my fist with his nose as he released his grip on my top. "Say all you want about me. But never speak Mia's name again. You don't know shit about us."

Tate huffed out a sarcastic laugh. "Good luck with the Scorpions. Coach Burrows will eat you alive, and Jon Morgan makes me look like the fucking fairy godmother."

He turned on his heel and headed through a door to the right, no doubt back to Graham's office.

I'd lost everything—the people who believed in me the most.

As soon as I pushed out the back door to the private parking lot, I leaned on the hood of my black Mustang and emptied the contents of my stomach onto the ground. Tears rolled down my cheeks, and my body shook as I brought my fists down on the metal over and over again.

I'd done exactly what I had known I would. I'd taken her happiness and selfishly absorbed it until there was nothing left to give and my dark world seeped into hers. The only saving grace was my dad would never know the real reason behind my trade, and therefore, he'd never find out about Mia. I could keep her at a safe distance.

When there was nothing left in my stomach to puke up, I raised my head and saw the image of Mia leaning against my windshield, a memory from when we had gone stargazing in the cornfields. Her black hair was swirling around in the freezing winter air, held down only by her fluffy earmuffs. Her smile was brighter than the summer sun beating down on my clammy skin.

"Always?" she'd whispered, her eyes full of hope.

I beat my fist once more on the hood, and pain shot through my wrist. I ripped my phone from the back pocket of my jeans and brought up the pictures app, opening the password-protected file with the photos we'd taken during the months we snuck around. One by one, I deleted them, desperate sobs punctuating my actions.

When I got to the final photo of us, one I'd taken when she slipped into the locker room after I deliberately stayed late for practice one night, I paused over the red button.

"I'm so fucking sorry," I said, bringing my thumb down until the screen turned black.

CHAPTER TWENTY-SIX

JESSIE

It's been a week of this—me absolutely killing it on the ice. I'm the first to arrive and the last to leave practice sessions. Unleashing my game has never felt so natural.

Especially when I haven't touched a drop of alcohol since the night Mia turned up at my apartment with flowers. It's easy to break the habit when the reason you chose to drink is remedied by the return of the greatest thing to happen in your life. Mia doesn't just numb my pain or make me feel like life is worth living. She makes me want to live the best life I can. Not just for her and for us, but for me too. I just hope I can keep holding it together when the difficult times inevitably find me.

We're right in the middle of a power play when our center steals the puck, passing it straight to me. We're deep in the third period and zero to zero at home with Colorado. We need this win to stay within our playoff hopes, and so does the opposition. The game has been tight all night, neither side giving an inch.

I assess my options; there're at least three defenders between me and the goal as I travel with the puck down the right wing. I can wait for backup or take them on myself.

"Bring it." Zach's words repeat in my mind.

When I slow my speed slightly, it gives one of our forwards a chance to catch up with the play. But I've zero intention of sending him the puck. His assist in this goal will be as a decoy.

I take the Colorado center out when I cut inside and open up my body, faking to pass with an inside move. He takes the bait and positions himself, ready to intercept the puck, giving me the perfect chance to spin away and hit the jets, sending the crowd a few decibels louder.

Maybe the last two defenders think I'm at top speed when they come barreling toward me, one on either side and ready to take me out.

Their assistant captain makes the first mistake, driving in to steal the puck, but he only finds his ass when I throw a backhand to forehand move.

Kind of humiliating.

I take out their captain with a slip straight through his legs. Powering away from him, I hit top speed as I set eyes on their goalie. I can't remember the last time I traveled with the puck at this kind of speed; my hazy brain has never been able to keep up. But today, I see it all unfold in front of me. I know exactly what the goalie is going to do as he backs away toward the net and hits the splits, showing his cards first.

Tucking the puck away upstairs, I hit the brakes just before I hit the boards, sending a wave of ice up in front of the crowd.

I turn to see Zach and the rest of the team flying toward me, his stick tucked under his arm and fist outstretched to congratulate me on what I know is the finest goal of my career so far.

"I have never in my fucking life seen anything like that move. I mean, where the fuck did that come from?!" Zach screams at me, throwing an arm around my shoulders.

I pull out my mouthguard and look at him. "Her."

Just before he skates off, he nudges me in the chest with his glove and winks. "Well, whatever she's doing, tell her your captain orders more of it."

Skating down the bench, I bump fists with each player, but come to a halt when Coach grabs me by the forearm.

He leans in, his expression unreadable. "I don't know what's changed in you, Callaghan, and I'm not about to ask questions. In ten seconds of gameplay, you just answered years of doubt. That move will be replayed for decades to come. Now give them more material."

That's exactly what I do for the remaining ten minutes, securing a hat trick for me and a shutout for Jensen.

"Fucking hero."

"Top-tier decoy," I reply to our rookie winger, O'Connor, and clamp a hand on his shoulder as I walk through the locker room and head toward my bench.

"Crazy Callaghan." Jensen shakes his head at me, awe on his face as he pulls off his helmet and dumps himself down next to me. "I'll be the first to admit that I knew you were good, but—fuck me, kiddo—that"—he points toward the ice on the other side of the locker room door—"was a fucking master class. A work of art." He shakes his head and leans down to untie his laces. "Poetry in goddamn motion."

"Thanks," I casually say, reaching behind and pulling my jersey overhead.

Jensen's head whips up as he stands in front of me and chuckles. "*Thanks*? Is that all you have to say? Our fans turned up tonight, expecting to see a hard-fought game between two teams battling it out for a playoff spot. Instead, what they—*and the whole fucking world*—got was a spectacle. That final period was …" He smiles proudly. "I don't have the words right now to describe what it was."

"Me realizing my potential—exactly what I should've been doing for years," I offer.

Drawing his lip between his teeth, my best friend looks off to the side as Zach enters the room, heading straight for us.

Jensen quickly refocuses his attention back on me. "Don't you even fucking think about turning tonight into a reason to hate on your past mistakes. That final period was a glimpse into what Jessie Callaghan is capable of. The world will be going feral over you right now, and so they should. Enjoy it, man."

"There are actual bras on the ice right now." Zach thumbs behind him, his shoulders shaking with laughter. "They're throwing their underwear at you."

"Don't suppose any of them are lacy and dark blue?" My response is out before I can stop it, adrenaline loosening my tongue.

Zach's brows furrow, and Jensen snickers.

"I'm gonna go out on a limb with this and say that was a reference to a forbidden someone."

I nod, my high dropping a few notches. "Just wish she could've been there tonight to watch. With the girls in the family box, cheering me on."

"Sucks ass," Jensen acknowledges with the only appropriate response.

"I think it's time we met the girl behind the game."

Jensen looks at Zach. "What you got in mind?"

Zach casts a cautious glance around the room, every player is deep in animated conversation over tonight. "It's well overdue, and Luna has been threatening to organize it for way too long. This coming Sunday is a day off and cheat day. How about a house party at ours on Saturday night? Just our group. We have enough space for everyone to stay over; even the twins can have their own room."

Jensen looks at me, nodding his head in appreciation. "What do you say, superstar?"

I swipe a hand across my mouth, assessing the risk, which seems minimal. "I'll talk to Mia."

MIA

"Not just generational, Leo. Never been seen before, probably never will again." Hugh points at the TVs above the bar as Tara sets a bowl of wings in front of me and takes a seat opposite me in the booth.

"I feel like I barely get to see you." She side-eyes Leo, who's still preoccupied with postgame analysis and Jessie's insane hat trick.

I feel another surge of pride as I replay his first goal in my memory.

Taking a bite out of a wing, I shrug a shoulder. "Picked up extra hours at work, and I've been living in the library."

She cocks her head to one side, throwing me a look. "Bullshit."

"What's bullshit?" Leo cuts Hugh off mid-flow and looks at us both.

I feel the blood rush to my cheeks as I scramble for an answer.

"Oh, Mia thinks she's going to fail the journal critique assignment we just submitted," Tara responds.

I could reach across the table and kiss her for saving me twice in the past couple of weeks.

With his hands folded together and his elbows resting on the table, Leo leans down to the side, bringing his mouth closer to me, and I feel the way his breath fans my ear. "You're way too smart to fail anything, Mia."

His compliment should please me, but somehow, it doesn't feel sincere.

"Thanks," I push out.

Tara looks between us both, her brows slightly raised. Maybe she can tell I'm uncomfortable.

"Tara! I've got orders stacking up over here!"

She looks over at her manager and jumps up from the booth,

straightening out her skirt before rushing off, leaving me alone with the boys.

Call me suspicious, but when Hugh gets up from his seat and leaves the bar, making a fake-ass excuse that he forgot to submit the assignment I know he turned in, the fact that I'm alone with Leo feels all too convenient.

Discreetly, I shift a couple of inches away from him, trying to put some space between us.

Leo does the same, closing the distance I created. He unfolds his hands and drops his right one onto the cushion between us. "Tara's right though. Feels like I haven't seen you much since that night at Riley's."

I smile at him innocently. "Like I said, I've been really busy."

Leo clears his throat, the awkwardness unbearable. "I get that; what with trying to balance hockey and studying, there isn't much personal time left for me."

He pauses and brings his right hand around my lower back. I want to pull away from the contact; instead, I freeze, shocked at how forward he's being.

"What time I do have, I want to spend more of it with you. Just you, Mia."

Frantically, I scan the room. Half desperate for Tara to rescue me, half hoping no one has seen us. But Tara is nowhere to be found, and the bar has emptied out since the game ended an hour ago.

I turn back to Leo and sit forward on the bench, breaking the contact above my ass. "I'm not looking to get into anything with anyone right now, Leo."

"Okay, well, we could still have a lot of fun. I've liked you for a while now," he says, bringing his hand back to my ass.

Touch me once without my permission, and I'll be shocked. Touch me twice, and I'm pissed.

Grabbing my bag and jacket from the floor beside me, I stand from the booth. "Look," I say, running a stressed hand through my hair, "I said I didn't want to get into *anything*. I'm just looking for friendship."

Leo narrows his eyes as he looks up at me from the booth. "You've been sending me mixed signals for months. Now you blow me off?"

I throw my hands up in front of me. What the fuck is this guy on? "I've done nothing to make you think I wanted anything more than your friendship. Whatever you've read into us is on you."

Leaning back into his seat with a thud, he dismisses me with a condescending wave.

I should really drop it and walk away. But this guy just pushed all my feminist buttons.

With my palm braced on the table in front of me, I lean closer to ensure only Leo can hear me as he continues to refuse eye contact. "Let me offer you some advice for future reference, Leo. Next time you try to impress a girl, wait until after you've got her in your bed before admitting you're a dickhead."

I stalk out of the bar, pushing through the door and out into the mid-February air. I'm terrible at confrontation, and my heart hammers in my chest the entire walk back home.

When I pull out my keys, the lights from my dorm building come into view just as a bus heading into town pulls up along the sidewalk, and a couple of students board, scanning their passes as they find seats.

Chances are, Jessie is heading straight to Riley's after tonight's win, but there's also a chance he isn't. I look down at the key he gave me, but never asked to have back …

Fuck it.

CHAPTER TWENTY-SEVEN

MIA

"Jessie?"

I'm greeted with the faint noise of music, but no one is in sight when I pocket Jessie's key and pull off my boots, hanging my jacket on the back of the door and leaving my bag next to the console table.

"Jessie?" I call out again.

Heading down the hallway, I walk toward the increasing sound of rock music.

When I push open the heavy door to a room I've not yet seen, Nirvana's "Smells Like Teen Spirit" fills my ears, and quickly, I realize this must be his home gym.

Holy hell.

Here I was, thinking the only secrets Jessie kept from me were about his past. But I was happily wrong.

It takes a moment for Jessie to register I'm watching, and I seize every single second as I admire him jump-rope expertly. I have zero idea what move he's pulling off, but when he crosses his arms over his chest, twisting the rope around his body in the process, I'm certain it's the hottest thing I've ever seen.

That and the black backward cap he's wearing.

With his attention on the opposite mirror, Jessie comes to a grinding halt, sweat trickling down his bare torso and stopping at the waistband of his black workout shorts.

He spins around to face me, a smile pulling at his lips when I walk toward him. "Hey."

"Don't stop on my account. I was enjoying the show," I say, coming to stand just in front of him.

Jessie switches the rope, holding it in his left hand as he takes me in from head to toe. "I wasn't expecting to see my girl tonight."

"What sort of girlfriend doesn't stop by and congratulate her man on the best game of his life?"

"No girl of mine," he replies, pulling out a small remote and turning down the music still beating through the surround sound speakers.

"I thought you'd be out celebrating," I say, taking in his black high-top Converse.

Jesus, he looks hot.

He shrugs. "Had too much pent-up adrenaline. I normally pick up a drink to calm myself down when I get like that." He steps toward me, his pupils blown. "But I'm working on myself, so I made my excuses and left."

"I didn't know you did this." I nod at the rope still in his hand.

He looks down at it and smiles. "When my mind is racing, this is a way to occupy my thoughts. If I'm in a good headspace, I pick up a rope instead of a bottle."

I look up at him and nod. "By the way you played tonight, I'd say you're in a pretty good place right now."

Jessie nods back, leaning down until our lips are almost touching. "Fucking right I am."

In a matter of seconds, my back is against a mirror, and Jessie hovers over me, a bead of sweat running down the side of his neck. I watch as it travels down to the center of his chest and stops in a light dusting of blond hair.

Since I first noticed his tattoos, I've never asked about them, not wanting to push him too far if they were meaningful. But every time over the past week we've gotten naked together, the dove that decorates the skin over his heart has made me more curious.

I point to the black-and-white tattoo. "Does this mean hope?"

He holds my chin between his thumb and forefinger, nodding once. "Yeah, I'd say it's my favorite of them all." He casts his eyes down his torso. There must be at least fifteen different tattoos, some reaching around his ribs, but they all fit together perfectly.

"None have color," I say, taking in an eagle that sits over his right rib cage. "And most of them are birds."

He brings my attention back to his face as he brushes his lips over mine. "Up until now, there hasn't been a lot of color to include. All I've ever wanted to do was grow wings and escape my life. So, I drew them on me instead."

"Up until now?" I whisper.

A sexy smile pulls at his lips. "Up until now."

My lips find his as I kiss him, sweeping my tongue inside his mouth.

Still making out, he leads me over to his weight bench and lowers onto it, pulling me down to straddle him.

He drops the rope on the floor and breaks our kiss, his chest rising and falling rapidly. "I want to have some fun with you, Mia."

I cock my head to the side. "What do you have in mind?"

His eyes fall to what I'm wearing. "When I saw you in this hot-as-fuck skirt in Riley's, I was pissed I wouldn't get to fuck you in it that night. Like hell am I passing up that chance again."

Leo's face flashes in front of me; that night in Riley's, I noticed the flirtatious way he was with me, and tonight, he stepped it up again.

"What is it?" Jessie asks, rubbing a hand over my shoulder.

"Nothing."

He quirks a brow. "Mia?"

I blow out a breath and I pin my bottom lip between my teeth, but Jessie reaches up and releases it.

"Tell me."

"You were right about Leo. He made a pass at me tonight. It's sort of the reason I'm here. Mainly because I wanted to see you, but also—"

"Because he's a fucking prick and he thinks he can put his hands on you? On *my* girl?"

I probably shouldn't be turned on right now, but I am.

"Nothing happened," I clarify. "I told him where to stick it and left."

Jessie's jaw tics as rage paints his face while he looks off to the side.

Gripping his chin, I pull his attention back to me. "We've got bigger issues to worry about than Leo. He means nothing to me."

"If he ever tries anything with you again, I want you to tell me."

"Okay."

"Mine." Untucking my sweater from my skirt, Jessie pulls it over my head and then reaches behind and unclips my bra. "Every single part of you belongs to me, Mia. You good with that?"

"Yes."

His lips fall to my neck. "Such a good girl."

"What if I don't want to be a good girl all the time?" I whisper, gasping at the way he works his tongue over my collarbone. "What if I want to be bad?"

"I'd say that's inevitable with the way I plan to corrupt you." Jessie's hands come under my skirt, palming my ass. Only my black tights and thong separating us. "Lift up and turn around for me, Sweetheart."

His hard cock rubs against my ass when I lower myself back onto him.

"I can't touch the floor." I laugh, pointing my tiptoes toward the gym matting as I perch on top of his thighs.

"But look at how beautiful you are." Jessie nods in front of him.

Looking straight ahead, I take us both in, Jessie resting his head on my shoulder.

"We look pretty good together, don't we?" I reply.

"Spread your legs for me. I got you."

Opening my knees, I can already see the wet patch forming on my dark tights, and Jessie opens his thighs with me, spreading me further apart.

"Do you have more than one pair of these at home?" he asks, plucking the sheer material.

"Yes."

"Good." His hands fall to my center, and he rips a hole in them, exposing my thong-covered pussy.

I throw my head back into his shoulder and laugh. "One pair less now."

My laughter turns to gasps as his tongue finds the crook of my neck again, and I feel the way his hard dick grows even harder beneath me.

Still sucking and nipping at my sensitive skin, he trails his right hand up my inner thigh, stopping at my pussy.

"When you come over to mine at night, I won't always be here. Sometimes, I'll be away with the team," he whispers into my neck. "When my hands can't touch you, I want to know my girl can still get herself off. You told me you've never been able to do that, right?"

"Right," I gasp.

He shakes his head and tuts softly, looking at me in the mirror. "That just won't do, Sweetheart."

With his other hand, he takes one of mine and joins them

together, bringing them over my pussy and pulling my panties to one side, exposing me.

"I'm going to show you how to finger this pretty cunt properly, and then I'm going to fuck it while you watch. Any questions?"

I shake my head, heat pooling between my thighs. "No questions, sir."

A rumble reverberates against my back. "Make sure you take lots of notes."

My mouth pops open when he takes my middle finger with his and pushes them both inside me.

"Do you feel how tight you are?"

I tilt my head up to the ceiling, already close to coming from the experience alone.

"I need you to watch so you can learn, Mia."

I find our reflection, admiring the way Jessie smiles at me through the mirror. "I've never been this tight before. I'm already so close."

Jessie pulls his finger out, and I follow, pushing it back in when he does.

"Look at us, baby. Look at how well you're doing. Fingering this sweet pussy of yours. Can you feel it getting wetter?"

My head falls forward as we continue to pump our fingers in and out. "I'm dripping."

"All over my floor. But remember to keep watching because I'm about to switch things up."

I pick my head back up and watch as he withdraws his finger, and I instantly feel the loss.

"Does that feel empty?"

I let out a needy whimper and nod.

"Better add another then, yeah?"

I push a second finger inside myself as Jessie brings his to his lips and sucks it clean, watching me finger myself in the same way he showed me.

"I want you to curl your fingers forward and find your front wall," he says, bringing his hand over mine.

"I don't know what you mean."

Jessie smiles cheekily. "Just try. You'll know when you get it right, trust me."

As soon as I curl them toward my palm, a shot of pleasure shoots all the way to my toes. "Oh my god."

Jessie pulls my hair to one side, kissing his way up my neck. "Keep doing that until you soak my floor."

His thumb finds my clit as I continue to stroke myself, and he moves in rhythmic circles.

"There's so much pressure," I gasp.

"With the way you're working your pussy so well for me, there's a chance you might squirt. And if you do, I don't want to miss it. Open your legs as wide as you can for me, Sweetheart. Let me watch that pretty cunt."

One more curl of my fingers sends my release flowing down my thighs and onto the black matting beneath, powerful shudders overtaking my body.

"That's the hottest thing I have ever fucking seen." Jessie picks me up with one arm under my ass and steps over the bench. With his free hand, he pushes his shorts and boxers down and kicks them off to the side.

In less than a second, he's straddling the bench, and both hands are under my ass, hovering me above his erect cock.

He looks at us in the mirror, his eyes full of pure lust. "Now I want you to watch as I fuck you."

I'm still dripping when he lowers me onto him, the mirror showing the way I take every inch of his length.

As I stretch around him, our moans fill the room, along with the low-playing music, which has switched from Nirvana to Adele's "Make You Feel My Love."

Rocking my hips over his, he fucks me through another orgasm, and as I let out a desperate cry, he whispers into my ear, "You feel the way I love you, Mia? Your cries are a product of my years of wanting you, needing to feel you wrapped around me so badly."

"I love you," I whisper back. "S-so much."

"Don't whisper it, Sweetheart." He thrusts up into me hard. "Scream it."

"I love you!" I cry out. Another orgasm ripping through me.

He chuckles, happiness rolling off him. "Congratulations, Mia. You passed today's lesson with flying colors."

CHAPTER TWENTY-EIGHT

JESSIE

It's a big risk, picking Mia up outside her dorm, but I'm so fucking tired of her taking taxis and buses whenever we meet up. I should be able to treat her in a way that demonstrates what she means to me—everything.

If I didn't think it would affect Mia directly, I'd call Graham right now, tell him I was dating his daughter, and explain there was fuck all he could do about it. But I need to follow her lead on this.

Sitting outside her building reminds me of all the times I picked her up from her dad's place. Back then, my Mustang had tinted windows because it was cool. Discretion, unfortunately, wasn't at the top of my priority list when I bought my red BMW X6 last year and then stuck a vanity plate on it.

A few students pass by my window, no doubt on their way to the bars, and I duck my head down, lowering my baseball cap.

Come on, Mia.

	ME
	I'm outside and trying to avoid detection. You ready?

S

Trying to explain to Tara why I'm dressed up to go out, but not with her. Down in a second.

	I'm going to need more details on this outfit …

Well, you'll see it in a minute.

	Thank fuck.

Don't get smart with me, Callaghan. Only good boys get rewarded.

	And also caught. Tell Tara you'll fill her in on the details later.
	P.S. And you best believe I'm cashing in on my good-boy reward.

Five minutes later, Mia emerges from her building just as a couple of guys who look like seniors pass by, heading in the opposite direction.

"Keep walking, fucker," I mumble to myself as the dark-haired dude checks her out from over his shoulder.

Her little black dress sits mid-thigh, and combined with a cropped leather jacket and black ankle boots, I can't exactly blame the guy for looking. I know I'd have done exactly the same in college.

Too bad she's taken.

Pulling my cap as low as it can go, I step out of my car when she approaches and head around to the passenger door, pulling it open for her.

"Am I overdressed?" She winces, looking down at herself. "I can head back up and change."

There's no one around when I step forward and press her up

against my car, bringing my knee up and between her thighs, feeling her heat radiate through my jeans. "Now that I've seen you in that dress, there's absolutely no way you're taking it off." I press my knee into her center, and she grinds down on me, a whimper leaving her pink-stained lips. "That is until I peel it off you later."

"Is that a promise?"

"Fucking right it is, Miss Jenkins." My lips hover over hers as a couple passes along the sidewalk on the opposite side of the road. I lean down and press a kiss behind her ear. "I've never been a jealous kind of guy, but it isn't just Leo who appreciates what I have." I nod at the open door. "Now, get in my car and let me keep you all to myself."

The front door to Zach and Luna's double-fronted house swings open as soon as we pull into their driveway, the gravel crunching beneath my tires.

"That's Luna, right?" Mia turns to me, her eyes lit with excitement.

Picking up our joined hands, I press a kiss along her knuckles. "Yep." I point at the boy she's holding with matching auburn hair. "That's Aster. He's a month younger than June and Will, but he sure makes up for it."

Mia's lips twist to the side. "What do you mean?"

"Once you get to know his mom, you'll know exactly what I mean." I chuckle. "Despite being older, the twins and Aster had very similar due dates, it's just that June and Will came early. So Kate and Luna agreed they would celebrate their first birthdays jointly. Aster and the twins are inseparable; could've been triplets," I muse, a pang of sadness hitting when I think about how close I would've been to Will if he'd survived.

Mia hesitates for a second, her brow creasing like she wants to say something, but knows I need this moment to sit with my thoughts.

A beat later, Luna waves at us, pulling us back to reality and encouraging Aster to wave along with her.

"She looks like pure sunshine," Mia says.

"She absolutely is," I reply, pushing my car door open. "And I think you'll love her."

"It's so great to meet you!" Luna coos, bouncing on the balls of her feet as Mia and I climb the porch steps of their huge new home.

"So good to meet you too." Mia looks at her son, who's fighting to break free from Luna's arms. "And you must be little Aster?"

"He's a bit wiggly. Are you okay with that?" Luna asks.

She flips her hands toward herself, and I watch as my girlfriend takes him into her arms and balances him on her hip. She flicks her eyes up to mine and then back down to Aster.

I look across at Luna, who stands at the entrance to her house, and her gaze is locked on me, the corner of her upper lip tipping up.

What? I mouth.

She doesn't say anything; she simply winks at me in response.

"Okay, let's not heat the street," she announces, clapping her hands together. "Zach and Jon have spent all day in the kitchen, prepping food together, and the new knife set we recently bought has looked increasingly tempting to use the more time I've spent around them. So, I need you all to head inside and rescue me from an impending custodial sentence." Stepping aside, she motions through the door.

We find everyone else gathered around the white marble island set in the center of their grand kitchen.

"That's not what I said, Zachary." Jon huffs at his closest friend as they both peer over the counter with their backs to us. "Shortcrust pastry has to be rolled once chilled. You clearly rolled this at room temperature."

Zach props his hands on his hips and motions to whatever they're looking at. "Why the fuck would it make a difference?"

Jon drags a palm down his face. "Like I told you, it makes the pastry lighter in texture. This looks like you could anchor a fucking ship with it."

Throwing his apron on the side, Zach points at Jon. "You always have to get smart." He motions to what I can now see is a vegetable quiche. "Just take it out of its pastry casing, and you've essentially got a frittata. Boom."

"Daddy can't make those either. Can he, baby?" Luna plants a kiss on Aster's forehead, who's still in Mia's arms.

Zach pins his fiancée with a glare and pulls out his phone. "I'm ordering pizza. You can have everything else we made alongside it."

"I'll eat the spider plant in the bathroom if I don't get something soon," Jensen announces, walking into the kitchen, June and Will balancing on each shoulder, an arm wrapped around each of them. "Mia, hi," he says, stopping in his tracks.

"Mama," June says, pointing at Mia.

I watch as Mia's cheeks flush a cute pink.

"Oh, no, baby. I'm M-I-A. Not Mama."

Bringing a glass of water to her lips, Luna smiles around the rim at me. I know what she's thinking—babies.

"Pizza will be twenty minutes," Zach announces, pocketing his phone and rejoining the conversation. When he scans the room, he clocks Mia, and his eyes flare wide. "Sorry, Mia. Got sidetracked by my jackass teammates." He chuckles and crosses the kitchen, holding out a hand to greet her. "Zach Evans."

As he takes Aster from her in one arm, Jon hugs Mia into his side with the other. "Welcome to the family. My wife has told me a lot about you."

"That I have." A British voice filters into the kitchen.

When Jon releases Mia, Zach stands awkwardly for a second, and in response, Mia holds out her arms to him, offering a hug too.

"Bring it in, Zachary."

Throwing my head back, I burst out laughing, and when I finally refocus my attention on the group, I notice the way Kate observes me, a soft smile tracing her lips.

"Can we get you a drink? We have wines, cocktails, beers ..." Kate asks Mia, pushing off the doorframe toward the fridge.

Mia pins her lip between her teeth, her eyes flashing to mine for a brief second. "I guess I could have a wine."

I grab a soda from the side and unscrew the lid.

"You're not driving home tonight, right?" Jon asks me, tipping his beer bottle in my direction.

I shake my head. "Nah, I'm just staying off alcohol for now."

Zach's hand lands on my shoulder as he looks over at Jon. "Found his form and trying to keep it."

"I saw, like, three times." Jon shakes his head at me in awe. "That game against my former team? You blew Colorado out of the water."

"You watched the footage three times over?" Jensen asks, stepping forward into the conversation, June and Will still perched like parrots.

It's at that point I notice the girls, now with drinks in hand, retreat out of the kitchen, Mia following as Felicity takes Aster from Jon. I throw a quick smile at Mia as she glances over her shoulder at me on the way out of the room.

"Yep," Jon replies, taking another sip of his beer. "Once live, the second and third time with Jack. He wanted to watch the best player to ever grace the ice." He shrugs a casual shoulder at me. "I told him he already retired."

Zach chuckles from where he's setting out plates and napkins.

"How's he doing?" I ask Jon.

For what I thought was a straightforward question, my former captain suddenly appears uncomfortable as he looks down and shifts his weight from one leg to the other, and silence falls across our group.

Jensen looks over at me, raising his brows in question.

I shrug in response.

"What's the score, buddy?" Jensen finally breaks the silence.

Jon sets his bottle down and drums his fingers lightly on the counter in thought.

"Things are going … well for him. There's a bunch of NDAs in force right now, but my former agent, now his, has just entered into negotiations with a couple of teams."

Jensen's eyes bug out. "An opportunity in the AHL? Maybe I shouldn't be surprised. He was impressive when we came to watch."

Jon clears his throat. "Yeah. Maybe for a season. I'm confident after that, he'll be offered pro terms if he keeps his game up."

"Holy fu—" I stop myself at the last second, glancing up at June and Will.

Jon's lips tip up, pride written all over him. "Kid's awesome. Not only has he been killing it in the NCAA, but his grades have been insane too. He's always found studies to be difficult, but everything is going his way, and he deserves it all. He'll likely graduate near the top of his class. Felicity is so damn proud."

"So, why do I get the feeling there's another part to this story?" Jensen asks, addressing the elephant in the room.

Running his tongue across his bottom lip, Jon scratches at the back of his neck. "Well, that's where the NDAs come in. I can't say any more than that right now."

"Do you know any more?" Jensen turns to Zach, the twins now playing with his hair.

"Nope," Zach answers, eyeing Jon. "Won't tell me a damn thing."

"Well, whatever it is," I say, screwing the cap onto my soda bottle, "sounds awesome."

Jon nods. "Speaking of awesome …" He tips his head over his shoulder. "Felicity filled me in on the details. At first, I thought you were insane to go after Graham Jenkins's daughter—not just once, but twice. But now that I've met her, I get it."

"She's pretty amazing," I reply, already missing her.

"She's definitely out of his league." Jensen chuckles. "Only took him four years to get his sh—izzle together."

I throw him a death glare. "Says the guy whose girl wouldn't even look at him for the first eighteen months."

He smirks and steps forward, casting his eyes up to June and Will. "And now, I have the bling and the babies."

Jon's eyes grow wide as he turns to Zach. "Bling. That reminds me. We need to talk about—"

"No."

CHAPTER TWENTY-NINE

MIA

"Oh my God, so she tried to go behind your back and steal the client from underneath you?" Felicity scoffs as all the girls surround Aster on his play mat, where he's busying himself with a sensory book after dinner.

Kate nods once, her silky blonde hair falling around her shoulders as she pulls it down from a messy bun. "Yep, no word of it is a lie. Mrs. Garcia called me directly, saying she couldn't make our appointment on Friday since a personal issue had come up. I was like, 'There is no meeting scheduled for this Friday.' At first, I assumed it was a mix-up with reception, but when she explained she'd made the appointment directly with Nina Higgins, my blood ran cold. She *knew* I had every intention of taking back my entire client book when I returned from maternity leave, but she still went ahead and tried her luck anyway."

"Ugh, what an absolute B." Luna shakes her head in disgust.

Kate raises her wineglass in agreement.

"I assume you had it out with her?" Felicity questions.

Kate huffs out a dry laugh. "Of course. Ideally, I'd have marched right up to her desk, but she moved back to the New

York office. So, I had to settle for a phone call. And you know what her reasoning was?"

"That she's a B?" Luna replies.

"Girl, that goes without saying." Kate flicks her hair over her shoulder. "She was concerned I couldn't handle a full-time workload on part-time hours."

"B!" Aster shouts.

"Precisely, Aster." Felicity nods at him. She looks back at Kate and places a hand over hers. "Please tell me you told Mark."

"Who's Mark?" I ask.

"Joint owner of the firm we work at," Kate replies.

When I turn back to Felicity, a wry smile traces her lips. "Actually, no, I haven't said anything to him."

"Um, why not?"

"Because, Mrs. Morgan"—Kate clears her throat and leans in closer to us—"I intend to keep that little scandal safely under my hat. The delightful Nina now knows I have information on her that could land her in serious hot water with asses she spends half her life kissing. I like to think of it as my own little power play. At least, that's what I said when I informed her I'd just been offered senior counsel. The same position she was being considered for."

Felicity gasps and throws a hand to her mouth. "What?! You got it?!"

"You know it!" Kate squeaks.

Pulling Kate into a hug, Luna kisses her on the cheek. "Queen. That is all." She points to her stomach. "When I have this baby and get back from maternity leave, I'm going to need you to teach me your ways. I have half an eye on the head of the department."

Kate quirks a brow at her in response. "You just took your entire class from average and failing to achieving some of the best grades in the state. There isn't a better teacher in Washington. The job is yours. No question."

"Congratulations, Kate." Leaning forward, I clink my glass

against hers. I look around at the women sitting in front of me. "You're all such an inspiration. Your stories are exactly what I need to get me through these next few years in college so I can hopefully open my own practice one day."

Setting her glass down, Kate stands and walks around to my side of the blanket, taking a seat next to me and pulling me into a hug. "Successful women support successful women. Stick with the right people, and you can have or be anything you want."

Although she never met my mom, Kate's words are exactly the kind of thing she used to say to me. And they're everything I needed to hear.

Kate takes my hand in hers, and I squeeze it back. "Thank you."

"You look thoughtful." Felicity tips her head to the side.

This whole thing feels surreal—me, Jessie Callaghan's girlfriend, drinking and laughing with women I've mostly seen on screens. Two months ago, I was hiding my embarrassed face beneath my coat and racing out of the café in Whistler as they looked on with sympathy. Now, I feel like a part of their family.

I take a sip of wine and set the glass down on the coffee table behind me. The stone fireplace burns a few feet in front of us. "Ever wonder how your life can change so dramatically? One second, you're leaving behind all you've ever known and the next, you're in some strange city, trying to follow your dreams while simultaneously keeping away from the one guy who occupies them. Now, he's just through that door, and I'm sitting here with you guys, trying to process all this."

My eyes sting as everything that's happened slams into me, overwhelming my emotions.

Kate squeezes my hand in hers again. "You know, I never used to believe in fate. My whole life, I'd been brought up to believe you can—*and should*—control every aspect of your destiny. Leaving anything to chance was a lazy way of fumbling through life." She laughs and plays with one of the tassels on Aster's blanket. "Then I got pregnant and fell in love with the man I had been determined to hate. I hadn't planned on either, but they're the greatest blessings I've ever had. You can't fight fate, girl. And you shouldn't either."

I nod and drop my head, tears pooling in the corners of my eyes. "You're right. But my dad will never see it that way. At some point, I'll have to tell him about Jessie. I lost my mom seven years ago; I can't lose my dad too."

"Why does he hate him so much? I mean, I know the background story. But what's so bad about a guy who's clearly crazy about his daughter?" Luna asks.

I know the women sitting around me are as loyal as it gets. If there's one thing I've learned over the past couple of months, it's when it comes to the best people, you don't have to be friends with them for years to know you can trust them. But Jessie's life isn't mine to tell.

"I'm gonna need you in here, Princess." Jensen pokes his head around the living room door. "Jon is trying to take over the joint birthday party with Aster. He thinks we need another tier on the cake and there won't be enough giraffe balloons."

Kate releases my hand and narrows her eyes, rubbing her palms together. "Please excuse me for a hot minute. I have a Morgan to deal with."

DAD

I'll be back in town two weeks on Saturday for business. Thought we could meet up for dinner if you're around?

SITTING up in Luna and Zach's spare bed, I stare down at the message I received from Dad a couple of hours ago. Maybe telling him then would be the right time to do it. If it's face-to-face, I can at least try and stop him from murdering Jessie.

ME

Okay. Just let me know where, and I'll make sure I'm not working.

DAD

I know I didn't say it last time, but I'm proud of you, Mia. I'll be the first to admit that, initially, I thought Seattle was a mistake. But you're proving me wrong. Your mom would be proud of you too.

I bite on the inside of my cheek as I read his text over, convincing myself that if he knew the truth, he'd still feel the same way.

I set my phone down on the nightstand and pick up my textbook, focusing on the chapter I need to have read and summarized before Monday's class. The sound of the shower filters into the room from the en suite. Part of me wishes I'd said to hell with studying and joined Jessie, like he'd tried to get me to do—several times.

I'm halfway through the first page when Jessie's phone lights up on the opposite nightstand, and I reach across to grab it, seeing *Mom* lighting up the screen.

The call continues to vibrate in my hand until it goes to voicemail, and it sparks memories of the night Jessie cut our theater date short. He let the call drop that night, too, but clearly, he knew she needed him.

A second later, the phone buzzes again, and without thinking anything through, I answer.

"Hey, um, can Jessie ca—"

"Will, is that you?" a weak female voice cuts me off.

Will?

"No. This is Jessie's phone."

"Who are you?" she replies, her tone clipped.

"I-I'm just a friend. I can go get Jessie. Give me a second."

"Tell him we need more money. Sixty thousand this time."

My heart races in my chest as I fall silent.

"Are you still there? His dad, Wayne, he's mixed up with a couple of loan sharks. They're threatening him and—"

A crash rings down the line, and I pull the phone away from my ear, wincing at the noise.

"The fuck is this?!"

I know without even having to ask who just picked up the phone.

"T-this is Jessie's friend. I was speaking to his mom."

"Alice, you fucking idiot! Who are you spewing your guts to now?!" His voice is muffled, and I can tell he's covered the speaker, even though I can hear every single word he says.

My heart beats faster in my chest. "I'll get Jessie to call you back," I hurry out, ready to end the call.

"Wait a goddamn minute," he snipes. "I know exactly who you are."

My book falls from where it was resting on my knees and hits the floor with a thud. "You have no idea who I am," I respond. There's no way he could.

"Red fucking fingernails."

Frantically, I check the screen, panicking that I've switched it to video mode.

"Don't go all quiet on me now, Jessie's girl."

"I don't know what you're talking about," I push out, my voice shaking.

His laugh is low and evil-sounding. "Since you're with him right now, I have a favor to ask. Tell him we need a hundred thousand by tomorrow morning. I've got a few people I need to keep happy, and they know where to find Jessie if he doesn't give them what they want."

My throat runs dry as I look up and see Jessie standing in the en suite doorway, his mouth open and a white towel hanging low on his hips.

"I assume you can do that for me, *Sweetheart*. That's what the *S* in his phone stands for, isn't it? He used to have a sweetheart a few years back."

Bile rises up my throat, his insidious voice leaving me cold. "I'll let him know."

"You do that."

The call cuts, and I drop the phone into my lap.

"Who was that?" Jessie asks, slowly walking toward me.

"He wants a hundred thousand, Jessie," I whisper. "He got himself mixed up with loan sharks or something, and he needs you to pay them off." My voice cracks as trembles set in.

Scratching his nails down the side of his face, he looks down at his phone in my lap. "You answered the call?" He looks concerned, but his voice is sharp.

"I-I wasn't thinking."

"Did you tell him who you were? Anything about you?" Reaching forward, he grabs the phone, clicks a few buttons, and tosses it back on the bed. "Mia."

I straighten at his tone. "No. I just said I was a friend. He said something about red fingernails and called me Sweetheart. He said you used to have a sweetheart a few years back." I cover my face with my palms. "If you don't pay by the morning, he's going to give these men your address."

"Fuck!" he shouts, his towel dropping from the floor as he scrambles for his wallet.

"You can't pay him, Jessie. No matter how much he demands, he'll always want more. It'll never be enough."

His breathing is erratic, and when I reach out and grab his hand, his skin is ice cold.

"I can help you work all this out. I promise. Does Will have something to do with this?"

He snatches his hand away as his eyes fill with tears. "How do you know about Will?"

I sit back in bed and bring the duvet up to my neck. "When I answered the call, it was your mom. She called you Will. Your dad grabbed the phone from her and started screaming."

"I need to get home," Jessie rushes out, not looking up as he starts shoving clothes into his overnight bag.

"Jessie, you can't just leave. Everyone will start asking questions."

He stops packing and looks up at me, the shattered look in his eyes returning. My heart cracks clean down the center.

Please don't. Not again.

"I need to make some calls. Go to sleep, Mia."

"Jessie," I plead, "don't shut me out."

He pinches the bridge of his nose and holds up a hand, the eagle over his rib cage more visible since the bruising has completely faded. "Just ... leave it, okay?"

"Jessie—"

"*Leave*. It."

Tears tumble down my cheeks as I watch him throw on a pair of gray sweatpants and a black T-shirt.

When he gets to the door, he pauses with his hand on the handle and turns back to me. Desperation all over his face. "Even when I think it's safe, you're always in danger."

CHAPTER THIRTY

MIA

"Girl, I'm going to need you to take more notes. This class is going way over my head," Tara whispers, nudging her elbow into my arm as we sit in the second row from the back. "And what is it with you wanting to be way in the back here anyway?"

I shrug and shake my head slowly. "Got a headache coming. Wanted to be away from the screen."

"No kidding." Tara sits back in her seat, tapping her pencil on her empty notepad. "I need binoculars."

The professor's voice is nothing more than a murmur in the distance as he delivers the class that I was supposed to prep for, but instead spent all night on Saturday waiting for Jessie to come back to bed.

At around three a.m., I found him in the pitch-black, sitting on Zach and Luna's couch, staring down into a whiskey glass.

He didn't drink any, but even in the dark, I could see the anguish written all over his face. He wanted to. He was battling with himself, gripping the glass so tight in his hand that I was worried it would shatter at any second.

I wanted him to talk to me. He'd been downstairs for hours, sitting alone with his own thoughts, drowning in emotions that I knew were eating him alive.

When he finally looked up and saw me standing in the living room doorway, I watched the way his eyes glazed, shining in the moonlight.

He didn't fight me when I approached him and took the glass from his hand, setting it down on the coffee table in front of him. He stayed silent as I led him back up the stairs and into bed, curling myself around him as we slowly drifted off to sleep.

And when he dropped me back at my dorm on Sunday morning, we didn't make any plans to see each other.

I don't know if he paid his dad that money. All I know is, Wayne Callaghan is the kind of dangerous you read about in books, never really believing or comprehending that kind of person is out there. A monster that would rather see their own child burn before any harm came to themselves.

All I did was share a two-minute conversation over the phone with him. My boyfriend has endured twenty-six years of his behavior.

I look down at the minimal words on my notepad.

The truth is, I can read every single textbook in the library, critique every journal and study of trauma survivors. But nothing could have prepared me for the look of pure terror reflected in his eyes.

The past couple of days have killed me to be apart from him, especially when I know he's about to head to Dallas for an away series. But my gut tells me he needs this space to deal with the shitstorm.

On Saturday night, I got it. I got why he'd hidden Dallas Jessie from me.

And despite it all, I still want every part of him. The difference is that I'm not sure I know how to do that now.

Wayne's words play over again in my ears, but Alice's broken voice lives in my soul. Jessie's right; she needs to get out. If not for herself, then for her son. She is the only reason Jessie goes back home, answers his phone, and puts his financial future at risk.

When he told me she'd made choices that destroyed him, he wasn't just talking about his childhood. She's still making them now. Choosing her husband over her son.

And the kicker? I think she's so far gone that she can't even see what she's doing.

When the professor steps out of class to fetch some handouts, Tara nudges me in my side. "Let's get out of here. I can download the slides for us later."

I shake my head. "We can't just leave class halfway through. We—"

"Mia, look at me," Tara interjects.

I continue to stare down at my pad, the first teardrop smearing the few notes I've made.

"It wasn't a request," she replies, grabbing my things and shoving them into my bag.

"You have a message," she says, passing me my phone and taking my hand, leading us to the front of the hall and out into the main corridor, not stopping to say bye to Leo and Hugh, who deliberately sat at the front.

No doubt avoiding me.

Still being led by Tara, I unlock my cell with one hand and check who it's from.

> KATE
>
> I don't need to be a lawyer to work out something happened on Saturday night. Did you guys fight? If you need me to deal with a Callaghan, I'm ready and waiting. Here for you. We all are.

We turn a corner and stop next to a bench.

Tara points at it, her left brow raised in determination. "Sit there, please."

Too exhausted to argue, I do as she demands and watch as she disappears into the dining hall before returning a second later with a glass of water.

Handing it over, she takes the seat next to me and draws in a deep breath. "I want you to know you can trust me, babe. There's obviously been something going on since you're barely home. I didn't push you because you seemed happy, so I figured there was nothing to worry about. But that day with your dad got me thinking, and now you look anything but fine. So, I gotta ask, is it Pancake Boy?"

I sniffle out a laugh and shake my head. "No—well, sort of." I look up at her, her regular sunny smile pressed together into a worried line. "I need to know I can trust you."

She nods slowly. "Absolutely, you can. Shit, babe, did Leo do something? Is that why he's ignored us all morning?"

I shake my head again, choosing to keep what happened at the bar with Leo just between us. Like I said to Jessie, a cocky college player is the least of our worries right now. "It's not Leo."

"Then what is it?"

"Jessie Callaghan," I whisper.

She pulls back, her brows knitting together. "As in the starting forward for the Scorpions?"

Pressing my lips together, I look off to the side as people rush past us, heading to their next class. "Yes."

"I don't understand."

"I've been seeing him."

A broad smile crosses her face. "Ha, that's a good one."

"No, really," I say, looking her straight in the eye. "We've been sneaking around for the past month or so."

"Holy crap!" she announces, then winces and ducks her head. "You aren't fucking with me, are you?"

"That's where I was when my dad came round that day. I'd stayed over at his place."

Her hand comes to cover her mouth. "Jesus. And you're upset about this? Wait, did he break up with you or something?"

She shakes her head. "Asshole. Slept with you and then ghosted you, right? Clearly a stupid asshole to do that to a GM's daughter."

"It's not like that. We're still seeing each other, but … ugh, it's really complicated. My dad doesn't know about us. No one really does. That's why I need to trust you. You can't say anything."

Pulling her thumb and forefinger across her lips, she throws away the key. "You're looking at a sealed vault. But my initial reaction stands—*holy crap*, girl. Tell me he's as good in bed as the books make out."

I smirk, thinking about the collection of hockey romance books that line her bedroom wall. "I don't kiss and tell, but I will say this: when it comes to my boyfriend, nothing about those books is fictional."

Her eyes flare wide. "As in he …"

I hold up a hand. "That's all you're getting."

I bend down and grab my phone from my bag, shooting a quick text to Kate, telling her I'm doing okay and not to worry.

Then I turn back to Tara. "It's already past four, and I have back-to-back shifts tomorrow. I need to head to the library. Maybe we can download the slides and try and work out what we missed?"

Tara leans back in her seat. "Ugh. Do we have to?"

This time, I take her hand in mine and lead her down the hallway. "Come on. I'll buy you a coffee. Caffeine can get us through."

It's past eight p.m. when we finally emerge from the library.

"I've never studied so much in my life." Tara giggles, holding the door open for me. "Neither have I ever left the library in the dark."

"Feels kind of good though, right?"

She quirks a brow. "I guess, but best believe I'm watching trash TV to cleanse my brain when I get back."

I smile, continuing to wear a brave face. Today has been a total write-off. Approximately zero of the notes we downloaded have sunk in, as my mind is still whirling over Jessie.

We walk for another five minutes until we reach the place Tara works at, and she stops next to me. "I need to check my shifts. Meet you back on the couch?"

"Yeah, sure," I say when my phone rings in my bag, and I fetch it out, showing her *J* written on the screen.

"Now I know what the *J* stands for." She smiles before turning and waving over her shoulder. "Trash TV for one then. Have fun."

"Hey," I say after hitting Answer before voice mail can pick up.

"Hey, Sweetheart," he replies, sending tingles to my toes.

"Where are you?" I ask, continuing to make my way home.

"About twenty yards away."

Standing under the same streetlight he was that night he stayed at my dorm and slept on my floor, Jessie watches me approach. A smile growing on his lips, the closer I get.

When I'm within a couple of feet, he pulls me into him, wrapping his arms around my waist.

"You still haven't cut your hair," I say, reaching up and pushing his floppy hair out of his eyes as it peeks out beneath his black beanie. "But at least you're wearing a jacket tonight."

He looks tired but in control, and I push out a relieved breath into the space between us when I realize he hasn't been drinking either.

Releasing me for a second, he drags the zip down on his dark gray winter jacket and steps back, holding it open. "I'm heading to Dallas tomorrow for an away series."

"I know," I say, bringing my arms around his warm body, and he wraps his jacket around us.

He blows out a long breath. "I needed to see you before I left."

I look up at him. "Did you pay your dad?"

When his warm lips meet my forehead, my eyes flutter shut. "Yeah."

"Jessie, you can't keep—"

He cuts me off when his mouth presses against mine. "I know, Mia. I know I can't. But I'm here tonight to say I'm sorry about what happened on Saturday."

I shake my head. "You didn't do anything wrong. I get it. Everything."

He nods in response. "Try telling that to Kate Jones. She said you looked upset before we left yesterday, and she was convinced it had to do with me."

With another kiss to my lips, he lightly sweeps his tongue inside, massaging against mine. There's no one around us when I bring my hand to the back of his neck, deepening our connection and drawing a whimper from his chest.

Jessie pulls back, his blue eyes sparkling beneath the streetlight. "No more secrets. I'm here to tell you everything I should've said on Saturday."

"About Will?" I ask.

He wraps his little finger around mine, closing his eyes. "Yes. About my mom. I'll give you every answer to every question you have. But I also don't want you to worry. My dad doesn't know who you are."

"I know," I whisper. "There's no way he could've just from a photo of my hand and a stack of blueberry pancakes."

He huffs out a weak laugh. "You mean everything to me, Mia. There's nothing I wouldn't do for you."

CHAPTER THIRTY-ONE

JESSIE

"Tara not home?" I ask, scoping the place out when we walk in. A single floor lamp is lit in the corner.

She shakes her head, pulling off her jacket and boots, and I do the same with my coat and sneakers.

"No, but she will be soon." She turns to me, uncertainty in her eyes. "Wouldn't matter anyway. She knows."

I throw my coat over one of the barstools, it's pointless hiding my stuff in Mia's room. "You told her?"

Standing in the center of her living space, looking like everything I want, she twists her hands around in front of her. "I, um ... I got a bit upset today in class, and with that and my mysterious disappearances, she kind of demanded to know. She had given me an alibi when my dad started questioning where I was the first night I stayed at your place, so I felt like she wouldn't say anything. I should've checked with you before I told her, I know. Just with Saturday night and your dad and everything, it all got a bit too much, and I blurted it out."

I make my way over and rub my palms up and down her arms. "If you trust her, then so do I. You have nothing to be sorry for. We both know your dad has to find out. It just needs to be at the right time."

She presses her lips together and takes a seat on the couch. Holding one of my hands in hers, she pulls me down next to her. "We need to talk about the right time to approach my dad, but I'm not ready yet."

Releasing her hand, I pick her up so she's sitting across my knees, and she wraps her arms around my neck. "When you give the go-ahead, we'll tell him together. Preferably in public so there are witnesses." I chuckle before bringing my mouth to her lips.

I have no idea how long we make out for like that. Ten, maybe twenty minutes? Not long enough.

I break the kiss and rest my forehead against hers, our breathing heavy and mingling. "I came here tonight to tell you everything. To lay it all down for you, Mia. I want you to know everything about me, about my past. Zero secrets. Some of the things my dad did to me and my mom are pretty bad. But I want you to have it all before you decide whether you truly want this with me, with us."

Bringing her hands to the sides of my face, she cups my head between her palms. "There's nothing you can tell me that would ever make me want you less. There's nothing in your past that will ever make me love you less, Jessie Callaghan. There never has been."

By the time I squeeze my eyes shut, the tears have already started to fall down my cheeks, and my hands begin to tremble. "I've never told anyone before. Not all of it."

"I know, Jessie. Take your time."

Picking her up off the couch, I walk us through to her room and kick the door shut behind us.

After I lay Mia on the single bed, I peel off her jeans and then pull her black T-shirt overhead, leaving her in only her underwear.

When I reach behind my head and pull off my hoodie and

shirt in one go, I watch as Mia's eyes fall to my chest, slowly traveling to the deep V protruding above my sweatpants.

Crawling over her body, I pull the duvet up and around my shoulders, forming a cocoon around us.

I swallow back the nausea as I will my brain to do something it never truly has.

Remember.

"When you came over to Kate and Jensen's, you asked me if I was an only child. I told you I was because I didn't know what to say. Jensen and the group know I had a brother who died, but I knew if I told you, then I'd want to tell you about his death and how it affected my mom. The trouble is, I've never been ready to talk about Will. I've never been ready to say it all out loud. I didn't want you to see me as the broken boy with so much sadness in his life. Because you make me anything but sad, Mia."

"I don't see you as a broken boy, Jessie. I see you as a phenomenal person who makes me happy."

I close my eyes, letting her words wash over me as I prepare to share my past for the first time. "Mom went into spontaneous labor, and Will was born twenty minutes after she delivered me. We were thirty-six weeks." I blow out a shaky breath and focus on Mia beneath me. "At that many weeks old, we both needed neonatal care. But Will was smaller and weaker than me. He needed more help with breathing."

Reaching out, Mia runs a gentle hand through my hair, encouraging me to keep going.

"I haven't had many chances to speak to my mom about what happened to Will, but on the few occasions I have, she told me that after a couple of days, I was strong enough to come home, so she and Dad brought me back to the house."

I swallow hard, but the lump in my throat won't shift; it feels like I'm choking, and I know it's on painful memories. "He, um ... he died that night. Mom said it was an infection that took him. But they never made it back to the hospital in time. I'd spent all night crying and wailing. Mom couldn't settle me; she said it was like I knew something wasn't right. They say that twins, you know, even as newborns, we instinctively feel what the other one is experiencing."

I drop my forehead to her shoulder, dampness coating her skin. "He was so damn small, Mia. One day when I was around ten years old, I found the ID band that the doctors had put around his ankle."

I fight to inflate my lungs, but each time I try, it feels like the vise fastened around them tightens. "I don't know all that happened after Will's death since I was a baby too. Mom was always a heavy drinker, but as the years went on and I got older, she spiraled out of control. She blamed herself for Will's death. Grief tore her apart, but alcohol never gave her a chance to heal."

"And your dad, he blames you, right?"

Picking my head back up, I shift a piece of loose hair from her face. "Dad has always been an asshole. My mom's parents hated him from the second they met them until the day they died. I was young when Papa took his last breath. Papa had been my rock and the only member of my family who believed in me and my hockey career. They never knew the horrors of what went on behind closed doors, but they never trusted Dad either."

Mia kisses the tip of my nose, letting me know she's here and listening.

"My dad told me I was the reason Will was so small, I was the reason he was too weak to survive, and I was the reason they never got to say goodbye. Funny thing is, I don't think he really cares all that much about Will; he just uses his death as a reason to be cruel and hate on me."

"I just can't understand how someone can hate like that, especially their own flesh and blood," Mia whispers.

I run my trembling lips over hers. "Those are answers I'll never be able to give you, Sweetheart. Because I'm nothing like him. I'm nothing like the person your dad thinks I am. Turning into him has never been my fear. Becoming my mom has. Every time I have a drink, I know I'm sinking further into her mold. Watching her destroy herself broke me. My dad beat me every night; he beat her too. But the bruises you see from him are just surface-level wounds."

Picking up her hand, I place both of ours over the dove that decorates my heart. "The true bleeding is in here. It bleeds for my mom; it bleeds for my brother. But it keeps beating for you."

"I love you, Jessie."

"Even when you thought I was shutting you out of my life and running away from you, you were saving me. You saved me, Mia. You did back then, and you do every day now."

"I just believed in you, Jessie. You are the reason you're standing here today. *Never* take that away from yourself. It takes incredible strength to keep going against all the odds, and it takes even more courage to know when to ask for help. Thank you for trusting me."

The golden fleck in her eye shines in the soft lighting of her side lamp, and the urge to bury myself deep inside my girlfriend, along with my darkest memories, hits me square on.

I sit back on my heels, threading my fingers through hers, and she sits up with me, the duvet still wrapped around us.

When my hands find the clasp on her red bra, she looks up at me. "Can I ask you one more question?"

"Anything," I reply, releasing the clasp and her stunning tits.

"When you joined the Scorpions, your number was ninety-eight. Then, the next season, it was forty-four. No one ever really knew why you'd changed it."

She noticed.

I lay her back down and bring one of her nipples to my lips, swirling my tongue around it until it peaks in my mouth. She groans at the pleasure, and the sound pumps blood straight to my dick. With a single hand, I push down my pants to free myself.

"When things got really tough for me mentally, Coach

Burrows and the GM asked me if there was anything they could do to help. And I asked if I could switch up my jersey number. Number ninety-eight had been allocated to me at the last minute, and I hated it from the start. Will was born at eight minutes past nine at night, and every time I look at that number, it triggered memories I couldn't handle. It's not normally something a team does, but I was granted special permission to change it."

My hands fall to the waistband of her thong, and I pull her panties down and over her legs, tossing them on the floor alongside her bra.

Pushing myself down the bed, I dangle my feet over the end, spread her legs apart, and swipe my tongue through her soaking pussy. "Forty-four is an angel number. It also means tenacity, belief, and manifestation. You can have the life you truly want if you believe in it enough. I never stopped believing in us, Mia. I never stopped loving you. If I couldn't put my name on your back, I'd wear our number."

"Fuck me," she pleads, and I feel the way her pussy contracts around my tongue as I push it into her. "Now. I need you inside me."

I rise onto my knees above her, the only way I want to take her tonight is to be as deep as possible. "On your hands and knees for me, Mia."

I watch as she does as I ask, her eyes never leaving mine as she turns around, her silky black hair falling over her shoulders.

"What do you want me to do now?" Her voice is full of need as I bring my palms to her ass and spread her wide, and she gasps at the sensation.

"Come all over my face," I command, sucking her pussy into my mouth.

She drops her head into the pillows. "Oh my god."

"Jesus Christ, you're so damn ready for me," I rasp against her, swiping my tongue over her entrance. The pressure building in my cock is virtually unbearable. "Let me drink you in, Mia. Come for me."

Fisting the sheets beneath her, she struggles to stay in place as she unravels into my mouth for the first time, and I wrap an arm around her waist to hold her steady.

When I pierce her pussy with my tongue again and then rub my finger gently over her asshole, she jumps forward, turning over her shoulder. "That's my—"

"Ass?" I finish for her, swiping her release from my bottom lip with my tongue. "You like that?"

She nods, her cheeks flushing pink. "A lot."

"Such a dirty girl. You want me to play with it some more?"

"Mmhmm."

"Do you have any toys in here?" I ask, pointing at the single drawer in her nightstand.

A cheeky smile breaks over her face. "A vibrator."

I pull the drawer open to see the pale pink wand sitting alone inside. Grabbing it, I click the button and start it on its lowest setting. "Do you use this and imagine it's me buried inside you?"

"Yes, every time."

My cock jolts at the image of my girlfriend getting herself off to thoughts of me fucking her. "But you never came with it?"

"Every time I got there, I'd get in my head and think you and I would never happen in real life. Then I'd lose it, and the pleasure would fade."

Notching the toy at her entrance, I push it in only a centimeter, and I can tell by the way her cheeks flush that she's already so close to coming again.

"Let me show you how to use this so when you're in this bed on your own and I'm on some away series, fisting my cock to thoughts of you, we can both come together."

Leaning over until my lips meet her neck, I push the vibrator inside until it's fully seated. "The key is to take it nice and deep, Mia. Just like the way I fuck you. When you think you can't take any more of my dick, your pussy always stretches."

"It's so deep," she moans.

She turns her head so our lips meet, and we breathe into each other.

Pulling the vibrator out, I run it over her clit and then push back in quickly.

"Yes, right there, Jessie. Right there."

When I hit the next setting on the vibrator, her head falls to the pillows.

"Come back up here," I demand. "I'm not done with you yet, Sweetheart."

I bring her mouth back to mine, running my tongue across her bottom lip, and she parts for me. Taking the kiss deeper, I push the vibrator in a little further until it hits a wall, and she moans into my throat.

I'd smile so fucking big right now if I didn't want to kiss the shit out of her more.

"When you feel like you're right there, I want you to tell me so I can give you what this pussy was meant for."

I switch the vibrator to its highest setting, and Mia moans against me.

"I can feel how wet you are. You're dripping down my hand, Sweetheart."

"I'm right there. I'm gonna come. Shit, I'm gonna c—"

Pulling the vibrator out quickly, I toss it to one side and line myself up to her pussy.

I close my eyes and will myself not to blow straight away when I push inside and feel how tight she is, how close she is to coming.

I look down at the connection between us and blow out a steadying breath. "You've got it all now, Mia. My heart, my head, my cock. Now let me give you my cum too."

With my hands planted firmly on her hips, I rock into her, and she cries out. If Tara came home, there's no way she can't hear her roommate fucking right now.

Another pump, and her release coats my dick.

"Are you ready to come for me?"

Her head falls forward, and quickly, I reach out and wrap my hand around her hair, gently pulling her back up.

"Don't collapse on me now, baby. Just give me one more on my dick, and then I'll let you rest."

For maybe an hour.

Mia squeezes around me so tight as a deep wail leaves her throat, and I have no doubt this is the hardest she's ever come.

And that's it. I'm gone, fucking done. I'm over the edge and never coming back as I spill everything I have inside her.

I fall to my hands on either side of her shoulders and kiss the back of her neck. "Un-fucking-real."

CHAPTER THIRTY-TWO

JESSIE

"Someone's got a spring in their step." Jensen smiles at me as we board the team plane to Dallas.

Never did I think I'd be practically skipping onto a flight back to my hometown. But after last night, there's no bringing me down. "Life's good right now. What can I say?"

We take a seat next to each other, and Jensen turns to look at me. "You could start with, *Thank you for always being right and pushing me to go after the girl.*"

I roll my eyes and pull my headphones and cell from my carry-on bag. When I open up the playlist, it's set on Adele's album, and the last track played was "Make You Feel My Love."

I inwardly smile and set my headphones over my ears.

Jensen looks over at the album playing and mouths, *Simp*.

"All right, listen up." Coach Burrows closes the overhead bin and turns to the rest of the team. He points at me, and I pull off my headphones and wait for him to speak. "Thanks for joining us, Callaghan. All right, tonight's game is a late one. It's a grueling game, and that's why this morning's skate was light. I need you to be as rested as possible. Take on extra fluids, eat well, grab a massage from the trainer when we land and get to the hotel. The key to this win is preparation."

Jensen dips his head down to me. "What about you, Jessie? Have you eaten well?"

I quirk a brow. "What I ate is none of your damn business. But my fist is on the menu if you want that."

He throws his head back into the seat and laughs.

"Something funny, Jones?" Coach props his hands on his hips.

"Nothing. Just having a bit of fun with Callaghan here."

"Figures. Well, save the joking around until after we get the W." Coach spins around and takes his seat at the front.

From a couple of rows down, Zach unclips his belt and walks toward us. Leaning his forearm on the empty seat in front, he lowers his voice. "So, you know how Tate Coulson gave up the C at the start of this season?"

Jensen nods. "Yeah, taking a step back in preparation for retirement."

Zach's lips pull to the side as he looks down at the floor and then back up at us. "I don't know if it's because they expect the game to be physical or one of their first-line defensemen is carrying an injury we aren't aware of, but word is, he's gonna be starting tonight."

My stomach twists. "So, you're telling me they want to give a slower, older guy more ice time over younger alternatives?"

Zach shrugs. "That's what I said to Jon when he texted me to say there're rumors circulating in the press that he's being favored over Sanchez."

"Probably picked something up in early practice. Or it's bullshit, and they deliberately started a rumor to try and force Burrows's hand to make changes to our lineup, only for Sanchez to start anyway," Jensen replies.

Zach taps the seat once with his fist. "Yeah, maybe, but all I'm saying is, something doesn't feel right. He's no longer the captain, and he doesn't have the same expectation on his shoulders to set an example for the team. I should know—once an enforcer, always an enforcer."

"I don't like this," Zach says from his bench as we make the final preparations to head out onto the ice. "Warm-up felt weird; the entire atmosphere is weird."

"It's just a big game getting in your head, Cap." Jensen claps a hand on his shoulder as he strides out of the locker room.

Zach stops me with a hand on mine as I follow him. "Has Tate said anything to you?"

"In the warm-up?" I shake my head. "No."

"Would he normally?" Zach asks, chewing on the side of his mouthguard.

Pulling on my helmet, I blow out a breath. "I'll admit, it's strange that he's in first line tonight, but Coulson hasn't said a word to me since the second I got traded. We didn't exactly part on good terms."

Zach's brows knit together. "What do you mean?"

"Mia. He had a thing for Mia and his head firmly up Jenkins's ass. But that was years ago, man."

"Is there a chance he knows?"

I shake my head, remembering Mia's confidence in Tara. If her dad knows, then there's no way Mia wouldn't, and we definitely wouldn't have been having text sex an hour ago. "No chance."

As I step into the rink, I raise my hand and acknowledge a crowd who, over time, has accepted me back onto their home ice. At first, my trade was controversial, and I lost a lot of fans, but as I skate past the boards, a bunch of Destroyers fans show their appreciation. There's a small part of me that would like to see the end of my career back in this arena, but I know that would mean moving back to a city where my dad could get to me and those I love more easily.

When I skate past Zach to get into position for the puck drop, he tips his head at me, reminding me to keep my eyes up.

There's no denying that there's zero love lost between me and my former captain, but I've been on the ice with him plenty of times since I got traded to the Scorpions. Tate would need to look at me to take me out. And since the day I left the Destroyers, he's barely acknowledged my existence. Sure, he's an asshole, but he's no Alex Schneider—the former New York Blades defenseman who nearly killed Zach a couple of seasons back with a dirty hit, all because of his former girlfriend.

It must be ten minutes into the first period when I pick the puck up from our center, the move eliminating two players, one of them Coulson.

With an inside-outside move similar to the one I pulled off against Colorado, I take out their final defenseman and slot the puck home with a snapshot that catches their goalie off guard. When I light the lamp, it takes my tally to thirty for the season so far, and as I pump my fist in the air, keeping it low-key since it's my former team, I can't deny I have one eye on Wayne Gretzky's record for most goals in a single season.

"All right, that's how we fucking do it!" Rob Jackson, our center, bangs his glove on top of my helmet. "Fucking goal machine, bro!"

I point back at center ice, my focus locked in and my head already running through the next play. "There's another fifty minutes of game time. We're gonna need at least another four to seal the W."

"Damn right we are."

When Jackson skates out of my line of vision, I see Zach raise his glove at me, pointing to my left.

"What?" I shout, knowing full fucking well he won't hear me over the noise.

"Finally got your shit together, Callaghan." As Tate Coulson pulls up alongside me, he throws ice up, causing the Destroyers fans to bang on the glass behind us.

I don't know if they're anticipating a fight, but they should know I'm not one to get into it on the ice.

"Did you trade your voice for some class?" Coulson sneers as I ignore him and push off.

I know I shouldn't, but my newfound game confidence gets the better of me, and I spin around at the final second. "Nah. Just found a captain I actually want to play for."

He throws his head back and laughs before refocusing his attention on me.

I don't like the look in his eyes as he slides up closer.

"Or is it more to do with the pussy you were inside last night? You'd think she'd have wised up the first time around."

My heart hammers in my chest as I fight to keep my expression unreadable. "The fuck did you just say?"

Replacing his mouthguard on a smile, he skates forward and then stops right next to me. "Jenkins knows. But don't worry; it can be our little secret for the next fifty minutes. Can't promise it won't hurt though."

My head is spinning out when I take a seat on the bench, watching the game play out in front of me.

How the fuck does he know?

Tara. It's gotta be Tara.

"Callaghan, you're back in. I want the same performance again." Coach's booming voice snaps me from my trance as I rejoin the play and immediately pick up a loose puck, handing us a turnover.

When two defensemen come charging for me, I consider the option of pulling off a similar move as last time. But neither of them is Coulson, who hangs back down the wing.

As much as I'm shitting myself over the prospect of Graham knowing, I'm pissed that Coulson thinks he can threaten me and talk shit about Mia.

I know he's slow and he doesn't stand a chance when I hit

the jets, and that's exactly my game plan as I head straight for him.

The deke I throw offers me the perfect chance to thread the puck through his open legs, embarrassing the shit out of him, and I'm sure he can hear my laugh as I hit overdrive and accelerate away, my head up and ready to pass the puck off to Jackson to put us up by another goal.

But as I set up, ready for the pass, my stick doesn't connect with the puck; instead, my jaw does when I hit the ice so fucking hard that the noise of the crowd fades in my fight to stay conscious.

When I roll over, Coulson's face is the first thing my blurry vision recognizes as I bring my gloves to my jaw.

"Fuck you, Callaghan!" he shouts, spitting on my jersey. "You think you can just disrespect the man who gave you everything?!"

"Nah, bro, fuck YOU!"

I watch from my back as Zach lands the first punch against the side of Coulson's head, sending him straight back and into the boards.

Climbing to my feet, I look down to see a puddle of my blood freezing on the ice. Blood has never bothered me, so I know the nauseating feeling rolling through my stomach is either from the pain or a concussion.

"No one messes with my wingers!" Zach spits, landing another punch on Coulson's helmet, and it flies across the ice. "I fucking knew you were gunning for him!"

My vision is shit, but even I can see the fury in Zach's eyes as he lands punch after punch, each one sending Coulson closer to the ice until he lands flat on his back.

Zach doesn't stop beating on him until the ref pulls him off. Calling a major penalty against Coulson for taking my legs out with his stick and the same for my captain for fighting.

"Game's over, son." Coach Burrows wraps his arm around my shoulders as I step off the ice, my glove clutched to my chin to help stem the bleeding.

I shrug off his arm and turn to him as the team doctor shouts for me to follow for treatment. "I need to speak with Graham. Where is he?" I say, knowing he'll have eyes on me from somewhere in the arena.

The empathetic look on Burrows's face turns to stone. He knows I would only be asking for Graham's whereabouts for one reason. "No fucking idea, Callaghan. But if you're asking for the reason I think you are, I'd say there's a fair chance he'll find you. Now, get off the ice and get that jaw looked at."

CHAPTER THIRTY-THREE

JESSIE

"Four stitches? I'd say you got away lightly with that."

"Yeah, guess so," I reply to Jensen, rushing to button up my dress shirt so I can get out of the arena and call Mia.

"Coulson received more, apparently." Zach sidles up alongside me, adjusting his tie. "All that was to do with Mia, wasn't it?"

He doesn't speak loudly enough for the others to hear, but Jensen's head whips up at the mention of her name.

"You think he knows? I thought he was just being the asshole he'd always been."

"Oh, he knows. And so does Jenkins, apparently," I say, looping my tie and glancing down at my phone in my bag. "I don't know if Mia does yet. Coulson made it out like it was just a secret between him and Graham right now."

Jensen runs a palm over his mouth. "I don't get it. Who would out you guys? There's nothing in the press. If there were, we'd sure as shit know about it."

Now fully dressed, I snatch up my wash bag and grab my phone. "By process of elimination, it has to be Mia's roommate. She found out yesterday."

"Has she got some kind of vendetta against you or Mia?" Zach asks.

"Not that I was aware of, but like I said, she's the only one who knows."

Swinging my bag over my shoulder, I wave my phone at the guys. "I need to call Mia. See you on the team bus."

A tattooed hand comes to my forearm as I make to leave the locker room, and I turn to see a serious look on Zach's face.

"Does this compromise your position with the team?"

I shrug and bite the inside of my cheek. "I did what you'd advised. Played hard and made myself un-benchable. Burrows is close to Jenkins, and, yeah, he's gonna be pissed at me for rocking the boat." I turn to look at him, the past few weeks with Mia flashing through my mind. "But at this point, there's nothing I wouldn't risk to be with her. I walked away once, and it was the biggest mistake of my life. There never has—and never will be—anything more important in my life than Mia Jenkins."

I'm already scrolling for her contact when I step into the empty hallway.

Hitting dial, I bring the phone to my ear and lean against the wall, keeping a check around me for eavesdroppers.

Mia picks up on the first ring, her voice rushed and panicked. "Jessie, are you okay? I saw the fight, the way Coulson brought you down. I always thought he had your back in Dallas."

"I'm okay, Sweetheart. It was a few stitches and bad bruising; I got away without breaking anything."

"Oh, thank fuck." She breaks off and goes silent. When she speaks again, her voice is way more measured than I ever expected it to be. "Dad knows. He texted me, saying he knew, but wasn't ready to talk about it."

"Fuck, this isn't how it was supposed to be, Mia. I'm so sorry."

"I know." Her voice shakes, and I can tell she's trying to hold back the tears.

I switch the call to video mode. If I can't hold her, the least I can do is let her look in my eyes when I promise it's all going to be okay.

She isn't wearing any makeup, and her hair is unwashed and thrown on top of her head when she comes into view.

She's never looked more beautiful.

"Jessie, your face." She reaches toward the camera. "Coulson did this because of us, didn't he?"

I nod. She has no idea what happened between him and me when her dad kicked me off the team, but it's too much of a coincidence. "Yeah. That's how I know about your dad finding out. Coulson told me right before my ass hit the ice."

"Asshole," she bites out, looking off to the side.

"I'm gonna make this right with your dad, I promise."

She winces and looks down at the ground. When she looks back up, her eyes are red and glassy, and I want to reach inside the phone and pull her to me. This is exactly the way I didn't want things to play out with Graham. This is worst-case scenario number one.

"Fuck!" I shout to no one in particular, my frustration and anger getting the better of me. "Why is it that no matter how hard I try to keep you safe, my life always finds a way to hurt you?"

She shakes her head and spins around to take a seat on a couch, and it's then I notice that she isn't in her dorm. "This isn't your fault, Jessie. I shouldn't have trusted Tara."

"Where are you?" I ask, my blood beginning to boil at the fact that she can't even be in her own dorm.

"Kate and Jensen's. When I got Dad's text, it was halfway through the game, and I panicked. Only people I could think to text were the girls. Tara was out, so I packed an overnight bag, and Kate came straight over to grab me." She brings a palm up to cover her face. "I can't go back there."

"And neither can I because I can't be held responsible for what I might say to her," I hear a voice say, belonging to Kate.

If there's one person I'd want with Mia right now, it's definitely Kate Jones.

"I'm gonna make this right with your dad," I repeat and bring the phone closer to me. "I'm gonna go see him before I leave Dallas, and then I'll charter my own fucking flight so I can get back to you ASAP. Then I'm bringing you back to mine, and you won't leave my arms. I promise it's gonna be all right, Mia."

Just as Mia opens her mouth to reply, a throat clears from down the hallway, and I look up to see Graham's ominous figure at the end, his arms crossed over his black suit jacket.

"I gotta go," I tell Mia.

"He's there, isn't he?" she replies in barely a whisper. Her eyes wide.

I nod. "It's gonna be okay, Sweetheart. I promise."

"Jessie, I—"

"Promise," I tell her before I cut the call and pocket my phone.

When he uncrosses his arms, one hand finds the pocket of his dress pants, and the other reaches out and opens a door to his right.

Pushing off the wall, I stand up straight and face him. I'm a pro hockey player, and I have taken more beatings in my life than I can count, but this moment right here is intimidating.

This is the father of the girl I love. Whatever he hands out to me, I'll take it. For her.

"You wanted to talk." He points to the open door and steps through. "Let's talk."

The walk down the hallway feels like I'm making my way to some kind of death chamber, my palms cold and sweaty.

"Look, Graham," I say the second I cross the threshold.

The door slams behind me, and in a millisecond, my back is against the wall, and his hand is around my throat. His face is bright red, anger twisting his features as he pins me in the same way he did in Mia's bedroom.

"Give me one good fucking reason why I shouldn't be in custody tonight," he spits, rearing his fist back, ready to strike.

"Let go of me, and I will," I choke out.

"I fucking knew it. I knew it when I saw her in Seattle. Just couldn't leave well enough alone, could you, Callaghan?"

"I love her." My words are barely a whisper.

"Love. You don't know the meaning of it."

Raising an arm, I push him hard in the center of the chest, and his grip loosens.

"You failed me as a kid, and you're failing me now," I push out.

Graham grinds his molars. "Failed you? I *made* you. You were never hungry for it, for true success. You've always gone the easiest route in life. And now you have the balls to tell me that *I* failed you?!"

"Made me?!" I gasp, bringing a hand around my neck and stepping forward. "You've got no idea what I went through to even be here, do you?"

"Oh, I do. Half the fucking volleyball team and now my daughter!" he sneers.

Shoving my hands in the pockets of my dress pants, I look down at my loafers. A pair my best friend bought me last season.

I raise my head and look at Graham, I don't care that he can see the tears in my eyes. "You wouldn't see it. Because from the second I was born, I've spent my whole life hiding." I point at my chest and step forward. "Do you know what it's like to be hungry, Graham?"

He doesn't respond.

"To go to practice on an empty stomach because the last beating you took caused you to throw up the last meal you had eaten. To puke up the food you'd had to steal from a fast-food joint because there was nothing in the cupboards?"

"I, um—"

"Do you know what it's like to pull on your hockey pads and inwardly scream at the pain? You can't work out because of your back from sleeping on the floor night after night or the cracked ribs your father just gave you. Or maybe"—I pause and inhale a deep breath, the first tear hitting my cheek—"maybe it's because you're so fucking exhausted, trying to carry your mom up the stairs since your dad had left for another two days and she drank herself into the fucking abyss."

His eyes grow wide.

"That's right; no one really knows what it's like. Not unless they've lived in those four walls." I swallow hard, bile rising into my throat. "Do you know how many times over the past four years my dad nearly got his wish? With dark thoughts taunting me and alcohol running through my veins, I convinced myself no one would miss me. That no one wanted to hear my story. That the only thing I was good for was hockey, and even that was a fucking shit show."

"Jessie, I—"

"Shut up!" I shout back. "Just shut the fuck up, Graham. You spent that much time focused on my stats; you didn't stop to think about why they had been dropping. Or what I was trying to hide when I skipped massages and went home."

We're practically eyeball to eyeball when I step up to him.

"Do you know who didn't fail me, even when I was failing myself? Mia."

Silence stretches across the room. I give him a chance to speak, but he chooses not to.

"While you were busy *making me*, she was spending her life trying to make *you* happy. All she's ever wanted is to make you happy and proud of her."

"I am proud of her."

"Are you?" I prod my finger into the center of his chest. "Are you, Graham? Because you sure have a fucking funny way of showing it. All I see is your patriarchy."

More silence.

"Years ago, I walked away from the girl I loved. The girl who didn't know what I was going through, but somehow got me. She wanted me for who I was. In the moments we had gotten together, I had fallen so fucking hard for her. My parents had stolen my childhood, and then I let you go and steal my girl too."

Bringing my hands to the top buttons on my dress shirt, I undo the first few, and Graham's eyes fall to the dove. "I got this the week I arrived in Seattle. For her, for me, for us. Maybe she did turn up in Seattle, hoping to find me; maybe it's possible she has the same level of feelings for me that I do for her. But let me tell you one thing I do know, Mr. Jenkins: as soon as I get a chance to put a ring on her finger and make her my wife, you'd best believe I will. With or without your blessing. So, I'll say it again. I love her. There is no one other than *her*. From the second my hazy, fucked-up brain laid eyes on your daughter, I wanted to know more about her."

I step back and give us both space, my shirt still open at the front.

Graham swipes a palm over his mouth and looks back at me. "Is it true about your dad? Were you abused, Jessie?"

I hold up a hand. "I had a childhood I wouldn't wish on anyone, and my dad is someone I work to keep as far out of my life as possible. The only person who looked out for me as a child was my papa." Tears fall more freely from my eyes.

"I'm s—"

"I don't want to hear your apologies right now because I won't be able to accept them. I just want to get back to Seattle and my girl."

I turn to leave, my hand on the door handle, ready to walk out and find a flight, when I pause and swing back around. "Call your daughter and apologize to her. She's just been betrayed by her friend and roommate. The least you can do is give her your support."

"Wait. Roommate? What are you talking about?"

I spin back around and face him. "Tara. The only person who knew about us. Fuck knows how she knows you, but she just went behind Mia's back and betrayed her trust."

Graham pulls his phone out of his pocket. "It wasn't Tara."

My brows shoot to my hairline. "What?"

"I have a player on the program who is in her class and actually made friends with her. I asked him to keep an eye on Mia and make sure she was doing okay. I won't name him, but he's one of my most trusted, and when he saw you outside her dorm building last night, he sent me a message asking if I knew she was dating you."

I look up at the ceiling and blow out a single harsh laugh. "You really are a fucking idiot at times, aren't you?" I step back into the room, a smile spreading across my lips.

Who the fuck does he think he is, keeping tabs on his grown-ass daughter?

"I don't need you to give me a name. I already know it. Leo."

Graham's eyes grow wide for a second time.

"If I were you, I'd be really fucking careful who you consider to be your most trusted. Last time Mia saw Leo, he tried to get in her pants." I thumb over my shoulder to the hallway. "So, yeah, I'm gonna go and be with my girlfriend now. Right after I punch your latest prodigy square in the face."

CHAPTER THIRTY-FOUR

MIA

JESSIE

I'm heading back to Seattle. I'll be with you ASAP. Stay with Kate and don't go back to campus. Tara isn't the one who told your dad, and I want you nowhere near that son of a bitch.

My heart races. Who else could it have been?

ME

I need to see you. Who was it?

JESSIE

I'm boarding the flight now. I just came straight from the arena. It was Leo. He's known your dad for a while, and he plays on his program. Your dad asked him to keep an eye on you. He saw us outside your dorm building last night and sent Graham a message asking if he knew we were dating.

"Oh fuck," I announce, causing Kate to spin around from the sink.

> **ME**
> You think he was using me to get ahead with Graham?

> **JESSIE**
> I think he wanted you—because what guy wouldn't? You turned him down and bent his ego, so he took revenge on us, and it was a convenient way to get ahead with your dad. Speaking of which, has he called you?

> **ME**
> Bastard. I could punch him. And, no, not yet. Not holding out much hope for that.

> That's my job, Sweetheart. Sit tight. I'll be there in a few hours. And I meant what I said earlier.

I frown down at the message.

> **ME**
> What do you mean?

> **JESSIE**
> You're coming home with me. I love you.

Setting my phone down in front of me, I watch Kate move about the kitchen, the twins asleep upstairs.

"It wasn't Tara."

She spins around to face me, drying her hands on a towel. "Excuse me?"

"Tara. It wasn't her. It was Leo."

"Who the fuck is Leo?"

I swipe at my tired eyes, resting my face in my hands. "He's a part of the same friend group I made, and he's a hockey player. Takes some of the same classes as me. Last time I spoke to him, I basically told him to go fuck himself since he made a pass at me. Turns out, he plays for Dad's foundation—he just failed to tell me that part. Then he saw me and Jessie as we made out last night and told my dad about it."

Kate rests a hand on the kitchen counter. "Sounds like one of my cases."

I burst out laughing when my cell starts vibrating on the side with a call from my dad.

Kate points to it. "Whatever he has to say, it needs to start with a whole heap of sorry before you even think about hearing him out. It's time he started treating you like the strong-minded woman you are. Also, tell him you don't have long to talk since you need to try and rebuild your friendship with Tara. Which is also his fault."

Smiling at Kate, I press Accept and put the phone to my ear. "Hi."

"Mia, it's Dad."

I climb off the barstool, moving into the hallway and up the stairs, closing the spare bedroom door behind me. "I know."

He blows a long breath down the phone. "Tell Jessie the first thing I said to you was sorry."

I cock my head to the side in confusion. "Why do you care what Jessie thinks all of a sudden?"

He doesn't say anything for a few beats, and I hear him adjust, maybe from his bed since it's really late in Dallas. "He told me, Mia. About his mom, his dad, and how he feels about you. In all my time on this earth, I have never witnessed a grown-ass man pour his heart out in the way he just did. I should've called you earlier, but to be honest, I'm still trying to process everything he said. Did he go hungry as a boy?"

My throat feels like it's closing up at thoughts of Jessie starving. "He went through a lot in his childhood. Back when we were in Dallas, I didn't know much, but I knew he wasn't the guy you made him out to be. He made me happy, and he was everything I wanted. You've had him all wrong for a very long time, but you were too pigheaded to see it."

"I'm sorry." His voice cracks on the final syllable, and he draws in a heavy breath. "I've spent so much time worrying about protecting you. Whenever I saw Jessie, I saw that guy locked up for your mom's death. He drank a lot too. All I saw was a boy throwing away his talent and betraying my trust."

"No, that would be Leo Walsh," I reply, deadpan, tagging on his last name with disdain.

My dad clears his throat. "Yeah, Jessie told me about him too."

"Yeah, well, you really missed with this one, Dad." I bring the back of my hand over my mouth, the soft white pillows on my bed looking all too comfortable. "I need to call Tara and make sure she's okay, and then I need to try and get some sleep. You shouldn't have done what you did with Coulson. That was a real dick move."

"I know. What can I do to make things right, Mia?"

Looking down at the soft carpet beneath my feet, I shake my head. "Tell Burrows to lay off my boyfriend and support the fact that I love him."

"For what it's worth, Mia, I already do support it. I don't think there are many men out there who would do for their woman what Callaghan just did for you. I meant what I said over text the other day. I'm proud of you."

Tears sting my eyes. "Thanks. Now, I gotta go."

"Mia."

I stir and roll over onto my back.

"Sweetheart."

When I crack a lid, Jessie's face comes into view.

Other than his gorgeous blue eyes, the first thing I notice is the stitches across his jawline, along with the black bruising. "Fuck, Jessie." Reaching up, I bring my palm to his cheek. "It didn't look that bad over the phone."

"It's fine," he replies, leaning over me and bringing his face down to mine.

"That is so not fine," I retort. "Have you taken any pain relievers?"

He rolls his eyes. "For a girl who worked with hockey players for several years and is now dating one, you sure don't know much about our pain threshold."

I quirk a brow. "You're right, and I'm quickly learning that you're just standard men. Refusing to take direction or medication when it will help."

He pulls back and smirks. "You've been spending too much time with Kate. Best get you back to my bed before she corrupts you anymore."

Brushing our lips together, I part, and his tongue finds mine, kissing me with so much intensity that I feel my pulse in my ears.

"Did you speak to your dad?" Jessie asks, starting to kiss down my neck.

"Yeah. Right before I spoke to Tara."

"Is she okay?"

I nod, the sensation of his lips over my skin making me pool with heat. "She got it. But I think Leo lost another friend."

Jessie chuckles into my neck. "The way I want to send him a photo of me making out with you. See if he wants to forward that to your dad too."

I giggle as I feel his hard length grind between my legs. "Baby, I'm all for showing you off to the world. But I think I've about had enough of my dad seeing you all over me to last a lifetime."

Bringing his hands to the waistband of my leggings, he slowly pulls them and my panties down in one. Leaving me bare from the waist down with a pink cami top and no bra on my top half.

Jessie brings his finger to his full lips. "Shh. No screaming. It's really early in the morning."

I pulse in anticipation. "Is Kate awake?"

He smiles and wets his lips. "Jensen too. Not that I give a shit. He fucked her right next door at their own wedding."

Another giggle bubbles out of me. "I don't know if I can be quiet."

Pausing with his mouth over my pussy, he runs a finger through me and brings it to my lips, and I open for him, tasting myself.

"See how sweet you are? There's no way I can resist you right now. So, be a really good girl for me and be nice and quiet while I eat your pussy. I'll let you scream later when you're riding my cock."

As I lift my hips up off the bed, he rests both my legs over his shoulders.

The first swipe of his tongue has me jolting upward, and Jessie brings an arm over my waist to hold me in place.

He sucks my clit into his mouth, massaging it with his tongue, and I reach out, grabbing a pillow to cover my face.

"Oh my God," I moan into it, my voice low and muffled.

Licking me from one hole to the next, he circles the entrance to my pussy with his tongue, lowering me down to the bed.

"Spread these for me, baby," he instructs as his callous palms find the inside of my soaking wet thighs, pushing them apart. "So goddamn beautiful."

I get lost in the way he eats me out, and the fact that I can't see what he's going to do next only adds to the intensity.

When two fingers slide inside me, slowly pumping in and out, I draw my bottom lip between my teeth, desperately trying not to scream. The only sound is the noise my pussy makes as I slowly unravel for him.

"I'm going to fuck this pussy all night once we're back in my bed," he rasps against me.

"Jessie, I'm going to come," I speak into the pillow.

"Soak my face with this pretty pussy."

His dirty words send me right there, and I feel my release over his hand and into his mouth as I come apart at the seams.

He continues to finger me as I come down from the high, pulling the pillow away from my burning cheeks.

"Can you give me another, Mia? I'm so fucking addicted to this cunt."

"Make her come all you want; you've had a shit twenty-four hours, so I'll give you a free pass. But just know, you're taking the sheets home with you to wash."

The pillow is back in front of my face the very second I hear Jensen's voice filter in from the other side of the door.

Crawling up my body in hysterics that I do not share, Jessie pulls the pillow away and smiles down at me, kissing the tip of my nose. "You bad girl, messing up my goalie's sheets."

I swat at his chest, my face no doubt turning redder. "He can probably still hear us."

Jessie shakes his head and brings his hand between my legs, running his fingers through me before pushing one inside. "Nah. We're close and everything, but he's not into listening to me get it on with my girl."

I moan into his mouth as he kisses me and continues to finger me slowly.

With his other hand, he pushes down the waistband of his gray sweatpants, and I feel his cock naturally notch at my entrance.

"I told your dad I loved you, and I do, Mia."

He pushes inside me, and my jaw falls open at the way I stretch around him.

"I want you to move in with me. Tara will get it—the need to move in with a hot hockey star." He chuckles and grinds his hips against mine.

"But you live across town," I say between groans of pleasure.

"I'll buy you a car."

I shake my head and bring my hands to his ass, pushing him deeper inside me. "No. You need to keep the money you have."

"Then take my car, and I'll catch rides. I couldn't give a fuck how I get home as long as it's to you each night."

Still riding my high from before, I come hard when Jessie rolls his hips into me again.

Tipping his head down, he kisses my chest, and I feel the way he jerks inside me.

"Yeah, okay," I whisper into his hair. "Let's do it."

CHAPTER THIRTY-FIVE

MIA

As we pull into the parking lot of my dorm building, Jessie puts his car into park and pulls off his glasses.

It's a bright early March morning, and the first signs of spring are pushing their way through on the trees.

Right after he finished giving me my third orgasm, we took a nap together in Jensen and Kate's spare bed.

"Do you have the sheets?" I turn to him, a playful smile on my face despite being nervous to be back on campus.

Leo could literally be anywhere, and he's absolutely the last person I want to see.

Flipping his black baseball cap backward, he leans across the center console and smiles against my cheek, setting a kiss on my cheekbone. "You're so fucking cute. I stripped the bed and put them in the washer before we left."

Through the passenger window, I look across at my dorm building. "I'll be a few minutes while I grab some stuff. Tara is home, so I want to explain that I'm gonna be staying with you."

He rests his forearm over the steering and twizzles his glasses around on his fingers. "I'm coming in with you, Sweetheart."

Getting out of the car, he rounds the hood and pulls my passenger door open, taking my hand in his, and we start walking across the lot.

We're halfway to my dorm when Jessie pulls up, and I stop alongside him, my eyes searching his when I realize there's something eating at him.

He takes a deep breath and looks across to my dorm building. "The second we go public is the second pictures hit the internet. I want you to know that's what I want, too, more than anything, but it will mean *he* will know who you are."

With his free hand, Jessie pulls off his cap and runs a stressed hand through his hair, the stitches on his jaw already starting to heal. "I want you living with me for so many reasons, Mia. But as your boyfriend, I also need to know you're safe, and I'm confident you will be if you're in my secure apartment building and sleeping in my bed. I'm going to look into us moving right away so he doesn't have my address anymore, but for now, this is the only way we can have what we both want. I know he won't know your address here, but when he finds out what college you go to, it won't be hard, and trust me, I know their security systems here are about as good as the heating."

An icy sensation creeps up my spine. "You really think he'd go that far? Like, come after me and those you love?"

Running his tongue across his bottom lip, Jessie sets his cap back on his head. "There's only one thing in the world Wayne Callaghan cares about—money. And I'm his meal ticket. I need to get my mom to Seattle and cut off his funds. When that happens, he'll do everything in his power to hurt me, and you will be priority one. Even with a restraining order, he'll do what he can to get to us."

I drop my gaze to the ground, my hand starting to tremble in his. "What if you just go to the police over him now?"

Jessie must feel my anxiety when he brings my other hand into his. "Sure, I could, but they'd just open a child abuse case, and Mom would get dragged into it. He'd do more damage while they were investigating what had happened twenty years ago."

He pauses and looks off to the side, his eyes becoming glossy.

"If you don't want to do this with me, if you want to walk away or wait until my shit show of a life is in a better place, then I get it. I can't stand here and lie; it would break my fucking heart to be without you. But I'd do it. I'd let you go to know you were safe. At this point, there isn't anything I wouldn't do for you. Just say the word, and I'll step into oncoming traffic or throw myself off High Steel Bridge. I'll literally do anything to keep you happy, even if it tears me in two."

I don't hesitate when I bring one of his hands to my lips, kissing his knuckles softly. "I'm not scared of Wayne fucking Callaghan. The only thing I'm scared of right now is going right back to where we were—apart or trying to be together and hiding."

Dropping our hands, I pull him across the parking lot and toward civilization. "Now come help me pack."

Two guys are pushing through the entrance to my building when we approach, and Jessie takes the door handle.

They stop dead in their tracks when they recognize his face and then across at me standing with him.

"Uhh, um, thanks," one of the guys stutters as they move away, the other looking back over his shoulder, nearly walking straight into a bench.

Jessie leads the way up the stairs, taking them two at a time, his fingers still laced through mine.

After so long of sneaking around and years of having to hide who we were to each other, the feeling of being out in public feels crazy in all the best ways.

When we reach my door, Jessie holds out his hand for my key and takes it, opening the door and pushing through. The broad smile on his face tells me he's feeling the same kind of way—that we made it. We're finally getting our chance to be together for real.

"Babe, I thought you said th—" Tara waltzes out in her nightwear and robe, her head down and in her phone. When she looks up and registers who I'm with, she stops dead.

"Shit, sorry," Jessie says awkwardly, scratching at the back of his neck. "I thought with it being the afternoon, you'd be, umm ..." He waves a hand at Tara.

"Dressed?" she replies, quirking a brow.

I stand next to my boyfriend and fight back laughter as he flushes.

"Yeah."

She shrugs a shoulder and walks over to the fridge. "I had a late night last night, and today is my only free day, so it's a pajama day for me."

Jessie nods and looks around the space as we take off our shoes. "I'm gonna use the bathroom if that's okay?"

Tara points at the door. "Just over there. But maybe you already know that since this isn't your first rodeo."

I flare my eyes at Tara as Jessie steps into the bathroom and closes the door behind him.

Tara's casual demeanor drops the moment the lock clicks, and her head whips to mine. "Fucking hell," she whisper-squeaks. "He's even hotter up close. You actually weren't shitting me, were you? H-he really is your boyfriend."

I can't help it as a big, cheek-aching smile spreads across my face. "Nope, not shitting you."

Tara pours herself a coffee and takes a sip. "We're good though, right?"

Crossing the kitchenette, I wrap my arms around her and bring her into a hug. "Absolutely, we are. It should be me apologizing again. I jumped to conclusions, and I shouldn't have. I had literally no idea about Leo, so by process of elimination, I panicked and pointed the finger at you, and I'm sorry."

She waves a hand in front of her like it doesn't matter, but I can see the sadness on her face. "Honestly, it's fine. At this point, I'm more pissed at that asshole." She sets down her cup and blows out a breath. "And the fact that we were all supposed to be going back to Riley's after the game next week. I guess that isn't happening, and I'm kinda gutted. I like their cocktails."

"You can still come," Jessie says, coming back into view. "Just sit with us. We'll be there after the game. You can even come to that if you like. There'll be enough seats in the box, and I can get my hands on an extra ticket."

Excitement lights up her pretty face. "Are you kidding me? My dad will go wild when he finds out I'm not only going to a Scorpions game, but I'll also be hanging out with the players afterward."

Jessie swings his arm around my shoulders and kisses me on the side of the head, and I watch as Tara visibly melts.

"Let me know his name and I'll get him a signed jersey."

"Ugh, I've died and crossed into some kind of alternate, way better universe," she replies, making me chuckle.

Thumbing over his shoulder to my bedroom, Jessie turns to me. "Want me to get started?"

When I messaged her this morning to say we'd be stopping by, I hinted that I was going to be staying with Jessie for a while. I nod, and my boyfriend takes off in the opposite direction.

I turn back to Tara, taking her hand in mine. "I hope you know this has nothing to do with what happened. We just need to spend time together. Like I told you last night on the phone, we've been apart for so long, and I—"

She squeezes my hand in hers. "I get it. Like, really, I do. Plus, he's giving you his car, and in all seriousness, babe, what girl wouldn't want to spend each night beneath ..." She nods her head in Jessie's direction.

A schoolgirl giggle bubbles out of me. "I have zero complaints, trust me. But seriously, come to the game and then Riley's afterward."

"Oh, I will; do not worry. My lunch buddy, Charlotte, is going to lose her mind when I tell her later."

Remembering Tara isn't like me and makes friends way more

easily makes me feel less guilty for leaving the dorm. Knowing she has loads of people around her on campus.

She leans into me. "Also—and don't take offense here—every time I've brought a guy back, I've had to be quiet, and let's just say, I'm not usually, so I can definitely be a little louder now."

I shake my head and smirk in response.

"I'm not looking forward to our next class with Leo."

Groaning at the thought, she refastens her robe. "I'd say, based on the text messages we exchanged last night, he will be making himself as unnoticeable as possible for a while."

"What did you say?"

"Similar to what you did that night in the bar. He told me that you called him a dickhead and he was pissed at the mixed signals you'd been giving him. I said what he did to you and Jessie was one thousand percent little-dick energy, and I'd be making sure all the girls on campus know he was a crap lay and an absolute asshole."

With that, she plants a kiss on my cheek and saunters off. "I expect you to pick me up in that posh new car of yours next time I see you. Oh, and ...hot." She spins around, fanning her face with one hand, her coffee cup in the other, as her eyes motion to Jessie before she disappears inside her room.

CHAPTER THIRTY-SIX

JESSIE

> MOM
>
> You didn't come home when you came back to Dallas last week. You always come and see me when you're back. I miss you, Jessie.

I have no idea how to reply to my mom's message as I stare down at it from the booth in Riley's Bar. The next time I see my mom, it will be as she steps off a plane at the Seattle airport. All I have to do is find the right words to convince her that she absolutely has to leave Dallas.

"Everything okay?" Mia asks from beside me.

Closing out the message, I pocket my phone and bring a hand to the side of her face, kissing her hard.

And, yeah, that's right. Out in public, for everyone to see and take photos.

The past week of us living together has been the best five days of my life. Also the most sex I've ever had.

I slide my other hand up the inside of her left thigh and

underneath her skirt when Kate clears her throat from opposite us.

"Listen, I know you guys aren't used to public displays and all. But sex in a busy bar is a fast way to get yourself arrested."

Breaking the kiss for just a second, but never taking my eyes from Mia's, I contemplate stopping our make-out session altogether.

"Fuck it," I respond and bring her lips back to mine.

"Maybe you don't give a shit about the custody part, but you sure as hell will when I empty the contents of my stomach onto you both," Zach shouts from across the table.

We both look at him as Luna swats him on the arm. "Leave them alone. They aren't hurting anyone."

"Yeah, well, I might be getting a little FOMO." He drops his head and kisses her behind the ear, his hand coming to her round stomach as he runs a palm over it.

"Another cocktail, Tara?" Felicity asks as she turns her head over her shoulder, searching for a waiter.

Mia throws Tara a *you're underage, and you know it* glare, which earns her a quirked *don't you dare rat me out* brow.

Pulling Mia's face back to mine, I whisper against her lips, "You aren't fooling me with that good-girl exterior any more. Not when I know the nasty girl you are behind closed doors. Kind of my dream girl, come to think of it."

"The sheets cleaned up great, thanks for asking," Jensen pipes up, interrupting us.

With Mia pinned to my side, I look across at my closest friend. "You're welcome."

He narrows his eyes at me, but I can see the smile fighting to break out on his face. Briefly, he glances at Mia and then back at me, his smile only getting more obvious.

"Fucking traffic," Jon announces as he slides in next to his wife and brings his hand to the back of her neck, kissing her deeply.

"Can you, like, not do that?" Jack, Felicity's only son, takes the last seat available opposite them. Pulling off his beanie, he runs a hand through his floppy brown hair.

Jon looks back at his stepson, clearly enjoying winding him up. "Do what? Make out with your mom?"

"It's possible to change your mind about someone—you know that," he replies, his English accent still noticeable despite him living in the States for several years.

"We all did that years ago, buddy." Zach chuckles, bringing his beer to his lips.

Jon throws him a face and then turns to Felicity. "You want a drink, Angel?"

"I just got them. Cocktails for everyone, soda for you." She smiles at Jack, who rolls his eyes in response.

"You know I'm twenty-one now, right?"

Felicity ignores him and then looks at me. "I ordered you a beer, Jessie."

Mia's eyes find mine as I sit up straighter in the booth and look down at my empty soda glass.

"He's still on an alcohol ban as he pushes for Gretzky's record," Mia chimes in.

Felicity winces. "Shit, yeah. Sorry."

"It's fine. I'll take the spare beer." Jack smiles at his mom.

From under the table, I squeeze Mia's thigh in appreciation. At some point, I probably need to share with my friends the battle I've been through with alcohol. If I owe my honesty to anyone, it's to Jensen—the guy who's always looked out for me and had my back. The thing is, the second I unload my secrets, the more questions will come my way.

Right now, the only person I want to see me fully is sitting tucked under my arm.

From her position next to me, Mia suddenly stiffens, and I watch the way Tara does the same.

I lean down to whisper in her ear, "What is it?"

Leo, Tara mouths at me and then points across to the other seating area.

You have got to be kidding me.

Turning over my shoulder, I watch as Leo and his usual friend take a seat in a booth on the opposite side, a couple up from us. From his position, he can watch everything we're doing, but I have my back to him. And I don't like it.

"Ow. Fuck, man," I say to Jensen as he kicks me under the table.

He nods his head behind me. "That the prick who ratted you out to Jenkins?"

I roll my eyes and take a sip of my fresh soda after Jon passed it over to me. "Yep."

Jensen's brows rise slightly as he leans forward, resting his forearms on the table. "He's got some balls to show up here—I'll give him that."

"Ugh, he's a right prick," Jack says, clearly having picked up on who we're referring to. He nods his head in Leo's direction, and Jon turns over his shoulder to look. "Don't look, Jon! For fuck's sake, we're trying to be inconspicuous here." Jack rolls his eyes and picks up his beer.

Zach points to Jack. "I don't know where you're headed next year since your coach won't tell us shit, but you can come and play for us. Your banter game is solid." Reaching down the booth, he fist-bumps Jack.

"Oh, yeah," Jon says, ignoring them both completely. "Complete prick. You know those guys who have next to zero talent, but make up for it by being an agitator on the ice?"

Jensen smiles at Jon. "Yep."

"Well, that's Walsh." Jon tips his head behind him.

"Well, as I've always said to my husband, takes one to know one," Felicity sings, winking at Jon.

Jon drops his head between his shoulders, laughing along with everyone else. "Yeah, gotta admit, I walked straight into that one, didn't I?"

"Don't get too down on yourself, Cap."

Picking his head back up, Jon looks at Zach, who's busy watching Luna. "Why?"

"Well, we kind of had a change in plans. We're still getting married in the Caribbean, but we want you all to be there." Luna pauses and looks at Jon. "Our planner hasn't been that great, to be honest. Look, we know it's last minute, but we were wondering if—"

"Yep," Jon announces, slapping the table hard with a hand. "I will be your planner. Abso-fucking-lutely. One hundred percent."

"For fuck's sake," Jack repeats, dropping his head to his forearm. "The guys on the team are never going to hear the end of this."

I'm still laughing when Mia nudges out from under my shoulder.

"I'm heading to the restroom."

I wrap a hand around her upper arm, my eyes flicking to Leo, who's busy talking with his friend. "You want me to come with you?"

She shakes her head and knits her brows together. "I'm literally fifty feet away. Stay with the group and celebrate tonight's win."

When Jon and Felicity stand to let her out of the booth, I can't tear my eyes away from my girlfriend as she saunters over to the restrooms, her perfect ass swaying under tonight's red miniskirt.

When Mia disappears down the hallway, my eyes momentarily land on Leo, and I don't know if I'm seeing things, but I swear I see his gaze flick from mine and back to his friend when he notices I'm watching.

Staring down into my soda, I feel the way my molars grind together.

He doesn't even get to look at her.

"Go," Jensen says, giving me another sharp kick under the table.

Twisting around, I watch as Leo gets up from the booth.

"Oh, hell fucking no," I announce, already ushering Jon and Felicity out of the way as Jensen chuckles from behind.

"Play nice, Jessie," Zach calls after me.

But I'm gone, already halfway to the restrooms, zeroed in on the back of Leo's head.

MIA

"Oh, yeah, convenient bathroom break." Jessie's boom echoes down the dark hallway to my left as I step out of the restroom.

I walk toward the voices, and they come into view a second later.

"What's going on?" I ask, coming to stand by Jessie's side.

He nods at Leo, who's standing a few feet in front of us, his back to the emergency exit. "Why can't you just take a hint?"

Leo scoffs. "I was heading to the bathroom."

"Like hell you were," Jessie says, leaning down to whisper in my ear. "Go back to the group. I'll be there in a second, Sweetheart."

I wrap my hand around his thick forearm, pulling him away. "Just come back with me. Ignore him."

As he crosses his arms over his chest, a mock smile paints Leo's face. "Yeah, probably best not to hurt Graham's top defenseman."

I turn back to him. "You mean my dad hasn't kicked you off his program yet?"

He snarls, "That's between me and your daddy, nothing privileged bitches like you need to worry about."

Jessie lurches forward and out of my grasp, his right fist balled at his side. "What *the fuck* did you just say to my girl?"

Leo tips his head up to the ceiling and barks out a laugh. "Oh my God, she's got you wrapped around her little finger." He centers his attention back on Jessie. "Let me guess. You fucked your way to the top, taking handouts from daddy's little princess."

When Jessie's fist connects with Leo's face, even I'm not about to stop him.

The bones audibly crunch, and Leo flies back, out through the door behind him and into the parking lot.

Jessie looks down at his fist and smirks. "Didn't even scratch me."

Stepping out into the night air, he grabs Leo by the scruff of the neck, pulling him a couple of inches off the ground so he's at the same height as my boyfriend. "Let me make this really fucking clear for you, Leo. Overall, I'm a pretty reasonable guy. But there are a couple of scenarios that turn me from nice-guy Jessie Callaghan to a monster you do not want to meet." He cocks his head in my direction. "Fucking with my girl is at the top of that list. Now, she didn't want to fuck you the first time you tried, and she absolutely does not want to this time around either. Why? Because you're so far beneath her that I'm surprised you're actually above ground. That and the fact that she comes home to our bed every night. To me."

Leo looks to the side and spits blood onto the ground.

"So, at this point, you have a couple of options. One, never look in her direction again. Even during classes. Or two, refuse to comply, and I'll remove both eyes so the first is never a possibility."

Leo mumbles something inaudible.

"Sorry, what was that?"

"One. Option fucking one," Leo says louder.

On a smirk, Jessie releases Leo, and he meets the ground with a thud. "Thought so."

Grabbing my hand, he interlaces our fingers and never looks back as he slams the door behind us and marches us back up the hallway.

But just as we get opposite the ladies' restroom, Jessie pushes on a door and plunges us into darkness.

"What are you doing?" I ask, my heart beating out of my chest.

"Exactly what I should've done last time we were in this closet."

His mouth crashes down to mine as his hands fall to the hem of my skirt, pulling it up around my waist.

With one hand, he pins my arms above my head by the wrists and lifts me up, and I wrap my legs around him.

In the darkness, I feel his breath fan my lips as the sounds of him undoing his belt and unzipping his dress pants fill the room.

"Normally I'd lick your pussy for hours, but right now, I wanna fuck. You wet for me, Sweetheart?"

"Yes," I gasp.

He hooks his fingers into my panties, pulling them to one side, and I feel him smile against my neck, sucking the soft skin into his mouth. I know he's marking me, but I couldn't give a shit. He can own me.

"Fucking dripping, Mia."

I whimper with need.

"Does watching me claim you in front of another guy get you off?"

I nod, the desperation for him to fuck me hard getting to be all too much.

"Good. Because same. I've never been this fucking hard in my life."

In one movement, he thrusts up and into me.

"Yes," I cry out.

"Louder for me, Sweetheart. Let's give them all a show."

"Yesss," I scream above the beating music.

When Jessie's finger circles my asshole, already slick from my release, he pushes the tip just inside as he continues to fuck my pussy with his cock.

"Ugh," he groans. "So good. Fucking you is so damn good."

"I'm going to come. Like, everywhere." The same pressure I felt in Jessie's gym is already building.

"Now?"

"Any second, yes."

"Unwrap your legs, Mia."

Jessie thrusts into me one more time and then pulls out, dropping to his knees but holding me in place against the wall, his fingertips digging into my thighs.

"Squirt down my throat," he commands, sucking my clit into his mouth.

"Oh my god, oh my god," I repeat over and over as I do exactly as he demands.

His mouth clamps onto me, his tongue continuing to massage my clit as he swallows me down.

When I've given him everything I have, he sets me down to my feet and leans over me, his cock still hard.

"My turn," I say, lowering onto my knees and taking him into my mouth.

One of his hands falls to the top of my head, and he threads his fingers through my hair, pumping his hips as I take his cock as far as I can go.

"Jesus Christ, you suck my dick so damn good."

I can still taste myself as I continue to work my tongue around his shaft. Knowing this came from him fucking me a second earlier makes me pool with more need, and I suck him harder, tightening my palm around his length.

Jessie sags above me, and I can tell he's close.

"I need that pussy again," he groans.

In an instant, I'm back against the wall in the same way I was before, but this time, my legs are even wider as his grip spreads me further apart and open for him.

When he drives himself inside me, all I can see is the way his hair falls over his forehead, his eyes shining in the very faint light creeping in under the door.

Warmth spreads inside me as I feel my boyfriend's cum pour into my pussy.

His damp, parted lips find mine, and he holds himself there, not kissing me, but not moving either. "Goddammit, Mia Marie Jenkins. I'm so fucking gone for you; you have no idea."

CHAPTER THIRTY-SEVEN

JESSIE

In the first couple of seasons after I joined the Scorpions and whenever Coach announced we had one-on-one practice drills, I'd be thinking of excuses to explain why I wouldn't be coming out on top.

I trained too hard in the gym the night before.
I picked up the flu virus that was going around.
I'm not happy with my skates.

Anything, literally anything, to pass off why, Jessie Callaghan —arguably the fastest guy in the NHL with the stick skills to match—couldn't perform in a drill that was made for him.

The only practice worse than that? Sprints and agility tests between cones. Alcohol slows you down, especially when you still have last night's session sitting in your system.

It got to the point where I'd forgotten what it was like to feel like myself, not only on the ice, but to actually think straight. All I could focus on was when I'd be able to have my next drink to ease my mind and help push reality back into the box where it belonged.

But right now, those days feel like a distant nightmare and have since the day Mia came back into my life.

We're sitting in the briefing room before this morning's practice, but rather than listen to the conversations going on around me, all I've been able to think about is my girl and how she's turned my life from something I despised into an existence where I can actually look in the mirror and not hate the person standing in front of me.

"I want you to all watch the video replay of Callaghan and focus in on the following observations." Coach breaks me from my trance, pointing to footage from a sprint drill I absolutely nailed last week. "One, weight distribution. This might sound really fucking obvious to you as pro players, but too many of you aren't keeping your weight on your heels. Two, balance. I want to see more of you working on core exercises as part of your free time in the gym. Balance comes from the core, and I'm tired of repeating the same message."

Coach Burrows looks across at me and quirks a brow, inviting me to add anything to what he just said.

I clear my throat and lean back in my chair, the video paused on me taking a corner. "Yeah, I'd agree with that, Coach. But speed is pretty pointless if you aren't thinking two or three plays ahead. Obviously, we're all great at that, but if you want to get faster, your game analysis has to get faster too."

Right there, that was my problem in college and for the majority of my career. My head was so far up my ass; even if my body was moving at twenty miles per hour, my fucked-up brain was making all the wrong decisions.

"Couldn't have put it better myself." Coach rounds the table and claps me on the shoulder.

The feeling of praise is all too foreign. Since that day I had it out with Graham, Coach has never breathed a word about Mia to me. Something tells me I have my girlfriend to thank for that.

He walks across to the door and pulls it open, looking back

at the guys. "This morning, I want to see attention to the basics, and I want to see them done right."

"Planning on going home at any point tonight?" Jensen stands at the entrance to the ice, fully dressed and showered.

I shake my head and focus back on the line of pucks in front of me, taking my first wrist shot and burying it in the top right, the exact spot I picked out.

"Damn," Jensen responds. "I'd say you've got that down."

I shrug and line up another puck, winding up and hitting exactly the same place.

"Want to get a lift with me to the party?"

I shake my head, still focused on the drill. "I'm gonna get an Uber and meet you all back there. Doesn't start for another couple of hours, right?"

"Still don't know why you don't just buy a car. Also, you know being late to this birthday party is the equivalent of signing your own death warrant. Even I'm scared of my own wife right now."

Truth is, I could afford it. But my financial priority is buying a house for me and Mia and setting my mom up when I can get her to Seattle.

"I won't be late, just finishing up," I reply, tipping my head over my shoulder and smiling at Jensen.

Tapping his hand on the on the board, he turns to leave. "You're really going for Gretzky's record, aren't you?"

"Yep. If I make it, then we'll lift the Stanley. No doubt."

"All right, catch you in a bit," Jensen says, and I hear his footsteps fade out down the hallway.

It must be another fifteen minutes when I hear a side door to the rink open and close behind me.

Expecting it to be one of the maintenance staff, I carry on my routine, having moved on to slap shots.

"That's probably the hottest thing I've ever seen."

I whip around to see Mia standing exactly where Jensen was. "How did you get in here?"

She taps her finger against the side of her head as I make my way over to her, pulling off my gloves and setting my stick against the side. "I have my ways."

When I wrap my arms around her ass and lift her up, she loops her legs around my waist and I skate us to center ice, spinning us around slowly as she hovers above me, her arms thrown over my shoulders and her bag in one hand.

"Breaking and entering now. This good-girl mask of yours is slipping further, Sweetheart."

"Jensen gave me the code," she admits with a giggle, the sound giving me life. "I knew you'd still be practicing late, so I came to pick you up. I also knew you wouldn't be checking your phone, and the last message from Kate read something like, *If anyone is late, I cannot be held responsible for my actions.*"

Gliding back to the edge of the rink, I step off the ice and carry her down the hallway to the locker room. "Better get going then."

The second I push through the door to what I know is an empty room, Mia pinches her nose. "Ugh, Destroyers or the Scorpions—both locker rooms are equally gross."

I set her down on her feet and take a seat on the bench, undoing the laces on my skates. "I don't remember you complaining about the smell the last time you were alone with me after practice. In fact"—I sit up straight and pull my bottom lip between my teeth, taking in how gorgeous she looks in a gold skirt and purple top—"I don't remember you saying all that much at all."

She props her hands on her hips, fighting a smile. "Is that right?"

"Come here," I say, flipping my hands toward me.

When Mia steps up to me and sets her bag down on the

bench next to us, I reach forward and pull her down onto my lap, and she sits across me, her arms around my neck.

"I think this was one of my favorite moments we shared," she whispers, resting her head against my shoulder.

I nod, remembering Mia sneaking into the locker room after practice in her hot-as-fuck black suit. I'd stayed late that night as well, not because I wanted to practice my shots, but in the hopes that she'd come and find me.

Tipping her chin up with my finger, I bring her in for a kiss. "Remember the photo we took right after we finished making out for, like, ten minutes straight?"

She chuckles and bites down on her bottom lip. "The selfie?"

I roll my eyes. "The one where I had to get the angle just right."

Reaching behind her, she pulls out her phone from her purse and unlocks it, bringing up a saved gallery. When she finds the photo of us both, she holds it up in front of us at the exact same angle we took it. "Ugh, I look so much better there."

I can't help the emotion as it floods my senses, and I drop my head down, taking a second to center myself.

When I pick my head back up, I look at my girlfriend, tucking a piece of hair behind her ear. "Trust me, there is nothing more beautiful than you in this moment. Will you take another for me?"

Her eyes scan mine as she hovers the phone above us. "Yeah, sure."

The click of the photo echoes around the silent locker room as she brings the phone toward her and inspects the photo. "It's like a then-and-now kind of thing."

"Can you send me both shots?"

She looks up, her brows slightly knitted. "You don't have the original?"

I swallow down the lump in my throat. I told Mia I'd answer every question she had. "When it all ended, you and me, I was told a trade was the only option. I let everything go." The moment my thumb hovered over the Delete button replays in my head. "I was convinced that I'd never see you again and thought I didn't deserve to either. So, I deleted every memory, thinking it would somehow erase the pain." Bringing my hand to the nape of her neck, I pull her as close as I possibly can. "Turns out, love isn't pixelated, and you can't just erase the emotions."

When she pulls her leg around to straddle me, I swear I can feel her heat through my pants.

"Everyone you have in your life—me, your friends, your fans—you absolutely deserve, Jessie. If there's one thing my mom taught me, it's that some of us find our people sooner than others, and sometimes, we find them too early as well." She presses a palm over her heart. "I know if my mom had been around to meet you, then she would've fought for us to be together sooner, and she definitely would've told my dad to hear you out. She never believed that every piece of a puzzle had to fit perfectly in place for it to make sense. I know we still don't have all the pieces, but the picture looks pretty perfect to me. You're perfect to me."

I go to open my mouth, but she places a finger against my lips.

"You don't need to say anything because you know I'm right."

I press my lips together in a smile. "I was gonna say, you're definitely right about not having all the pieces."

She looks down at her sneakers as they dangle above the floor. "I never thought I'd say this, but maybe the only way to get your mom to Seattle is to go see her and talk face-to-face. Go at a time when you know your dad is at work or when he goes out."

I consider her suggestion and finally nod. "I think that's my best shot. Didn't work last time, but I have to try again."

"She is worth so much more than him. No one should stay with someone like that."

Pressing a kiss to her forehead, I close my eyes, appreciating how special the woman in front of me really is. "I know; I've lost count of the times I told her that. I just need to help her see that there's a better life."

Mia climbs down from my lap and grabs her bag. "I'm going to use the bathroom. But I say call her, leave her a message if she doesn't pick up."

When Mia pushes through the door, I lean down and grab my phone from my bag, the two images she sent lighting up my home screen.

There is a better life.

Taking a risk that Dad might be around, I hit dial on Mom's number and wait for the phone to go to voicemail like it always does when she can't pick up.

"Mom, hi," I say as her voicemail connects. "It's Jessie. I'm sorry I didn't come home last time I was in town; things were kind of crazy and … yeah." I inhale a deep breath. "Listen, I wanted to talk to you about something. I have a couple of days between games and practices next week, and I was thinking of coming over. Maybe I could take you out for food or something if you're up to it. Just like the old days. Yeah, anyway, call me back, okay? I … I care about you."

CHAPTER THIRTY-EIGHT

JESSIE

"Wow, I feel like I've stepped into Disney World or something," Mia says from beside me as we walk out into Jensen and Kate's garden for Aster and the twins' joint first birthday party.

"Their very own Animal Kingdom," I reply, trying to take in one of the most lavish first birthday parties I've ever seen.

As soon as she sees us, Kate approaches, a glass of champagne ready to hand to Mia. "You made it! And on time." She looks to me.

"Wouldn't miss this for the world." The garden is huge, but somehow, they've managed to fill it with balloons, activities, and huge models of giraffes, elephants, and every other animal you can think of. "Where are they?" I say, looking for Aster, Will, and June.

Kate points toward a window in their house behind me. "Oh, Jensen, Luna, and Zach are changing them into their costumes."

"For real?" Mia asks with a squeak, obviously not fazed by this one bit.

"Yep. So, Aster chose to be a lion, June is a hippo—God

knows why she chose that—and Will also wanted to be a lion, but we convinced him he made a better crocodile."

Taking a soda from the tray as the waiter passes, I look down at the animal-themed straw sitting in my glass. "Jon is behind this, isn't he?"

"Actually, no, thank you. He is not. This is all me and my husband. Zach and Luna too, obviously."

"Well, you went to town. I don't think I've seen anything like it." Mia suddenly gasps, and I practically spill my Fanta down my white shirt. "Look!" she says, tapping her hand on my arm. "There they are."

When Jensen walks out, holding Will, and they're in matching crocodile outfits, the drink I try to swallow nearly sprays across my girlfriend.

Jensen's mom, Claire, is the first to run across to the twins with Zach's mom, Rachel, hot on her heels.

As soon as he hands Will over to his mom, Jensen makes a beeline for us, his scaly tail swaying behind him.

"What do you think of the look? Nailed it, right?"

My eyes ascend his costume slowly and pause on his painted green face, hiding inside a long and pointy mouth, complete with sharp white teeth. "It's a look—I'll give you that."

He shrugs. "Kate likes it. She likes the bad-boy image."

His eyes drop to the gift bags in my hands. "Oh, there's a designated present table in the tent. You can just put them in there if you want. We're going to open them all later."

He must see the disappointment in my eyes and rolls his. "All right, you can give them to him now." He tips his massive head over his shoulder to locate his wife, who's over with June. "But if she gets pissed, I never knew a thing."

The second I stand in front of Will—a mini version of his dad—he reaches his arms out to me, and I pass the bags across to Mia as Claire hands him to me, a bright smile on her face.

"Hey, buddy."

When I make eye contact with Mia, I see the understanding

in her eyes. My teammates' children are like family to me, but my connection with Will is something special.

"Do you want to open it?" Mia asks Will, pulling his present from the bag and offering it out to him.

His little hands take it from her, and he giggles as he turns the wrapped cube around in front of him.

"Go for it, buddy," I say.

"I still can't guess what it is."

I turn to Mia. "Time to find out."

As I help Will pull back the green wrapping paper, the first picture comes into view, and Claire gasps as the glitter swirls around it inside the plastic cube.

"Oh my, it's a picture snow globe. Jessie, it's beautiful."

When all the wrapping is on the floor by our feet, Will shakes the cube, and multicolored glitter swims around inside it. Each side displays a photo of Will throughout his first year. Two of them include me—one at the beach, taken when he was four months old, and another at his first Christmas. One is with Mia at Luna and Zach's house party. One with Jensen, Kate, and his sister in front of their fireplace—I took it at Thanksgiving last year. The last two were snapped on the day he was born—one just with his mom sitting up in bed, holding him and June, and then with the whole group together.

"Wait, there's a picture of me with him too," Mia says, bringing her hands to the cube, and Will passes it to her, still mesmerized by its sensory nature. "Jessie, this is beautiful."

"Wait, you started open—" Kate cuts herself off as she catches sight of what Mia's holding.

Will's mom has always struggled to show her emotion—something we've always understood about each other, even if we've never said it out loud.

Tears gather in the corners of her eyes as Mia hands it to her.

I watch Kate as she studies the images. "I don't have many pictures of my childhood, but there is this one of me with my mom on the couch in our living room. It's pretty special to me, and I thought maybe Will would like something he could keep. Something that reminds him that he's been loved by a lot of people from the moment he was born."

When Kate looks at me, the tears are now trickling down her cheeks, and she turns to my girlfriend. "Mia, would you just take Will for a second?"

The moment Will is in Mia's arms, Kate's are around me. "I know we don't talk about it much, and that's okay. But I want to say thank you, Jessie. Thank you for being a great friend to my husband, a great friend to me, and the greatest uncle my children could wish for. All I've ever wanted was for my children to feel loved. I know you get that."

I swallow thickly. "I do, Kate. I'm so happy you got your happy ending."

She pulls back and tips her head toward Mia, who is busy helping Claire count Will's fingers. "You got yours too."

MIA

"Do we break them up now … or later?" Felicity drawls as I stand in the backyard with her, Luna, and Kate, watching Jon, Jensen, Zach, and Jessie race around a makeshift track on Hopper Balls.

I fight to hold back laughter as Jessie bounces up and down on something that is designed for elementary children.

"I don't know," I say with a smirk. "We could take bets on who's going to end up on their ass first."

"They were meant for the children!" Luna brings a hand to the side of her mouth and shouts.

"He looks like a giant green dick." Kate points at her husband. "He started talking about more kids last night, and for a while, I was considering it. Now, I need to erase this image from my mind forever."

I turn to Kate and waggle my eyebrows. "He said you liked the costume."

"When he's holding my son and daughter, yes; when he's bouncing around like an overgrown child, no."

"Somehow, they have to turn everything into a competition." Felicity shakes her head as Jon breaks from the group and bounces toward us.

When he reaches his wife's feet, he looks up at her. "Hop on, Angel. There's space."

Felicity looks over at us and then back at Jon. "I've got a better idea. How about boys versus girls? There's another four Hopper Balls, right?"

I swear I see Jon visibly gulp. "Yeah, there're a few spares, but …"

Before Jon can finish his sentence, all four of us are across the grass. Kate, Felicity, and I grab the Hoppers, and Luna takes Aster from Rachel.

"I'd better not since I don't want to go into labor this early."

Zach pulls off his sunglasses and eyes her as I bounce up alongside Jessie, stopping at the makeshift line Jon drew earlier with white chalk. "Watch the master at work, Rocket."

Flicking her auburn hair back, she brings Aster's hands between hers and claps them together. "We're cheering for the girls."

Jon looks down the line at the rest of us. "All right, three laps around the circuit. First to cross the line wins. I'll go easy on y—"

"Three, two, one, GO!" Felicity rushes out, setting off at a crazy speed.

In protest, Jon throws his arms in the air. "Hey! Wait up. I didn't—damn it!"

He sets off after her, and I hit the gas, chasing after Kate, Jessie, and Zach.

"This is hard work!" Kate shouts a couple of places ahead of me as we take the first corner, and Zach almost skids off the ball, desperate to catch up to the front.

"My ass is already going numb!" I holler back, painfully aware I'm in a skirt and there are at least a dozen other people watching us with their children.

When Felicity overtakes me on the second lap, I quickly realize that this is probably not my wheelhouse.

"Yep, Hopper Balls are not for me," I shout ahead.

"It's the taking part that matters, Sweetheart." Jessie laughs as he overtakes me too.

"Oh, really?" In a last-ditch move to save face, I bounce to the right and straight into him, knocking him off course. "Ha-ha-ha-ha-haaaa!"

He narrows his eyes at me and straightens himself up, ready to bounce back toward me, when he suddenly stops and lets go of the handle on his Hopper, redirecting his hand to the pocket of his pants.

The second he pulls out his phone and looks at the screen, I can tell something isn't right.

Abandoning his Hopper Ball, he stands and rushes off in the opposite direction, speaking into the phone, although I can't make out anything he's saying with the noise and music around us.

I jump to my feet and call after him, stumbling over one of the blankets set out with toys as I chase my boyfriend down across the yard. "Jessie?"

When he pulls up at the bottom of the stairs leading up to the house, he drops his head between his shoulders, and my heart sinks into the earth beneath us.

Oh no.

"Jessie?" My voice breaks this time.

"Okay," I hear him say. "I'll be there. Yeah, on the next flight."

As soon as he disconnects the call, he spins around, his eyes red; he's stressed and breathing erratic. "I have to go."

He's not even looking at me.

"Jessie, I'm here."

Blinking a couple of times, he focuses on me and scratches his nails down the side of his face. "My mom," he pushes out. "The stairs. She fell down the stairs, and I need to get back home. Now."

I step up to him, throwing my arms around his neck and standing on my tiptoes.

"Everything okay?" Jensen asks, approaching us carefully.

"I need to get to the airport, like, right now," Jessie says to him, his hands coming to my waist. "My mom is … she's in bad shape, and I need to get back."

"Wait, I can come with you."

Jessie looks down at me and shakes his head. "No, Mia. I need you to head back home and wait for me there." He looks back to Jensen. I know why he isn't asking me to drop him at the airport, because I'll insist on taking the flight with him and he wants me nowhere near his dad.

"Let me grab my keys," Jensen says, already unzipping his costume.

Setting a kiss on my forehead, Jessie pulls away from me and races up the stairs.

"Is she okay? When will you be back? I don't care if he's there. I can come," I blurt out.

When he spins back around, I see the tears in his eyes.

"I don't know. I'll call you when I get to Dallas." He brushes a hand over the scruff of his jaw. "Just stay here, where you're safe, yeah? For me."

CHAPTER THIRTY-NINE

MIA

"I need to go with him."

"Just come inside, babe. He'll call you when he lands." Kate wraps an arm around my shoulders as we stand at the end of her driveway and watch the boys tear away in Jensen's white Tesla.

I wrap my arms around my waist. "It's not that simple."

"What do you mean?"

I think hard about my next words. "He had a really tough childhood."

Kate nods and plucks a piece of stray hair from my T-shirt. "I guessed as much. He once mentioned that he had a brother. I know Jensen named Will after him, but honestly, that's as much as I know. I think Jensen knows a little more, but not a lot. If he's let you into his life, then based on what I know about Jessie, I'd say that's a huge step for him."

I inhale a steadying breath.

Kate's hand squeezes my shoulder. "Until I got pregnant, I was the most skeptical person when it came to love. I didn't think it was possible to find *the one*. But let me tell you this: the way Jessie looks at you, that isn't just love; that's a connection on a level so deep that no one will ever be able to find the words to describe it. I know I can't. But to witness it? Now, that's something really special. If I'd known you both the first time you were together? I'd have flown you to Seattle myself. He might've had a really tough start, but to find that kind of love? Trust me when I say he knows how rich he is right now. He'll do anything to protect you."

I turn and look at Jessie's BMW parked in the driveway. "Which is why I have to go to him. Everything you just said, I feel it too. Would you go to Jensen?"

She looks off to the side and down the road where they disappeared a few minutes earlier. "Wait here."

A couple of minutes later, she reappears with my jacket, purse, and a small overnight bag. "I literally just dumped some spare clothes of mine and a cosmetic bag in here; there's also a spare toothbrush in the front. That way, you don't have to go home."

I reach up and wrap my arms around her neck. "Thank you."

"I just have one condition."

"Fire away," I say, pulling the keys out of my purse and unlocking the car.

Kate's face turns lawyer serious. "Call me as soon as you find out how his mom is. I want to know you all are okay."

I nod. "Promise."

Any hopes I had of making the same flight as Jessie crashed and burned the second I hit a gridlock on the freeway and got to the airport, only to be told I'd just missed check-in for the last afternoon flight to Dallas.

Luckily, there was another flight with an alternate airline departing only an hour later, so I jumped on that.

And that's where I am now, about to touch down in Texas with a packet of half-eaten Lays chips in my lap and a Minute Maid between my knees, typing out my hundredth text to Jessie and immediately deleting it.

If I write him and say I'm on my way, he'll tell me to get right back on a return flight, and that isn't happening.

There's not a chance in hell I'm leaving him to care for his mom alone. Even if he's done it his entire life.

I only have one issue.

I have zero idea where his parents live since he never took me back to his home, and there are kind of a lot of houses on South Boulevard.

When the plane wheels touch down and I step out into the Dallas spring air, there's only one person I can think of who might know where he lived.

Even if I'm still not fully over what he did.

The second he picks up, I hear the road noise and know he's driving.

"Mia, hi. Are you okay?"

"Hey, Dad," I say, raising an arm to flag down a taxi.

When silence falls between us, the only thing that breaks it up is the sound of his blinker and the plane passing over my head.

"I'm okay. But actually, I called to ask for a favor."

I hand the taxi driver my overnight bag, and he puts it in the trunk. I say a quiet prayer that my dad won't go off on me for what I'm about to ask.

"Go on," he replies cautiously. "I'm driving, but on Bluetooth. It sounds like you're at an airport."

"I'm in Dallas."

Dad huffs out a long breath. "Please tell me you aren't going to say it went wrong between you two."

"Where to, ma'am?" the taxi driver asks.

I lift a finger, asking him to give me a second.

"Nothing has happened. Well, it kind of has, but it has

nothing to do with me and Jessie." I pull the car door open and climb into the back, and the driver takes his seat. "When Jessie was playing for you, did you have his home address?"

"Like the apartment we rented out for him? Probably, yes ... but why, Mia?"

"No, not when he was playing for the Destroyers. His home address on South Boulevard. From when he was a boy."

"I'm not sure that's a good idea."

I squeeze my eyes shut and blow out a frustrated breath. "With all due respect, Dad, your decisions lately haven't exactly been good. His mom had an accident, and I need to support my boyfriend. I don't have a lot of time." I glance up at the driver, who's eyeing me in his rearview mirror. "Do you have the address, or should I think of another option?"

Nothing.

"Dad, please."

"I'm sorry, Mia. But I can't give that to you. This isn't me being difficult. If you're calling me for it, then there's a reason you aren't getting it from Jessie, and it must be a good one. Turn around and get back on the plane, Mia."

As I stare out of the passenger window, my heart sinks.

He's never going to treat me like the woman I know I am.

I miss you, Mom.

"Okay, fine. I'll find another way," I bite out.

Pulling my phone away, I hit End just as I hear my dad call my name.

"Ma'am—"

I hold up a hand and stare down into my lap. "Just give me a second, and I'll get out. I'm sorry for wasting your time."

"Ma'am—"

"Just a second," I repeat, picking my phone back up and scrolling through my contacts, aimlessly searching for someone who might be able to help.

"Is it Jessie Callaghan's address you need? The one on South Boulevard–Park Row?"

Picking my head up, I stare at the dark-haired taxi driver. "H- how do you know that?"

He shakes his head. "Nah, I'll probably get fired if this gets out," he mumbles to himself.

"Please, tell me," I blurt out. "He's my boyfriend and his mom's hurt. I just need to get to him, but he thinks it's a bad idea." Opening the gallery on my phone, I flick to the picture we took in the locker room; it feels like a million years ago, even though it's only been a matter of hours. "Look, that's me with him. I'm still wearing the same outfit because it was taken today. I just need to get to him."

The driver drops his head between his shoulders. "If you're some kind of stalker or a woman scorned and looking for revenge, then just know that I have a family and I'll lose my job."

"I'm just a girl trying to support her boyfriend."

A couple of beats pass before he speaks. "I gave him a ride a while back. It was to South Boulevard–Park Row. I gotta tell you, miss, it's ... bad. The house is bad. Are you sure you want to go there? Because your dad sounded kinda reluctant."

I wipe the tear from under my eye. My voice is way stronger than I feel. "You said you have a family. So, you have someone you love or did once upon a time, right?"

He nods, keeping eye contact with me in the mirror. "My wife."

"What lengths would you go to for her?"

Without a word, he cranks the engine.

CHAPTER FORTY

MIA

"This is it."

"Okay," I say, unclipping my belt and reaching into my purse for the fare, my head firmly down.

I will not show my reaction.

When I finally look up and offer the driver thirty dollars for the ride, he waves his hand in front of him. "Keep it," he says, passing me his contact card. "If you run into trouble, I'll be around the area for the next few hours."

I take the card and push open the door, leaving the cash on his back seat. "Thank you, but I can't accept the free ride."

The driver rounds the car, pulls open the trunk, and hands me my bag. "Sure you'll be okay, ma'am?"

"Yep." I smile at him, not nearly as convinced as my response sounds. "Thank you again."

When he gets in his car and takes off down the long street, I turn back to the front porch of the house where Jessie grew up.

It's devastating.

Honestly, I don't know what I expected. I tried to imagine

what having nothing looked like. What four walls of horror might appear like from the outside.

But no amount of visualization could have prepared me for the dilapidated state in front of me. Homes don't need to be fancy or big or even tidy. It just needs to feel safe, like love and hope exist there.

By that definition, this isn't a home.

Pulling the screen door open first, I push at the front door, the handle virtually redundant, and enter the house. The door closes on its own behind me with a creak.

The inside of the house looks like it's been ransacked, barely resembling a livable space. But it's not the mess that hits me first; it's the smell.

If depression had a scent, I'm pretty sure that this house would be it.

Bringing my palm across my face, I peer down at the coffee table in front of me. No one is around, but the ashtray is full of butts, some look fresher than others.

My throat is dry and thick, but when I hear movement from upstairs, my heart beats faster in my chest. "Jessie?"

There's no response as I stand and wait for a couple of beats. "Jessie?" I try again, feeling sure he'd said he was going back home.

A bang ricochets across the ceiling, followed by, "Fuck!"

The voice is male, but it doesn't belong to my boyfriend.

Wayne.

As fast as my trembling body will carry me, I turn and head for the front door, pulling it open. When I get to the screen, it's wedged in the doorframe. I keep pulling on it, but it won't budge.

"Red nails."

A hand wraps around my arm, spinning me around to face an older version of my boyfriend.

He looks like him, but he's nothing like him, all at the same time.

His eyes are blue, but hold no warmth, like his son's.

"I was looking for Jessie." It's the only thing I think of to say as he peers down at me.

When he releases my arm, I think about my chances of making a run for it. If Jessie isn't here, then neither is Alice.

"Struggling with the door?" he asks, tipping his head up and over my shoulder.

"Is he here?"

Running his tongue across his bottom lip, he scans my body. The insidious tone in his voice that night on the phone is mimicked in the way he looks at me, and I take a step back into the screen.

"He's at the hospital."

"W-which one?" As much as I try to hold back my fear, it's impossible to hide. I can stand up as straight as I want, but my voice gives me away.

He laughs, but there's nothing amusing about the way it sounds. "I'd say, at this point, it really doesn't matter."

"Why not?"

He looks off to the side, and I follow his gaze to a picture on the wall. One with Jessie as a baby, sitting on his mom's lap. "She died shortly after she got to the hospital. He'll be there since I asked them to call him before I left." He shrugs his shoulder and slides his hands into his pockets. "I don't currently own a phone, so I couldn't do it myself."

"She's dead ...why aren't you still there with her?" The question leaves my mouth before I can stop it.

He stares at me for a long second and then blows out a breath. "Did you not hear me? She's dead. There's nothing more I could do. Sitting by her side isn't going to bring her back, is it?"

"I ... I guess not." I turn around to leave, praying this time, I can figure out how to get past the screen door. "I'll call Jessie and find out where he is."

"Not so fucking fast." His hand comes around my arm again. "He doesn't know you're here, does he?"

In around half a second, my mind searches through the contents of my bag, remembering the pepper spray I stashed in there when I started college.

"He knows I'm here," I lie. "He's probably on his way over right now."

With my back to him, I feel *and smell* his breath fan my ear. The stench of booze is unmistakable, and I shut my eyes in the hopes that it will disconnect my other senses too.

"Come on now, Mia. He has no idea you're here, does he? I'd go so far as to say he doesn't even know you're in Texas."

A shiver licks up my spine when he says my name. As Jessie predicted, the minute we went public, Wayne would know my identity. He only needed to check the gossip sites to work that one out.

Not waiting for him to do it himself, I spin around and face him, tipping up my chin. "Why are you so bothered, Wayne? I mean, I could stay here and talk with you, but you sounded pretty busy up there." I motion toward the stained staircase. "So, I'll be on my way and leave you to do ... whatever it was you were doing."

Assuming he has a system full of alcohol, his reflexes take me by surprise as he reaches up and snatches my bag off my shoulder, throwing it across the room and onto the couch, the contents spilling out, including my cell.

"If he's on his way, then there's zero point in you leaving."

"I don't want to stay," I reply, my voice significantly less steady than before.

He leans down, bringing his face inches from mine. "Why not?"

I know it's an illusion, but I can't help believing it's real when I stare past Wayne's shoulder and into the tiny kitchen behind him, seeing an image of a young Jessie climbing onto the counter to search the cupboards for food.

I wonder where Wayne beat Jessie when he was last here.

Maybe right in front of the broken TV or upstairs and away from his now-dead mother.

Rage builds inside me, impossible to push down. I can't ignore it, and I don't *want* to anymore.

My heart aches for the man I love because, today, he lost his mom, and I know deep down in my gut that it was to the same monster he fights every day of his life—alcohol.

As I bite my cheek, I know this is a mistake. But somehow, an error in judgment has never felt so good.

My lips curl into an involuntary snarl. "Because I can't stand the sight of you."

I don't know how I expected him to react, but it's not the hysterics he breaks into, practically doubling over.

He holds up a hand, his other arm wrapped around his waist. "Sorry ... just give me a second. That was way too funny."

I'm confused and intimidated, but the sight of my phone ringing silently on the couch catches my attention. *Dad* lights up the screen.

Maybe I should've listened to him and Jessie. Why didn't it click that his mom would be in the hospital? Why am I so goddamn stupid?

"Okay, I'm good now."

I've only ever felt like I couldn't breathe twice before in my life. The first time was when I fell off a pony as a young girl, and the second was when my dad told me my mom had passed away.

This time, it's when my back hits the wall so hard that all the air is knocked out of me.

His fingers wrap around my throat, giving me zero chance of catching my breath as he holds me against the wall, my feet dangling above the floor.

This is it. Where I die.

At the hands of a man Jessie repeatedly told me was dangerous.

At the hands that have repeatedly beaten down my boyfriend.

"Please," I beg, my voice strangled and barely a whisper, the tears flowing freely from my eyes. "You don't want t-to—"

"Don't want to what, Sweetheart?" He brings his face to my neck, inhaling my hair. "Why are you all the same? Alice used to beg and plead too. It's not attractive."

Thrashing my body from side to side, I try to kick him in the shin, but he jumps back, and laughter spills out of him once again. This is all a game to him.

"Oh, now, maybe I get it. Why my boy likes this pussy. It's got fight. Does he make you fight him, Mia? Does he like that his posh little rich bitch is feisty?"

My attempts to fight back slow as my energy reserves dwindle, and the room around me starts to dim.

"Get your fucking hands off her!"

I fall to the floor, but the thud I hear is way louder than the noise my petite frame should make.

"I should've done this way before now!"

On my hands and knees and still gasping for air, I lift my head, trying to find the voices.

When my vision slowly recovers, I see Jessie over his dad as he lies flat on his back, his hands shielding his face.

"You killed her, didn't you? You let her fucking die on the floor," he shouts between sobs and punches. "You could've called for help earlier, but didn't."

He continues to beat down on his dad, his fists connecting with whatever part of Wayne's body he can find.

"Jessie," I whisper.

The sobs he releases ricochet through my own body, and my tears tumble to the matted carpet beneath me.

"Jessie," I repeat, a little louder this time, but it still doesn't register.

Forcing my exhausted body to move, I crawl toward him.

"I hate you. HATE YOU!" he screams, landing another blow to his dad's nose, blood spraying everywhere. "Piece of fucking shit."

Jessie isn't a violent person, and these punches aren't aggression. With every strike, he's purging years of abuse, of silence. Every hit and wail he releases carries a different purpose than to simply inflict pain. His dad's body might be traumatized, but Jessie is the one bleeding out.

"Jessie." I try one final time, bringing a hand to his shoulder as he straddles his father.

It's then I catch the first glimpse of something I hope never to see in his eyes again. Fear. True fear. Unadulterated fear that I've only read about in books and tried to describe in assignments I submitted.

"You're going to kill him. You don't want that on you," I whisper.

"He watched my mother die and assaulted my girlfriend!" he spits.

I'm not even sure he recognizes that it's me he's talking to.

"You don't want to do this, Jessie. He's not worth it. You're worth more than all of this."

Sliding my hand down the arm that's closest to me and currently wrapped around his dad's throat, I trail my fingers over his as his other arm hangs in the air above Wayne's bloodied face.

"It's okay." I soothe, hooking my little finger around his.

I barely use any force, pulling his hand away with ease.

His dad stirs but is barely conscious when Jessie climbs off his body and onto mine, wrapping his arms around my shoulders.

"I need you, Mia." He brings my legs around his waist and lifts me to straddle him. Rocking us back and forth, he buries his face into the hair over my shoulder, his tears soaking into my shirt. "I need you."

As I stroke a palm down the back of his head, I don't say a word, just rock with him.

When he releases a gut-wrenching wail that shakes the foundation of the house, I hear it echoing in every room, every wall. This roar of pain is on behalf of his brother, his mother, and every year of his own life where he's seen and felt indescribable torture.

Looking down at the zip-up hoodie he wasn't wearing when I last saw him, I notice the initials *JJ* stamped on his chest as I unzip it and pull one side open and then the other. "Wrap it around us, baby."

He lifts his head from my shoulder, and the dark circles under his red eyes are still visible in the fading light outside as he takes me in.

"You're safe under here," I reassure him.

As he stretches the large hoodie around us, we don't say anything for at least thirty seconds; the only noise is the traffic outside and the shallow breathing of his father lying next to us.

"We need to call the police and nine-one-one," I finally say to him.

Nodding slowly, I know he understands why.

"We need to make statements," I whisper as calmly as I can.

"The doctors said the internal bleeding my mom died of was advanced. They couldn't be sure, but they suspected she'd been like that for a while before he used her phone and called the paramedics. He'd left her. I know he did. His body shudders with another sob as he delivers the earth-shattering reality.

"Tell me he didn't hurt you," he pleads. "Tell me you're okay."

I close my eyes and run my palm across the nape of his neck, and he collapses his face into my chest.

"I'm okay. You got to me in time."

"It's okay, Mia. I got you both."

Two hands land on my shoulders from behind.

"Dad?"

Crouching down beside us, my dad checks Wayne's pulse and then pulls out his phone, hitting three numbers and the Call button. "I knew you'd find a way to get here. I'm just sorry I don't drive a rocket ship. He's messed up pretty bad, but the fucker deserves worse." Putting the phone to his ear, he scans my body quickly, landing on the red marks that no doubt paint my neck. "Are you okay, Mia?"

I nod, still clinging to Jessie. "We're both okay, but I need to get him out of here ASAP."

Jessie tangles his fingers in my hair, twisting the strands around.

"I'm sorry. I should've listened to you. I shouldn't have come. I just made it worse."

Inhaling a shaky breath, he brings his lips to my forehead. "You should've listened, but when Kate called me to say she hadn't heard from you since you'd landed in Texas, I knew where you'd be. I knew because I'd stop at nothing to be right here, too, if this were you."

"I'm a stubborn bitch at times," I reply as my dad stands and walks to the other side of the room, confirming the address.

"I just want to go home with you."

"We will, baby," I say, rocking him again. "Promise."

CHAPTER FORTY-ONE

JESSIE

It's been four days since I walked into the ER and was told my mom hadn't made it.

My agent has advised that, this time, I don't try to bury the news, that I show the public the real Jessie Callaghan.

Except I thought I was starting to like him, and now I feel like I'm right back to nothing.

If there's nothing I like about myself, then how will the world find any redeeming feature?

All her death took was a slip at the top of the stairs on the wobbly legs I'd watched her climb so many times.

All she needed was to get medical attention sooner.

All her safety would have taken was for me to step up and get her to Seattle.

Life today could've looked so different.

But it doesn't.

The picture of me as a baby, sitting on her lap while we watched TV together, was taken by Papa, and it now sits on my nightstand. Courtesy of Mia and her quick thinking before we left the house.

When I roll over onto my back, the morning light streams through the blinds. The ceiling is still just as white today as it was the day before.

"It happened again," Mia whispers, turning over and resting her head on my chest, her dark hair fanning across my skin.

"I know," I reply, motionless.

She trails her red fingernails across my stomach, and the feeling of her touch is the only comfort to me. "Did you get any sleep?"

Shaking my head, I already know that tonight will be the same. "Every time I start to drift off, it happens. Like someone's choking me."

Waking up, gasping for air, is nothing new to me; it's been happening for as long as I've been battling my mental health. Since we got back to Seattle, it's gotten way worse. Last night, just as I was falling asleep, I bolted up in bed, gagging and retching.

She yawns against my warm skin and then looks up at me, her chin resting on my sternum. "I wish I could do something to help."

I want to keep her awake at night for all the right reasons. Not this.

But, fuck me, is she so naturally beautiful.

I reach across and curl my hands under her bare ass, lifting her onto me. We're both naked, and her gorgeous breasts and pink nipples harden in the morning air. The white bedsheets are a perfect contrast to her dark hair as it falls in front of her face and shoulders.

Threading each hand through hers, I intertwine our fingers and rest our joined hands on each of her thighs. "What are your dreams, Mia?"

She pinches her brows together, confused at the random question.

Except it's not random at all.

"Dreams ... you mean, like, my ideal career?"

She shifts forward slightly, the warmth of her pussy wrapping around my hardening cock. Despite my state of mind, my body still responds to her like the tide going out each day. Without question and like it's the most natural thing in the world.

I squeeze her hands in mine. "No, Sweetheart. You've already got all that down. What are *your* dreams?"

"You mean, like, personally?"

I nod and wait for the answer I'm already sure she's going to give.

Her face instantly morphs from consideration to delight. "Oh. Well, that's simple—you, me, and a great big Saint Bernard."

I blow out a laugh. "What? You've never even mentioned a dog, let alone a huge one before."

She shrugs and briefly lets go of my hand, pushing her hair back over her right shoulder. It's then I notice the red fingerprints that still mark the side of her throat.

My heart plummets at the sight, landing in the lobby three floors down with a thud.

He's still out there, having made bail.

Reclasping our hands, she leans forward, her peaked nipples rubbing across my chest.

When she places her mouth over mine and kisses me, my pulse goes from barely registering to beating uncontrollably.

I release her hands and flip Mia onto her back, spreading her legs and settling between them.

When I pull the white sheets up and over our heads, I find her neck and will the physical memories away with my mouth.

The truth is, the marks will fade, but she hasn't spoken to me about the effect the attack has had on her. She told the police she was fine and made her statement to press charges against my dad.

I get the feeling my girlfriend is just as skilled at hiding her scars as I am, and the thought chips away at my armor just a little more.

"What about you, Jessie? What are your dreams?" she asks, tilting her head to give my lips better access to her neck.

I pause against her skin, realizing this isn't a question I can answer easily.

Feeling the way she stiffens in response to my hesitancy, chips at another piece.

"What do you want, Jessie?" she repeats, her voice less relaxed than before.

My lips ascend the side of her neck, and I close my eyes. "You," I whisper, feeling the way her muscles relax.

Squeezing my eyes a little tighter, I know I owe her all the honesty I've always promised. "For as long as I'm here, on this earth, while blood is running through my veins, my existence will always revolve around you. Even if one day, your dreams don't involve me, mine will always be of you, Mia."

She pulls back and twists her head to face me. I can't make out if it's hurt or confusion in her green eyes. "You think there will be a point when I don't want you anymore?"

I go to kiss her, words failing to express what I mean when she pulls back again.

"No, wait. You don't get to kiss me right after you just said that."

"Mia—"

She holds up a hand, her eyes glassy. "No."

"That's not what I meant. I wasn't questioning your love for me; I was …" My frustration ramps up to the point where I want to tear my hair out at the roots.

How is it possible that I'm fucking everything up right now with the one person I have left?

With a palm to the side of her face, I wipe a stray tear away with my thumb. "Every image I have of the future belongs to you. Not to hockey, not to anyone else. They're all of you. There just aren't that many of them. I can't see beyond today or even how I'm going to get out of this bed. My mind is at sea, and I'm drowning. You're my life raft, holding me up, but I know I'm getting heavy. What happens if my weight is too much? What if I stay here, trying to tread water, but slowly, I'm sinking us both? What if I never stop blaming myself for my mom? What if the temptation to head three blocks down to the nearest liquor store gets to be too much? What then, Mia? Would I be your dream then?"

She presses her lips into a thin line, and I watch as her throat works, the marks still just as prominent.

"What you just described is the very definition of conditional love."

"I described a situation where I'd never blame you for walking away. I've always told you if I'm going down, you aren't coming with me."

"Except my love for you isn't like anything you've ever had, Jessie. You don't get to have a say in that either. You are my priority, and you always will be. I love you unconditionally."

I close my eyes and let the sincerity in her words sink in, willing them to override my years of fucked-up love.

When she reaches down and brushes her soft palm over my cock, it stirs to life, and I focus back on her.

"Make love to me, Jessie. Because I need you. I need us."

We haven't had sex since before I left for Dallas—by far the longest time we've gone. Even when I've been away with the team, we've gotten each other off over the phone.

Every cell in my body wants the woman lying in front of me, asking me to bury myself inside her.

"Me too, Sweetheart."

She's already wet when I swipe a hand along her entrance.

My girlfriend whimpers quietly, pulling my face down to hers. "If your mind won't listen, then maybe your body will."

"All I want is to be the man you absolutely deserve, Mia."

"Then show me."

As I hover over her, I kiss my way down her neck, stopping at the red marks. "No one is ever going to hurt you again, and that includes me. You're so fucking precious to me."

She knows my tongue is making its way to its favorite place when I circle it around her navel and lift one of her legs into the crook of my arm, spreading her wide open.

Sliding all the way to the bottom of my bed, I tease her clit with the tip of my finger, and she squirms, the tiniest giggle rippling out of her.

With my finger now pressing just inside, I pause and look up at her as she pins her bottom lip between her teeth, gazing down at me. "Want to talk me through the best way to finger you?"

She smirks. "Are you testing if I've been listening in class?"

A smile pulls at my lips, and I'm confident she's the only one who can—and will ever—make me feel this way. "You bet I am."

When I push deeper and let a second finger join, her mouth falls open, and she presses her head further into her pillow. "Deeper. Go deeper."

I do as she says and reward her by sucking her clit into my mouth and teasing it with my tongue.

"What now?" I ask, releasing her with a pop. "I'm at your beck and call, but I need more instructions."

"When you get as deep as you can go, you need to curl them forward and find that wall."

"Like this?"

"Yesss ... right—there," she cries as the first release washes over my fingers.

"You've done so well, Mia. Want me to take over?"

She nods quickly, and I can't help but let my smile grow wider. The look of pure pleasure painting her face somehow finds its way to me, inflating my chest.

When I withdraw my fingers, she whimpers at the loss. Her eyes quickly fall to my mouth, and she watches me lick my favorite flavor from them.

"Don't worry, Sweetheart. My cock can fill you up good too. This time, I want you to ride me, but go slow. I want to watch the way I satisfy you."

When I fall to my back beside her, she climbs over me, straddling my hips and lifting up onto her knees.

She takes my cock into her hand and pumps it once, lifting her eyes to mine. "This reminds me of the time I straddled you in your car at the theater. I wanted to sink down onto you then too."

As she lowers herself, she has zero hesitation, taking me all the way inside her until I bottom out.

Mia throws her head back and rocks her hips over me once, twice, and on the third time, she moans into the silence of the room. "Oh my god, you feel so good, Jessie."

I bring my hands to her hips and steady her, wanting her to take from me what she needs, happy to let my body show her how special she is.

"You gonna come for me?"

Her hands come to my shoulders as she continues to ride my dick, slow and deep. I know I'm not far away from coming inside her.

"I'm so close. I can feel it building," she gasps.

When she loses rhythm, the overload of an orgasm crashing toward her, I take control and sit up slightly, drawing up my knees and spreading them apart. "I got you, baby. Let go for me, Mia. Come all over me."

On a cry that I'm sure everyone in downtown Seattle can hear, she comes hard, and I feel the way she drowns my dick, tipping me right over the edge with her.

"I'm coming too."

Continuing to rock over me, she makes sure I'm fully finished as I shudder beneath her, digging my fingertips into her soft flesh.

Pieces of her hair stick to her slick forehead as I roll us over and hover above her, my cock still deep inside.

With a gentle kiss to her forehead, I rest mine against hers, our erratic breaths mingling. "I love you."

"I know you do," she says, running a hand through my messy hair.

Tipping my chin up with her finger, she asks me for the eye contact she knows I'm struggling to give right now, as my mind is racing with confusing emotions. "Always."

The eighteen-year-old Mia, sitting on the hood of my car and asking for the same thing, flashes in front of me. Except this time, it's not a question.

With every goddamn ounce of me, I want to say it back. I want to promise her my always. I want to promise her I can hold it together.

I swallow thickly as she watches me fight a battle with myself.

"It's okay, Jessie. I'm not asking this time. I'm telling you. You came back to me, you fell in love with me, and I fell right after you. It's okay to trust me when I say it's forever."

CHAPTER FORTY-TWO

JESSIE

> **JENSEN**
> You home?

> **ME**
> Yeah. Why?

> Because I've been standing outside your door for the past five minutes. I know it's not for another six months, but I'm buying you a smart doorbell for your birthday.

Dropping my rope over the weight bench, I grab my shirt, throw it on, and make my way to the front door.

When I pull it open, Jensen wastes no time stepping inside and taking a look around before his eyes land on me. "You can tell a girl lives here now."

I cross my arms over my chest. "Why?"

Striding over to the kitchen in his post-practice gear, he pulls open the fridge and fetches out a Gatorade. Twisting the cap, he takes a mouthful and holds the bottle in one hand. "Because it's tidy."

I take a seat on a stool at the island, lifting up the bottom of my shirt and wiping the sweat from my forehead. "Did you need me for something?"

He stands opposite me, bracing his hands on the counter. "We don't want to crowd you, man, so I said I'd come alone. It's been a few days since ... everything happened, and I wanted to check in. Mia said you've been hiding in the gym for most of it."

I sit back in my seat, and my arms instinctively fold across my chest again. My mind casts back to this morning, in bed with Mia, knowing I need to be strong for her and for us. I can't keep hiding in my apartment, where the darker thoughts get louder in the silence.

"I'm coming back to the ice tomorrow."

"Are you okay to do that? I mean, with everything that happened."

The agitation that's been simmering inside me since my dad got released on bail, pending an investigation, builds. I know my friends are only trying to look out for me, but honestly, they know nothing about what I've been through. What they see is a guy who lost his addict mom in a tragic accident on the stairs and a dad who's being questioned about his assault on Mia, along with his story of why it took so long to call nine-one-one. He said he was out at the time and came home to find her in that state.

Fucking liar.

My heart pounds wildly into my throat as I draw in a deep breath and hold it for four.

Jensen doesn't say a word, but stays in exactly the same place, waiting for me to speak.

I drop my head and squeeze my eyes shut, knowing I'm anything but okay. I'm powerless to hold in my emotions, and they spill over. "I'm a piece of shit who should've tried harder to save her."

"It wasn't your fault, Jessie," he replies. "None of it was."

"Then why does it feel like, other than one part of my life, everything else is fucked?"

"Mia?"

"Yeah. Why is she still here? With me? With the guy who couldn't protect his own mom? What does that say about me as a person? I chose to fuck off to Seattle and run away from my problems. I chose the easy route while she rotted away. She had so much alcohol in her system when she died that the medics aren't even sure she was fully conscious before she fell. What sort of *person* lets their own fucking mother get in that state? Huh?!" My hand flies to my chest as I beat against my sternum. "I'll tell you who, Jensen. An oxygen thief. Just like he said I was. Just like I've always been."

"Jessie, I—" He rounds the island and throws an arm over my shoulder.

"All I'm good for is being on the ice. But you know what?" I unhook his arm and stand up, walking over to my balcony, my arm outstretched as I point to the outside world. The word vomit spills out of me, and my secrets unravel under the weight of my knowing I'm on the verge of losing it all, maybe even my mind. "I'm sick of this shit. Sick of pretending to be some great guy who doesn't want to drink himself into the fucking oblivion every second of every goddamn day. Because I do. All I want is to pick up a bottle and drink until it doesn't matter anymore. Until my face feels so numb that it's impossible for my brain to process anything. *That's* the relief I need."

He takes a couple of cautious steps toward me. "Jessie—"

I cut him off. "No one really knows what happened. You know why? Because I can't remember. My brain can't remember! Moments, memories, beatings from my dad—they're in there somewhere." I bang my inner wrist hard against my temple. "All that goes on in here is sadness, overwhelming fucking pain. I've told Mia all I can remember, but the rest … the rest died with my mom. My brother had died because I was stronger than him, and my mom died because I was too selfish to put her over my shoulder and march her out of that godforsaken house."

I crouch down onto the balls of my feet, the self-hatred spiraling to uncontrollable levels. The red mist descending.

"If it wasn't for your wife, I wouldn't have saved my girl. I wouldn't have even known she was with him. I was too busy in my own head, dealing with my bullshit excuse for a life, while another part had my heart pinned against a wall."

Jensen walks over to my couch and takes a seat, resting his elbows on his knees as he looks at me. "How long have you been having these thoughts, buddy?"

I tip my head up to the ceiling and smile. "It's probably easier to ask me when I haven't."

He scrubs a hand over his jaw, his eyebrows raised in shock at the realization of the depth of my struggles. Maybe surprised at the effective way I've hidden everything from him and the rest of the boys for all these years.

"All right. When is it not so bad? The drinking, the thoughts?"

I look over into the kitchen, Mia's coffee cup rinsed and overturned on the drainer. The last time I saw her was when she left for college before I got up. "When she's near me. When I'm anywhere in her proximity, but mostly when she looks at me. I've never had anyone look at me like that before."

"Like what?"

I stare at him. "Like I might actually count for something. Like if I break, then they'll break too. She practically told me this morning that she's in it with me, no matter what, that we're unconditional. And you know why it'll be my fault when I inevitably drag her underneath with me?"

"You won't, buddy."

"Because I can't keep away from her. I couldn't help myself when I went to her in the college library, hoping to catch a glimpse of the girl who was so far out of my goddamn league that

I wasn't even playing in the same universe! I couldn't even keep my hands off her in bed this morning."

Silence.

"Graham was right the first time." I shake my head. "I just couldn't leave well enough alone—because I am my dad. He steals oxygen with his fists." My hands come to the top of my head. "I just suck the life right out of people."

"Mia is happy with you."

"Is she?" I look up at him, dropping my hands from my head. "Because she still had the red marks around her throat when she left this morning. She thought I didn't notice when she stood in front of the mirror and covered them with concealer. How much more is she hiding, Jensen? What bruises is she keeping from me because she doesn't want me to see? How many times does she cry in silence? I'm the one who's supposed to protect her!"

"Mia's okay, Jessie. She told Kate she's doing okay. She's spoken to a therapist; she's working through it all. You both protect and support each other." He points to a picture of us taken in Riley's Bar. Tara snuck the photo of us kissing and gave it to Mia, who framed it and put it on a bookcase.

I stare at the photo—my hand's wrapped around the nape of her neck, pulling her into me.

"Every time I touch her, I feel like I have no right. Every time I wrap my body around hers, it feels like she'll evaporate right there in front of me. Because she can't be real."

"You deserve her, buddy," Jensen argues.

"And do you know what makes all of this especially fucked up?"

He stays quiet, letting me get everything out.

"Now, she's gone—my mom. I'm free. Free to cut ties with every part of my past, apart from my brother and the couple of memories I have of her when she was sober. When I walked into that hospital, they told me she'd already passed. I felt relief. For me." My nose and eyes sting with emotion. "What kind of person does that make me, Jensen?"

My emotion reflects back in his eyes as he looks over at me and smiles. "It makes you human, Jessie. I told Kate once that nothing her parents had done to her had any bearing on who she was as a person. That they were the fucked-up ones, not her."

"But I am fucked up. I'm broken."

"So, that's it, is it? You're going to push Mia away for a *second* time because you're worried that you're going the way your mom did? Is that what this is about? Because that sounds every bit like your dad winning."

I nod, knowing he's right. "Last year, the team psych, Ashley, diagnosed me with complex PTSD. She wanted me to start a course of treatment that would help me process what had happened to me. The memories I can't remember. Only once the gaps have been filled can my mind file them away."

"Did you take it?"

I scratch at my chin. "Not really. One or two sessions maybe, and then I backed out. It just made me feel worse. Then, around the time Mia moved to Seattle, I agreed with Coach to go back into therapy. But then my game started improving, I got my drinking under control, and I figured I didn't need it anymore. Maybe Coach did too."

Jensen takes a second to work through everything I told him before he speaks. "I think maybe you do. I'm not an expert, but I think you need to make peace with not just your past, but yourself. I don't need to know the details of what happened to you, Jessie. I've read between the lines of the small snippets you've offered me over the years to know you deserve every good person in your life. I'd also hazard a guess that your mom would think that too."

"I don't know if I have it in me. To walk through the memories. I'm scared, Jensen."

Rising from the couch, he disappears down my hallway, reappearing with something black in his hand.

When he hands me the puck from the great game I played against Colorado earlier this season, I take it from him and turn it around in my hands. He knows I keep game memorabilia on a shelf in my gym.

Crouching beside me, he reaches across and taps his finger over my heart. He's seen my tattoos before, but never once asked me about them, instinctively knowing they were likely to do with my past and respecting the privacy I obviously needed at the time.

"I don't think I've ever met another person like you, Jessie, and I don't think I ever will. On or off the ice. You're a warrior, and I'm honored to walk alongside you. To call you my friend. I'm even more honored that you shared everything you just did with me—I know how much courage that took. But know that this day, right now, marks the start of your healing."

He bites on his bottom lip and exhales slowly. "At twenty-six, you've lived a life where most people would have faltered. How many times have you gotten back up, man? Off the floor, off the ice. How many times have you shared your problems with the bottom of a bottle, but still, you got back up? I wanted to know more about your battles but respected the fact that you weren't ready to tell me. But now, you have. You've shared the strain, so let me take some of that weight, brother."

He stands and wraps his hand around my forearm, pulling me to my feet with him. "You want to take to the ice with us tomorrow? Then, this time, you do it, knowing we have your back. Your girl has your back and your whole fucking heart too. You aren't going anywhere, and you know it. You aren't going to let her or yourself down either. You're way too gone for her. You've come too far together. So, this time, when you rise up, you won't fall back down. Because this time, you have us."

CHAPTER FORTY-THREE

JESSIE

I've stepped out onto the ice more times than I can count.
To be honest, at this point, I'm not sure which my body feels more at ease with—the ice or a regular walking surface.

Graham Jenkins picked me up as a young kid and gave me a chance to play the game I loved. But it was my papa who first introduced me to the ice, taking me to the local rink one Saturday morning.

Despite being a huge fan, he never got a chance to go to a Destroyers game because he didn't have the money for tickets. When they got first pick and drafted me, that was my only wish at the time. I wished he'd still been here to see me sign the contract he had been convinced I'd secure one day.

Dad always said he was a dreamer, a factory worker with visions of grandeur that did no one any good. Before I was earning big money and lining his pockets, he said I'd be better off ditching hockey and living in the real world. People like us didn't make a name for ourselves.

Papa died when I was ten, but he did get to see me enter

Graham's program, and I'll never forget his face when I told him Graham had contacted my school, asking about me.

That was the thing about my papa and the reason why he bucked the trend when it came to my family. His tears of joy weren't for anyone but me. He knew I was destined for greatness, and he told me that every damn day.

He also told me the second I played for the headlines, the fame, the money, or for anyone else, then it was over.

I had to play for me.

Every game was just like in the little leagues.

Every time I laced up my skates, it was to pursue my dreams and no one else's.

Somewhere along the way, I lost my papa's voice. Initially, I thought it was because my love for the game had disappeared, and I was left doing exactly what he'd pleaded with me never to do—to play for someone or something other than me.

But now, I know my love for hockey never disappeared; it was just buried beneath the weight of trauma, unrecognizable as I searched for self-validation and a reason to feel worthy. I was trying to score goals for all the wrong reasons.

When my first blade hits the fresh ice before I kit up for regular morning practice, the feeling I get is anything but normal.

Finally, I can hear myself. I can hear my skates as they cut through the ice.

I feel lighter—and not just because I've gone weeks without touching a drop of alcohol.

For the first time since I can remember, I'm doing this for myself. For the love of the game. I can hear my papa because he isn't being drowned out by the goddamn bullshit noise in my head.

The ice is empty since I got here before my teammates.

When Mia asked me why I was leaving so soon, I told her I needed to get ahead of the others and be alone with the ice for a while. She didn't question it; she just smiled and kissed me goodbye.

Without giving it much thought, I head over and pick up a stack of red cones set out on the side, ready for practice.

Skating around the ice, I arrange them in the formation I know Coach Burrows has planned. Red cones are reserved only for sprint and agility tests.

I wait for the fear of failure to take hold and tell me I can't do this. I wait for the excuses to come barreling toward me as I finish laying them out along the ice.

Except I don't feel any of those things when I pull up at the center line and close my eyes. When I draw in a deep breath, all I can smell is the freezing ice beneath me. All I can feel is my heart as it beats in a regular pattern. All I can hear are my own welcome thoughts. And all I can see is Mia as she lay beneath me this morning, her cheeks matching the color of her rosy lips as I pushed inside her and took us both to the brink of ecstasy.

When I hit the first corner, I don't overthink or analyze my weight distribution. I'm on autopilot, my body powered by my unhindered mind.

The freezing air whips past my face as I take the second corner.

It's this part right here, halfway around, when I usually slow up. The adrenaline working against me as I convince myself there's no way I made the time. I don't deserve to make a good time.

But my brain doesn't even go there.

Because this lap is for *me*.

As I cross the line and hit the brakes, I throw my head back and stare at the bright lights overhead, my hands propped on my hips as I take in oxygen.

"Fuck, that one was fast," I whisper into the silent arena.

"I'd say your fastest yet, kid."

My head follows the sound of the voice until I land on Graham, sitting on the away team bench.

I don't say anything, unsure if this entire thing is just a hallucination. I approach him and lean my forearms over the boards.

With his face hidden underneath an orange-and-black Destroyers cap, he holds the stopwatch in his left hand. The time reading thirteen seconds flat.

He still hasn't looked up at me, continuing to stare down at the watch.

"There wouldn't be a roof left on this arena if you'd just pulled that off in the All-Star game."

I rest my elbows on top of the boards and pull down on my black beanie.

That's when he looks at me. I'd say properly looks at me for the first time in years.

"What are you doing here?" I ask.

He wipes a hand over his mouth and nods across to the other side of the rink. I turn around and see Coach Burrows standing at the entrance to the ice, watching us, his hands in the pockets of his pants.

"I wanted to speak to you alone. Mia told me you'd be here, and Mike let me in. I've been sitting here for at least five minutes." Reaching into his pocket, he takes out his phone and snaps a picture of the time displayed on the retro stopwatch. "Don't ask me why I still carry this around with me when I could just use my phone." He shrugs. "Old habits die hard, I guess."

"You came here to talk to me?"

He nods once, rising from the bench. "Always liked this rink. It was one of the few away games I enjoyed. Being away from my family was hard, but coming here was somehow—I dunno—comforting."

I don't say anything as I watch him take in his surroundings.

"You were right, Jessie. I did fail you."

I drop my gaze toward the ice. That morning in the Destroyers boardroom crashes forward from where I buried it deep in my brain.

"You ..." I begin but then stop. Unable to lie and tell him he didn't.

"I should've asked myself more questions about your state of mind and living arrangements. I should've asked myself why you needed more support when your papa passed away. I should've concentrated more on what was behind the boy standing in front of me and not the player I desperately wanted to see."

Noise filters in from behind us, and Graham's eyes flick toward where my teammates' voices come from.

"I can't turn back the clock and protect you from what he did and what you went through. Neither can I offer you the family and safety you needed back then. It's too late for that."

He holds out the stopwatch, the time still written across the small screen. "If one of my players recorded a time like that, I'd tell them their future in this game was fucking bright, provided they could keep their head in it."

Taking the watch from him, I don't move my eyes from his.

"I think it's going to take a while for my daughter to forgive me for the way I treated you." He huffs out a laugh. "She's turned into one hell of a woman."

"I love her."

"I know. I know," he breathes out. "And I don't know if you'll ever find it in yourself to forgive me for what I said, what I did ..."

The moment I open my mouth, he holds up a hand, asking me to let him finish.

So, I do.

"I want you to know that I see it now. My daughter's future. I thought I did, and I thought I had it all laid out for her. I thought what I had planned for her was what she wanted, what she needed. I couldn't have been any more off track. What she wants is you."

The stopwatch in my hand blurs, and I quickly swipe the wetness away.

"Your dad is a piece of shit who deserves to do time for what he did to you and your mom. I can't change my past failings, but I can tell you that if, one day, you can find it in yourself to forgive me, then I'd love to be back in your life for all the right reasons."

Words stick in my throat as I roll my lips together, and he claps a hand on my shoulder, squeezing it in his palm.

"At the risk of this sounding condescending, I'm so fucking proud of you, Jessie, and I want to offer you whatever help you need to process and deal with what you've been through. Even if it's just an ear." He looks over my shoulder as my teammates take the ice behind me. "Something tells me you've got plenty of those though."

Tipping my head over my shoulder, I catch a glimpse of Jensen leaning against the boards on the other side of the ice, watching us intensely as he takes a drink from his bottle.

"I do," I say, turning back to Graham. "But I could always use one more."

Something like relief crosses his face. "You've been through a lot."

I pocket the watch in my sweatpants and tap my knuckles on the boards. "There's this form of therapy I've been offered a few times. It's a lot, and takes it out of people as they revisit some of the worst moments in their past. I'll be the first to admit it scares the shit out of me. But this time, I want to do it. I don't want to go for hockey or my career. I want to go for me ..." I pause and take a deep breath. "I want Mia to be my wife and give her more than just tomorrow or next fucking week. To do that, I think I need to take my psych's recommendation. I know the trauma will be there forever, and I'll never be able to turn back the clock for my mom. But I want to try to be everything your daughter deserves."

He shakes his head. "You already are that, Jessie."

"I want to get to a point where I'm waiting for our children to be born, not for the next chance to open a bottle. Instead of drowning my emotions, I want to embrace them. Good and bad."

I reach out my hand, and he takes it in his and then wraps his other palm around it.

"I get it, Jessie. I get it."

I stare into his green eyes, and for the first time since his wife died, I see the warmth of his daughter in them.

"Here's the thing, Graham. When I promise Mia forever, I want to fucking mean it."

CHAPTER FORTY-FOUR

MIA

I can't claim I'm not like the other girls and that shopping doesn't do anything for me because it does.

But grocery shopping? That can go to hell.

I would literally order takeout every night just to avoid going to the store if I thought my waistline could take it.

And the absolute worst part of it all? Hauling the bags you just paid way too much for, thanks to inflation, from your car and into your apartment and then throwing out the food you bought the last time you were on a health kick and replacing it with a fresher version.

The only redeeming part of this entire thing? Half the ingredients that are now sitting in our refrigerator, I'll be using them tonight to cook beef tacos for Jessie when he gets home from a four-night away series in Boston.

Kate, Felicity, and Luna weren't kidding when they said the days they were on the road felt way longer than a regular twenty-four hours.

With an iced latte in hand, I take a seat at the kitchen island and bring up the method for tonight's meal on my phone.

I might be a terrible cook, but I'm determined to do something nice for my boyfriend, especially since he's always the one making dinner for us.

I'm halfway through learning about homemade guacamole when my phone buzzes in my hand.

JESSIE
Where's my girl at?

I catch myself smiling down at my screen.

ME
Nursing an iced latte at the kitchen island. Also—and I'm not ashamed to admit it—I'm clock-watching.

JESSIE
Me too.

The clock-watching bit, not the iced latte. Fucking gross.

It's got a caramel shot in it too.

I love my girlfriend, I love my girlfriend, I love my girlfriend.

I was actually busy arranging a surprise for you before you rudely interrupted me. How can I help you?

Oh, yeah? Clue?

Ummm ... you can eat it.

Baby, we're still an hour away from landing, and now all I can think about is you sitting on my face. Play fair.

I burst out laughing and quickly type a response, crossing my legs under the counter.

ME

> Not sure my pussy is a surprise for you anymore.

JESSIE

It is when I still can't process the fact that you're mine and I get to be your man.

Only Jessie Callaghan—drop-dead gorgeous NHL superstar forward and current lead goal scorer, who could get any girl he wanted—could think he wasn't enough for me. I don't care how many times I have to say it, even if I'm repeating the words on my last breath; he will one day believe that he's everything to me.

ME

> Well, best start believing it. When will you be home? It's only, like, ten a.m. here. You're way earlier than expected.

JESSIE

Yeah, the guys voted on getting home ASAP since three-quarters of the team have families now. Actually, can you do something for me?

> Yeah, sure.

Meet me downstairs in the lobby in, like, two hours?

> You're making me suspicious, Callaghan. What are you planning?

Let's just say, it's something I've been wanting to do with you for a while.

> That's literally all I'm getting, isn't it? Also, I was planning a surprise for you tonight.

> There are so many ways I could reply to this message, but I'm sitting next to this really fucking annoying goalie who won't stop reading over my shoulder. So, all I'll say is, yep, that's all you're getting ... for now.
>
> P.S. Will be home in time for your surprise.

> Hi, Jensen.

> Don't encourage him, Sweetheart.

WHEN THE ELEVATOR doors open to the lobby, I see my boyfriend standing on the other side in all his navy-dress-pants-and-white-shirt glory.

A smile tugs at his lips when he sees me. "Hey, Mia."

Not giving a fuck, I launch myself at him, wrapping my arms around his neck and burying my face into his chest.

"What are you doing?" He laughs as I inhale him.

"Your smell on the pillows was wearing off. So, I'm getting my fix."

When he tips my chin up to look at him, I rise onto my tiptoes as a few people move around us to enter the elevator.

"Well, we need to remedy that, don't we?" He brings his lips down against mine, swiping his tongue across my lower lip. "Yeah, I'm going to need to stop actually." He pulls away slightly and takes a look around.

"Why?" I say, trying to work out who he's seen. "We don't need to hide anymore, remember?"

He looks down between us, and that's when I see it—the tent forming in his pants.

A giggle bubbles out of me.

"Oh, you think this is funny, do you?" he mocks. "Robbing your man of all his dignity out in public?"

I shake my head and inconspicuously brush the back of my hand over his dick. "I'm really sorry."

He closes his eyes and drops his forehead against mine, his hair tumbling forward. "Yeah, you sound really regretful. Let's get out of here before I abandon this idea altogether and take you back upstairs." He scans what I'm wearing. "You knew what you were doing when you wore my favorite black skirt, didn't you?"

I shrug and bite down on my bottom lip, pleased my outfit hasn't gone unnoticed. "Where are your bags?" I ask. "You came straight from the airport, right?"

Jessie tips his head over his shoulder. "Yep. The concierge is looking after them for me. We need to get going."

He wraps his little finger around mine, smiling down at me. I can tell he wants to kiss me again, and, God, do I want him to.

"Let's go. There's a car waiting outside for us."

With our fingers still joined, he leads me through the double glass doors and out into the fresh spring air.

Climbing into the back of an executive SUV, I look across at Jessie as the driver takes off without any instruction.

"Where are we going?"

He retakes my hand across the back seat, a satisfied grin spreading across his face. "You'll see."

As I playfully narrow my eyes at him, I don't say anything; instead, I observe the lightness in his face.

In the past week, even though he's been on the road for most of it, I've caught glimpses of the real Jessie Callaghan. The version of him that was buried alive with fear and pressure. He spent every day being crushed under the weight of anticipation, worrying about everyone but himself.

I still see heaviness there. Guilt over his mom and that he couldn't save her. I know he blames himself not only for her death, but also for the way he's feeling right now. Relieved. Knowing that her passing gives him an opportunity to break free from the shackles her addiction locked him in. Sometimes, I catch him staring at the picture of them sitting on the couch when he was a baby. The morning before he left for Boston, I know I heard him talking to her when he was in the bathroom. That was the same morning he found out Wayne didn't want to hold a funeral for her, claiming it wasn't Alice's wish.

I don't believe him, and neither does Jessie.

My heart breaks for him that he won't get a chance to say goodbye properly. If there's one thing the grieving mind needs, it's closure.

When I squeeze his hand a little, he turns his head from where he was gazing out of the passenger window to look at me.

"When I moved to Seattle, it's true that I needed the money, but do you know the real reason why I got a job as a florist?"

He shakes his head. "Why?"

Drawing in a breath, I steady myself. I've never shared this with anyone before, not even with Jessie the first time around. "I have more photos of my mom than I know what to do with. Album after album of me growing up in her arms. I've spent a lot of time flicking through those pages, trying and hoping to feel her arms wrap around me again. To feel that comfort only she could bring me as a child, you know?"

He swallows thickly, his eyes shining in the bright sunlight filtering through the windows.

"Then, one day, I was walking through town. It had been a really shit week."

I clear my throat and push down the lump forming there. "I really missed my mom, but that day especially, I needed her. I needed to feel the safety of her arms. Everything felt like it was spiraling—my emotions, my thoughts, I was even struggling to imagine her voice anymore."

Jessie squeezes my hand back, but doesn't say anything, just letting me know he feels everything I'm saying.

"I knew what was happening—that I was struggling with depression. But it wasn't like I could really go to my dad since he was even worse off. I'd wake up to faint noises of him crying from his room and go to sleep to the same sounds. In that moment, I felt like I'd lost both my parents, and as an only child, it felt like my world was pretty dark all of a sudden. I'd gone from worrying about the length of my school skirt to wondering whether my dad was potentially suicidal."

Jessie wraps his hand around the back of my head, leaning across and burying his face into the crook of my neck. "Sweetheart, I'm so fucking sorry. And then I went and broke your heart all over again."

"It's okay," I whisper. "I'm not telling you this to make you feel guilty. I get why you had to do what you did."

On another deep breath, I continue, "That was when I walked past this florist. It wasn't new or anything. I'd just never really paid attention to it before. It was the smell of the freesias they had on display that had me stopping in my tracks. I guess you could describe them as a warm hug in the fall. When I picked up a bunch and smelled them, I just remember feeling grounded, and that's when it came to me—she used to keep them in a vase on our dining table. They were her favorite flowers, and Dad used to buy them for her. So, I did. I bought a bunch and took them home with me."

I blow out a soft, tearful laugh. "It's amazing what five stems of flowers can do—because they filled the room with my mom. When my dad got home that night, he dropped his bag at his feet by the door. At first, I thought maybe I'd made things worse for him. But when he saw them sitting there in the center of the table, he smiled. The same smile he reserved just for Mom."

Holding my chin between his thumb and forefinger, Jessie brushes his lips over mine. "You know, each time I look at you, I convince myself there's no way you could get any more beautiful. You can though, can't you? Because your beauty is coded not just into your body, but every part of your soul, Mia."

I sigh into his touch. I know I'll never take the way he makes me feel for granted. "Is there maybe something that would help you feel connected with your mom?"

When he drops his eyes, a pang of despair hits me, as I'm reminded about how different our childhoods looked.

"Ginger. Whenever I smell ginger, I think of Mom," he whispers. "It makes me think of Will too. She told me that when she was pregnant with us, she used to eat it to settle her nausea. When she lost Will, other than the booze, she'd comfort-eat ginger biscuits. She still did right up until the day she passed. I guess the smell of them is warm and comforting, you know? When I was a kid, I used to sneak a couple when I could, and sometimes, she'd break one in half and share it with me. Whenever I smell ginger, it takes me somewhere. Reminds me that Will was here once and maybe now my mom too."

I kiss him, and then the driver takes a sharp left, bringing us back to reality and reminding me that Jessie was taking me somewhere.

"We're nearly here," he says, looking past me and out of my passenger window.

In the time we've spent talking, I didn't notice we'd driven out of town and into rural surroundings.

"Where are we going?" I ask once more, trying to get him to break.

"You want to know right now? We're only, like, a minute away."

"Yes. I'm impatient." I groan.

He chuckles and sits back in his seat, our hands still clasped together between us. "Hawthorne Hills."

My brows furrow. "That means nothing to me."

"It's a quiet town with great views." He turns to look at me. "Close to your university too."

My heart leaps in my chest. "W-why would that matter?"

Right as the question leaves my mouth, our driver turns onto a private driveway.

Rolling down his window, he speaks into an intercom. "Hi. Mr. and Mrs. Callaghan are here to view the property."

I choke on my own breath as it leaves my lungs in a whoosh, and Jessie throws his head back, chuckling.

As the gates open, he turns to look at me, his head still resting against his seat. "Just as I thought."

"Thought what?"

He smiles brightly. "I told the driver we were married—which was risky for the rumor mill, I know, but I couldn't help it. I needed to know what it would feel like to hear you take my name."

A giddy smile pulls at my lips. "And?"

He shrugs and dips a hand into his pocket, pulling out a set of keys and dangling them between us, and I look up and take in the big white house with double doors and a glamorous porch.

"Just like this house that I want to buy for us. Fucking perfect."

CHAPTER FORTY-FIVE

MIA

"So, how did you like the house?" Kate asks as she pushes the front seat forward.

"It was actually amazing—like, absolutely perfect for us," I croon and climb out of Felicity's Mini, knocking my head on the roof as I go.

I look back at the tiny car and then across at Felicity as she shuts the driver's door.

"What?" she asks, pressing her fob and locking the car.

I look over at Kate as she smirks back at me. "I just see now what Kate was saying and why Luna didn't get a ride with us."

"Mmhmm," Kate hums from beside me, pointing at Felicity's car. "It's hard enough, getting in Martha when you aren't carrying another human—or two."

Felicity props her hands on her hips and sighs. Looking down at the green Mini, she mentions that Jon has tried to trade it on more than one occasion. "Yeah, to be honest, it might be time to say goodbye to the old girl." She reaches out and rubs a hand over the roof.

Kate looks like she's been shot as she shoots backward in the parking lot to the boutique we just pulled up in. "Sorry, come again? You want to get rid of her?"

Felicity eyes her best friend. "Would it be a problem if I traded?"

Kate hooks her bag onto her shoulder, flicking her blonde hair back over her shoulder. "I mean, no. I guess it would be the end of an era, but ... I'm just shocked, is all." She tries to sound unaffected, but the sadness in Kate's tone is unmistakable.

Jessie has told me all about Martha and that Felicity brought her over from England when she moved to Seattle several years back. According to my boyfriend, everyone, especially Jon, pretends like Martha is a ridiculous choice of car for a busy US city and the biggest inconvenience, but really, she symbolizes their friend group.

Clearly Felicity is all-too aware of this as a smile breaks out on her face, and she turns and walks off in the direction of the boutique. A sense of triumph in her step.

Tipping her head over her shoulder, she dangles the keys from her fingers, swinging them merrily. "My husband was delighted when I told him I'd decided to trade Martha in for a new car. He even booked us an appointment at Range Rover for the day after tomorrow." She pauses as her smile turns kind of evil-looking. "I just need to find the right time to tell him that I have, in fact, ordered another Mini."

"WHAT?!" Kate shouts, laughter breaking free.

"But!" Felicity announces. "I have decided to go slightly more practical, which I know will please him. I'm getting a convertible. Perfectly practical for the upcoming summer months. It's also perfect timing since it will be arriving on my driveway in around" —she looks down and checks her watch—"oh, two hours."

My hand flics to my mouth. "Nooooo! Jon will go nuts!"

"Whoa, whoa." Kate points at Martha with a look of relief. "I thought you said you traded her?"

Her best friend shrugs. "Meh, minor detail. I *planned* to, but when it came down to it, I just didn't have it in me. My daughter can use it when she comes over to visit, which is getting more frequent."

"Oh, Darcy will love that, she's wanted Martha for ages." Laughing hard, Kate loops her arm through Felicity's, and they giggle like a pair of witches plotting their next move.

"Hey," Kate shouts over her shoulder as I catch up to them, striding across the parking lot. "Where's my other girl?"

Propping her other hand on her hip, she holds her arm away from her side. "Bring it in," she says, and I loop my arm through as our trio makes for the bridal store.

"Okay, where is the blushing bride?" Felicity announces as we step into the all-white store.

Bright crystal chandeliers fill the long space above us with two rows of dresses lining the length of the room.

The assistant steps out from one of the dressing rooms, a measuring tape hanging around her neck. She smiles at us and moves to one side.

"I couldn't wait, so I started," Luna announces from behind the curtain.

"We aren't even late," Kate replies, taking a glass of champagne from a tray another assistant holds out to each of us in turn.

Felicity waves off the drink. "I'm driving, thank you." She picks up one of the glasses and passes it to me, smiling. "Here you go, babe. Have one for me."

I take a sip, and the bubbles dance on my tongue, warming me as I swallow them down.

"I know; I know," Luna says. "But it's just so damn pretty. I got here, like, a half hour early, and I couldn't wait. It's been an entire three weeks since I last tried it on. Then I came in after work twice this week just to stare at it. I think I have a problem."

Kate looks at one of the assistants, and she rolls her lips

together in response, her amused look confirming that Luna isn't lying.

"So, how many times have you tried this dress on now?" Felicity asks.

"Ummm ... only a couple. I just look at it mainly. But I wanted you all to see me in it before I commit to it fully."

"I'd say it's the one, babe," Kate replies.

"But you haven't seen it yet."

Kate shakes her head even though Luna can't see. "Doesn't matter what we think. It's all about how it makes you feel. I'm just here for the bubbles."

"Same," Felicity agrees.

"Me too," I pipe up, taking another sip.

The fizz nearly leaves my mouth as I fight to keep it from spraying across the room when another assistant pulls back the curtain, revealing Luna in a Grecian-style ivory dress.

"Christ on a freaking cracker," Felicity announces, sinking into the plush white couch behind her.

Pink rises on Luna's fair complexion, staining her cheeks. "What do you think?" She looks around at the three of us, all motionless.

Kate moves first, setting her champagne glass down on a table. Walking across to Luna, she steps up onto the platform her friend is standing on and takes both of her hands in hers.

Luna's dress is long and flowy with a thin white band that sits just below her breasts; the flawless material cascades over her baby bump and falls all the way to the floor, where it pools around her feet. The deep V neckline features the only detail on the dress, crystals lining either side of the V, leading all the way up to the thin white straps that tie around her neck.

She looks like a true goddess.

"You know how I said that it doesn't matter what we think?" Kate says to Luna.

In response, she nods. "It's how I feel?"

Releasing one of Luna's hands, Kate swipes under her left

eye. "Well, I take that back. Because you absolutely need to know that I have never ever seen a more beautiful bride in my entire life."

Luna throws her arms around Kate's neck. Her auburn hair falling over her shoulders.

"What do you think, Felicity?" she asks.

Felicity cocks her head to the side in a way that reminds me of the first time I met her in Riley's Bar as her green eyes shine bright. "Tell me, do they have good health care in Barbados?"

I turn to look at her, completely confused.

"I mean, I think so," Luna answers. "Zach has researched the shit out of it just in case I go into labor, like, two months early."

Felicity nods. "Well, let's just say, it won't be you needing the medical treatment because he will be in full cardiac arrest when he sees you in that. And I can absolutely see why you've been stalking it these past few weeks."

Smiling at Felicity, Luna then looks at me. "What do you think, Mia?"

I continue to stand there, transfixed by her beauty. "I think there's a fair chance Felicity is right. Stunning. Absolutely stunning."

JESSIE

"So many memories in these four walls," Kate says as the girls enter our favorite Italian restaurant, Luigi's.

She takes a seat next to Jensen. He plants his arm behind her and leans across to kiss her on the cheek.

"I think a personal highlight has to be you breaking the pregnancy news here," Felicity adds, sitting next to Jon.

Kate winces. "Oh my God. The sheer panic I was in."

"Why?" Jensen laughs.

Side-eyeing her husband, she points over to the table where I assume they were sitting. "I'd found out a couple of days before, and I was convinced when I told you, you'd run for the hills."

Jensen brings his lips to Kate's cheek again, and this time, he runs a hand across her stomach. "And what actually happened, Princess?"

Although she tries hard to hide it, it's obvious she's flustered. Turning to him, she smiles coyly. "The opposite happened."

He runs his hand over her stomach one more time as the noise in the restaurant cranks up, and I can barely hear what they're saying, but I swear he mouths, *Just let me know when.*

Mia comes to sit beside me, and I lean across and kiss her on the side of her neck.

She looks around at everyone, taking in the huge table we always book when we come here. "You have a lot of friends, Jessie."

Tonight, there are even more of us.

Jack takes the remaining seat next to his mom. He pulls off his college team cap and shakes out his brown hair before grabbing a menu. "Did we order yet?" he asks as conversations continue around the table. "After that practice, I'm going for one of everything."

When I catch sight of Zach palming Luna's stomach, a flush of something that feels like permanence shoots through me.

Family.

I turn back to Mia, who's scanning the menu. "Yeah, I guess I do have a lot of friends." Underneath the table, I rest my hand on Mia's upper right thigh. "They're your friends now too, Sweetheart."

I'm busy gazing at my girlfriend as she chooses her entrée when Kate picks up her empty wineglass and stands, tapping her fork against it lightly.

"Okay, okay. I know we all came here to eat, but first, Luna has a special announcement."

In response, Luna's cheeks turn the color of her hair as she glares at Kate and then looks around the restaurant to check who's watching.

She takes a sip of water, clearing her throat. "So ... I found the one!"

Zach brings his fiancée in for a kiss. "Tell me, what is it like?"

"It's big and white," Jack interjects, earning an eye roll from Felicity. "She can't reveal that, bro," he finishes.

"Jack's right; I can't give you any details about my dress. It's bad luck." Luna agrees.

"Just know this, Zachary: you are going to lose your shit," Kate confirms, crunching on a breadstick.

"Congrats, Luna," I say, raising my soda. "Only three months to go now, right?"

"One hundred days exactly," Jon chimes in. "I assume everyone has their flights booked?"

Mia's head whips up as she looks at me and mouths, *Flights?*

Squeezing her thigh again under the table, I lean down until my lips touch the shell of her ear. "I booked them last week."

As she closes her menu, she turns her head slightly, and I watch the way the delicate skin on her neck pebbles at my proximity. "Them?"

"Yeah. It's only a few days. You can get some time off work, can't you? College is finished for summer break."

I feel her shift under my touch. "I can. I just didn't want to assume I was invited."

The temptation to tell her that she isn't just invited, that she's actually a bridesmaid alongside Felicity and Kate, is strong. Instead, I keep that secret to myself and give Luna the honor of asking her when she's ready.

"You're definitely invited, Sweetheart."

"Okay," she replies. "How was therapy?"

While the girls were with Luna for a dress fitting, we had a morning skate, and then I had my fourth session on a new course with the team psych, Ashley. In reality, over the years, I've had way more sessions with her, but we agreed that with the new course I'd be taking, we'd take things right back to the beginning. Opening up to her has been as hard as I expected it to be.

"Better," I reply. "I don't have a huge headache, for one."

"When does she think you'll be ready to begin the course of therapy she's recommended?"

Tucking a piece of hair behind her ear, I remind myself that I'm not only doing this for me, but I'm also working through everything for us too. Eye Movement Desensitization and Reprocessing, or EMDR for short, is something Ashley and I are preparing for, but to carry out this course of treatment, it takes some initial groundwork to identify what areas of my memory we want to explore and recall.

"In a week or so. I need a couple more sessions first," I reply.

When she takes my hand in hers under the table and squeezes it, I know whatever my mind unearths over the next few months, I absolutely have my girl by my side.

"Have the owners accepted your offer yet?" Jon asks me across the table, bringing all conversations to an end, including mine and Mia's.

I shake my head and take a sip of soda. "The signed offer was sent to their agent a couple of days ago. Still waiting to hear."

"Oh, it's in the stars, trust me. I'm so excited for you both," Luna squeaks. "I just know in a few months, we'll be all sitting in your yard, having a barbecue, while the kids are in the swimming pool."

"Oh yeah, that reminds me to thank you, babe," Kate replies. "That sitter you recommended?" She gives a chef's kiss. "Perfection. Will and June love her. She's already sent me, like, three videos since we got here."

Luna holds up her phone and plays a video of Aster knocking down a huge tower of building blocks, his laughter ringing out across the table. "Me too," she replies. "We have fantastic sitters."

Pulling out his phone, Jon taps the screen a couple of times.

"Yeah, we can all get live updates of our babies; I have around-the-clock footage of my new Porsche."

It's as if time stands still when his eyes blow wide, his brain catching up to whatever's on his screen.

"What is it?" Zach asks, slightly concerned.

Pointing to his screen, he opens his mouth, but words clearly fail him for once in his life. "Uh ... there's, uh ..."

"There's what, baby?" Felicity asks, her lips shaking with obvious laughter.

His head whips to her as he continues to point at the phone in his hand. "There's a brand-new fucking Mini Hatch in our driveway."

Completely unfazed, Felicity leans across to look at his screen. "Technically, no. It's actually a convertible."

CHAPTER FORTY-SIX

MIA

"I literally cannot believe our freshman year is almost over," Tara says from beside me as we sit, listening to the professor wrap up our late afternoon class.

"I know," I reply. "I have zero idea where the past three months have gone."

Tapping her pen against her notepad, as she always does, she keeps her eyes straight ahead. "Yeah, if I'd spent them mainly beneath an NHL superstar, I guess all my days would blur into one as well." She side-eyes me, pursing her lips together. "They do say time flies when you're having fun."

A couple of rows in front of us, I watch as two girls look behind and at me for the hundredth time in the past hour. They turn back to each other and smirk, clearly saying something, which I'm guessing is about me and probably not a compliment.

"Want me to say something?" Tara asks, her eyes still trained on the professor, but I know she's referring to what I'm looking at.

Since Jessie and I went public with our relationship, I've mainly been left alone by other students. But there's always the few who like to make shit up. The latest rumor is that I'm knocked up and I tampered with my birth control to trap an NHL player.

At what point will women realize that spreading shit about other women only perpetuates negative stereotypes? I mean, so fucking what if I was pregnant? I'm not, but why try to shame me for something that, for one, has absolutely nothing to do with them anyway?

I lean back in my seat and close my notes as the professor gathers a stack of marked assignments, ready for us to collect as we leave class.

My stomach knots in anticipation. I could really do with a high grade on this paper since social psych is exactly the area I want to major in.

I shrug a shoulder. "Nah, it's fine. Haters gonna hate. I don't need to waste my energy on false rumors. Especially when they clearly aren't my girls."

She tilts her head slightly to the side, and I'm surprised when Tara's face fills with emotion.

She swallows thickly. "Listen, I know I don't often say serious things, but I want you to know that I'm so glad we met this year. I've got friends I made before I was out of diapers, but somehow, I feel closer to you. I guess how much time you've known someone doesn't always count for much. It's how they make you feel."

I watch as Leo and Hugh collect their marked assignments from the front. Scanning the paper, Leo throws his head back and squeezes his eyes shut. I'd say that is not the look of a happy student.

Shame.

As Tara goes to get up, I take her by the hand and pull her back into the seat next to me. Keeping ahold of her hand, I wait for a couple of students to clear from behind us.

"A lot of really good people have either come back into my life this year, or I've met them for the first time. You are absolutely one of those people. You are loyal to a fault, and I'm so sorry I questioned you that day."

She smiles and squeezes my hand tighter. "I always got you."

We get up from behind our desks, and I draw in a deep breath as I stare down at the last two papers on the table.

When we take the stairs down to the front, Tara stops in her tracks. "If this grade is terrible, then there's only a month left of the year and one more grading. There's no way I can pin all my hopes to pass on that."

I collect both the papers, Tara's result sits on top, a huge black *B* scrawled across the front.

On a smile, I hand it to her, still not brave enough to look at my own.

When she registers what she scored, she lets out a high-pitched squeak and clutches it to her chest. "This is absolutely thanks to your late-night library sessions!"

Gritting my teeth, I fold my paper in half and go to put it in my bag, but at the last second, Tara snatches it from me.

"Don't you dare! I want to share in your victory."

"Ugh, it's going to be bad, isn't it?" My hands fly to cover my face as she slowly opens it up. "Actually, no, don't tell me."

"Hmm, you sure about that?" she asks.

"Yep. Absolutely positive."

"Well, that's a shame since you smashed the absolute shit out of it."

When I pull my hands away from my eyes, the big *A* greets me with a note from the professor congratulating me on one of the most comprehensive accounts and understanding of environmental factors and how the behaviors of others could have an effect on the mind, both short- and long-term, especially at a young age.

Tears well in my eyes as I stare at the grade and note.

"You okay, babe?" Tara asks.

"Yeah," I say, thoughts of Jessie, my mom, and the impact they've both had on my life rushing forward.

"Okay," Tara says, handing me the paper. "Well, I say that's enough tears for today. I'm not working tonight, so how about we head to the bar to celebrate?"

I nod and take one last glance at my paper before putting it in my bag. "Yeah, sounds perfect."

"Okay, well, mocktails are better than I initially gave them credit for," Tara says as we push through the door and out into the early April night. "When you told me you were driving and couldn't drink, I was kind of disappointed, but to be honest, I'm now grateful," she explains as we walk toward my car, parked at the back of the lot. "I might even take the opportunity to study some more when I get home—you know, since my head isn't fuzzy."

I'm about to ask her who she is and what she's done with my friend when a pair of lights flash at the end of the lot.

"Is that at us?" Tara asks, peering into the dark.

The lights flash again, and I get a better look at the red car. But it isn't mine—or I should say Jessie's—although it's parked next to it.

Looking around, we're completely alone when the lights flash several more times.

"Yep, it's definitely at us," Tara confirms.

My phone buzzes in my bag, and I root around inside, pulling it out and opening a message from Jessie.

> JESSIE
> Are you just going to stand there all night or come over here and kiss me?

Leaning over my shoulder, Tara rests her chin on it. "Does he have a brother?"

I know she didn't mean anything by the statement, but I

can't help but feel the pang of sadness over Will and on behalf of my boyfriend.

"Only child, like me," I reply, typing out a message.

> ME
> What are you doing here, and whose car is that?

> JESSIE
> Get your ass over here, and you'll find out.

Lifting her chin from my shoulder, Tara sets a kiss on my cheek. "I'd say you should walk that sweet ass over to him because I think he just bought you a car. I'll catch you tomorrow in class."

"Let us give you a ride," I say.

Tara shakes her head and smiles at me. "No way. The campus bus is due in, like, one minute, and whatever Jessie has planned for you both, something tells me it's meant to be alone."

My eyes are wide as I take a couple of steps forward and turn over my shoulder to wave goodbye. "You think?"

She quirks a brow. "Living the dream, girlfriend."

Jessie's already out of the red BMW Coupe and leaning against the hood, his hands in the pockets of his post-practice sweatpants.

"Come here."

Opening up his hoodie, he brings me into a hug, wrapping it around us. And when he pulls back the collar of my jacket and sets an open-mouthed kiss against my collarbone, a swarm of tingles unleashes throughout my body.

"Do you like your new car, Sweetheart?" he asks.

I take it in. "You really bought this for me?"

He holds out his hand and wraps his little finger around mine, leading me to the driver's side. "I've been wanting to spoil you, and, well, now, I can buy you everything you deserve without anything hanging over my head."

The engine is running, and the interior is nice and warm when I take a seat and run my hands along the leather steering wheel, the new car smell mingling deliciously with Jessie's cologne.

He shuts the driver's door and jogs around to the passenger side, climbing in next to me.

I turn to him. "This is really nice, Jessie. An amazing surprise."

He leans across the center console and tips my chin up with his finger, our lips almost touching as his eyes sparkle with excitement. "I have so much to tell you, but first ..."

I about double over with laughter as he squeezes his frame between the seats, asking me to join when he finally makes it into the back.

On a smirk, I get out the car and then climb into the back, using the provided rear door.

"Smart-ass," Jessie jibes, pulling me inside and shutting the door behind us.

He maneuvers me so I'm straddling him in the middle seat, my head almost touching the roof.

"So, what else do you have to tell me?" I ask, twizzling a piece of his hair around my forefinger, our noses practically touching in the small space.

Lifting his hand from my waist, he pulls at the ponytail, and my hair falls around my shoulders.

Instantly, I feel the mood between us shift from joking around to something more serious. I can tell by the look on his face that it has something to do with his dad.

Smoothing a palm down the back of my head, Jessie keeps his eyes on me as they glisten in the soft street lighting that illuminates the sidewalk. "My dad got taken back into custody today."

I pull back, my hands now planted on his shoulders. "He did?"

He nods. "A couple of days ago, I decided to make a statement to the police. I'd never felt like I could speak up, but I got to thinking about what you and Ashley have been saying to me. The support Jensen's been giving me too. Plus, some of the therapy unearthed memories involving my dad that I couldn't stay quiet over. I needed to find peace and closure, and speaking up felt like the right thing to do as part of my journey. Maybe even sending a message to others that it's never too late to come forward and call out their abuser."

"Jessie ..."

He brings his lips to mine, halting me in my tracks.

"I know I should've probably told you about my intention to formally report it, but until the second I made the call, I wasn't sure I could go through with it."

I swallow hard, my emotions rising into my throat. "I'm so proud of you for doing that, for speaking up."

He drops his forehead against mine. "Some of the memories that have come back to me involve domestic abuse against my mom. Others potentially explain how some of my scars I covered with tattoos got there. I think I finally worked out why I got the tattoos and why they're birds."

"Why?" I ask.

His lips shake with emotion. "I think it was all subconscious like the memories I had were trying to break free and be heard. But I covered them, knowing they needed to be acknowledged, but I was too scared to show my scars. Burying all of this only hurt me more, and as a kid, I didn't know what to do. So, I just got inked."

"I-I don't know what to say," I reply, relieved tears tumbling down my cheeks on his behalf.

He draws in a steadying breath and wipes at my cheek. "My mom stayed silent for years, probably out of fear of what he'd do. But he can't get away with it, Mia. I know I'll have to testify in court. I know it will be in the media. I'm so damn scared, but I have to do this—for me, for her, for us. I have to make sure he doesn't walk free. The case won't go to court for a while, but your dad wants to help support me through it financially; he's going to pay for my lawyer, who thinks my dad will get the book thrown at him and be made an example of. Texas law allows charges to be pressed against him for crimes committed many years ago. Graham told me I should use all the money I earn to make a life for us both. So, I am."

He tucks a lock of hair behind my ear as his blue eyes scan my face. "We got the house, Sweetheart."

My hands fly up to cover my mouth. "Really?"

He reaches up and pulls them away. "Really. But don't cover those pretty lips. I like it way more when I have access to kiss them."

I shake my head. "I can't believe it. It's beautiful, but we're going to rattle around in it—you know that, right? It's huge for just the two of us!"

He smirks. "Technically, three, and we'll probably need all the space we can get with his huge ass knocking around the place."

Reaching into his pocket, he fetches out his phone and taps the screen a couple of times.

My eyes struggle to focus on what I'm seeing. A big mass of fur is the image in front of me.

"He's still a puppy, but a rescue," Jessie says. "We can go meet him tomorrow and collect him in a few weeks."

My hands cover my mouth again as I stare at the beautiful Saint Bernard puppy. "You didn't … you got me a dog?"

He nods and swipes to another picture. This one of him lying on his back and playing with a red toy.

"I don't know what to say," I reply, taking the phone from Jessie's hand and staring down at the photo. "He's beautiful."

Jessie nods. "The only thing we need is a name. The shelter asked me to think it over before tomorrow so they can complete his paperwork. But I said it was your choice. So, give it some thought."

I shake my head, already knowing. "I don't need any time to

decide." I bring my hand to the side of his face and smile. "I want to call him Ginger."

Looking down at the phone in my hand, Jessie's eyes are glazed when they return to mine. "None of this would be happening if it wasn't for the strength you gave me. Turning up at that library was the best fucking thing I've ever done, Mia. Shutting out all the noise, telling me I had to keep away from you, and listening to my heart—it hasn't just changed my life. It's given me the one person I needed to haul me off a path I didn't want to be on."

Setting down his phone beside us, he reaches across into the car door pocket and pulls out a black-and-white top.

When he unravels it and holds it out in front of him, more excitement fizzes inside me.

"Your jersey," I whisper.

"Wear my name and our number while I eat you, Mia. I'm fucking starving."

My pussy pulses as I shrug off my jacket, and he pulls the jersey over my head. It's way too big as it hangs off me. But I've never felt this sexy while wearing anything before.

I never want to take it off.

His breath hitches in his throat as his eyes trail over me.

Reaching down between us, he slips his hand underneath the hem. "You look like total perfection in my jersey. Now, sit on my face and let me lick your pussy while you wear it."

I look around at the tiny space, my pussy throbbing. "In here?"

A cheeky smile traces his lips. "Right here."

Reaching down and to the side, Jessie adjusts the electric driver's seat, sending it all the way forward, giving him just enough room to slide down beneath me as I rise to my knees and hover over him on the back seat.

When I feel his warm breath against my already-dripping pussy, I expect him to push my panties to one side. Instead, material tears as he rips them off me with both hands, throwing them onto the floor beside him.

"Lower," he commands.

I spread my legs wider, and his face disappears beneath his jersey.

When I feel his tongue tease my clit, I whimper, already so close to coming.

On a growl, his hands come to my hips, pushing me down. "I said I was starving, and I meant it."

"I'll suffocate you," I cry out as his tongue fucks my pussy.

Lifting me up for a brief second, he swipes his tongue through me as one of his hands traces the curve of my ass, dipping underneath the back of the jersey. When he gently slides a finger into my soaking wet asshole, I cry out into the silent parking lot, the windows of my car steaming up around us.

"If I die right here, with your cunt in my mouth, my fingers teasing your sweet ass, and my name stamped across your back, I'll have zero complaints, Sweetheart."

I lift the hem of the jersey so I can see what he's doing, and he pulls out his finger and brings it to his lips, sucking off the taste of me.

"That's so hot," I tell him.

He offers me a cheeky smile and then spits onto his fingers. "I warned you I have a filthy mouth, and now I want to finger your ass properly. Can you be a good girl for me and hover that pussy over my mouth while I do it? Because I guarantee you'll squirt."

My head falls forward onto the headrest in front of me. "Yes."

"Good girl. I'll make a slut of you yet."

Taking more of my release onto his finger, he reenters my ass and slowly pushes it all the way inside. His other hand grips my left hip, pushing me down onto his face.

"Jessie!" I cry as I lean forward into the headrest, granting him easier access to my ass as he pumps his finger, touching deep inside me.

Since his mouth is full of my pussy, he doesn't say anything in response, but by the way he growls against me, I know I'm giving him everything he wants.

After a couple more strokes of my ass, my moans increase as I dangle over the edge of coming harder than I ever have before.

He must know I'm not far away by the way I'm contracting around his tongue, and he pulls me back up. "Grab the headrest, Mia, and spread those gorgeous thighs as far as they'll go for me."

Wrapping my arms around the two headrests, I slowly ease my thighs apart until I'm practically doing the splits over his face.

When he pumps me again, pressure builds inside me, and I know I'm about to release all the way down his throat.

"I'm coming!" I gasp. "Take me."

At the final second, he lifts the jersey up with his free hand, letting me watch the way he swallows me down as I gush straight into his mouth. I'm gripping the headrests so hard that I'm sure my nails are damaging the leather, but I don't care.

I'm so turned on.

His hand falls to my upper thigh as he slowly grinds me against his face, his other hand still gently fingering my ass.

"I'm so in love with you," I whisper against the noise of him playing with my wet pussy. "You are everything, Jessie Callaghan. Fucking everything."

His finger speeds up, wanting to wind me up again. I don't know how much I have left to give, but there's no way I'm moving from this position.

On the third pump of his finger, he strokes deep inside me, and I come again, but this time in silence since I want to listen to the way he moans around me.

Finally, when he's convinced I've nothing left, he pulls his finger out of my ass, and I instantly feel the loss. I want his cock to take me in there someday; I know it.

As he lifts me up, he swipes his tongue through me and over my sensitive clit. "You did so fucking well, Mia. I love all the ways you let me corrupt you."

When he slides back up to a sitting position, I straddle him and watch as he sucks me from his fingers again.

With no panties on, I know I'm leaking all over his gray sweats, and somehow, that turns me on more.

"I want to fuck," I plead, grinding myself against him, already desperate for more.

He throws his head back into the rest and chuckles. "And I want to leave you like this—bare, in my jersey, and driving home in your new car, thinking about the way I'm going to rail you so fucking hard the second we walk through our door."

"From behind?" I ask.

Placing his hand at the nape of my neck, he pulls me in for a long, passionate kiss. "Fast, slow, from behind, with you riding me, in every way possible, and all night long, tangled up in each other. Just you and me, Mia. Just you and me."

With my emotions riding high, I take in a deep breath, feeling like now is the right time to ask the question I've held off for over four years.

"Always? Are we always, Jessie?"

When his eyes pool with tears and a single one trickles down his cheek, I know there's nothing sad in his reaction.

"Yes, Mia. Always."

EPILOGUE

END OF JUNE

JESSIE

"You still have the rings, right, man?"

Rolling his eyes like it's the craziest thing he's ever heard, Jon reaches into the pocket of his gray casual pants and pulls out two small black boxes, showing them to Zach. "Yep, I still have them."

Zach turns back to look at himself in the mirror, adjusting his collar for the tenth time.

"It's all good. Everything's going to go just"—raising his hand, Jensen pinches his thumb and forefinger together—"perfectly."

From behind, Zach's dad places his hands on his son's shoulders. "Everything looks great out there."

Holding both of Aster's hands above his head, I walk him over to his daddy. He looks so fucking cute in a matching suit.

"Hey, buddy." Zach picks up his son and swivels back around to speak to him in the dress mirror. "Ready for Daddy to go marry Mommy?"

"Yeah," he answers and then points a slobbery finger at them both. "Da-daaaa."

My heart squeezes in my chest as I hope, one day, I'll hear my own child's voice.

Truth is, if Mia got pregnant tonight, I would be ecstatic, but I know we're a few years off that while she finishes school and establishes herself as a kick-ass therapist.

Jon checks his watch and points at the door. "Okay, it's time." He looks between us all. "You remember the order of proceedings, yeah?"

On a salute, Jensen walks over and opens the door to our hotel room. "It's burned into my memory, Morgan."

"Then my work here is done," Jon replies as we all step out of the room, dressed in various-colored linen pants and white shirts.

I look down at my blue pants and wonder what Mia will look like in the midnight-blue dress she picked out with Luna. When she found out she was going to be a bridesmaid, I don't think I'd ever seen her so emotional. It meant everything to her to be part of a day our group had been waiting for since the moment Zach had proposed on Lake Washington.

We reach the end of the hallway and turn left, ready to head out the side exit and step out directly onto the soft white sand.

That's when I see Kate, Felicity, and Mia step out of their room at the end of the hall with small white bouquets in hand.

She's only a couple of weeks from turning twenty-three, but as I approach her with the rest of the guys, I pray she'll be next to me for the rest of my life.

When she steps toward me and away from the others, the long, silky blue gown she wears pools around her feet, hugging every gorgeous line and curve of her body. The neckline rests just above her breasts, and the tiny straps holding the slinky fabric make me think she isn't wearing a bra.

My dick stirs—I can't help it.

"Down, boy," she whispers against my lips as I take her mouth with mine. "We need to keep this PG—at least for a while."

Someone clears a throat from behind me, and I turn to look at Jensen, who immediately drops his gaze to June and Will. On wobbly legs, they hold on to each of his hands.

"I gave you a free pass with the sheets, but I will accept zero petting around my children."

I narrow my eyes at him as we all get into order.

"Okay, this is where I leave you." Jon squeezes Zach's shoulder. "I'll see you down the aisle with your wife."

Since Luna's dad is basically an estranged asshole and her mom said she couldn't make the wedding as she'd already booked a vacation with her new husband, Luna asked Jon to give her away.

Dropping his head between his shoulders, Zach takes another deep breath and then leads us out onto the sand, and when we all reach the simple white flower arch that looks over the perfectly still ocean, you can literally hear a pin drop.

"It's beautiful," Felicity whispers to Kate.

Only the officiant and our group can be seen on the private island Jon suggested they book.

I lean across to Jensen, who's standing next to me on the other side of the archway, still holding June's and Will's hands. "I gotta hand it to him," I say. "Jon absolutely nailed this in the end."

Jensen nods. "I'd say this is a bigger win than the goal-scoring record you secured or lifting our third Stanley this season."

"J—"

I look down to where the tiny voice came from and see Will holding his free hand out to me.

"Oh, wow." Mia is the first to speak.

"Did he ..." I say to Jensen, not sure if I heard it right.

"He definitely did," Zach agrees.

Jensen's brows lift as he looks down at his son. "What was that, little guy?" he asks.

When Will stretches his hand up toward me again, I know he wants me to hold him.

"Can I?" I ask, my eyes shooting to my best friend.

An easy smile breaks out over his face as he picks Will up and hands him to me.

I bring him face-to-face with me, and Will stares at me, his brown eyes wide and matching his dark hair swirling in the coastal breeze.

"You trying to tell me something, buddy?"

"J-Jessie."

The air in my lungs escapes in a whoosh.

"Jesssssie," Will repeats.

"Oh my God," Kate says from across the archway. "Did he just say your name?"

"And his first word," I croak out.

Tears surface before I can stop them. "Hey, Will."

Will's tiny palm comes to my cheek as he continues to stare at me. In his gaze, I see the reflection of the tiny waves as they creep up the shoreline.

Jensen's hand lands on my shoulder, and I turn to look at him, his eyes as watery as mine.

"I don't think we could've wished for a more perfect first word. You earned it, buddy. You mean the world to him."

"I definitely have inadequate tissues for today." Felicity wipes underneath her eyes and then focuses her attention ahead of her as Luna and Jon appear at the end of the empty aisle.

"Breathe, Zachary," Kate reminds the groom as he holds his breath at the sight of his girl.

"You weren't kidding, were you?" he says to Kate as Jon and Luna walk slowly toward him.

Her eyes are pinned on Zach, dropping to Aster as she comes to stand next to him under the archway.

Wrapping his hand around the nape of his neck, he grips hard, trying to push back the emotion as it tumbles down his cheeks. "I don't have words. You look ..."

"Like our happily ever after?" she asks.

I look over at my girlfriend as she stands behind Kate, facing Zach and Luna, tears pooling in her green eyes.

She catches me looking at her, and a smile pulls at her lips in response.

Zach nods. "Yeah, Rocket. Exactly like that."

THE FOLLOWING morning is exactly like the previous day—still, peaceful, and with bright sunshine filtering through the blinds of our beach bungalow.

We barely got any sleep last night, the celebrations drifting into the early hours. And when I finally got my girl alone, I had absolutely zero intention of spending the rest of the night in any way other than buried deep inside her.

Mia's still sleeping when I climb out of bed and pull open the glass door, which leads directly onto a small, decked area and then out onto the beach.

"What do we think, Will?" I speak into the morning air, hoping the ocean breeze will somehow carry my question to him. I look across at my suitcase sitting on top of the trunk at the foot of our bed. "Is it now like we planned?"

A large wave crashes to the shore, stirring Mia awake, and I turn around to see her sitting up in bed, stretching her arms out above her.

She looks perfect, dressed in a silky white nightdress.

Before she can register where I am, I lift the lid on my case and swipe what I need, dropping it into the pocket of my athletic shorts just before she looks up at me and yawns again.

"Hey, baby. What time is it?"

I bring my finger to my lips and hold out my other hand for her to take. "Still early. Take a walk with me?"

She looks around the room. "Sure. Let me grab my robe."

When she takes my hand and we step onto the cool sand, I

feel my body begin to tremble. Although this time, it's not anxiety or fear that takes over my body's reaction.

When Mia lets go of my hand and steps into the shallow water, I watch as she turns back to me with a bright smile framed by her dark hair blowing in the wind.

Reaching into my pocket, I turn the small velvet box around in the palm of my hand. It wasn't hard to find a ring; there could really only be one. When I told Graham about my plan to propose and he gave me Jayne's engagement ring, I knew I wouldn't be able to hold out on giving it to her.

With my dad still in custody, awaiting a trial, which will almost certainly see him behind bars for at least a decade, I finally feel like I have some kind of closure on my past.

But with the help of regular therapy, I've never felt closer to Will and Mom. Last week, I even caught myself laughing at a memory I shared with Papa and her at the local diner when I spilled a strawberry shake all over his brand-new pants.

"What are you thinking about, Jessie?" Mia steps toward me, her head cocked slightly to the side in question.

"Just everything," I answer.

She giggles, the sound inflating my chest. "Well, you wouldn't be my boyfriend if you weren't overthinking everything, even surrounded by the calm ocean."

I bring my eyes to hers. "What if I told you I don't want to be your boyfriend anymore, Mia? What if I wanted to be something else?" I slowly drop to one knee in front of her as I reach into my pocket for the box. "Like your husband?"

She brings her hands to either side of her face, and I open my palm out in front of me, my hands still trembling, and pop the lid.

As soon as I do, petals fly out, scattering across the sand around us, but one stays where it is, caught inside the thin white gold band.

"My mom's," she gasps, reaching out to touch the delicate

ring. Her eyes flick to mine. "And ... freesias. Oh my God, Jessie, freesias."

Tears tumble down her cheeks just as mine do the same.

"I'm not perfect, Mia. I guess no one ever really is, and I can't promise you that I won't struggle at times." I take a deep breath. "I once told your dad that I wanted to get to a place where I could sit with even the hardest of thoughts and still feel like I was the man you deserved."

With my other hand, I pull out the ring and hold it between my thumb and finger.

"I know it's taken a long-ass time, but in my heart, I know I'm there; I'm ready to not just survive, but to spend every second I can making you happy."

Standing up, I take her left hand in mine and hover the ring over her finger.

She releases a long breath as the tears continue to fall down her cheeks.

"I've gotten to the point where forever with you means so much more than it did. Everything in me wishes I could somehow find a way to merge our souls, so there's no way I can ever lose you because I'm never letting you go, Sweetheart. Not in this life or the next."

When I push the ring to her knuckle, she looks up at me.

"So, while I find a way of making us eternal, I can offer you this ring and my promise to make you the happiest wife who ever lived. So, will you marry me, Mia?"

She doesn't hesitate, not even for a millisecond. "Yes!"

She leaps into my arms, and I hold her tight against me as she wraps her legs around my waist.

"I can't wait to spend my life with you," I whisper into her neck.

She pulls back, and I catch a tear that falls from her long lashes and into my palm.

A few beats pass between us as she looks out to the ocean. "I wish Ginger could've been here. We'll have to get him a doggy passport next time."

"Actually, I got a message from Coach this morning."

Mia smiles. "Oh, yeah? Is the sitting going well?"

I blow out a laugh. "Yeah. Not sure who's sitting who, but Ginger's happy."

Cheering filters from behind, and we both turn to find where the whooping is coming from. Jon, Felicity, Luna, Zach, Aster, Kate, Jensen, and the twins all stand on their verandas, clapping and punching the air.

Taking Mia's hand in mine, I walk her back up to our friends. They all knew I planned to propose this morning.

Everyone circles around us as Mia shows the girls her mom's ring, the inside engraved with her parents' wedding date. Something I plan to add to when we set a date ourselves.

Jensen holds out his hand for me as Zach and Jon join us. "So fucking proud of you, man. Congratulations."

"Literally couldn't have asked for anything more perfect. The best setting," I say, looking over my shoulder at the ocean.

Jon smiles. "This is just the beginning too, Jessie. You think it doesn't get any better, but when she's that damn special"—he pauses and looks over at his wife—"you could go anywhere, be anything, and still feel like the luckiest guy alive."

Narrowing his eyes at his best friend, Zach swipes a hand across his mouth. "Getting a little philosophical on us for an early morning, aren't you, Cap?"

In response, Jon drops his eyes to the sand beneath his feet and shrugs his shoulders. "I guess I'm just saying that not everything stays the same."

"Okay ..." Jensen drawls.

From over my shoulder, I watch as Mia shows June, Will, and Aster her ring, but as I'm about to turn back around, I catch sight of Felicity, who looks at Jon, nodding just once at him.

Zach looks at his best friend. "What's this all about, Jon?"

Running his tongue across his bottom lip, Jon puffs out a

slow breath. "Seattle has been really good to me. I found my family here, and over the past few years, I've looked on as my friends have built a life for themselves." He looks to Zach. "You with Luna and Aster, another baby on the way."

He tips his chin at Jensen and then over his shoulder at Kate and the twins. "You finally got the girl you wanted to love you, JJ."

And then his eyes finally land on me. "And you've got everything ahead of you, Jessie. It's been an amazing journey. Seattle has changed my life, but now ... now, I need to help make my stepson's dreams a reality. In New York."

Zach's eyes practically leave his head. "Wait, what?"

"He got signed by the Blades, didn't he?" Jensen asks.

Rolling his lips together, Jon nods. "I haven't been able to tell you until now, but he signed his contract last week. He'll spend a year in the AHL, and if he impresses management, they'll likely offer him pro terms in the NHL."

"Wow," I say. "Jack Thompson, taking on the NHL. He'll kill it; I know he will."

"Well, that's the other thing." Jon smirks, running a hand through his hair. "We're about to enter a new Morgan era. He's taking my name."

"And you absolutely love that, right?" Jensen laughs.

"Yep." He pops the *P*. "When he told me he wanted to take my name and play as a Morgan, I gotta admit, my heart exploded. Can't say I was too excited about him wearing his dad's family name either."

"I'll say. So, other than the return of a Morgan to the league, where do you fit into this?" Zach asks.

A smile breaks out across my face as the pieces all fall into place.

Since the season when the Blades' assistant captain, Alex Schneider, took out Zach on the ice, they've been cycling through coaches, trying to find the right fit to rebuild their struggling team and culture without success. I'd take a guess that they think Jon is the guy they've been searching for, and they'd be a hundred percent right.

"They offered you the coaching job, didn't they?"

"They might be our rivals, but it was an opportunity I couldn't turn down," Jon replies. "And when Felicity got her transfer to the New York office, I knew it was time."

Blowing out a long breath, Zach plants a hand on Jon's shoulder. "Fuck me, man. I guess all I can say is congratulations. This is huge."

When the rest of the girls join us with the kids, his wife wraps her arms around Jon's neck.

With emotion in her eyes, it's obvious Felicity just broke the same news to the girls. "I guess all chapters come to an end at some point," she says, leaning across and planting a soft kiss in Kate's hair. "I'm sorry I couldn't tell you sooner, babe. We just had to wait for confirmation on everything."

Swiping under her eye, Kate smiles at Jon and Felicity sweetly. "It's fine. Now we have the best excuse for retail therapy in Manhattan."

"Ah, blissful. Maybe we could even take in a Broadway show when we visit," Mia coos.

I reach my hand out to the side, wrapping my little finger around hers. "Exactly. Amazing things ahead for us all."

Luna nods. "If there's one thing I've learned over the past couple of years, it's that when you truly love each other, distance really doesn't matter."

"Damn straight," Jon agrees.

Bending down and picking up June, Jensen holds her in his arms. "What a journey we've had though, right?"

"Only more to come."

Jon looks at Zach, an all too familiar expression on his face. "Definitely. But I don't plan on taking it easy on you, buddy."

"We won't need it," I retort.

From beside me, Mia giggles. "Okay, this sounds like a whole heap of fun."

Lifting his chin, Zach holds out a hand to his former teammate and captain, and as Jon takes it, they both crack huge smiles.

"It's gonna be real fun, lifting that cup next season."

With his shoulders shaking, Zach drops his gaze to the ground before lifting his eyes to Jon. "Bring it."

THE END

JACK'S STORY is book one in the Blade Kings, a next-generation hockey romance series, and will release in March 2025. Pre-order now!

ACKNOWLEDGMENTS

My Husband: Another book where you have been by my side as I carve out the story that has sat in my heart for so long. Thank you for being my rock and safe place as I told Jessie's story.

My Dad: Thank you for always believing in me and, most importantly, for encouraging me to believe in myself.

My little boy: Thank you for giving me the strength to sit down and write. Even on the hardest days, you always make me smile.

Sam: You know this one was especially hard for me to write. Thank you for listening to my rambling voice notes!

Nay: Another book with you by my side, reassuring me and sending me an endless supply of chocolate! Hand on heart, I'm not sure this one would've been possible without you.

To all at Wordsmith Publicity: Autumn and the whole team at Wordsmith, thank you. I'm endlessly grateful for all you do. My books are the best they can be because of your guidance. Here's to many more in the future.

To the Bookstagram community: So this is it, the final book in a series that you've loved, shouted from the roof-tops and flooded my DMs talking about over the course of a year. Thank you for making this journey so incredibly special. I know this is, in many ways, is a sad moment—saying bye to the characters we've grown to love so much. I can't wait to share the next part of my journey with you...Jack!

To all my readers: Most importantly, to everyone who has picked up and read Boarded Hearts, Frozen Over, Dead Rinker, and now Ruled Out, THANK YOU. I continue to be blown away by the response to my debut series, and I can't wait to introduce you to the next chapter...The Blade Kings. From the bottom of my heart, thank you.

ABOUT THE AUTHOR

Ruth Stilling is an avid romance reader turned writer. Having spent many years reading about and dreaming of her ideal book boyfriend, she finally decided to create her own and to share them with the rest of the world.

Living in a small town in Derbyshire, England, Ruth is an introvert by nature and spends much of her time talking with her equally book-crazy friends from across the globe.

When she isn't writing your next book boyfriend, Ruth enjoys watching all kinds of sports and is an Aston Villa and Derby County fan. The outdoors is a real favorite, and if the British weather were kinder, she would spend all her time writing outside.

Ruth is a wife to her best friend and number one cheerleader, whom she married in 2015, and a mom to her beautiful son, who has shown her a new perspective on life—enjoy and celebrate who you are as a person and cherish those who are there for you through rain and shine.

Ruth is incredibly excited to share Ruled Out, the final installment in her Seattle Scorpions Series!

You can follow Ruth and keep up to date with what's coming next via Instagram and TikTok by searching @authorruthstilling

Printed in Dunstable, United Kingdom